The Devil's
Menagerie

Also by Louis Charbonneau

The Magnificent Siberian

White Harvest

Stalk

The Ice

No Place on Earth

Night of Violence

Nor All Your Tears

Corpus Earthling

The Sentinel Stars

Psychedelic-40

Way Out

Down to Earth

The Sensitives

Down from the Mountain

And Hope to Die

Barrier World

Embryo

From a Dark Place

The Lair

Intruder

The Brea File

Trail

As Carter Travis Young

The Wild Breed

Shadow of a Gun

The Savage Plain

The Bitter Iron

Long Boots, Hard Boots

Why Did They Kill Charley?

Winchester Quarantine

Winter of the Coup

The Captive

Blaine's Law

Guns of Darkness

Red Grass

Winter Drift

The Smoking Hills

The Pocket Hunters

The Devil's Menagerie

A NOVEL BY

Louis Charbonneau

DONALD I. FINE BOOKS
New York

DONALD I. FINE BOOKS
Published by the Penguin Group
Penguin Books USA Inc., 375 Hudson Street,
New York, New York 10014, U.S.A.
Penguin Books Ltd, 27 Wrights Lane,
London W8 5TZ, England
Penguin Books Australia Ltd, Ringwood,
Victoria, Australia
Penguin Books Canada Ltd, 10 Alcorn Avenue,
Toronto, Ontario, Canada M4V 3B2
Penguin Books (N.Z.) Ltd, 182–190 Wairau Road,
Auckland 10, New Zealand

Penguin Books Ltd, Registered Offices:
Harmondsworth, Middlesex, England

Published in 1996 by Donald I. Fine Books,
an imprint of Penguin Books USA Inc.

1 3 5 7 9 10 8 6 4 2

Copyright © 1996 by Louis Charbonneau
All rights reserved

ISBN 1–55611–494–X
CIP data available

This book is printed on acid-free paper.

Printed in the United States of America

For Joshua Bilmes,
for his support, friendship
and labors beyond the call

Eight Years Ago

REMEMBERING THAT NIGHT always gave him a quick-charge. It was like seeing the scared, unmoored expression in a woman's eyes at the instant when she first realizes that she has made a mistake, that the usual coy games won't save her. Sometimes—he didn't examine this fleeting thought closely—he wondered if his mother had ever seen that shocked comprehension in his eyes. If she had *enjoyed* seeing it.

He shuffled the memories like snapshots, pausing to study the good ones. He was still in the Air Force then, stationed in Wiesbaden, Germany. Off duty, he had gone into a village overlooking the Rhine, not far from the base. It was November and darkness came early. The day had been cloudy and damp, and intermittent drizzles persisted into the evening. The air felt dirty and bitter cold. The atmosphere matched his mood.

He spent the evening in a village beer hall getting half-drunk. He had always been able to hold his liquor well. When he went to the men's room he could feel the heaviness in his limbs, but his mind stayed cold and clear.

A copy of the letter was in his jacket pocket. Once in a while he would pat the pocket with his fingers, feeling the folds of the sheet of paper, as if to verify that it was still there. He kept the original in a waterproof pouch at the bottom of his trunk, like a treasured artifact. Once, late in the evening, he fished the copy out of his pocket and carefully unfolded it. The blonde across the room who had been giving him the eye for the last hour watched him, a faint smile on her full, pouting lips. German girls had this habit of pushing their lips out, pursing them as if inviting a kiss, even when they didn't mean it, as if they had all gone to the Elke Sommer school of acting.

He felt rage rising, bile in his throat. He swallowed it, held it down. The blonde was probably making guesses about the letter. A love letter from home in the States? From his wife? A girl friend? Why else would a man brood over a letter late at night amidst the noisy confusion of a dimly lighted bar? He thought about walking over to her, not hurrying, and smearing that little smirk across her face.

The heat had always been there, an invisible part of him for as long as he could remember, like hepatitis in the blood. Banked coals, always ready to burst into flames. Sometimes, even as a boy, his temper had got him into trouble. At school he was big for his age, and because he fell behind early in his studies he dropped back to a class a year younger. In schoolyard fistfights he took a joyful relish in hurting kids who were younger, smaller and weaker, punishing them, never letting up until he was dragged off. After a while no one wanted to fight him. He became a casual bully, unchallenged.

At home, with a woman who was five feet four and weighed a hundred and twenty pounds, he was the victim, she the bully. In the summer of his thirteenth year he punched her out. Scared her so badly that she never looked him directly in the eye again. The screaming didn't stop, the wrenching emotional scenes, the tirades against his absent father, the drunken orgies of self-pity, but the physical bullying ended.

When he was seventeen he enlisted. It felt like being let out of a prison. He never went home again.

The violence remained in his blood. Sober, he frequently didn't sleep well. Counting sheep, or fantasies of compliant women, left him wide-eyed. At some point he began to use other fantasies to ease his way to sleep. Images of his fists smashing into soft flesh, breaking brittle bones, splitting fragile mouths. Blood spraying the blackness behind his eyelids. He didn't need sleeping pills, antihistamines, even pot or other drugs. If he was tossing and turning, he would think about violent images, wait for them to take shape, create scenarios that gave them focus and intensity. Most of the time the dramas never played out to the final curtain. The anticipation was enough, the tranquilizing effect of those first moments of imagined rage. He would drift, sedated on a sea of savage blows.

The blonde was not the only woman in the crowded hall who had noticed the handsome American soldier with the staff sergeant's stripes on his sleeve and the row of brightly colored ribbons over his left-hand chest pocket (the pocket where he returned the folded copy of the letter). Something about him commanded their attention. He had regular features that barely escaped blandness, close-cropped sandy hair, cool gray eyes behind tinted gold frames. He resembled a young William Holden, the Golden Boy of another era, but heavier, with wide shoulders and a deep chest. He was an inch under six feet tall and weighed just over two hundred pounds. His face was unmarked but his hands were scarred and calloused, with one knuckle oversized from being broken. He wore a plain gold wedding band on the third finger of his left hand.

The cool gray eyes, magnified slightly by his glasses, were the feature women noticed particularly, perhaps mistaking their mocking glint for good humor. That and the easy way he moved, with the controlled power of an athlete. When he pushed away from his table and walked toward the door the blonde watched him hungrily all the way. She was no longer smiling.

Beringer half hoped she would try to follow him.

The damp cold shocked his senses without quite sobering him. His glasses, warm from the overheated beer hall, steamed up from the cold. He removed them and carefully polished the plastic lenses with a soft white handkerchief he carried solely for that purpose, whistling softly between his teeth as he worked. When he put the glasses back on and set off he felt very light on his feet, intensely alive, invulnerable, moving through the darkness like a tiger through tall grass.

Ahead of him an ancient bridge crossed the Rhine, its shape obscured by night fog. Two figures passed through a pool of light and disappeared into the mist. *Snapshot: scene from an old spy movie in black and white.*

A couple, Beringer thought. A uniform and a girl, leaning into each other. He felt an odd singing in his brain, as if he could sense the electrical impulses racing along the network.

Without even thinking about it he started to follow the couple. They materialized briefly from the misty darkness when they passed under one of the light stanchions on the bridge. The yellow glow of the lights was too feeble to penetrate more than a few feet into the shadows. The figures were imprecise, loosely drawn in gray and black watercolors and kissing, their bodies bowed inward at the waist as if their pelvises were attached. *Click!* The river mist curled around them.

Just as Beringer reached the foot of the bridge they broke apart, skipped into the mist hand in hand and vanished.

Their disappearance gave him a moment's beery confusion. Where could they have gone? He walked after them, alert and excited, working out the puzzle. They weren't jumpers, not the way they were acting with each other. And there was no way off the bridge.

He found the answer near the center of the bridge: a door where a door had no place being, set into a concrete frame. In the mist and darkness, finding a door there was like one of those creepy moments in a film about a haunted house when someone accidentally presses the right button and discovers a secret opening in a solid wall.

Stairs leading down into the darkness.

Beringer had a flash of opening the door and stepping into a void, plunging through the night into the cold black waters a hundred feet below, as if the door had been put in the middle of the bridge as a sick joke.

He took off his glasses, folded them into their case and clipped the case over his right breast pocket. Quietly he opened the thick wooden door. It swung silently on oiled hinges. He peered down, squinting without his glasses. In the pitch blackness several seconds passed while he assured himself that there really was a flight of stairs. They seemed to lead down into a bottomless well.

Then he heard the girl laugh, the sound warm and gurgling like bubbles spilling up in tepid water and bursting at the surface. The laughter, swirling up out of the dark emptiness below the bridge, gave him an eerie sensation. But the sound was too real, too much the echo of a woman's naked yielding, and the crawling on Beringer's neck gave way to a stirring in his loins.

The steps led down to a platform, some kind of observation or service platform (he never went back in daylight to see it), and the G.I. had the girl down there.

Beringer tiptoed silently down the steps. He was halfway down when the animals-rustling-in-the-leaves noises from below abruptly stopped. By this time his eyes had adjusted enough to the deeper blackness so that he could make out the two figures on the platform. The girl scrambled to her feet, brushing at her clothes as if they were dirty, rearranging herself. *Snapshot: a white breast being pushed back out of sight.*

Then the young soldier, who was as thin as straw, no more than twenty years old, did a thing so ridiculous that Beringer laughed whenever he thought of it. He retrieved his cap, which must have fallen off during his grappling with the girl, and as Beringer paused on the bottom step the soldier carefully put on his cap while he stared upward.

"What the hell—?" the soldier said.

Beringer didn't say anything. He peered toward the girl, only a few feet away, backed against a waist-high safety rail. Up this close his vision was good enough without his glasses. The photographic image recorded in his memory was of a spill of blond hair, the pale softness at her throat, the round dark pools of her eyes, her open mouth.

"Who are you?" the soldier demanded. Beringer heard a quaver in his voice. "What do you think—?"

"Get lost, junior," said Beringer, without raising his voice or taking his eyes off the girl.

"Fuck you!" Anger and fear made the young soldier's voice shrill.

"Jimmy, don't!" The girl spoke in English with a strong German accent. "Let us go . . . just go."

"Not you," Beringer said to the girl. Finally he turned to the young soldier. "You can go, Jimmy."

The soldier jumped him. He managed to get in a wild blow,

but Beringer hardly knew he had been hit until he felt the sticky warmth of blood on his lip. His brain was singing louder. He hit the thin soldier once, a solid punch to the face. Jimmy folded over the railing as if he had no spine. He did, though. He pulled himself off the railing and came back. Beringer was grinning now, feeling fine, hearing the girl's frightened protests and the soldier's wheezing struggle to breathe through a broken nose. Beringer grabbed the kid soldier and wrestled him back to the railing. When he picked him up, Jimmy seemed weightless. It was like lifting a child, like the times Beringer would toss his son into the air until he shrieked with delight. But now it was the girl who screamed. When the soldier felt himself in the air, high over the protective rail, he made only a bleating sound that was maybe an oath and maybe a cry and maybe just the unconscious reflex of disbelief.

"Bye-bye, Jimmy," Beringer said.

For an instant after releasing his grip he stood there by the rail, breathing easily, listening, waiting. All he heard was the thin catcall of traffic somewhere overhead and what might have been the turgid motion of the river far below. And, immediately behind him, the girl's hysterical whimpering.

When he swung around, the girl scurried toward the steps. Beringer caught her arm and easily pulled her back. He felt the weight of her, a little plump, not like the skinny soldier. His left hand grabbed her bottom, pulling her closer. Solid curves where there were supposed to be curves. At a visceral level the discovery pleased him. He hated stick women. Slovenly in her dirty house-coat, skinny legs sticking out, bathing him in the warm milk of mother's love one moment, yelling at him the next, snapping his head back with a hard slap . . .

"*Gott in himmel!* What have you done to my Jimmy?"

"Maybe he can swim. He sure as hell couldn't fuck you the way I'm gonna fuck you."

"You . . . you can't do this! It is crazy—please!"

"I don't feel like arguing about it," Beringer said with a smile.

She struggled as he held her, and he liked the feel of that, the chunky body writhing against his, those full soft breasts loose under the thin cloth coat and a blouse. He reached in with one hand and caught the top of the white blouse, one button still unbuttoned, and ripped downward, popping buttons and tearing the fabric. When the girl raked at his face with her nails, he jerked the coat down over her shoulders, imprisoning her arms. The action parted the coat. Indelible image of the torn blouse and the white globes peering at him out of the darkness.

He tried to pull her down to the floor of the platform. They fought, the girl silent, desperate. Somehow she wriggled free of the cloth coat and broke for the steps again. When his hands fell heavily on her shoulders, hauling her back, she found her voice. *"Bastard!"* she screamed. *"Bist du des teufels?"*

She struck at his eyes, claws out.

Beringer's anger exploded. He began to scream back at her, each word accompanied by a blow: "Lying—cheating—fucking—whore!" The first punch knocked the resistance out of her. The second snapped her head back and made her mouth go slack. The next, a smash to the chest, broke something and she crumpled.

She was lying inert on the platform, Beringer kneeling astride, the refrain drumming in his brain, over and over.

The image that came to him afterward was of a butcher pounding a slab of red meat.

LATER, RESTING ON his haunches beside the body on the platform, he picked up the purse she had dropped, intending to toss it over the railing toward the dark waters far below. Some keys spilled out, a wallet, a tube of lipstick. Picking up the wallet, he fingered through it, searching by touch. He extracted a few German marks and a U.S. ten-dollar bill. He came across a plastic folder with several cards inside. One was an identification card with the girl's picture. In the darkness he could not make out her face.

Beringer extracted his eyeglasses from their case and put them on, being careful with the earpieces, which were easily bent. He had to strike a match to read the name on the ID card. A gust of wind blew out the first match. The second flickered over the name: Lisl Moeller. Alongside the name a pretty face peered eagerly into the camera. The face dissolved as the flame guttered out.

In that brief flare of light Beringer understood for the first time how fate had intervened to show him the way to his personal magic kingdom. It was a yellow brick road, he thought—every twist and turn laid out exactly as it was meant to be!

He dug his Swiss pocketknife from his pocket. He smiled in the darkness as he crouched over the girl's body.

It was the most exhilarating moment of his life.

THE FBI AGENT, who was stationed at Bonn, was called in by the German police as a matter of form because the girl had been seen frequently with an American soldier. The agent's name was Karen Younger. She was twenty-four years old, one year out of the FBI Academy, with a BA in psychology from Penn State and a law degree from Georgetown. She had never seen a murder victim before, much less a young woman mutilated and beaten to death. She walked shakily out of the morgue and staggered to a nearby bathroom, where she vomited into the toilet. When she looked into the bathroom mirror she thought she saw the pale face and haunted eyes of a dead woman.

The stolid German detective who had driven her to the morgue waited for her in the white-tiled corridor. She surprised him by insisting on examining the body more closely. Aside from the victim's battered face, which would torment Younger's sleep for years to come, what riveted her attention was the initial, approximately three inches high, carved crudely into the dead woman's abdomen. The same weapon had been used for vaginal penetration and a savage vertical cut. According to the medical examiner's preliminary report the raw slashes had been made with the point of a small blade, not very sharp. The minimal bleeding indicated that both wounds were postmortem.

"What does the letter mean?" Younger wondered aloud.

The German policeman shrugged. "It is her initial," he said. "Her name was Lisl Moeller."

"And she was last seen with an American soldier?" the agent asked after a moment, still trying to breathe slowly and deeply.

"*Ja*. She was seen with him many times before."

"They were lovers?" Was that what this was? A crime of passion? "Has the soldier been identified?"

"He is Corporal James Crowell of your United States Air Force," the detective said in precisely correct English. "He is stationed at the Air Force base near Wiesbaden. He has not reported back to the base."

"I guess we'd better find him."

The soldier was found the following morning by two young boys who had gone down to the river to fish. The body, in the water more than thirty-six hours and carried two miles downstream from the bridge by a strong current, was in poor condition, but Karen Younger was able to note two details of particular investigative interest. One was the soldier's broken nose and the purplish bruising beside it, suggesting that Crowell had been in a fight. The other was Crowell's hands, which were unmarked.

It hadn't been much of a fight, she thought.

One

THE INDIAN SLIPPED through brush and smoke, invisible until he popped up next to Dave Lindstrom. Startled, Dave lurched back a step.

"I scared you," the Indian said.

"You sure as hell did. How do you do that?"

"It's something my people learned fighting the cavalry."

"You're too young to have fought the cavalry."

The smoke-blackened Indian was a Navajo, no more than twenty-five years old, Dave guessed, one of a team of firefighters flown in the day before from Arizona. His name was Jim Roget. "Like the champagne," he had said when he introduced himself.

"Where did you acquire a French name?"

"It's a long story of oppression and deceit. You wanta hear it?"

"Not really," Dave had answered with a grin.

The Navajos were experienced firefighters, and Jim Roget had been assigned as a crew boss for Lindstrom and his group of volunteers. They fought the fire with shovels and McLeod rakes and Pulaskis, the latter a double-edged ax and hoe, each of these tools used to cut down, clear away or bury combustible brush and grasses. Right now the volunteers were strung out along a service road on the east flank of San Carlos Canyon, halfway up the slope, trying to widen the gap created by the road before the fire reached it. Farther along the road Dave could see the line of fire engines, four-wheel-drive brush rigs and pumper trucks, and a tangle of thick hoses strung across the road like spilled intestines.

Dave had been on the lines for thirty-six hours. It was hot, punishing work and every muscle ached. His blisters had blisters. Roget, he noted, looked as fresh as he had when the buses dumped him and the other Navajos at the base camp in San Carlos Regional Park the previous day.

Unlike the Navajo, Dave Lindstrom was not a professional fire-fighter. He was an assistant professor in the Film and Television Studies program at San Carlos College. He had taken volunteer training with the county fire department, plus two weeks with the Forest Service, and this was the second year he had been called upon to help battle a major fire in the hills on the outskirts of San Carlos. Some of his academic colleagues thought he was crazy, and right about now Dave was inclined to agree with them.

The time was the last week of September, the beginning of the fire season in Southern California. No rain since last April, and the brush on every hillside was—as the television anchors kept re-peating—tinder dry. Set a match to it, or even throw a cigarette carelessly out of a car window, and the brush literally exploded. This fire had been started farther up the canyon two days ago. Some thrill-seeking arsonist slipping out of his car at the side of the road in early morning darkness, catching the glitter in his eyes as the first flames crackled in the brush.

So far six thousand acres had burned and twelve homes had been destroyed along with their lifetime accumulations of posses-sions and memories. Most of the houses had burned the first night of the fire, hillside homes above Canyon Drive where the blaze had started.

Off to Dave's left there was a loud explosion. A tall palm tree burst into flames, a dazzling fire on a stick like a fireworks display. Through the pervasive smoke Lindstrom could barely see the strike force of firefighters who were making a stand before some threat-ened homes, hoping to stop the relentless march of the fire before more dwellings were gutted.

A helicopter flapped overhead, one of the larger, twin-rotor choppers hauling a huge bucket of water at the end of a long cable and moving toward the threatened homes. Working his shovel, sweat pouring down his face, Dave peered through a film of his own making as the helicopter dropped its load. The water fell on a finger of flames, turning that little patch of hillside into a black smear. He felt like cheering, but the flames beyond the dousing seemed to leap higher and race even faster through the brush.

Someone was shouting at him. Dave saw several of the other volunteers straightening up, clambering onto the service road. "Pull back! Pull back!"

Lowering his head, momentarily blinded by white ash, Dave stumbled as he tried to climb. A strong hand gripped his arm, preventing a fall. Jim Roget, encased in his fire-retardant Nomex jacket and pants and matching yellow helmet, grinned at him. His black eyes peered through a coating of white, as if he wore warpaint. "Hang in there," the Navajo said. "Help is on the way."

"What? The wind's shifted?"

"Naw, a couple of Super Scoopers are gonna hit this side of the hill. You know, those big mothers scoop the water right out of the ocean on the fly. We're pullin' back. Now."

He went along the line, informing and encouraging the crew. One by one they climbed onto the road, peered at each other through the gloom, and began to trudge up the slope toward the ridgeline. Laboring after them, Dave wondered if the Super Scoopers were as effective as claimed. Even more effective than the helicopters and the C-130 tankers that were used to drop either water or fire retardant onto the fire, the banana-yellow Super Scoopers were able to scoop up 1,600 gallons of water at a pass, repeating the maneuver again and again without returning to base.

Above him Dave could now make out the phalanx of equipment and firefighters massing along the ridge above him. This, then, was the next line of defense. Beyond it, on the far side of the hill, were not isolated homes but the beginnings of a crowded subdivision, Mountain Ridge Estates, expensive homes overlooking San Carlos and the coastal hills on out to the Pacific Ocean.

Nearing the ridge, Dave had a panoramic glimpse through a rent in the curtain of smoke. Along the side of the canyon scores of men in their yellow gear were clambering up the slope, like an army in retreat. And the fire, as if sensing a rout, blazed higher, leaping over terrain the retreating firefighters had surrendered. A stand of trees ignited, one after the other, sharp explosions succeeding each other like the crash of big guns. A sinuous thread of fire, licking through a cut in the hillside, merged with another, and the flames suddenly soared thirty feet into the air.

The retreating firefighters were scrambling now, stumbling with exhaustion and a hint of panic, for the fire raced up the hillside faster than they could run. For Dave Lindstrom and the others, the heat was now a force, two thousand degrees at its heart, sucking the oxygen from the air and from their lungs. He was winded, exhausted, his legs wobbling like the Straw Man in *The Wizard of Oz*. Ray Bolger on a bad day, Dave thought.

Suddenly there was a thunderous pounding almost directly overhead. Dave looked up in time to see the big, gleaming yellow shape of the highly touted Super Scooper aircraft swoop low across the canyon. A wall of water spilled down onto the advancing flames. Dave felt the moisture in the air, fine and hot against his face like scalding spray.

Then he was being pulled onto the road at the ridgeline, hearing scattered cheers through the general turmoil. The road was crowded with men and equipment, everyone moving, shouting. Dave was pushed into a line with other volunteers at the side of the road, setting to once more with their shovels and axes and rakes. The smoke was now so thick that the entire scene was obscured. Digging and hacking away at tangled brush, Dave had no idea what was happening with the fire. He could hear the roaring of the flames even though he couldn't see them, the hissing from the fire hoses, the shouts of crew chiefs barking orders. More than once he thought he heard the Super Scooper returning, and he had a glimpse of one of the water-dropping helicopters as well. He knew that some backfires had been set, a thin red line spilling over the slope toward the main fire like a small squad of suicidal soldiers. The whole scene was like a battlefield, thought Dave, who had never been in a battle. He had read that real military combat was often much like this, troops blundering along blindly the best they could, no one knowing what was happening more than a few yards away, confusion everywhere . . .

*   *   *

IT WAS DARK when Jim Roget again pulled Dave Lindstrom from
the line onto the ridge road. "Break time," he said.

Dave saw a truck waiting, blackened faces piled in back. A
friendly hand shoved him toward the vehicle.

"Where to next?" Dave mumbled. He swayed on his feet.

"You're being relieved—you and your buddies. Get some grub
and a few hours rest. You can bunk down at the camp or go home
if you live close enough."

"What? I don't . . ."

"We've stopped it for now," the Indian said. "Those damned
banana planes are good. We don't have the fire contained yet, but
we can start giving the crews a break in shifts. Back here at midnight, okay?"

Dave climbed into the truck. Home, he thought numbly. Saw
Glenda's face, anxious, worried about him. Hadn't seen her since
early Thursday morning. What was it now—Friday? He had missed
two days of classes. Out on the fire lines, where everything was
reduced to fundamentals of survival, it was easy to lose track of
days.

The truck lumbered down the twisting grade and the bedlam
on the ridge vanished as if it had never existed. Only the smell of
the smoke persisted, filling the interior of the truck, clinging to
clothes and hair. No one spoke. Each was immersed in his own
bone-deep weariness. Dave felt it like one of those lead blankets
they throw over you when you have X-rays taken. But way down
beneath the fatigue was something that he would remember longer
. . . a flicker of satisfaction.

The emergency camp set up in San Carlos Regional Park was
a sea of confusion that reminded Dave of an episode from the old
television series Mash. There were lights strung from trees and
poles, Jeeps and fire trucks rumbling along dirt roads, rows of tents,
trailers that served as command and communication centers, a mess
hall and an emergency medical center. Dave stumbled past tents
to the parking area, where it took him five minutes to find his four-

year-old Nissan Sentra. He could have grabbed an empty bunk in one of the sleeping tents but making his choice wasn't much of a contest.

Minutes later, funneling down the last grade out of the San Carlos Mountains, he had no sense of rushing toward disaster. That lay behind him, marked by a black smudge of smoke ten miles long that slowly dissolved into the enveloping darkness of the night sky. Ahead of him a sprinkling of lights outlined the city of San Carlos, sparkling like luminous dust motes scattered across the valley floor. In the distance, rising above treetops, Dave glimpsed the lighted clock tower on the campus of San Carlos College, where he taught. The glowing lights marking the wide, safe, tree-shaded streets of the college town brought a comforting familiarity.

He was almost home.

Two

"SO HOW WAS it?" Glenda asked.

"It could have been worse."

"I didn't expect to see you tonight—the fire news is still bad, in Laguna and up in Malibu and here."

"We got some help from those big tanker planes, and the winds eased off. I have to report back at midnight," Dave added apologetically.

Glenda tried to hide her concern. "You need more rest than that—that's only a few hours."

Dave shrugged. "I'm lucky to get this much of a break."

"I worry about you, you know."

"You don't have to worry for the moment. You can even sit closer."

They were on the black leather sofa in the den, where Dave had collapsed and Glenda had brought him microwave-warmed leftovers of pot roast and brown potatoes. Dave thought he'd never tasted anything as delicious. Glenda leaned against him with a smile and his arm fell around her shoulders. For a moment they stared idly at the television set across the room, where stark pictures from other parts of the Southland mirrored the disaster Dave had left behind in San Carlos Canyon. From upstairs in the large old house came other voices, sometimes rising sharply. Friday nights the two kids—ten-year-old Richie and five-year-old Elli—were allowed to stay up later than usual, Richie having no homework. To Dave's surprise the boy was still working on a chemistry project. Maybe he had a calling.

"You smell all smoky, the way you used to when you still smoked those vile cigarettes."

"Those weren't vile cigarettes, they were manly Marlboros."

"They smelled vile."

"Well, they're a distant memory now."

"I still remember the way your shirts used to smell. I think you'd better change this one. Maybe the rest of those clothes too."

"Not much point . . . unless that's some kind of excuse to get me with my clothes off." He glanced at her sidelong, seeing mostly the top of her head where it nestled against his shoulder. Her hair was the same honey blond he had first seen bent over a peanut butter and jelly sandwich on a bench on the UCLA campus six summers ago. After more than six years and a second child, her figure was still as trim and sleek and given to sudden fullnesses as a small sailboat running before the wind. The humor, once tentative, had confirmed itself around her eyes and the corners of her mouth. She was now . . . What was it, exactly, that was different? More relaxed. Self-confident. Mature. A girl then, a woman now, and the woman improved on the girl—a feat he would once have believed impossible.

"I don't need an excuse, and you're too tired. You're going upstairs for a couple hours sleep."

"I'm not sure I can. I'm too wound up. Besides, there's tired and there's *too* tired. This is just tired."

"Are you sure you're not just trying to live up to those macho stories you told your fellow firefighters? I mean—"

A shattering crash from upstairs cut her off. Dave felt her body flinch, and even when the explosion was followed instantly by a youthful voice shrill with accusation, a faint tremor continued to pulse through Glenda's body.

"I told you not to touch it!"

"I didn't mean to!"

"They pick the damndest moments," Dave muttered, rising from the couch.

"They don't know about Daddy and his moments."

"Well, they're about to find out."

Before he could reach the open doorway to the den footsteps

pounded down the stairs to the front hallway. Elli, all legs and hair and wide, panicky eyes, burst into the den. From behind her came a furious shout. "I'll kill you!"

Dave caught Richie as the boy flung himself headlong through the doorway. The impact of a sturdy ten-year-old in full flight knocked Dave back a step.

"Daddy, stop him! He's gonna kill me!" Elli's tone of panic became shriller in the safe presence of her parents.

"That's enough!" Dave said sharply. "Nobody's going to kill anybody."

Richie twisted so violently in his struggle to reach his sister that Dave had to brace himself. He tried to push the boy back lightly, but at that instant Richie went limp. Without the expected resistance, Dave's shove turned into something much more vigorous than he had intended. Richie flew backward. His head smacked audibly against the wooden door frame.

"Richie!" Dave heard Glenda's gasp, saw the boy's sudden tears. "I'm sorry, but you shouldn't—"

"Go ahead!" Richie blurted, struggling against tears. "You always take her side."

The words shouldn't have meant anything important, they were nothing more than a normal childish complaint, but they hit Dave like a block of ice sliding down a chute and thudding into his stomach. "Only when you're out to commit mayhem," he said.

"It's true! You're always on her side just because—"

"Richie!" Glenda did not raise her voice, but a clear, sharp warning cut through the boy's anger and silenced him. He glared across the room at his younger sister, who stood closer to her mother than necessary.

Dave Lindstrom glanced from one to the other of his children, feeling the perplexity their constant quarreling awakened in him. It was only a phase they were going through, Glenda said, probably because they were five years apart in age. If the disparity were greater, she said, they wouldn't have the same kind of rivalry; and if they were closer in age, they would be able to share more things. This sounded to Dave as if she had been reading too many of the child psychology books that filled one whole shelf of the bookcase in the den.

On the face of it, the younger Elli, named after Glenda's mother Ellen, was the troublemaker. A blue-eyed blonde like her mother, she was a skinny, long-legged girl with no waist or hips at all. Dave's heart ached with parental joy whenever he looked at her. With no trace of malice in her makeup, but impulsive, thoughtless and irrepressible, she had a talent beyond her years for goading Richie into one of his temperamental outbursts. The boy was of a much stockier build, his hair a slightly darker shade, his eyes pale gray. Unlike his mother, who was quiet and restrained and kept things to herself, Richie had a very low boiling point. His was a case where popular psychology seemed to have it all wrong. Dave could hear his father, who was fond of adages, saying, "It's no good to brood on things, Dave. Get 'em out in the open where you can take a good look at 'em and they shrink in size." Not with Richie, Dave thought.

"All right, let's have it. What happened up there?"

"He was gonna hit me," Elli said quickly. "I was only—"

"She knocked over my experiment," Richie retorted. "I *told* her not to touch it. I told her what she'd get."

"Your chemistry experiment?"

"She ruined my cultures."

Dave glanced at Elli, trying for a stern expression. "A lot of work went into that experiment," he said quietly.

"I didn't mean to break anything. He just didn't want me to touch it, that's all."

"Was he wrong? You did knock it over, didn't you?"

"Well, I . . . I didn't do it on purpose!" Elli wailed. Her defiance dissolving in sobs, she stumbled into her mother's arms.

Dave waited a moment before turning back to Richie. "Was it an accident, Richie?"

"Well, yeah . . . I suppose. I guess it was. But she shouldn't have been messing around."

"Point taken," Dave said. "Suppose you let it go at that . . . as soon as Elli apologizes."

"That's not fair," Elli protested, her sobs miraculously under control. "It wasn't on purpose!"

"You heard what I said. You aren't *glad* you knocked it over, are you?"

"No. . . ." Suddenly the girl became sheepish and the crisis was over. She lowered her huge eyes, then raised them shyly, so perfectly mimicking the coquettish manner of a silent movie heroine that Dave nearly burst out laughing in admiration. Instead he watched gravely as Elli shuffled her feet and whispered to Richie, "I'm sorry."

It wasn't much, but in keeping with the peculiar code of childhood it seemed to be enough. Richie appeared mollified.

"Okay, suppose you both go see how much of the damage you can repair. And if there's any more fighting . . ." Dave smiled. "We'll all put on gloves."

He caught Richie's quick grin, followed by a ripple across the square face that might have been embarrassment. Dave squeezed his shoulder and pushed him gently toward the doorway. Elli looked up at Richie as she followed him to the stairway. In a moment their voices could be heard murmuring amiably.

Dave sighed wearily. "I don't exactly feel like Solomon."

"You stayed on your feet."

He dropped onto the leather sofa beside her. During the quarrel Glenda had touched the mute button on the remote control, silencing the TV reporter who was now standing at the foot of a street in Laguna below the blackened hulks of burned-out houses. For a moment they watched the silent tableau.

"Is it me?" Dave wondered aloud. "Or do all brothers and sisters fight so much?"

Glenda pulled his head around, not gently. She stared hard into his eyes, then kissed him firmly on the mouth. "If you're worrying about what Richie was going to say, I'll smack you with the coffeepot."

"Is that what they call the carrot and the stick?"

"Call it whatever you want."

She knelt on the sofa close to him, her knees pressing into his thigh, the wide curve of her mouth an invitation that was only half jocular. He swung an arm around her waist and pulled her onto his lap. "This is the Ramon Navarro technique. Sometimes it breaks her back, but if she survives . . . ."

"You've been watching too many old movies."

He smothered her mirth with his lips. After a few seconds she stopped giggling. Her mouth opened to his and their tongues probed. The muscles of her thigh tightened where his hand rested.

A low whistle broke them apart. Richie grinned at them from the doorway.

"Don't you ever bother to knock?" Dave growled.

"You oughta sell tickets."

"I'm surprised you and Elli haven't thought of it." Dave felt a twinge of regret as Glenda slipped off his lap and smoothed her slacks with a show of nonchalance.

"We did, but we decided to keep the show to ourselves."

"Fresh kid," his mother said. "I don't know why we put up with you. Why aren't you putting your cultures back together, or whatever they are?"

"There was only one slide broke." Richie wandered into the room, in no hurry to leave. "It sounded worse than it was."

"As long as everything's all right, you'd better start getting ready for bed. Both of you."

"Hey. I'm older," Richie protested. "I should be able to stay up later."

"One hour, that's all. Tell Elli she's to start getting ready for her bath. I'll be there in a minute."

"Okay. Hey, Elli, you have to go to bed!"

As Richie started down the hall the phone rang. It was on the oak secretary in a corner of the den by the doorway, an antique Dave and Glenda had found in Santa Barbara on their honeymoon. Richie said, "I'll get it," and picked up the phone.

Dave fell back on the couch, wondering if he should have stayed at the fire camp after all.

"Yes, this is the Lindstrom house. I'm Richie," the boy added, as if answering a question. "Sure. Mom's here. Who's calling?"

For a moment Richie listened. Dave could faintly hear the sound of the voice on the phone. Richie's cheerful expression segued into a series of emotional masks, surprise and consternation and something like grief, like changing images superimposed over each other in a movie from the thirties, Spencer Tracy's Jekyll turning into Hyde, or a boy's face becoming that of an adult and then an old man.

The blood drained from Richie's face. It happened so suddenly and clearly it was like watching red liquid seep out of a test tube.

"Stop it!" Richie cried. "Why are you calling? Why don't you leave us alone?"

Glenda reached the phone ahead of Dave and snatched it from Richie's hand. "Who is this? Damn you, don't you dare hang up!"

She stood trembling for a long moment before she put down the phone. "He hung up," she said.

She and Dave both stared at Richie. He was shaking visibly, his face pale, shock and hurt in his eyes.

"Who was it, Richie?" Glenda asked gently. "What did he say?"

Richie shook his head, a gesture almost violent.

"He must have said something," Dave said. "Was it a man?"

Richie nodded jerkily, still unable to speak.

"Did he say who he was?"

"He said I . . . I should tell you he was back. That you'd know."

"What . . . ?" Glenda looked as if she had been slapped.

"Maybe you'd better sit down, Richie," Dave said. "Take it easy. Just tell us—"

"No!" The boy pulled away. There were real tears in his eyes and he made no effort to hold them back. "He . . . he said you weren't my dad."

David heard the quick intake of Glenda's breath. He felt the skin tighten over his cheekbones. The cake of ice slammed into his stomach. "You knew that, Richie. You've always known."

"Yes, but . . . he said *he* was!"

Three

RALPH BERINGER DROVE slowly along the tree-lined street. It looked more Midwest than Southern California, the street wide and shaded by tall oaks rather than palm trees. The mature oaks with their wide overhangs screened much of the light from the occasional streetlamps, leaving the sidewalks deep in shadows. This was the Old Town section of San Carlos—big, two-story frame California bungalows with wide, friendly front porches and broad green lawns littered with autumn leaves, shadowy tricycles and wagons and, on the steps of one white-shingled bungalow, a one-armed doll staring out toward the street. To Beringer, after more than eight years in Europe, it was like a movie set, an idyllic vision of yesterday.

He hated it.

The Lindstrom house was one of the older ones on the street, dating back to the 1930s. Its wood siding and facia shingles were painted blue with white trim. It had a bed of roses along one side of the driveway, all in full bloom. Like the purple bougainvillea rioting over one half of the long porch, the late September roses placed the house in Southern California, not America's Heartland.

Beringer coasted along the dark street past the house. There were lights on downstairs, and more lights turned the drawn shades yellow over the upstairs bedroom windows set into a wide front dormer. Their room? he wondered. What were they doing now? In bed, sitting up, questioning each other about the unexpected phone call? Beringer didn't know much about David Lindstrom yet, but he knew sweet little Lennie. And he knew she wouldn't be getting much sleep tonight.

That knowledge gave an edge to his anger as he stared at the comfortable old house, the shutters and the glowing lights making it appear warm and snug, sheltered from any evil that might stalk the cold darkness outside.

He clamped his foot down on the accelerator and the gray Taurus shot forward. He slammed it around the next corner, tires squealing as the car leaned hard. He resisted the temptation to circle the block and cruise past the house again. He had already driven by twice. Quiet neighborhoods like this one, Neighborhood Watch signs posted all over the place, it was easy for an outsider to draw attention to himself. Beringer's rented car was anonymous, both the model and the color, and he had taken the precaution of muddying the license plates so they could not be read easily. Even so, it was much too early in the game to take chances. There would be time enough to reconnoiter the house and the neighborhood.

Besides, the night wasn't over. The phone call tonight had been a hearty dose of what was to come for the Lindstroms, only an appetizer for him.

"ARE YOU GONNA be all right?"

"I'm fine."

"I don't like to leave you like this."

"I told you, I'll be fine. You can't be thinking about me when you're looking into the throat of that fire. Promise me you won't."

"Okay. How was Richie when you went in there just now?"

"He's confused. He doesn't know how to take it. I'll talk to him while you're gone." Her anger, barely under control, burst out. "The bastard! How could he do that to Richie? His own son, for God's sake!"

"Take it easy, honey."

"Don't tell me to take it easy. I *won't* take it easy." She sucked in a sharp breath. "I'm sorry. Go. Go on. We'll be okay. We can talk when you get back. Be careful."

"Don't worry, I always am."

I have so much to come back to, Dave thought. It had always

seemed so secure, so untouchable. He knew that any human happiness hung on a very thin thread, but he had considered theirs blessed, the thread unbreakable.

It was close to midnight when he went out into the night, heading back to the fire lines. For the first time that he could remember, as he backed the Sentra out of the driveway, he found himself scanning the street, searching the shadows, seeing how menace could hide in the long dark nave created by the street's overhanging oaks.

BERINGER DROVE PAST the San Carlos College campus in the southwestern quadrant of the town, snugged up against the hills. Modern brick and glass buildings, winding walks, tree-shaded grounds. Even at this hour some students strolled along the lighted paths and clustered around the steps of the Student Union building as well as a lighted gymnasium where there was late evening activity. There were even lights in some of the classrooms, but Beringer figured classes ought to be about over, past eleven o'clock on a Friday evening.

He continued past the campus. More wide streets with more old houses, their lawns coated with white ash as if it had snowed. At this end of town, closer to the fire in the hills, drifting ashes were more visible. They washed over the hood of the gray Taurus like an attack of tiny feathers.

Lindstrom was a volunteer firefighter, Beringer had learned. Something to think about. A do-gooder. Lennie was a sucker for that kind of crap. Didn't she ever ask herself what kind of man would go off to play firefighter, leaving his wife and kids alone?

He reached San Carlos's main street, Washington Boulevard. The long center islands were planted in old palm trees. Large, gracious, two- and three-story brick homes flanked either side of the boulevard. Closer to the center of town these dated mansions gave way to small shops and stores. Here, for four blocks, vehicular traffic was shunted to one-way streets on either side of the boulevard, which became a pedestrian brick walkway where shoppers and strollers walked beneath picturesque gas lanterns past small boutiques, elegant shops, bookstores, coffeehouses and a variety of restaurants.

Beringer parked in a city lot north of the pedestrian mall and followed a winding brick path to the main street. The promenade was crowded. Several shops, two bookstores, a Mexican restaurant and no less than three coffeehouses were open, doing a brisk business. Try this in downtown Los Angeles late in the evening, Beringer thought. Leave your wallet home and make sure the insurance is paid up. San Carlos was different. Trendy, mostly white, quiet and safe.

That was about to change.

A well-built six-footer in his thirties, wearing khaki slacks and a green-striped knit golf shirt, obviously fit, probably worked out on the machines at one of the local health clubs, Beringer blended readily among the strollers enjoying the mild autumn evening. Any glances he drew were mostly from women, and always favorable. His was a tanned, strong-boned outdoor face, sandy hair no longer in a military crop but allowed to grow long over his ears and neck. He might have been an actor, one thought. His eyes were somewhat distanced behind tinted lenses set into gold-framed aviator-style glasses. The tinting affected his night vision slightly but he was used to that, and bright light hurt his eyes, which were a pale gray behind the light blue lenses. The intricate tracks fanning out from the shoreline of his eyes suggested that here was a man who laughed a great deal; the protective lenses hinted that he might simply be one who squinted often against sun glare.

For a half hour he strolled along the promenade, stepping inside a few of the open shops or peering through storefront windows. He bought an ice-cream cone—pralines and cream—from a Baskin Robbins and ate it sitting on a bench, watching the passersby. Close to midnight he sat at a tiny table in one of the coffeehouses and ordered a cup of cappuccino. The room was crowded with young people, students from the college. A mousy girl with long straight hair hanging over her eyes read a poem at the back of the room. Only occasional words were audible over the babble of conversation at the tables, but she didn't seem to notice. The poet didn't interest Beringer but he could feel the excitement building inside, the edge he had waited so long for. The right one would show. He could feel it. Tonight.

He was aware of covert glances his way. He smiled at a green-eyed redhead young enough to be a college student, but let his gaze drift away. Not her.

He spotted one who could be right when she left a table near the back. Blond, willowy, a pretty face wearing the confidence of a woman who knows what she looks like, a kind of arrogance in her posture and the carriage of her head, as if she were sniffing the air suspiciously. She wore a white T-shirt with a cat's face and the slogan "Cat's Meow" on the front, firm high breasts pushing at the shirt, long legs set off by a stone-washed denim miniskirt.

She walked out alone, but a moment later an older man who had also been sitting in the same part of the room hurried after her. Twice her age, Beringer thought. Silk shirt, expensive slacks, full head of silver-gray hair. One of her professors?

Beringer followed him out.

The man caught up with the girl when she turned off the brick promenade along one of the side paths leading toward the parking lots. Then they walked together, the teacher doing the talking, the girl staring straight ahead while he glanced nervously over his shoulder. He was her senior, Beringer thought, but she was in command, calling the shots. Why had they pretended not to be together when they left the coffeehouse?

Beringer trailed well behind them, offering no threat. He stopped in the shadow of a pepper tree at the edge of the parking area. The couple walked straight to a red Japanese sports car. The girl had the keys out, she was the driver. Teach got into the passenger seat.

Backing out, the car's backup lights illuminated its license plate clearly, and Beringer felt a jolt as powerful as a cattle prod. The car was a Nissan 280Z. The personalized license plate said EDIES Z.

Beringer ran across the parking lot to his car. Anxiety drummed in his chest. *You can't lose her, not her, she's the one!* He careened out of the lot with a squeal of rubber. One-way street, they could only turn one way, left.

Then he saw the red car up ahead, stopped at a traffic signal, and he released a pent-up breath. *Gotcha.*

The couple in the sports car drove to a supermarket parking lot in a shopping center on the southwest side of town, not far from the college campus. They sat for a few moments in the car. From his vantage point on the far side of the lot Beringer watched the heads glue together. Then the man climbed out, gave the girl a wiggle of his fingers and turned to the car parked next to the 280Z, a silver Lexus. Matched his hair, Beringer thought. Edie and Beringer both watched him drive away.

She sat there and lit a cigarette. Smoke filled the interior of the car while more smoke from the fire in the hills drifted overhead. Beringer lit up himself, so excited now that his hand shook holding the lighter. *Come on, Edie, you know you're mine but it can't be here. Where is it gonna be?*

She made the decision for him, and he was wrong. It wasn't going to happen out on the highway or in the shadows beside a college dormitory but right here in the parking lot of the Alpha Beta market. The door of the Z popped open and Edie's long slim legs carried her across the macadam and into the market.

Appraising the situation quickly, Beringer realized that the location wasn't as impossible as he had first thought. Risky, but Edie and her teacher had taken the precaution of parking around to the side of the market, away from the lights and activity out front. Didn't want to be seen together, he concluded, confirming his hunch about the way they had acted in the coffeehouse and afterward. Teacher, if that's what he was, was on his way home to the wife and kiddies, leaving Edie all worked up and no place to go.

Beringer drove across the parking lot, easing into the open space next to Edie's Z that her lover had vacated moments ago. Forcing himself to breathe slowly and deeply, Beringer slid over to the passenger side of his car and eased the door open. Earlier he had taken the routine precaution of disconnecting the interior light that normally went on when a door opened. Now he removed a pair of smooth black leather gloves from the glove compartment. They were extra large but his knuckles were tight against the leather. From a pocket of the London Fog jacket on the seat beside him he removed a leather sleeve holding a row of steel balls the size of large marbles. The sleeve fit comfortably into the pocket of his balled right fist.

He adjusted the side-view mirror so that he could watch the front of the market. He didn't have long to wait before he saw the girl coming around the corner and walking toward him, the sweet scissoring of those legs under the miniskirt. The parking lot was clearly illuminated at the front, but someone ought to complain about the side area, Beringer thought. Widely spaced lights didn't do a damned thing, and the night was dark, overcast not only from cloud cover but also from the pervasive pall of smoke. Not far away another woman alone loaded her groceries from a cart into a station wagon, but she had her back to Beringer and there was no one else close, no one close enough to see what was happening when Edie came near her car and Beringer pushed his passenger door open and stepped out.

Edie stopped short, maybe a little wary but not alarmed as she took in the appearance of the tall, tanned, well-built man facing her. Beringer smiled easily and backed against the Taurus, offering her room to open her driver's side door. The courteous gesture calmed any concern she might have had. With a faint smile touching her red lips she moved forward, unlocking her car door with a touch of a remote button on her key chain, ready to slip into the bucket seat.

Beringer said, "Hi, Edie."

Her eyes leaped toward his, startled. "What? Who—?"

He hit her once, hard, in the stomach. The air exploded from her lungs in one whoosh and she sagged like a pile of rags. Beringer caught her easily, levered the door of the Taurus open behind him and swung her onto the passenger seat. He folded the long, lovely legs into the car, dropped her plastic bag of groceries at her feet and closed the door with the door lock already set. Edie's face was pale behind the window, her mouth open and struggling to suck air like a fish in the bottom of a boat.

Walking quickly around the front of the Taurus, Beringer scanned the parking lot. The woman in the station wagon was driving away. No one was looking his way, only a few stragglers in sight intent on their own small errands. Into the Ford, all doors locked, the wide package tape ready in its holder, slap it around her wrists, taping them together in her lap. Tape around her ankles too; good, no trouble now. Tape her mouth as well? She was coming out of it a little, panic leaping into her eyes when she realized her hands and feet were tied. He didn't really want to tape that pretty mouth, he had better plans for it, so he hit her on the side of the face, holding the roll of steel balls, and saw her lights go out.

Driving slowly, the excitement singing in his blood, Beringer left the shopping center and drove south, following the coastal route on the ocean side of the burning hills.

Four

BIKE TRAILS HAD been laid out just off the coastal highway south of San Carlos, where the road traversed some protected wetlands, a sanctuary for migrating birds. The trails were popular with weekend bicyclists. There was the ocean off to the west, beyond the highway, and a quarter mile of sand dunes, and inland there were some twenty thousand acres of relatively untouched nature teeming with ducks and cranes, occasional Canadian geese and a variety of smaller birds.

Harry Malkowski, a reed-thin chemistry student in his third year at San Carlos College, tried to get in a full fifty-mile bicycle run every weekend, following the trails south from San Carlos along the coastline. He liked to get out early, before the trails were packed with other cyclists or the joggers who never seemed to get the idea that the bike trails were for people on bikes, not on foot.

This Saturday he was out early as usual, a thermos of coffee strapped to the carrier behind the seat of his Yamaha ten-speed, the sun not yet up when he hit the trail shortly after five o'clock. The hoped-for onshore flow of air had moved in late Friday night, bringing early morning coastal clouds and the cooler temperatures that meant relief for the firefighters in the hills. Unlike many beach-goers who loved the dry, warm Santa Ana winds and hated the usual coastal clouds and damp fog, Harry enjoyed these misty mornings. They muffled the beat of city noise behind him, leaving him alone with the distant crashing of the surf, invisible beyond the dunes, and the tranquil beauty of the wetlands as far as he could see. This morning veils of mist curled over the marshes like the fire smoke that blanketed the San Carlos hills. Through the mist Harry glimpsed a family of ducks swimming along one of the estuaries, a white crane standing one-legged in shallow water as still as a post, a colony of mudhens, and there, by God, yes, two honkers drifting on the water, must have flown in during the night.

Where the highway spanned one of the many creeks that threaded through the wetlands and the bike trail ran parallel to the road over its own wooden bridge, Harry saw the body. Shock pelted through him. He veered to the right, nearly colliding with the railing of the overpass. He stared down at the foot of the highway bridge, his heart pounding. A young woman, naked, lay facedown in the mud on the bank of the creek. For Harry, whose nights were often filled with fantasy images of naked women, there was nothing titillating about the sight of this one at all. She looked pathetic rather than sexy lying there. She looked dead.

Harry Malkowski didn't want to stop riding. He didn't want to give up his Saturday outing, he didn't want to get involved. For a long moment he sat motionless on his bike, sweat drying under his fleece pullover and pants, a chill beginning to penetrate—and not only from the damp, cool air and drying perspiration.

He couldn't leave her there like that, eating mud, dumped like a bag of garbage below the road. He just couldn't.

There was a telephone next to a roadside cafe, the Bright Spot, about a mile back. Harry made it in record time on the ten-speed.

Detective/First Class Timothy Braden of the San Carlos Police Department's Investigations Unit got the call at 6:08 A.M. that Saturday morning. He had had one of those nights where he went to sleep around midnight, woke up at two-thirty in the morning, the air heavy and the sheets clammy, and was still awake at four, watching the end of a 1940s *film noir* in which Dick Powell acted like a tough guy and the cops acted like surly jerks. Pretty much the way cops still acted, Braden mused.

Bleary-eyed and unshaven, he made it out of his apartment in ten minutes and pushed his unmarked car hard through the empty streets.

Mist swirled over the highway as he pulled up behind the flashing red and blue lights on a pair of black-and-whites. Two uniforms were waving curious drivers along. There wasn't much vehicular traffic, but even at this hour—Braden logged in at the scene at 6:39—there were gawkers on the highway and along a bike trail on the inland side of the road. Braden immediately sensed the potential for a jurisdictional problem. The uniforms were sheriff's deputies. Braden was San Carlos PD, and he wasn't exactly sure if this wetland strip was within San Carlos city limits or was county land. More likely, it was U.S. government property.

Braden parked a short distance down the road on the apron and walked back to the bridge. The highway crossed a shallow creek, its bed about ten feet below the road. There was another bridge about thirty feet or so in from the highway, a wooden structure about five feet wide. It was here that most of the gawkers were clustered—morning joggers and bicyclists in their designer exercise outfits and Nikes. Braden had given up wondering what drew people to gape at scenes of blood and mayhem.

Braden nodded at two deputies who stood at one end of the bridge. He knew the older one, Al Borland, a beefy man with close-cropped gray hair, the mottled complexion of a heavy drinker and the generally skeptical view of humanity that cops acquired after twenty years on the job. Braden, whose own disposition was often questioned, got along with him fine.

"Morning, Al," he said, nodding also at the younger deputy, whom he didn't know. "What have you got?"

Borland stepped aside, giving Braden his first glimpse of the green plastic sheet at the edge of the muddy creek below them. "An ugly one," he said.

Braden suspected he wasn't talking about the victim.

"We haven't touched her, just covered her up. We're waitin' on the techs."

"You see enough to fill me in while we're waiting?"

"Yeah, sure. She's a young woman, maybe twenty. Caucasian,

no ID. Not a stitch on her—that's why the deputy used the tarp. Those footsteps on the bank, those are Deputy Reardon's. He's the one covered her." Borland caught Braden's glance and said, "Shit, Braden, you can't blame him. There was already a crowd building up on that path over there. Some of those ghouls even have cameras, for Chrissakes. They'll be peddling pictures all over the college campus by this afternoon. This is . . . she was a good-looking woman. Talk about sickos . . . these gawkers are almost as bad as the perp."

"How was she done?"

"There's a little blood, not much. She wasn't done here. That's why Reardon figured he wasn't messin' up a murder scene goin' down there. There were no tracks. That's soft mud and sand on the creek bottom, and the bank's soft too. She wasn't carried down. She was just dumped from this bridge."

Both sides of the creek between the highway and the pedestrian bridge had been sealed off with yellow crime scene tape, but at least a dozen onlookers hung over the railing along the bike path, staring down and whispering to each other, the way people do in the presence of the dead, as if loud voices might disturb the departed spirit.

Borland followed Braden's gaze. "I know," he said. "Time I got here it was too late to secure that part of the scene, the gawkers were ahead of me. Anyways, she had to be dumped from this side."

"Maybe he had trouble lifting her over the side," Braden said, more to himself than to Borland. "There might be something."

The parapet for the highway bridge was cement. Like the paved highway, it offered little promise for trace evidence but would have to be thoroughly checked out.

"I want to have a look at her."

"No problem," the deputy sheriff said.

Braden went down to the creek twenty feet east of where the victim lay under her green plastic cover. He approached the body slowly along the edge of the creek bed. Water sloshed into his shoes. Ignoring the stares of the curious bystanders on the bike path above and behind him, he squatted and lifted a corner of the sheet.

The girl lay facedown in the mud. A small amount of blood

had seeped into the moist earth, looking black in the gray morning light. Under other conditions the victim would have been beautiful, Braden saw. A slender, shapely figure with nice long legs. Dirt smeared her buttocks and thighs. He wondered what time the tide had gone out and whether she had rolled at all. No, he decided, examining the creek bank. She had been dropped right here, a ten-foot drop from the road, more like twelve from the top of the parapet, and the impact had created the depression in the sand she lay in. There were no visible cuts or bruises on her back or on the backs of her legs. She lay facedown, and gravity was already pulling the blood downward. He could see signs of lividity that would be more obvious when she was turned over.

Braden carefully lifted her wrist. It remained flexible and there was little resistance. He touched her hair with the tip of his fore-finger, gently moving the strands aside. A blue eye stared up at him.

Unnerved, Braden let the plastic sheet drop over her.

He climbed to the top of the bank and stood there quietly, thinking about the young woman under her shroud. There was a good chance she was a San Carlos College student, given her age. All of her dreams and aspirations, the hopes and fears of her par-ents, all of it ended before her life had really begun to find its shape and purpose.

He wondered when the medical examiner and crime scene technicians would get there. Everything at a scene waited for them. Maybe there was nothing for them to find other than the victim herself. Borland was right, this wasn't the murder scene. But every-thing was on hold all the same.

The damp morning chill penetrated his jacket, causing him to hunch his shoulders. He was suddenly aware of being stared at, whispered about, though he did not turn his head toward the bike path. He was used to the stares and whispers, but that didn't make them any easier to ignore. *That's him. How could they let him near her?*

Borland coughed, standing beside him. Braden shook himself. "Who found her?" he asked.

"We got a 911 call at . . ." Borland consulted a small spiral notepad. ". . . 5:42. Kid said he was out biking, came over that wooden bridge behind you. He saw the body."

"That early in the morning?"

"It's a popular trail. Some of those bikers, joggers too, they're out while it's still dark. They have the path to themselves then, I guess. Anyway, he pedaled back to that coffee shop just off the highway, the Bright Spot? About a mile back? He called in from a public phone there. The call's on tape."

"You talk to him yet?"

Borland shook his head. "Only got here five minutes before you did. Kid's name is Harry Malkowski. College student. He's back there at the Bright Spot havin' coffee. I got a deputy baby-sittin' him, Officer Pritkin."

Braden had received his own call from the watch officer at the San Carlos Police Department at 6:08, which was only twenty-six minutes from the time the 911 call was clocked at the sheriff's station. Pretty fast work, he thought. He wondered what that meant.

"You want this one, Braden," Borland said, as if answering Braden's unspoken question, "we got no beef. Thing is, I don't have one homicide detective isn't up to his ass in alligators. We don't need this one. Might be yours, anyway, if she's from the college and got picked up in town. This isn't where he did it to her."

Borland was making the same assumption Braden had: the dead girl's killer was male. Not much of a reach, he thought.

He was relieved to hear there wouldn't be a jurisdictional quarrel over the case. The sheriff's department was predictably swamped in violent criminal investigations. By comparison San Carlos was an enclave of peace and tranquility. Braden had been there a year. This case, if it fell into his lap, would be his first murder investigation since leaving the LAPD's Homicide Division.

"I'll be glad to take it."

"Uh . . . might be one problem."

"What's that?"

"These wetlands are U.S. government property. The feds might want to get in on it."

Braden groaned aloud. "Not the FBI."

Borland shifted his feet. He was a heavy man, with a cop's big feet in heavy black leather shoes. Braden knew the deputy sheriff was glad to get the case off his hands—it had the look and smell of something that wasn't going to go away—but something was bothering Borland. Before he could speculate further Borland answered the question.

"Thing is, Braden, the sheriff's part of this liaison arrangement with the FBI's NCAVC . . . the VICAP thing? This is the kind of crime they want feedback on, you know? The sheriff won't want to let that pass. I mean, the forms are voluntary, but if I was to let him know you'd send 'em in, he'd be happy. That might keep the feds off your back too. Otherwise, you know how they are, they might want to take over the whole investigation."

"Great," Braden muttered, thinking of the endless pages of a VICAP questionnaire.

The NCAVC was the National Center for the Analysis of Violent Crime, headquartered at Quantico, Virginia, the site of the FBI Academy. VICAP—the Violent Criminal Apprehension Program—was one of its most important tools. Fully operational after ten years of development, VICAP was essentially a computerized program storing data on violent crimes reported by police departments throughout the United States, cataloging and cross-referencing detailed information about the crimes, the victims, the perpetrators and their MO's and profiles. Braden had no doubt the program was a significant crime-fighting advance, enabling an investigator in Hobbs, New Mexico, say, to link a murder weapon or a fingerprint found at a local crime scene to a similar crime recorded two years previously in Boston. Not after days, weeks or months of laborious plodding, but in the nanosecond burst of a computer match. What made him feel a little old was the prospect of filling out more forms.

"Tell the sheriff to send over the forms," he said. "I'm not sure I have them."

Relieved, Borland plodded off to his vehicle to make a call. Left alone, Braden shook a cigarette from a nearly full pack—he was trying to cut down—and flicked his Zippo lighter with his thumb, cupping his hands to shield the flame. There was a momentary lull in the traffic on the highway, and in the silence Braden heard a familiar whirring sound.

He turned quickly. A young man on the bikers' overpass had a camcorder snugged against his cheek, its lens staring straight at Braden.

Anger flared. Braden opened his mouth, but at the last second bit off a shout. Letting them see how easy it was to get to him would only make things worse.

Braden had put in nine years with the LAPD, the last two with the Homicide Division at Parker Center. He was a rising star in the department. They said he had a gift for it—not only for the painstaking attention to procedure and detail that were part of any homicide investigation, but also for those flashes of intuition or insight that jumped past the physical evidence toward another kind of truth.

Then came the Incident. Braden's fifteen minutes of fame, recorded in a jumpy black-and-white video by a witness. The key moments—less than thirty seconds of film—were played over and over again on the nightly news, local and network stations, *Hard Copy* and *A Current Affair*. In those thirty seconds Braden's career at Parker Center went down the tubes.

He blocked off the bitter memory. He kept his back to the man with the video camera and stared down at the unidentified victim of a brutal murder, his face as expressionless as a block of wood.

He was relieved when he saw the flashing light of an ambulance up on the highway and, closer, the familiar small, neat figure of the county medical examiner walking toward him.

Five

TED NAKASHIMI LOOKED more like a high school dropout than one of the county's best medical technicians. He wore faded jeans with a hole in one knee, dirty Reeboks, a polo shirt with some visible stains and a red headband he used to keep his lank, shoulder-length black hair away from his face. He was short, round-faced and breezy, his brown eyes perpetually amused behind coke bottle spectacles. Braden knew for a fact that the DA's prosecutors hated having to call him as an expert witness in criminal court cases, not for lack of competence but because of the impression he made on jurors. In truth, Nakashimi's careless appearance and breezy manner disguised a sharp-eyed, serious professional, a perfectionist in a profession that measured its daily achievements with microscopic precision.

"Hey, what you got for me, Braden?" the ME asked as he arrived at the end of the bridge.

"I always save the best for you, Doc."

Nakashimi examined the ground carefully before stepping down the bank toward the shape beside the creek under the green plastic sheet. Before lifting the sheet he peered closely at the surrounding area. From the bridge above him a police photographer began taking pictures.

"These footprints belong to you guys?"

"That's right," Borland said.

"Nobody else been down here, right? I want some pictures before I move her."

While he waited for the photographer to finish, Nakashimi

glanced over at the bystanders on the wooden overpass. An expression of distaste flickered across his normally impassive features. "If we're not gonna sell tickets, I need a screen here. Get me another tarp, two of the deputies can hold it."

He had two deputies hold a tarpaulin shoulder high, creating a buffer between the victim and the gawkers, some of whom called out their protests. The technician ignored them. Going down on one knee beside the body, he beckoned to Braden, "You gonna be working this, Detective?"

"Could be."

"Unless the feds take it over, right? Isn't this a wildlife sanctuary? Protected government land?"

Nakashimi used a voice-activated tape recorder during his examination, but Braden made his own notes. The dead girl seemed unnaturally white in the growing brightness of the morning, her nakedness a cruel atrocity, taking away any shred of dignity she might have had in death. The tech murmured into his recorder as she examined the victim's back and legs, noting the minimal degree of rigor and lividity, both of which would help to determine the approximate time of death, examining her fingers and fingernails carefully. The latter had false nails attached, bright red and perfectly shaped except for one that had been broken off. Nakashimi, who took swabs, smears and samples as he worked, putting each into separate plastic bags, seemed surprised at the condition of the fingernails. "Either she was washed thoroughly or she didn't put up a fight," he noted, glancing up at Braden. "Maybe because he had her taped up good."

"Can you tell me what kind of tape?"

"What, you think I'm a magician?" Nakashimi pursed his lips as he picked up one of the girl's wrists. "Sticky stuff. Maybe heavy-duty package tape. There's some residue on her ankles, too. I'll run some tests."

He turned the woman over. Braden heard a raw intake of breath from one of the deputies behind him. "Oh shit," the medical technician muttered.

The girl had been battered savagely about the face and body. Lips pulped over broken teeth. Her nose was a smear. One eye—

the one that had peered sidelong at Braden when he lifted up her hair—was clear, but the flesh around the other was so swollen and discolored that the eye itself was no longer visible. Similar swelling and discoloration marked the abrasions and contusions over her chest and stomach.

Nakashimi paused as he examined her belly closely. After taking samples of blood, sand and dried mud, he used a damp sponge and a soft brush to clean the blood-smeared stomach. As he did so, something unexpected was revealed. Both the tech and Braden stared down at it in silence. The cuts that crisscrossed the victim's abdomen were neither random slashes nor deep, penetrating wounds. The shallow cuts—three horizontal slashes and one vertical—traced a large capital letter "E."

"Cause of death?" Braden murmured.

"We'll have to wait and see. She's got broken ribs, maybe a punctured lung. She was hit on the neck, the larynx may be crushed. But the cuts . . ." Nakashimi shook his head ". . . not deep enough."

"He beat her to death."

"That's not a medical conclusion, Detective, but it's a helluva good guess. Maybe I can tell you more after the cut."

"How soon can you get to it?" Braden's tone was flat and hard.

Nakashimi raised an eyebrow. "This is Saturday, Braden. By midnight the county morgue will be knee-deep in bodies."

Braden stared at him. "We have a real bastard loose here."

"You've got a weirdo," the ME admitted.

"The colder she gets, the farther away he gets, you know that. How long has she been dead? There's almost no rigor."

"What do you need me for?" Nakashimi answered testily. "Okay, okay . . . she's been dead about three hours, give or take an hour. Don't hold me to that, but it should be pretty close."

Braden glanced at his watch. The medical examiner's estimate put the time of death at around four that morning. Or between three and five as the outside parameters.

Braden thought about the biker who had made the 911 call at a little after five-thirty. He wasn't completely out of the picture.

"What else can you give me, Doc?" he said after a moment. "Did he do it with his fists? Or did he use a weapon of some kind?"

"I don't like guessing, Detective," Nakashimi said with a frown. "But he couldn't have done that much damage with his fists in the ordinary way. Unless he's like that fighter—what was his name, Duran? Hands of Stone?"

"What are you telling me?"

"You know what it looks like, Sergeant? Like someone used good old-fashioned brass knuckles. Or maybe he was holding a role of quarters when he hit her. And there's something else. He was wearing gloves. Smooth leather gloves. There are no obvious pattern impressions in the skin. Also, lots of damage, but no obvious trace evidence of skin or tissue other than the victim's. We won't know for sure until I've done some tests." He paused. "This was no spur of the moment thing, Braden. Your killer came prepared."

"Was she sexually assaulted?"

"Oh yeah, he tore her up in at least two places. There's vaginal and anal tearing and bruising. But he practiced safe sex," the ME added with heavy irony. "He didn't leave us any semen."

"And the cuts on her stomach? You read that the way I do? The letter 'E'?"

"Could be a symbol of some kind, but it looks like an 'E' to me."

"And the vaginal cut? What does that tell you?"

Nakashimi shrugged. "It means he likes to play games, Braden. The cutting is a message, maybe a signature. Or maybe he's just laughing at us."

The medical technician stepped back. "Let's get the rest of the pictures and get her out of here. Maybe your perpetrator isn't as smart as he thinks. Maybe he left something behind as a calling card that he didn't think of. I won't know until I get her on the table."

"You'll get right on it?" Braden pressed him again.

Nakashimi studied him for a long moment. "I love working on weekends, Braden, you know that. It's the OT."

"I'd appreciate it."

For a moment the ME was uncharacteristically serious. "Maybe we should all hope this one was personal," he said, looking down at the body.

"Whatta ya mean, Doc?" Al Borland asked. The deputy sheriff had joined them in time to hear Nakashimi's last comment.

"That letter he cut. The alphabet has twenty-six letters."

As BRADEN WAS walking back to his car, Borland caught up to him. "Wait up, Braden."

Braden turned. The body of the murdered girl was being loaded onto the ambulance. The crowd of bystanders lingered on the pedestrian bridge. Southern Californians walked out of Dodger Stadium in the seventh inning, Braden reflected, but for a homicide they hung in there to the bitter end.

The deputy sheriff stared past Braden's eyes into the distance, as if embarrassed. "I been on the horn to the sheriff. He agrees we should work together on this," Borland said, as if he and Braden had reached such an agreement.

Braden tried to hide his irritation. He wanted the case, and that meant he didn't want a jurisdictional dispute dragged out. "How would we coordinate?"

"I got this deputy I can cut loose. The one I told you about? Officer Pritkin? He's back there at the Bright Spot with the caller. He's green, Braden, but he's eager. And he comes with a bonus."

"For Chrissake, Al—"

"He's the only cop I ever met doesn't hate forms. And he's in love with computers. You got to coordinate with VICAP on this, Braden, Officer Pritkin is your man."

Six

WITH THE FIRE largely contained, Dave's crew of volunteers were released at six o'clock Saturday morning. When he reached his street and turned into the driveway, he was just behind the paper boy who had tossed the morning *Los Angeles Times* into the rose-bushes. Dave couldn't remember anything about the drive out of the hills. It was as if he had been driving while asleep. A zombie. Appearing out of the morning mist like something from *Night of the Living Dead.*

Dumb movie, he thought. What made a cult classic? Oughta be an article in that. How about a seminar on cult films? His thoughts seemed fuzzy.

The children were still in bed, the house cool. Glenda was awake, opening the door for him, still wearing her nightgown. She had heard the car turn into the drive, heard the car door shut. They hugged silently.

"Would you like something to eat?" she asked. "Some hot chocolate?"

He shook his head. "Just sleep. I'm falling down."

She followed him upstairs and sat on the bed while he undressed and stepped into the bathroom to shower. He stood under the warm shower for five minutes, but when he emerged it seemed to him that the smell of smoke and ash still clung to his skin. He dried himself quickly and, shivering, tumbled naked into bed.

He stared up at her. "Did you get any sleep?"

"A little." He thought she was lying.

"If Beringer really has come back, we're going to have to deal with it."

She stared hard at him. "You think that's all this is?"

Dave started to reply and thought better of it. He sank back against the pillows. Glenda stalked over to the dormer windows facing the front of the house. The shades were raised halfway—they both liked an open window and fresh air while they slept. The Battenburg lace curtains stirred in the current of cool moist air coming through the window. The streetlight just north of the house was still on, its sensor fooled by the overcast morning, and Dave could see mist curling in the yellow light and flakes of ash falling softly on the roof shingles.

Glenda had her arms folded under her breasts. Her lips were tight and there was color in her cheeks. Dave thought she looked beautiful. How many old movies had used that line? *You're beautiful when you're angry, kid.*

"I suppose you think I'm overreacting."

"I didn't say that."

"You don't have to. I know you. Dammit, Dave, what Ralph did last night was deliberate! Calling up out of the blue, giving us no warning, then saying something to upset Richie. He *wanted* to stir things up."

"You don't know that, honey. Maybe he just wanted to remind Richie who he was."

"Then why hang up? Why didn't he have anything to say to me? Or to you, for that matter?"

"Talking to Richie probably upset him—"

"Oh my God! How can you defend him like that?"

"I'm not defending him, I'm only saying we should give him the benefit of the doubt, at least for the moment."

She stalked over to the side of the bed and stood hipshot, glaring down at him. Her breasts jiggled under the cotton knit nightshirt when she walked. The morning chill had made her nipples erect, hard under the shirt.

"You don't know him."

"Well, that's true, I never even met the guy. But he couldn't be all that bad or you wouldn't have married him. And he wouldn't have fathered a kid like Richie."

"You don't know," Glenda whispered.

Dave stared at her, sensing something in her that went much deeper than anger. After a moment he said, "Maybe you should tell me."

Glenda hesitated. She had never been able to bring herself to talk to Dave in any detail about Ralph. With strangers in her support group she had spilled out everything, but that was different. The people who had listened to her then were all battered women in one way or another, each with her own story to tell. There was never any need to explain.

"You'd have to know him, Dave. He can be . . . very cruel. He's mean, and he doesn't care if he hurts people—in fact, he enjoys it. What he did last night, that was to hurt me, knowing how I would react . . . but he didn't care if Richie was hurt as well. And you know he was."

"It was thoughtless," Dave admitted. "But look, honey, he probably hasn't been around kids much, especially his son. So if he blunders around, that's understandable. Doesn't make it right, but—"

Glenda shook her head sharply. "You're not listening to me. Ralph doesn't blunder. He knows exactly what he's doing. He's . . ."

Evil, she thought. Something Dave Lindstrom didn't believe in. Dave fumbled for excuses to explain the actions of drive-by shooters, for God's sake. Ralph Beringer was something totally alien to his experience.

Sometimes Glenda resented Dave's seemingly idyllic youth. He had grown up in Cedar Rapids, Iowa, and he spoke with fondness of Jefferson High, hayrides and Halloween pranks, kolaches from Bohemitown, trips to the Amanas with his parents and summer vacations on his grandparents' farm. He remembered it all without any warts or blemishes. On their trips back to Iowa to visit Dave's family—the trips were less frequent now that his parents were both dead—somehow he made it all seem real. In Dave's Cedar Rapids the Ozzie and Harriet Nelson family wouldn't even have stood out.

Dave's favorite Christmas movie, predictably, was *It's a Wonderful Life*.

"He's what?" Dave asked quietly.

Glenda shook her head again, still standing beside the bed. She shivered from the chill, glanced toward the window and the curtains stirring. Gooseflesh popped out on her arms. "You wouldn't understand."

"Maybe I would if you'd tell me."

How could she tell him now, after all these years? It would seem as if she had been hiding part of herself from him, as indeed she had. How could she even begin to make him understand?

She had tried to distance herself from the two and a half years she had lived with Ralph Beringer. Ralph was a career serviceman—a sergeant in the Air Force when he left the States eight years ago. She had married him when she was nineteen, overwhelmed by the sheer animal force of him, unable to resist his physical strength or the unsuspected wildness he tapped in her. She had been pregnant with Richie when they married, and after the baby was born she had endured increasingly violent abuse for two years before Ralph shipped out to Germany.

In Ralph's absence she had started to attend meetings of a support group of servicemen's wives, amazed to discover there were so many others like her trapped in brutal relationships. She had not dared to look for help while Ralph was there, but three thousand miles of ocean gave her the courage she needed. Four months of therapy and anguished soul-searching later, she wrote the Dear John letter she dreaded.

There was no reply. Ralph's silence was more frightening than any angry call or letter. For weeks she dreaded each strident ring of the phone; when the day's mail came she often sat staring at the accumulation of bills and trash mail without the courage to sort through it.

Then, three months after her letter, an envelope arrived addressed to her and bearing a German stamp and cancellation mark. Inside was a single sheet of notepaper. Across the sheet four words were scrawled in Ralph's nearly illegible hand.

It's not over, bitch.

The blunt warning—as cruel in what it left unsaid as in its vicious message—nearly undid her resolve. She wouldn't let it happen.

Glenda had left Georgia, where Beringer had last been stationed before shipping overseas. She had wanted to sever any connection with their life together, to get as far away from him as she could, moving all the way across the United States to California. She had not dared to conceal the move. She knew Ralph would find her if she tried to hide and punish both her and Richie for it. Instead she lived in terror of the day when he might complete his overseas service—or come back on leave.

That first Christmas in California there was another message. It came in an innocent guise—a present for Richie from his father in Germany. Because Richie saw the package and was excited over it, she could only watch helplessly while the boy eagerly tore at the gift paper wrapping. He squealed with delight over the brightly painted wooden toy, a foot-high nutcracker carved in the image of a woodsman with an ax.

Richie left the toy under the tree that Christmas Eve. Glenda could not tear her eyes from the ax in the woodsman's hand, reflecting a red glow from a nearby tree light.

Divorced and alone with a small child, Glenda had tried to rebuild her life. She found a job as an assistant in the office of the Dean of Men at UCLA. She began learning to survive.

She had never expected to fall in love—really fall in love—but two summers after moving to Los Angeles she met David Lindstrom. He was taking summer courses at UCLA in filmmaking and screenwriting, working toward a doctorate in Dramatic Arts, when their paths crossed.

Glenda was having lunch by herself, sitting on a bench in the sun, when someone sat down beside her. Long skinny legs in jeans, a denim shirt, unruly hair and a nice smile. "You brought your lunch?" he commented. "I envy you. What's that, peanut butter and jelly? My favorite, especially if it's on cheap, squishy white bread—"

She bolted from the bench, dropping her brown paper bag that still held an apple. She ran, heedless of the shouts of the slender man who had sat down beside her.

For a week she avoided going outside on campus during her lunch hour. When she finally did, Dave Lindstrom found her. He was carrying a fresh apple in a brown paper bag.

Only much later did Glenda learn how persistently Dave had mounted a campaign to break down her resistance, gradually undercutting her fear by revealing a man of simple decency. He was gentle, good-humored, quiet, with an incredibly even temper. After six years of marriage she had yet to see him fly into an uncontrolled rage. He was attractive—handsome in her eyes—six feet tall, thin, with lean, regular features and a generous mouth always curved upward slightly at the corners. He didn't have the animal magnetism that Ralph Beringer used like a weapon, but Dave was imaginative, playful and considerate in bed, a caring partner, a loving father to both Richie and Elli, the daughter born a year after their wedding.

She had never expected to trust a man completely again. Dave had managed the impossible, Made it so that the night sweats began to go away and the stark terror of awakening shivering at the slam of a car door. Eventually that thump in the night became an innocent sound, not the dreaded signal that *he* was home. In time she was able to go weeks without reliving the abject fear, the despair, the sense of worthlessness.

"You didn't get any sleep," Dave said. "Come to bed."

She crawled under the covers beside him and crept into the circle of his arms. Thin as he was, Dave radiated heat like an oven. On chilly nights she loved snuggling against him, spooning, sheltered within that aura of warmth. Not merely a physical warmth but a haven of love, peace, safety.

But there was no safety, she thought bitterly now, her momentary calm evaporating. There would be no peace.

This morning her body slowly warmed from the touch of her husband's, but deep within her a core of cold remained.

It's not over, bitch.

She shivered again.

"Hey, hey," Dave whispered.

"I prayed he would never come back."

"Are you so sure he has? We don't even know where he was calling from."

She wanted to believe him, but the frightened woman she had thought long buried knew better. Tears ran down her cheeks. Dave's hand trailed up her arm, his touch light, and when she resisted he turned her face toward his. His lips tasted tears.

"Whatever he did, it was a long time ago," Dave said. "No one's going to hurt you now—you or Richie."

Glenda didn't answer.

Seven

OFFICER JACK PRITKIN was no more than twenty-five, red hair in a brush cut, the clean-jawed look of a college halfback.

"You ever work a homicide before, Pritkin?" Braden asked him.

"No, sir."

"Borland says you're good with paperwork and computers. I'll need some help there. Like with this VICAP program? You know it?"

"You get me a copy of your crime scene report and the autopsy protocol and the rest of it, Detective Braden, I'll be logged on with Quantico the same day."

"Good," Braden said. Maybe this arrangement would work out after all.

He had pulled Pritkin out of the Bright Spot. Now he glanced through the water-streaked window into the diner-styled coffee shop, where Harry Malkowski sat alone in a red vinyl-covered booth.

"You talk to him at all?" he asked the deputy.

"No, sir. Sheriff Borland said I should just baby-sit him."

"Good. You can wait in your car or I'll see you back at the station. I don't want to crowd this kid too much."

"Yes, sir."

"And don't call me sir."

"Yes, uh . . . Detective."

"Call me Braden."

Deputy Pritkin grinned sheepishly. Braden left him outside and went into the diner. It was warm inside, with a background of muted jazz. When the set ended Braden recognized the voice of a

Long Beach DJ, one of those who served up vintage jazz and provided listeners with the names and personal histories of every instrumentalist.

When Braden slipped into the booth opposite Harry Malkowski, the young man jumped.

"Detective Braden," the detective said, offering Harry a flash of his badge before returning it to his jacket pocket. "You're Harry Malkowski?"

"Uh . . . yeah. That's with an 'l.'"

"Got it. You made that 911 call."—Braden consulted his notes, although it wasn't necessary—"at five-forty-two this morning."

Malkowski licked his lips. His right leg projected into the aisle and it kept jumping up and down. Braden figured his nervousness was normal. Most people were nervous when confronted by a policeman, especially under unusual circumstances like these.

Harry Malkowski was a thin, dark-haired youth, perhaps twenty-one years old, no more than a hundred and fifty pounds, maybe five eight when he stood up straight. Narrow chest and shoulders, small hands with long, sensitive fingers. Braden couldn't picture him lifting the girl over the guardrail of the highway bridge, but you never knew.

He couldn't picture those hands battering the girl to death, with or without brass knuckles.

A waitress with a full head of frizzy blond hair, a short skirt, button nose and an impudent smile brought him a cup of coffee. The name tag on her bosom read Iris. Braden sipped at his hot coffee, studying Harry Malkowski in silence. Harry couldn't hold his stare. His eyes jumped around the coffee shop as if searching for a way to escape.

"Tell me, Harry, what were you doing out on the highway at that hour of the morning?"

"I always go out early on weekends—I mean, with my bike. It's the best time, there aren't too many people out."

"See anyone else out this morning?"

"Uh, no . . . maybe one or two in town, but not on . . . on the highway."

"You nervous, Harry?"

"Uh, no . . . no, I'm not . . . it's just that, uh, seeing her like that shook me up. The girl . . ."

"You were on the bike path, right?"

"Yeah, you don't dare ride on the highway. Some of those drivers will force you off the road just for kicks."

"Did you notice any particular cars on the road? Before you came to that bridge?"

"No . . . I guess there might have been a little traffic, but I wasn't paying attention. There was hardly any, I know that. When I stopped at the bridge, you know, it was eerie, like I was completely alone out there. There wasn't a sound except for the birds. The fog was kinda thick, swirling around. I mean, it was eerie."

"What made you stop there?"

"I didn't stop. I mean, uh, I just saw her out of the corner of my eye. Shit, I ran into the railing, I couldn't stop myself. Uh . . . sorry."

"Don't worry about it. Go on."

"Well, I mean, that's it, you know. I saw her, and I stopped. I couldn't believe it at first. But when I looked I could see it was a girl, you know, just lying there."

"How close did you look, Harry? Did you climb down there by the creek?"

"No! No, I just looked over from the bridge—the wooden over-pass on the bike path. You can see for yourself, it's not very far from the highway. I could see her all right. I didn't have to get any closer."

"How did you know she was dead?"

"Well, uh, I just . . . it was the way she was lying there, face-down and, uh, not wearing anything, you know. I just assumed." Remembering that startling vision, Harry Malkowski turned pale. He licked his lips again. "I rode back to the Bright Spot as fast as I could and called 911. Wasn't that, uh, the right thing to do? I mean, should I have gone down there to make sure . . . ?"

"You did fine," Braden said.

He leaned back in the booth, glancing around the diner as he sipped his coffee, which had become lukewarm. The blond waitress, aware of him, grabbed the coffeepot and started toward him. Braden smiled at her and waited while she refilled his mug.

"Everything okay here, gentlemen?"

"Fine."

"You're a cop, aren't you?"

"That's right."

"You want a doughnut?"

Braden grinned. "Come to think of it, I haven't had breakfast. You got a cinnamon roll?"

"The best. Fresh this morning."

"You, Harry?"

Harry Malkowski shook his head. He seemed to turn a little paler at the thought of food.

"One cinnamon roll, coming right up," Iris said.

She bustled off, short skirt twitching above long, shapely legs that wore only their summer tan. Harry Malkowski was not too under the weather to notice.

Braden had not seriously expected the chemistry student to be a legitimate suspect, and after talking to Harry he was even less inclined to think so. It was not unusual for criminals, even murderers, to telephone the authorities about their crimes, but the method of choice was the anonymous tip. For a killer to make a 911 call and identify himself would be nervy as hell, and Harry Malkowski simply didn't fit that picture.

"Did you recognize her, Harry? Ever see her before?"

Harry shook his head almost violently. "No! I mean . . . d'you think she's a San Carlos College student? Oh shit . . ."

"We don't know yet," Braden said. "She's the right age, and the crime scene isn't that far from town."

"You think she was killed right there?" Harry was stunned, as if the possibility had not occurred to him.

"The crime scene is where the victim was found, not necessarily where she was killed," Braden explained. He fished in his wallet for one of his less beaten up cards. "Thanks for your help, Harry. Here's my card. If you think of anything else, call me, okay? You'll have to come into the station to make a formal statement. Can you do that today? Is that a problem?"

"Uh, no, sir."

Braden looked at Harry Malkowski's hands again as he took the card and slipped it into his wallet. Harry was a chemistry student, and Braden could picture those slim hands pouring liquid into a vial. He could picture them playing the piano or writing a letter home to his mom. What he couldn't picture was those same hands as lethal weapons.

Eight

DAVE LINDSTROM SLEPT all day Saturday. That night, watching a favorite vintage movie on cable, a thriller with Ray Milland called *The Big Clock*, he missed the television newscasts. As a consequence he didn't become aware of the murder of an unidentified young woman found in the wetlands south of San Carlos until he opened the paper Sunday morning. A half-dozen killings on a weekend being fairly normal for the Los Angeles area, the death of another Jane Doe did not rate a headline story. But it was on the front page of the *Los Angeles Times* down in the lower left-hand corner. The woman, according to the story, had been sexually assaulted and savagely beaten. She had been dumped beside a creek where her nude body was found early Saturday morning, without any identifying clothing or jewelry.

The story disturbed Dave. How could such things happen? Yet they had become commonplace in America, the stuff of countless news stories, films and novels, and even more nightmares.

Later that morning, after the family returned from church, Dave welcomed Glenda's suggestion that he take Richie for a drive to the beach. She wanted him to be alone with Richie, who had been withdrawn and uncommunicative since the stunning Friday night phone call. Glenda knew that Richie admired Dave far more than Dave realized. "See if he'll talk to you, honey. Maybe he'll open up. This is hard for him. He has to let some of his feelings get out."

Dave figured an outing with Richie would be good for both of them. He had forgotten that the road to the coast ran past the wet-lands mentioned in the lurid news story.

There was a traffic backup for a quarter mile north of the point where the highway narrowed for a bridge crossing a creek. A sheriff's car was parked along the side of the road, and some other cars had stopped on the shoulder on both sides of the bridge. There were also spectators gathered on the bike path just east of the highway, looking down at the creek where it ran under the bridge. Dave suddenly realized they were ogling the site where the murdered girl's body had been found.

"Dad . . . can we stop?"

"The deputy is waving us on. I guess they have enough people stopped there."

Clusters of flowers were tied to the railing of the wooden bridge on the bike path, along with candles, small cards and signs Dave couldn't read. Another phenomenon of our times, he re-flected, the creation of shrines to strangers who had been brutally slain or killed in automobile accidents. Telling ourselves that each of us matters.

Richie twisted around to peer back as they passed over the bridge, but his view was blocked off as Dave drove on, resuming highway speed.

"I wonder what it was," Richie said.

"An accident, probably," Dave said, justifying the white lie to himself. "Hey, you're the one who gets queasy at the sight of blood, remember?"

"Yeah, but . . . an accident's different." There were a lot of people hanging around for just an accident, Richie thought. And there were no wrecked cars on the highway.

They drove in silence toward the ocean. The discussion over the "accident" had broken the ice with Richie, and when Dave caught his first glimpse of the surf ahead he decided it was as good a time as any to try to draw the boy out.

"About Friday night, Richie . . . are you okay with that phone call?"

After a brief hesitation Richie said, "Yeah."

"What's bothering you—what he said over the phone, or the fact that your father is here after all this time?"

"I don't know . . . why hasn't he been to see me?"

"Maybe he's planning on doing that. It's possible he's not ready . . . and he wanted to get you and your mom thinking about him. He's been away a long time."

"I know."

"You were what, two when he left? Do you remember much about him at all?"

"Well . . . I remember him. I mean, I'd know him if I saw him."

"Sure, you've seen that picture your mom has of the three of you. She didn't want you to forget him. I didn't either, Richie. Do you understand that?"

"Yeah . . . I guess."

Dave turned south along the oceanfront, wishing the sun would come out.

Richie said, "Why did he hang up? Why didn't he talk to Mom or you?"

"I don't know. But you're old enough to understand that your mom and your dad had problems. Lots of married people do, even when they have kids. You must know some of your friends at school whose parents are divorced, just like your mom and . . ."

Dave was having trouble referring to Ralph Beringer as Richie's dad. More trouble than he had anticipated. This isn't about your feelings or your ego, he reminded himself. It's about Richie's being able to sort out *his* feelings.

"Why did he stay away so long?"

"He was in the Air Force. A soldier doesn't get to choose when he comes and goes. The service tells him."

It was a lame excuse, Dave thought. Soldiers in a peacetime army had leaves. Beringer hadn't returned to the States for eight years because he chose not to. And even if such a trip was impractical, he could have done more for his son than send an occasional Christmas card or present. There had been few enough of those, no more than a half-dozen contacts of any kind that Dave Lindstrom knew about in the last six years.

To be fair, during part of that time there was a Cold War,

along with a Gulf War and a number of other dustups involving the U.S. military. Ralph Beringer had not always had time on his hands.

"He doesn't care about me."

Dave sighed. "If he didn't care, he wouldn't have come back now. Think about that, Richie."

Dave parked in one of the big deserted parking lots at the beach and they walked across the white sand toward the pounding surf. The ocean looked gray and cold under the low clouds, but on the plus side the chilly weather had kept the usual Sunday crowds away, leaving the long expanse of beach relatively deserted. A few brave surfers were visible near the pier about a half mile distant, paddling out to catch a wave. A week ago, with the beach area enjoying warm Santa Ana winds and temperatures in the eighties, this strand had been paved with tanned flesh.

Carrying his shoes, Dave walked along the wet sand close to the breaking waves, while Richie searched for shells and interesting flotsam deposited by the tide.

Why had Beringer come back now?

Glenda was understandably upset. Perhaps she was afraid Beringer would demand visiting rights with Richie, a concern that had never surfaced while he was overseas. Suddenly the status quo was being overturned. The rules might change, dramatically altering the comfortable assumptions of their lives. Hell, Dave couldn't blame Beringer if the man wanted some time with his son. He didn't particularly like the idea, but . . .

What did Ralph Beringer really want? And what kind of a man was he to create such fear and revulsion in the woman he had once presumably loved?

Uncomfortable questions for a day at the beach. How did the line go? Life's not a day at the beach. . . .

Staring out over the gray expanse of ocean, Dave felt a prickling sensation, as if someone were watching him. He turned quickly. No one. The strand was almost deserted. Only the seagulls making spidery tracks in the wet sand as, like Richie, they searched the foam left behind by receding waves.

*　*　*

G<small>LENDA</small> L<small>INDSTROM</small> <small>FELT</small> as if she were breaking apart.

She had tried to keep up an appearance of normality that morning, through Sunday Mass, a family breakfast of pancakes and sausages, the Sunday papers scattered around the living room in the usual cheerful chaos. Because the Raiders were blacked out on television—Richie's favorite team—he hadn't resisted her suggestion that he and Dave head for the beach.

Now Elli was across the street at the Schneiders' house—five-year-old Connie Schneider was her best friend—and Glenda was alone. No need to smile now, to act unconcerned, to disguise her shaking hands with busywork.

She picked up the living room with a kind of frantic energy. Stacked the morning dishes in the dishwasher. Started a load of clothes in the washer. Walked back through the house and found herself peering out the front windows toward the street. Looking for what? No need to answer.

She went up the stairs, her hand absently caressing the polished banister. She loved her old house, the cornices and woodwork, the stairway, the details that couldn't be found in new construction. Too expensive, everyone said, even while finish carpenters were begging for work. But this morning the house felt different. Emptier. Quieter. She caught herself listening to every creak and crack. A scraping on the roof made her nerves vibrate. A branch of the huge old jacaranda in the backyard touched the roof, and Dave had been promising to trim it back. He wanted to do it himself. Tree surgeons in Southern California were tree butchers, he said, creators of stunted skeletons. With its lavender petals the jacaranda was gorgeous in bloom, and neither of them wanted to see it butchered.

The house felt colder. In part that could be attributed to the gray, sunless autumn day, but Glenda knew it was more than that. The house had always felt warm, sheltered, secure, even in winter.

Everything had changed in the instant a stricken Richie had turned toward her, holding the phone in a trembling hand.

"Damn you!" she said aloud. "Damn you, Ralph, how could you do that?"

Even as she voiced the question she knew that it was exactly the kind of thing Ralph Beringer would do.

Why had he come back now? What did he want?

She stood at the front bedroom windows and stared out again at the quiet street, as if expecting to see Beringer standing there, returning her gaze with mocking nonchalance. Even after eight years she would know him at a glance. And she was afraid.

Ralph Beringer was the reason her home felt cold, vulnerable, no longer safe.

Dave made her feel secure and happy—God, how happy he had made her! In her eyes he had only one serious fault: his unwillingness to believe the worst of people. Glenda had looked into the pit of man's potential for unimaginable cruelty and lived with the knowledge of its awful presence; Dave didn't even know the pit was there.

Even Friday night, right after Beringer's call, and again Saturday morning he had been infuriating. Listening to his patient attempts to explain or justify Ralph's callous action, she had fought back a scream. *My God, how can you be so blind? Don't you know what's out there?*

"Maybe he wants to try to make it up to Richie—not being there for him all these years," Dave had reasoned. "It's not surprising he doesn't know how to go about it."

He doesn't want forgiveness! He wants to destroy us!

"Has it occurred to you that he might not even call again? He could just have been passing through Los Angeles."

He's not just passing through. He's not going away, Dave . . . not until he does what he came for. I know him.

"Honey, we're going to have to help Richie work his way through this. We can't ignore it. If Beringer calls again, I want to meet him."

He's not a reasonable man. You can't talk to him. Aren't you listening to me? He's evil, Dave! He's never forgiven me for divorcing him and remarrying.

But Dave hadn't heard any of her cries because she had been silent, numbed by reawakened terror. And Dave didn't know about the beatings, the black eyes and broken rib, the dislocated shoulder, the bruises she had hidden from friends, the crippled spirit. He didn't know because she had never told him. Sparing him that kind of truth—and sparing herself having to relive those terrors—she had kept the memories buried deep, private, an ugly secret she was both afraid and ashamed to bring out into the light, fearing that it would somehow make Dave think less of her.

Nor had she told him about Ralph and Richie . . .

She could show Dave Ralph's cryptic response to her Dear John letter, she thought. Perversely, in spite of her fear and loathing, she had never destroyed the note. Like the buried memories of her aborted marriage, it was hidden away in the spare room closet, concealed inside a cardboard box containing other mementoes and old photographs. In the beginning she had taken it out of the box frequently, rereading the terse threat (what else could it be?) as if she might find hidden meaning in it. Gradually, as time went by and her fear ebbed, she looked at it only rarely, as if to remind herself that her newly found happiness, her joy in her family, her feeling of safety were all an illusion, erected on a foundation that could be swept away in an instant, like the hopes and dreams of those people whose homes were destroyed in the recent hillside fire near San Carlos.

She thought of Dave out there in the hills confronting a wall of flames, an irresistible force that engulfed everything in its path. Ralph Beringer in a rage was like that fire, a force of nature as pitiless as the devouring flames.

Glenda still lived with the terror that had enveloped her when she read Ralph's message for the first time. But would Dave comprehend her fear? "He was angry when he wrote that," Dave would say, oh so reasonably. "There's acrimony in a lot of divorces. It doesn't mean anything now."

Glenda knew better. She knew, for instance, that Ralph had sent the toy nutcracker to Richie on that long-ago Christmas as another way of unnerving her. Selecting a toy that depicted a man gripping an ax had been calculated.

Dave would scoff at seeing anything sinister in a wooden toy. But it wasn't paranoid if it was true, Glenda thought bitterly. She *knew* Ralph had been playing mind games with her. *I'm not through with you*, the toy was intended to say. *It's not over, bitch!*

And now Ralph Beringer was here in San Carlos. God in heaven, what was she going to do?

Alone in the house, listening to every whisper of wind or creaking board, she understood that there was one thing she had to do. She had to tell Dave everything, all that she had dreaded to reveal. He had to know the truth.

Nine

RALPH BERINGER HAD followed Lindstrom's car at a safe distance on its trip to the beach. He chuckled at the irony of passing the crime scene on the highway near the bird sanctuary. To see the black-and-white standing beside the road, uniforms waving traffic on, the yellow police crime scene tape winding down on both sides of the bridge, was a kick in the gut. He drove on, grinning. *Look up here, boys! Here I am!*

During the next two hours his good humor turned to silent, seething rage.

At first from his car, and later from a distance on the beach, Beringer watched the tall, lean man and the chunky kid stroll along the strand, watched them stop to talk or to inspect broken shells, watched them take off their shoes and walk barefoot along the edge of the waves washing up on shore. They seemed to be having a great time, not a care in the world. Hadn't they learned anything from his message Friday night? Didn't they get it?

That's *my* son, Beringer fumed. Not yours, Professor—mine.

Once, while the pair were far off along the beach, sitting side by side and staring out to sea, idly tossing pebbles as they talked, Beringer inspected the teacher's car. He spotted a yellow Nomex jacket on the back seat of the car and some soot-blackened work-boots on the floor. Obviously Lindstrom hadn't got around to cleaning and stashing them since his latest volunteer fire duty. The inside of the Nissan must smell like old ashes.

Later, following the man and the boy back to San Carlos, Beringer kept thinking about that yellow jacket. Possibilities nibbled at the corners of his mind, like suspicious fish poking at bait. Never mind, he would work it out.

He had the rough sequence of the coming days worked out. He had had eight years to plan it all. It was like the game plans conceived by that former coach of the San Francisco 49ers, Bill Walsh. He was the first who actually preprogrammed the first twelve or fifteen plays in a game, then ran them as planned. Of course, once the game started, there was always the unexpected, the quarterback checking off at the line of scrimmage or being flushed out of the pocket and having to improvise. Beringer had always understood that, once his planned sequence started, unexpected obstacles might surface and he would have to adapt to them. New twists and turns would have to be found.

That yellow fireman's jacket was something he knew he could use. He didn't know how, not yet, but he would figure it out.

Something else occurred to him. Pretty, sexy Edie Foster had been having it on with an older man, someone not unlike Lindstrom, possibly another San Carlos College teacher. She had admitted it to him, mouth taped, all the arrogance gone from those lovely eyes, nodding her head vigorously when Beringer asked the question, as if she hoped that confession might absolve her sin and save her. Could he use that information in some way, fitting it into his game plan? Thinking about it as he drove, Beringer decided it was almost too good to be true.

When Lindstrom and Beringer's son approached the old neighborhood where they lived, Beringer turned away. Too much chance of being noticed if he followed them there on a Sunday afternoon when everyone was at home, cutting lawns or planting bulbs. He had already taken more risks than he had intended.

Thinking about the hours he had had with Edie brought a rush that left his stomach muscles clenched, his hands shaking on the steering wheel, sweat breaking out on his forehead. That was one of the unexpected twists. He had planned his hits in cold rage, seeing each as a repetition of the first one in Germany eight years ago, a quick hard strike, taking what he wanted, meting out the punishment they all deserved. In and out fast, so fast the cops would be dizzy trying to keep up, taking no chances.

Edie Foster had derailed the game plan.

He had had sexy Edie to himself in the motel room for four hours, helpless, terrified. So much better to take his time, draw it out, let her see what was happening to her at every stage. By the end of that time she wasn't much, admittedly, he might as well have been banging a sack of grain, but before that . . .

Dangerous, though. For a time he had been out of control, caution to the winds and all that, and he couldn't let that happen again. It had been so long, that was the problem, he had been waiting for these moments so long, who wouldn't get carried away at first?

All the same, taking her to his motel room had been a definite risk. The girl herself had presented no problems, still unconscious when he hustled her from the car to his room. And it had been late, past midnight, his room down at the end and out of the way. He had used all that to rationalize the risk, but he had been conning himself. He had jeopardized everything for a quick fix.

Beringer wiped the sweat from his brow with his sleeve, then jerked the Ford Taurus over to the curb and stared across the road. *What the hell was he doing?*

The motel where he had spent half the night with Edie Foster was directly across the way, appearing a lot more drab and cheerless by day than it did at night. He had driven here without conscious intent, drawn by the electric charge of memory. What was that line about a murderer returning to the scene of his crime? You think that stuff is all bullshit, but here he was. *Stupid!*

Beringer had stayed in the motel only one night, of course, before moving on. The chances of anyone having seen him with Edie, and linking her with the murdered San Carlos College coed, were infinitesimal. The way he had worked it out long before coming here was, motels were filled with transients and they were too easy for police to check. They provided a name, sometimes a license plate, from the registration card, and if you stayed too long, the next thing you knew a cop was tapping you on the shoulder. The Travel-Ease Motel had been only a preliminary stop for Beringer while he looked San Carlos over and let the happy couple know he was in town. It had never been part of the agenda to take anyone to the motel, but once he had Edie in the car with him she proved to be just too perfect to enjoy for only a few fleeting moments.

Images from those hours with her flashed in his memory like neon flares. Edie when she still had some fight in her, even with her hands and feet and later her mouth taped, her eyes so big and round, all of her emotions playing themselves out for him in those eyes, the anger and outrage and fear, the anguish when her body responded in spite of her resistance, the pain and shock of disbelief, and then the terror gradually taking over as the knowledge dawned on her that the worst was still to come, that there was to be no reprieve, that this was all there was, end of the line, the last of her life a silent scream.

A black-and-white San Carlos police car cruised by. One of the uniformed cops glanced toward him, casual but curious all the same. What was he doing there, sitting in a car by himself? Beringer put the Taurus in gear and eased away from the curb, a half block behind the black-and-white. He drove slowly, eyes locked on the police car, not even glancing toward the motel.

Crazy coming back here even to look, but no real harm done.

He drove across San Carlos and stopped for dinner at a Denny's on the north side. It was at the far end of town from the college, so there were few students inside, mostly senior citizens and weekend travelers catching the nearby freeway off-ramp upon spotting a familiar coffee shop's sign.

Beringer was hardly aware of what he ate, couldn't even remember afterward. His brain churned with those neon flashes of Edie spread-eagled on the bed with the plastic painter's dropcloth under her, no blood on the sheets; those images interlaced with the anger toward Lindstrom hippity-hopping along the beach with the kid—Beringer's son Richie. And that cop giving him the eye, the sidelong glance lingering, a hint of suspicion there, that hard-ass look all cops had, got it from practicing in front of the mirror.

He had to calm down. He was still riding the high Edie had given him, and it was time to settle down.

Leaving Denny's, he consulted a San Carlos street map on the seat beside him and located Washington Boulevard, the town's main drag that cut all the way across town. Out here near the city limits was the big shopping mall, flanked on its southern wing by San Anselmo Drive, Beringer's destination.

He took Avenida del Sol to Washington, turned right and moments later came to San Anselmo Drive—several blocks of large apartment and condominium complexes on the flatland west of the San Carlos foothills, this one in Spanish motif with pink walls and tiled roof, the next an imitation New England village, the next all palms and South Seas decor.

Beringer had sublet a unit in a modern building. The owners, an older couple, were traveling to Europe for a three-month vacation. Beringer had answered their ad because he liked the sound of it, and he had lucked out. The old man had been in the Air Force in World War II, stationed in England. He and Beringer had been able to swap war stories. The old geezer had been so taken with Beringer that he hadn't bothered about references or credit checks or honorable discharge papers, any one of which would have presented a problem. When the old lady tried to ask some questions her husband shushed her up, winking at Beringer as if they were old Air Force buddies. He handed Beringer a set of keys to the house and another set for the blue Buick LeSabre in the garage.

The condominium complex had underground parking with a remote-controlled security gate. A stairway and elevator were nearby, offering quick and private access to the individual units under most circumstances. Not that Beringer intended to bring any of the others back where he was staying. That was a one-shot deal at the motel, a mistake really, a self-indulgence he had gotten away with. He couldn't risk a second time. There were too many unpredictable possibilities for disaster.

He had signed the sublease on Thursday. The old couple were scheduled to be on a United Airlines flight out of John Wayne International Airport in Orange County that Sunday morning. Beringer used his remote control to gain entrance to the underground parking and slipped the Taurus into the vacant slot next to the Buick. Too impatient to wait for the slow-moving elevator, he took the stairs two at a time. He held his breath when he turned the key in the front door and stepped into the cool interior of the apartment. He half expected to hear the shrill, querulous voice of the old woman saying, "I told you so! I told you he had shifty eyes!"

But the stillness of the apartment was total, as if it had been abandoned much longer than half a day.

Beringer walked through the silent rooms, turning on lights. There were mini-blinds everywhere and he closed them carefully. He checked out the master bedroom, a smaller room the old man evidently used as a den, the kitchen, the small dining area and, finally, the living room. He felt out of place amongst all the down-filled floral upholstery, the big La-Z-Boy facing a Sony big screen television set, crystal and knickknacks covering every surface, not an ashtray in sight. Beringer had spent much of his adult life in and out of various military barracks and the spartan lodgings available to enlisted men at military bases, along with a couple of hitches in the even more spartan surroundings of the brig. No sofas covered in cabbage roses, no La-Z-Boy to kick back in, no forty-inch TV.

He found a cold beer in the refrigerator, plopped himself down in the oversize recliner, stacked his heels on the glass-topped coffee table and grinned with satisfaction.

He was invisible now, right here in Glenda's college town, no way anyone could trace him, no paper trail, a phony name on the sublease he had signed for the trusting old soldier.

Where the hell was the remote?

DETECTIVE TIM BRADEN caught his first break on the Jane Doe murder Sunday evening when a coed at San Carlos College reported her roommate missing to the campus security office. After learning that the girl had gone out on a date Friday night and had not been seen for forty-eight hours, the security officer on duty, Ken Woodell, filed a missing persons report with the San Carlos Police Department.

Braden had asked to be notified immediately of any such report pertaining to a young woman. He was sitting out on the balcony of his San Carlos Beach apartment in the dark when his phone rang. The apartment wasn't much to look at, part of a 1940s development of small frame cottages and duplexes, but Braden liked the proximity to the beach, the lack of pretension, the funky bars and Mexican restaurants and surfer shops. The furnishings, with the exception of a comfortable leather couch, were garage sale utilitarian—a legacy from Braden's divorce three years ago. He had been too tired to fight over who got what. The apartment suited him for the little time he was there, and it was only fifteen minutes from the police station in San Carlos.

He made it to the San Carlos College campus in ten minutes.

The roommate, whose name was Sheri Kuttner, was waiting for him at the security office. She was Edith Foster's age, give or take a few months. She had long dark hair, perfectly straight, and sharp features. Her huge brown eyes were frightened. She was not as pretty as her former roommate, but about the same size. They could have shared petite wardrobes, Braden thought.

When he showed her a copy of the murder victim's face, cropped from a photo taken by the police photographer Saturday morning, Sheri Kuttner burst into tears.

After the girl had recovered sufficiently, she identified the murdered girl as Edith Foster, a third-year student at San Carlos College, Sheri's roommate for two years.

Sheri Kuttner was too distraught that night to drive to the morgue for a formal identification or to be interviewed at length. That didn't lessen Braden's elation. Kuttner was able to reveal that Edie had been going to a poetry reading Friday night at The Pelican, a favorite coffeehouse of hers in downtown San Carlos . . . and that she might have been meeting someone there.

The rest would come later.

At least he had more than a Jane Doe lying in the morgue.

Now he had a trail to follow, witnesses to find and interview, a personal background to explore. He had a case.

Ten

MONDAY MORNING, AFTER less than two hours sleep, Braden left his beach area apartment and drove to the San Carlos police station. The morning was cool, overcast as usual, but this was one Monday morning when the gloom did not match Braden's mood. On the contrary, he felt eager and alert in a way he hadn't felt for a long time. He didn't question the reason.

Deputy Pritkin was already at the station. Braden found the eager young deputy desk space with a computer terminal and dumped the weekend's accumulation of crime scene, witness and preliminary autopsy reports relating to the Edith Foster case onto the desk. Pritkin had brought along the lengthy VICAP questionnaire through which Foster's murder would enter the FBI's databank. The deputy acted as if Braden were doing him a favor, like a rookie pitcher being sent out to pitch in the big game.

Then the phone rang. Edith Foster's car had been found.

A checker working the graveyard shift at an Alpha Beta supermarket had recognized Foster's picture in the morning paper. She had alerted the store manager, who called the police. The responding officer had spotted a red 280Z in the parking lot and had run a make on the personalized license plate.

By the time Braden arrived at the scene the techs were already there and the 280Z was being examined, powdered, photographed and vacuumed for any possible trace evidence. Braden looked inside. The interior was undisturbed. There was no sign of anything amiss, at least to the naked eye.

The checker who had recognized Foster's picture was waiting

for him in the market manager's office. Her name was Sylvia Stern. She was a plump, middle-aged woman with blue eye shadow and short hair dyed a bright orange. She remembered Edith Foster coming into the Alpha Beta around midnight Friday and purchasing a few items. The store, which was open all night on weekends, had not been busy.

"How come you remember her?" Braden asked.

"Well, you couldn't help noticing her. Such a pretty thing. I'd seen her before, too. She'd shop here sometimes."

"Do you remember what she bought that night?"

"No . . . I'm sorry, Detective. I just ring 'em up, I don't take much notice of what customers buy. Oh, wait—I do remember one thing she bought. It was a package of Dove bars. I remember because we kidded about how she could eat a whole package of Dove bars and stay as skinny as a model like she was, when all I got to do is look at a Dove bar and my dress size changes." Sylvia Stern paused, her eyes suddenly moist. "She seemed a nice girl. Such a terrible thing to happen to her."

"Yes," Braden agreed. "If you think of anything else . . ."

He left another of his cards and made arrangements to interview other market employees who had been working Friday night at or near midnight. When he went back outside the techs were finishing up their preliminary tests before having the sports car towed away for more exhaustive examination. Braden studied the area, trying to visualize how the killer had worked it. He must have been waiting for her when she came out of the market, he thought. Unless they were together.

Even though the car had been parked at the side of the market, there was a good chance someone might have seen the victim and the killer together. Other stores in the shopping strip would have to be canvassed, along with employees and patrons of The Pelican, the coffeehouse downtown. The manager of the latter had agreed to supply Braden with a list of customers who had used credit cards Friday night. It always amazed Braden how many people used credit cards to charge the smallest purchases—even a cup of coffee.

He walked back into the market and found the redheaded checker. "Do you remember how Edith Foster paid?" he asked.

"Well, I'm not sure, but . . . that's a funny thing, now you mention it. I believe she used an ATM card."

Ten minutes later Braden had a copy of the transaction, including the last items Edith Foster had purchased in her brief life. Neither the magazine, the orange juice, the frozen waffles nor the package of Dove bars had been found in her car or on the ground nearby. The girl's killer had taken them.

THE NEWS OF Edie Foster's murder raced across the San Carlos College campus like the recent fire sweeping through the dry hills of San Carlos Canyon. Students clustered on the steps of buildings and in the hallways, talking of little else. Dave Lindstrom felt the excitement and the undercurrent of fear pervading his Contemporary Film Studies II class that met at eleven o'clock that Monday morning. The buzz was audible in whispers and low-voiced asides, visible in youthful faces more alert and anxious than usual.

Even violent films like Quentin Tarantino's *Pulp Fiction*, which the class had recently studied on assignment, could not compete with the emotional impact of real violence striking close to home, Dave reflected. Many of the students in his class had known the murdered girl, if only casually. Dave had known her himself. It had taken him a while to place her among the two hundred or so students who enrolled in his classes each year, but he remembered her now through association with the girl sitting in the front row to the right of his lectern, Sheri Kuttner. Kuttner and Edith Foster had both taken one of his courses in the last spring semester. They had sat together in the front row.

The Edith Foster Dave Lindstrom remembered had been a strikingly beautiful girl, very aware of herself, supremely confident. Bold glances and warm smiles, always a lot of leg showing. Frequent excuses to linger after class asking questions she already knew the answer to, or stopping by his office . . .

He would never have cast her as a victim, Dave thought.

He shook off the distraction, not liking the direction of his thoughts, which seemed to him uncharitable.

"So," he said, "is *Pulp Fiction* too violent?"

His question caught their attention. Mention of the title of Quentin Tarantino's film was the motion picture equivalent of a buzz word.

"Heck no!" one student said firmly.

"Why not? There's casual violence, gratuitous blood all over the place."

"No there isn't. Everything in that movie is appropriate to the situation and the characters. Hey, it's not like *Natural Born Killers* or one of those."

"That picture was gross," a girl said.

Playing devil's advocate to stimulate the discussion, Dave said, "Isn't that a little like the female leads who are always saying that baring their breasts and having sex on the kitchen counter are essential to the revelation of the character they're playing? Isn't that what Tarantino is doing with violence?"

There was laughter, followed by instant protests. "It's not the same." "No way."

"What's wrong with bare breasts?" another student asked.

"When was the last time you saw a guy's dong on the big screen in living color?" a coed retorted.

Dave let the discussion run a minute, until it threatened to digress completely. Pulling it back on track, he said, "In England the script for *Pulp Fiction* is the best-selling script ever published in that country. How do you account for that?"

"That's what I mean," one of the movie's defenders argued. "It's the language that makes it great. I mean, you have to pay attention. You read it, the violence isn't bad at all. What you have on the page is the dialogue, quirky characters, the humor."

"But isn't that the problem?" Dave persisted. "The impact of visual violence on the big screen? Isn't that simply too easy a way to grab your audience's attention? Dole out a little violence to make them squirm?"

"Tarantino's sending it up—that's the point!"

"He doesn't give us that Peckinpah slow-mo business," another student said.

Dave listened as the debate took hold. The students—a generation younger than he was—had a different reaction to film violence than he did. The way Dave saw it, younger filmgoers had become desensitized to violence, inured to a steady diet of severed limbs, flying heads, blood-soaked sheets and spattered walls. The graphic images no longer meant as much to them as they had to an older generation.

They no longer meant as much as they *should*. Violence had become a matter of indifference.

He thought of Glenda's accusation—that he didn't want to face the evil, ugliness and violence of the real world. Not true, he insisted to himself—he didn't want to glorify or exploit it.

Or was he hiding his head in the sand? America *was* a violent society.

"It's always against women," one of the students was saying.

Dave glanced at her. Sheri Kuttner. An intense girl, thin, long dark hair, attractive in her own way. He had seen her more than once on campus with Edith Foster, he remembered now.

"That's a good point," he suggested. "I'd like all of you to take another look at the films we've studied so far, from Hitchcock's *Psycho* to *Pulp Fiction*, and ask yourself what impact they have on the way we look at women and the violence that's done to women in our society."

"That's that old argument," a serious film student objected. "People don't kill people because they see someone doing it in a movie."

"What about you, Professor?" one student challenged. "What do you think is all right for us to see?"

Dave hesitated. He was saved by the bell.

SHERI KUTTNER LINGERED at the side of the room as it emptied out, approaching Dave's table as he was gathering up his lecture notes.

"Good morning . . . Sheri, isn't it?"

The girl nodded. Hugged her books against her chest. She seemed to be waiting for him to say something else.

"You were a close friend of Edith Foster, weren't you? I'm very sorry . . . it must be hard for you to lose a friend like that."

"A detective questioned me."

"Really?" How many crime films had he viewed, studied, dissected over the past fifteen years? Movie detectives were like old friends, but Dave reflected that in real life he had never actually spoken to one. "Oh . . . because you were close to Edith."

"Yes . . . I had to identify her. Last night from a photograph, and this morning . . ."

"You had to go to the morgue?" Dave asked, appalled. "That must have been awful."

"Yes." Sheri Kuttner looked at him solemnly. There were dark shadows under her eyes, as if she hadn't slept. "We were roommates. But you knew that. Edie would've told you."

"Edith would have . . . I don't understand, Sheri."

"I knew about you and Edie. Last semester, I mean, when you . . . well, you know. I didn't say anything to the detective yet, but . . ."

The unfinished sentence hovered ominously between them. Dave felt a chill of alarm. "What are you talking about? What didn't you tell the detective?"

Sheri Kuttner's body language changed subtly. She hugged her books tighter, took a small step backward, avoided Dave's eyes. "I knew how she felt. We talked a lot. Then when she started going out again this semester, I figured . . ."

"What—that it was me?" Dave exclaimed. "You have to be joking."

"You think it's funny?" Sheri burst out. "She was so . . . so beautiful. She had so much to give, and all you people do is take, take, take. Oh, I don't know if you were the one who . . . who did that to her. But I know all about you! I know . . ."

Abruptly she turned and ran to the door.

"Miss Kuttner—Sheri! Wait!"

But the student fled into the corridor. Dave started after her, then stopped. He couldn't chase her down the hallway. Not today of all days, with the whole campus on edge.

Sheri Kuttner was overwrought. The trauma of having to identify her friend's dead body must have been almost too much to bear. She wasn't thinking clearly.

Roommates, Dave thought. Girls of that age would have been very close. Close enough for long, whispered confidences in the small hours of the morning. Edie Foster revealing her feelings for someone, talking out her fantasies. But surely she hadn't actually named *him*! Why would she do that?

Dave flashed again to the sometimes provocative approaches the coed had made to him. Her open invitations took on more significance. Such situations were not uncommon for many college instructors, and Dave thought he had always handled them as well as possible, principally by acting as if nothing were wrong, as if long slim legs and vibrant bosoms were outside the range of his tunnel vision, and sexual invitations from girls scarcely out of their teens were incomprehensible to him. You couldn't respond to what you didn't see. No one's feelings had to be hurt.

He had acted that way with Edith Foster.

Dave stopped in his tracks in the corridor.

Had he angered the girl? Had his seeming indifference been translated in her mind into rejection, turning her hostile? He could no longer remember whether the girl's demeanor had changed toward the end of the spring semester, and since she had not signed up for any of his classes this fall, he couldn't recall even seeing her.

But what had she told Sheri Kuttner?

PREOCCUPIED, DAVE LINDSTROM stopped briefly at his office to leave his notes and gather up some student papers that had to be graded. Rarely did a teacher's work end with the last class of the day, and today was no exception. He usually took home a couple hours work or more, not counting the reading and research that were part of his ongoing absorption in the subject of films and their impact on twentieth-century society. Even going to a movie—a passion since early childhood—was both business and pleasure. "Like Siskel and Ebert," he would joke with Glenda, "only they get paid more."

He walked to his car in the faculty parking lot behind the Liberal Arts building, thinking about Sheri Kuttner and the implications of her brief visit. Could he also expect a visit from Sheri's detective? The possibility was both intriguing and a little intimidating.

He unlocked the driver's door of the Nissan Sentra, tossed his armload of books and papers onto the passenger seat and paused, not immediately knowing why. Something in his peripheral vision ... but the parking lot was empty except for a few cars. No one else nearby. In the distance, students strolled across the campus, absorbed in animated discussions. About St. Thomas Aquinas and Aristotle? Wordsworth and Shelley? Radio isotopes? Girls and boys? The Raiders and the 49ers next Sunday? Or was everyone talking about Edie Foster, wondering, speculating?

Nothing out there to alert him. It was something he had seen when he opened the car, then. No, he suddenly realized. Something he *didn't* see.

His yellow fireproof slicker. He had been assaulted that morning by the strong smell of stale smoke and ashes permeating the interior of the Sentra. Had he tossed the offending gear into the trunk? No, he would have remembered. But just to make sure, Dave opened the trunk to look. He found the spare tire, tools in a greasy pouch, his Ping Pal 2 putter and some golf balls. No fire equipment or clothing.

Walking back around the vehicle, frowning, he spotted deep scratches beside the lock on the passenger side door. The metal was actually indented slightly where someone had pried at the door.

Popped it open, Dave thought angrily. Stole his Nomex coat.

He drove straight to the campus security office, where he railed to Ed Willhite, the white-haired chief of security, about the stupidity of breaking into a car to steal something the thief couldn't possible have any use for. "Hell, if he wants to fight fires, all he has to do is volunteer and the fire department will give him his own gear."

"Prob'ly figured there might be somethin' else more valuable when he broke in," Whillhite said. He was a big, slow-moving man, a retired LAPD cop, with a garland of white hair surrounding a pink scalp. This afternoon, less than twenty-four hours after discovering that a girl from the college was the subject of a murder investigation, Willhite found it hard to get excited about a stolen slicker.

"And right in the faculty lot—in broad daylight!" Dave fumed. "What the hell are we coming to?"

"Tell me about it," the security man said as he filled in the complaint form. "You sure nothin' else was stolen?"

"There was nothing there to steal."

"Prob'ly vandals. They'll just dump the coat somewheres. If it turns up I'll let you know. You wanta sign this right here by the X?"

Walking back to his car, Dave looked out across the campus, which appeared tranquil and peaceful in the long shadows of the late autumn afternoon. It was beautiful, he thought, but no longer as innocent as he had always viewed it. Strange how the loss of the coat, the invasion of his privacy, affected him so strongly, although the incident seemed trivial in comparison to the murder of one of his former students. Glenda thought him naive, always reluctant to see the worst side of things. Maybe she was right.

We're not immune, he thought. None of us are.

Not anymore.

Eleven

LEONARD "BUDDY" COCHRANE was a legend in the FBI, one of the pioneers of the Behavioral Science Unit in the 1970s and 80s, of the growing art-cum-science of criminal profiling, of VICAP, the Bureau's Violent Crime Analysis Program, and of its parent National Center for the Analysis of Violent Crime. In large part through Cochrane's efforts VICAP's capability of matching data from one violent crime to another, in order to establish links or patterns at the earliest stage, was now on-line to police agencies in a majority of the fifty states.

Cochrane was past the Bureau's fifty-five-year retirement age but had been retained at the NVAVC simply because his superiors at Quantico were reluctant to let him go. He was a handsome man with patrician features, piercing blue eyes, a full head of pure white hair and, at sixty, the body of a forty-year-old aerobics instructor. This Tuesday morning, however, after a long weekend consulting on a particularly gruesome series of mutilation killings in the vicinity of Tuscaloosa, Alabama, he wondered if it wasn't time to go fishing. He was drained, physically and emotionally. His ulcer was acting up again, and a weekend falling off the coffee wagon hadn't helped. He felt old and worn out. Retirement had the glow not of sunset but of a beacon.

A knock on the solid mahogany door of his office dissipated the glow. The office was at the end of a long, carpeted corridor in the basement complex housing the offices and laboratories of the BSU and its logical offshoot, the Investigative Support Unit. Special Agent Karen Younger peered around the door.

"Come in," Cochrane growled, his tone hiding the pleasure he invariably felt upon seeing her.

"Good morning, sir. You wanted to see me?"

Cochrane grunted, waving her toward a chair beside his desk. He didn't like to talk across the desk or across the room to agents or visitors. Up close and personal was his style. It was also his way of penetrating a visitor's defenses. With Special Agent Younger the habit carried a bonus, he thought, detecting a faint trace of White Shoulders perfume. Identifying scents was one of his arcane specialties. He had a dog's nose, he said, and at least one famous serial murder case had turned on Buddy Cochrane's recognition of a particular men's cologne on a victim's clothing.

Karen Younger was pretty enough, with even features, a wide mouth, intelligent gray eyes with flecks of blue in them and hair the color of autumn leaves turned dark gold. But what struck Cochrane about her was the sense of bedrock honesty and integrity she projected. She walked straight, sat straight, looked you straight in the eye. There was never any dissembling or posing. She wore little makeup, but a flawless complexion made it seem unnecessary. Special Agent Younger, according to her personnel jacket, was actually thirty-two, with degrees in business law and psychology. She was five feet seven and weighed a hundred and twenty-seven pounds. A nice armful, Cochrane thought, who sniffed at the notion that undernourished meant beautiful. At sixty, with a wife, three children and seven grandchildren, and an impeccable reputation for propriety, he was not immune.

A hint of color in her cheeks, Agent Younger said, "Is it about the Tuscaloosa killings?"

"No . . . no, we've got the killer, I have no doubt of it. It's in the prosecutor's hands now. But something else has come up—something I want you to look at."

He tapped a file on his desk, fingering a corner absently as he watched the interest flare in her eyes. "Read that," he said without preamble, pushing the folder toward her. "See if you see what I do. Would you like some coffee?"

"No, sir."

"Well, I would, but I can't have it, of course."

He buzzed his secretary and asked for a glass of milk. When she brought it Cochrane tipped his leather swivel chair back and sipped the cold milk slowly, watching Karen Younger as she read, searching for any reaction. He wondered, again, if he was making a mistake. No, dammit! Her instincts were too good to remain cooped up in a basement cubicle for the next twenty years.

He had groomed her for fieldwork in the VICAP program, but an extensive part of her experience had been with the Criminal Personality Research Project, or CPRP, interviewing and profiling convicted violent criminals. Although she was a trained psychologist with special emphasis on criminology, and, in spite of her relative youth, had had field experience both in the U.S. and Germany, the face-to-face interviews with a series of the most monstrous criminals in the national's penal institutions had proved devastating. Severe stress reactions among investigators in the program were commonplace. They suffered such symptoms as rapid weight loss, heart attacks, ulcers, severe anxiety attacks simulating heart problems, gastrointestinal disorders, insomnia and nightmares. Karen Younger had developed an ulcer at the age of twenty-nine. She lost weight, going down to a hundred and ten pounds. She experienced chronic sleeplessness. Finally she came to Cochrane, her boss, and told him she had to leave the CPRP program, even if it meant resigning from the Bureau.

Cochrane wouldn't have it, of course. She was a fine profiler, in part because she connected so fiercely with the criminals she worked with. What was destroying her was the same sensitivity to evil that made her invaluable. Cochrane brought her out of the cold, assigned her to the ISU's internal staff, where her insightful analyses were everything he could have asked for . . . but less than he wanted from her. With the expansion of VICAP's liaison program with law enforcement agencies throughout the country, Special Agent Younger, in her boss's view, belonged in the field.

When she finished reading, Karen Younger closed the file and placed it carefully on Cochrane's desk, as if it burned her fingers. Cochrane read her reaction in her body language as well as the tighter set of her mouth and a bleakness in her eyes.

"It's not possible," she whispered. "It's been . . ."

"Eight years," said Cochrane.

"It's coincidence."

The file had come in late on Monday, shortly after Cochrane's return flight from Alabama. He had taken it home with him along with an armful of other files to read.

VICAP had made an immediate linkage between a new case report from California and an eight-year-old murder that took place not in the United States but in Germany. Karen Younger, a fledgling agent on her first field assignment, had been stationed at Wiesbaden, Germany, as liaison between the large U.S. Air Force base near Wiesbaden and German police agencies. The murder, the first Younger had been involved with, had left a profound mark. It had encouraged the interest in criminal psychosis that led her eventually to the ISU. It had also given her nightmares that resurfaced years later when she became involved with the criminal profiling program.

The new case file had originated in San Carlos, California, a small college town outside of Los Angeles. The murder victim in the case was a nineteen-year-old college student, attractive, blond, apparently sexually active. She had been kidnapped and repeatedly raped both before and possibly after she was beaten to death. The killer then carved her first initial on her abdomen, using a relatively dull knife.

"She was even dumped under a bridge," Cochrane pointed out—an unusual detail calling to mind the circumstances of the incident in Germany.

Younger shook her head as if to deny the similarities. "This man, according to the report, wore smooth gloves and possibly brass knuckles."

"Or he was holding weights in his right hand when he hit her. And your man in Germany didn't. He used his bare fists and left skin and blood samples. But eight years ago he may have acted on impulse. Presumably that was his first. This time he was more prepared."

"Why?" Karen Younger cried with a kind of desperation. "Why now, after eight years? It makes no sense!"

"In one respect it makes a great deal of sense. You always suspected the murderer was a soldier stationed in Germany. He may have been there all this time. That wouldn't be unusual for a career soldier. And now . . ."

Cochrane knew that what he was suggesting was Karen Younger's worst nightmare.

"He's come home," she whispered.

"I think so. It's your case, Karen."

"No . . . no, sir." She could not remember Cochrane ever calling her by her surname before. Her eyes darted around the windowless office, not meeting his, as if she were a trapped animal. "I can't."

"I believe you can. Sooner or later you have to find out. There's no question this is the time. You've been close to this man once. No one else has. And since then you've had a great deal of experience getting inside minds like this one. You're our best chance to get to him before he strikes again."

The words shocked her. She stared at Cochrane as if realizing for the first time what he was implying. "You think he's a true serial killer? But . . . eight years . . ."

"He's kept it bottled up for all that time, if it's the same man. Now it's out of the bottle. Do you honestly think he can stop now?"

Special Agent Younger stared at him helplessly. She was paler than when she had cheerfully entered Cochrane's office less than thirty minutes ago. Her face was drawn. No flawless skin ad now, Cochrane thought dispassionately.

"If it's him . . . no," she said. "He won't stop."

"I'm not asking you to catch him yourself—this isn't a novel or a movie. Your job will be to assist the police in every way you can. You can assess the crime scene, make suggestions, offer immediate access to our laboratory facilities, even do a personality profile of the killer."

"Who has the case—the San Carlos police?"

"The county sheriff's department is involved—we have a VICAP liaison there—but the principal investigator in charge of the case is a San Carlos detective, formerly with the LAPD. I see it as a multijurisdictional, cooperative investigation."

"What are you not telling me?" The question confirmed Buddy Cochrane's estimate of Agent Younger's acuity.

"I think you'll understand when you read the background material I've had put together."

Younger appeared puzzled. She stared at the thick manila envelope Cochrane added to the original case file she had read, but she didn't press him.

"You can read the rest of the material on the plane. I've booked you to Los Angeles on an afternoon flight out of Dulles. You just about have time to pack." The white-haired man rose, extending his hand. He wasn't going to give her a chance to say no. "Good luck, Agent Younger."

He did not add the words that immediately sprang to his mind: *You're going to need it.*

Twelve

EDITH FOSTER'S MEMORIAL service was held at noon on Tuesday in the campus chapel. She was not present. The body of the deceased, not yet released by the coroner, would be flown to her home in Minneapolis for a more formal funeral ceremony.

Detective Braden did not expect the girl's murderer to show up for the service, although conventional wisdom said he might. Nevertheless, he had two detectives in an unmarked Chevrolet parked with a view of anyone attending the service, one of them armed with a video camera—today's weapon of choice.

Most of those who came were college students, a preponderance of young women, along with a sprinkling of adults Braden assumed were teachers and other officials from the college community. He recognized the plump, motherly den mother he had met at Foster's dormitory, and her roommate, Sheri Kuttner, who had identified the victim's photograph Sunday night and confirmed the identification Monday morning at the county morgue. On both occasions she had been too disturbed to be questioned at length.

Braden sat through the service, moved by the emotional recollections of the dead girl's friends, made more poignant by the dreadful circumstances of her death.

Braden caught up with Edith Foster's roommate outside the chapel. She swung around sharply at his touch. As she recognized Braden she dabbed at swollen eyes with a tissue.

"Feel like talking now, Sheri?"

She nodded wordlessly.

"Would you like a Coke or a cup of coffee or something?"

She shook her head. Youthful grief allowed no room for such mundane pleasures. Braden had grown up in a family where Irish wakes were occasions for boisterous gatherings of family and friends in the home, with enough food and hard liquor to sink a battleship, as his mother used to say.

Perversely, the sun broke through the clouds as the mourners straggled away from the chapel and fanned out across the campus. Braden walked in silence beside Sheri Kuttner until they came to an empty bench beneath shade trees. "This good enough?" he asked.

"I'm sorry to be such a baby, Detective."

"Don't apologize. Crying isn't childish. Sometimes it's necessary."

She glanced up at him, brown eyes curious under thick, damp lashes. For her friend's memorial service Sheri Kuttner had worn a short pleated blue skirt, mauve knee stockings, a gray cotton turtleneck and a vest that appeared to be made of multicolored ribbons. The outfit was a celebration of color, not darkness, and he guessed that Sheri knew Edie Foster would have preferred it that way. It made Braden wonder about the cost of tuition at San Carlos College. Had Edie been in the habit of carrying around large amounts of money? Wearing conspicuous jewelry?

"Nice vest," he said.

"Thanks. Uh . . . I made it myself."

"You did? How'd you learn to do that?"

"I took a class . . . no, not here at college. A sewing class."

Braden smiled. "I would've thought you had enough classes without going outside school."

"I like sewing." Sheri looked away. "I was making one like this for Edie. She really liked this one." The tears flowed again. The tissue was a crumpled wet ball. Braden fumbled in his pockets for a clean tissue and came up empty.

"You weren't just roommates. You were close friends."

Sheri nodded again. The words were lost somewhere inside.

"You know we want to find out who did that to her. Anything you can tell us that would help . . ."

"I'll do what I can."

"When was the last time you saw her?"

"Friday night, just before she went out. That was about eight o'clock."

"Do you remember what she was wearing?"

They exchanged glances, the shared knowledge of Edith Foster lying cold and naked under a bridge. Sheri described a white T-shirt with a cat's face and a denim miniskirt Edie liked because it showed off her legs. "She had great legs," Sheri said wistfully.

"Was she wearing any jewelry?"

"She didn't wear much jewelry. I think her friend was giving her things, but she just put them away. I mean, she wasn't wearing anything special that night."

"Did she carry much money with her?"

Sheri laughed briefly. "Her folks sent her money but she always spent it, mostly on clothes she liked. You know, even if it was jeans, Edie wanted designer stuff."

"You said you thought she had a date—that she was going to meet someone."

"Well, you know, I think she would've asked me if she wasn't meeting someone. She didn't like to go anywhere alone."

"Do you know who she was seeing?"

"No. She wouldn't say."

"Was that unusual?"

"Well . . . sometimes. She was popular, she liked going out a lot. Sometimes a bunch of us would go out together, or we'd go shopping, Edie and me. She was someone guys wanted to be with."

Sheri Kuttner broke off as a group of students passed by along the walkway, glancing at them curiously. Braden wondered if any of them recognized the Corkscrew Cop. Sheri Kuttner hadn't said anything to indicate she did.

"They're wondering who you are," Sheri said. "I don't think any of them would know you were the one on TV."

Braden looked at her quickly. "You recognized me?"

"Uh, no, that is, one of the security officers said that's who you were. While I was waiting for you Sunday."

"I see."

They sat in silence, Braden wondering if his brief moment of fame was always going to get in the way of his doing the job. Oddly, Sheri Kuttner didn't seem to be bothered.

"Edie liked older men," Sheri said, as if the comment were a logical extension of the conversation. "She thought most of the guys in school were, you know, sort of immature."

"I can imagine."

"She was . . . sophisticated for her age . . . and smart, too. Sometimes older men turned her on."

Braden gathered between the lines that Sheri Kuttner tried hard but didn't think she was very smart or sophisticated or popular or beautiful, not the way Edith Foster was. Another thread in the girl's voice had become sharper and more distinct as she talked. She hadn't approved of some of Edie's older friends.

"These older men . . . were some of them married? Like professors, maybe?"

Sheri pursed her lips.

"Was there a particular one she was seeing lately? Someone you know about?"

"I . . . I'm not sure. The younger guys, she would usually say where she was going and who with, but lately, I mean since this fall semester started, she was meeting someone she didn't want to talk about."

"How long has this been going on?"

"Well, this is only our fourth week of classes, so it's about a month. We register a week early."

"And she never mentioned a name, or a particular class, or anything?"

"Uh-uh." Sheri Kuttner seemed about to add something else but changed her mind. Her lips compressed again. She harbored resentment along with her genuine grief, Braden thought.

"Where would she have gone on her dates? Besides this coffee shop, The Pelican?"

"Movies, she loved movies. Some other coffeehouses, you know, where everyone hangs out. She liked to dance, but . . ."

"What?" Braden prompted.

"I don't think she wanted to be seen too much with this guy in public. Or he didn't want them to be seen together."

"Wouldn't they be seen together if they went to a coffee-house?"

"Yes, but . . . you can get away with meeting someone there. Not like at a dance or a concert or anything like that. It could be, you know, like casual. Like you didn't come together."

Braden was silent a moment, long enough for the girl to become conscious of the weight of that silence. "You think she was seeing a married man, don't you, Sheri?"

"You can't make me say that! I didn't say that!"

"I know, but it's what you think. It's what we both think. That's why she was being secretive. Do you think it was one of her teachers?"

"I . . . I don't know."

She wasn't really very good at lying, Braden thought.

"I wonder if you could do something for me," he said. "I'd like a list of Edie's teachers and friends, anyone you can think of that she knew. Don't make a big thing about it. I don't want to point fingers at innocent people, and if the man we're looking for actually is on such a list, I wouldn't want him to know we were looking at him, you understand?"

"I think so."

"Can you do that for me?"

Sheri Kuttner nodded unhappily.

"And any clubs or special groups or activities she was involved in, on or off campus. Like a health club, anything like that."

"Do you really think it was . . . someone from here?" In spite of her own obvious suspicions, the young coed seemed aghast.

"I don't think anything yet. I just have to cover all the possibilities. You'll get me that list? And if you think of anything else, call me." Braden had replenished his supply of business cards, and he gave her a fresh one bearing the San Carlos PD shield logo along with his name and telephone number.

Sheri Kuttner stared at the card. When she looked up her eyes were troubled. "It could've been someone from town, someone really gross that would make her parents go ballistic if they knew. Not someone from the college. You know a lot of parents send their daughters here so they'll meet some nice guy from a good family with prospects. That's the word my mother uses—prospects."

The sun, which had warmed the bench where they sat, went behind a cloud and the afternoon turned suddenly chilly. Sheri Kuttner shivered. She hugged her thin chest with both arms.

"Well, Edie met someone," Braden said, "not so nice."

Thirteen

THE UNITED AIRLINES flight from Washington to Los Angeles was unusually turbulent. Seasonal storms scoured the central plains. The pilot tried to take the Boeing 747 above the weather but the ride remained bumpy. Flight attendants cautioned passengers to remain in their seats and fasten their seat belts. Although the in-flight meal was delayed, the attendants did a brisk business in liquor sales.

From her window seat Karen Younger's view above the storm clouds was of a dark, whirling chaos illuminated from within by flashes of lightning. The scene seemed an appropriate background for her thoughts.

She couldn't believe what was happening.

The murder of Lisl Moeller and her American soldier boyfriend eight years ago had changed forever Karen's view of human nature and its potential for evil. In her private life that experience had made her more hesitant, distrustful, warping relationships. She would always remember Ron's stunned reaction to her panic when, in the midst of a furious argument for which she was equally to blame, he had pressed her against the living room wall of his apartment, pinning her arms above her head and shouting, "Dammit, listen to me!"

He had seen the stark terror in her eyes. He had stepped back quickly, more unnerved than she was. "Jesus Christ," he had muttered, "what were you thinking? What did you think I was going to do?"

Downhill from there, Karen thought. The closest she had come to happily-ever-after, and she had blown it. Her lifestyle with the Bureau didn't exactly offer that many possibilities to find Mr. Right, and Ron had been the closest thing to it. He was an agent himself, someone who knew where she was coming from. That night it had been too late to tell him that she was reacting to remembered trauma, that she didn't really believe he was going to hit her. The unspoken pact of faith and trust had been broken.

Ron was the Assistant Special Agent in Charge of the New York office now. She had seen him during the past summer when he had attended an ASAC meeting at the FBI National Academy. He had used the trip to Quantico to pass his annual physical exam and qualification on the shooting range. They had had dinner one night, just friends. The evening had been painfully awkward.

Something destructive had started to grow inside Karen that gray morning in Germany when she was called out to the scene of a murder involving an American—Lisl's boyfriend was stationed at the nearby U.S. air base. It had been nourished during her later years with the Behavioral Science Unit as an analyst and profiler of violent criminals, particularly serial killers—the most cruel, savage and bloodthirsty of psychopaths. Vampires, especially in the romanticized view currently in vogue, were pussycats by comparison to some of Karen Younger's subjects.

She was aware of a strange sense of continuity in this bumpy flight across the continent. Eight years ago, returning to the States on another long flight, Karen had had a feeling of palpable relief at leaving the unsolved crime behind her. She was going home. Lisl Moeller's killer was no longer her problem.

The feeling had been fundamental: she had been running for her life. Her escape carried with it a mixture of relief and shame. The shame—the sense of having let herself down as well as Lisl Moeller—had been an element in her eagerness to join the BSU and then to volunteer for the Criminal Personality Research Project that was Buddy Cochrane's passion, a program founded on detailed, head-to-head interviews with notorious criminals from Sirhan Sirhan to Ted Bundy to Charles Manson, and the legion of brutal serial killers imprisoned during the eighties and nineties.

Karen had failed at that, too. She had thought she was tough, a Pennsylvania girl who had made it on her own with a hard shell and few illusions, but she had been wrong. When the physical ills and the nightmares became too much for her, with Buddy Cochrane's reluctant support she had retreated to the shelter of a cubicle in the basement warren of the FBI facility that was now called the Investigative Support Unit.

Now she was airborne again. Cut loose. Hurtling through the dark skies as if on the reverse leg of that earlier flight. This time she was going back to the defining experience of her career, the moment when, staring down at Lisl Moeller's battered face, she had peered into the heart and mind of a monster.

"We've cleared the worst of the turbulence," a calm, reassuring male voice over the intercom intruded on Karen Younger's thoughts. "Our flight attendants will be serving dinner shortly, and I hope you will enjoy the rest of your flight. The temperature in Los Angeles today is seventy-one degrees . . ."

Although thick clouds still obscured the earth far below, shutting off views of fertile plains and sinuous rivers and the snowy battlements of the Rockies, the storm was behind them.

But not for her. Nor for Edith Foster, a sophomore student at San Carlos College.

Long ago Karen Younger had convinced herself that Lisl Moeller's death had been a crime of passion, an explosion of rage or jealousy. Such passion alone explained what had been done to her. But if the VICAP match was valid, a different conclusion seemed inescapable.

Karen herself had entered information from the German girl's murder into the VICAP database, more as a sample exercise in the early stages of the program than with any expectation of a future linkage. But the system had done exactly what it was designed to do: match data from one violent crime to another. Where and when the two killings had occurred didn't matter. There were enough similarities for the computer to link the two cases.

That match told Buddy Cochrane that one killer had indeed

struck again, his crimes committed on two different continents, eight years apart.

And Karen Younger remained the FBI's Special Agent of record on the case. Insofar as the FBI retained any jurisdiction over a crime on German soil, its case file had remained open—and it was hers.

Lisl Moeller's murderer was now a repeat killer. If he had acted out of rage, something had held it in check all this time. If not, he was cold and calculating beyond her comprehension.

The Boeing 747 lurched and dipped sharply downward before righting itself. Wind sheer, Karen thought. Not a severe incident, but bad enough to bring gasps and little exclamations of alarm from the passengers in the cabin. Across the aisle from Karen a woman tried to wipe up spilled coffee with a napkin. Karen's stomach seemed to have been left a little behind.

She ate little of her defrosted meal, poking at something that purported to be lasagna and managing to eat a small Caesar salad and a half-frozen dinner roll. Afterward she folded her tray into the seat back and reached for her briefcase.

The police report from San Carlos was included in the case file along with the VICAP questionnaire faxed to the FBI late Monday afternoon. By that time a preliminary autopsy had been completed.

Karen reviewed the few details of the crime. The victim had disappeared around midnight Friday. Her body had been found early the next morning under a creek bridge in a government wetlands area. The autopsy protocol confirmed that she had died around four in the morning. Her face and upper body had been savagely beaten and she had been repeatedly raped. The killer had also carved her initial across her belly. For the next thirty-six hours she had remained unidentified, until a San Carlos College coed was reported missing to the college security office early Sunday evening. The missing girl's automobile, a Nissan 280Z with a personalized license plate, had been found Monday morning in a supermarket parking lot, where it had apparently been parked since Friday night.

So where did he have you from Friday night until Saturday morning? Karen asked the dead girl. *Why did he keep you alive for hours? What kind of horrors did he inflict on you?*

And why you?

In the spare, clinical details of the crime reports Karen could not find Edith Foster, a young woman surely full of juice and dreams. She would have to visit the crime scene, talk to Edith's friends, find out who she was. Had she died by pure chance, simply because she was in the wrong place at the wrong time? Was that—confounding Karen's original opinion—also true of Lisl Moeller? Had there been something in common about the two women that triggered the killer's rage?

Edith's faxed image was there among the pages of the file, but it was silent. Another shadowy image lurked there, faceless, anonymous, its darkness lit from within like one of those black storm clouds where lightning flickered balefully.

You bastard, Karen whispered to herself. *Who are you and where have you been hiding? What hole did you crawl out of?*

In that moment she was close to hating Buddy Cochrane. Her boss and mentor for more than six years believed in her more than she did herself. The knowledge was small consolation.

She started to close the file and slip it back into her briefcase when the name of the San Carlos detective in charge of the case leaped out at her. She paused, staring at the name, remembering what Cochrane had left unsaid.

Of course! That was just what she needed, a case involving a killer who brutalized his female victims in unspeakable ways, and a homicide investigator whose career with the LAPD had been derailed by a police brutality incident caught on some amateur photographer's video film. For a week, until America's frenzied media moved on to the next sensation, Detective Timothy Braden had been a celebrity.

Karen wondered who had filled out the VICAP forms so quickly and efficiently. Not Detective Braden, she was willing to bet.

She closed the file and locked it in her briefcase, settled back in her seat and closed her eyes. Shivered at a fingertip caress of cold.

Far below, a rift in the clouds showed the white ribbon of the Colorado River clawing through pink rock canyons, spearing the western half of the continent.

Fourteen

PLEASED WITH HIMSELF and the attention the Edith Foster murder was generating, Ralph Beringer returned to the San Carlos College campus Tuesday in time to watch from a safe distance as mourners left the small campus chapel after paying their respects to Edith Foster. Beringer would have relished joining them, but he knew better. Seeing the burly man talking to one of the coeds after the service confirmed his hunch. He didn't have to be at arm's length to spot a cop.

He turned away, a man at ease in his surroundings, evidently not in a hurry.

He had made himself familiar with the campus on Monday when he had hit Lindstrom's car. He smiled at the memory. He had had no trouble locating the faded red Nissan Sentra in the faculty parking lot behind the Liberal Arts building. The yellow fireman's coat was still in the back seat. There were a dozen cars in the lot. No one was about. Beringer had studied the back of the building long enough to assure himself that no windows overlooked the corner of the lot where the Nissan was parked.

Thirty seconds later, using a small pry bar, he had had the Nissan's passenger side door open. He had stuffed Lindstrom's yellow fireproof coat into a carryall, dropped the pry bar into the bag on top of the coat, closed the car door and walked away.

Now, as then, wearing the same long-sleeved blue cotton turtleneck and gray Dockers twill pants, he looked as if he belonged where he was. No one paid him any attention.

He noticed clusters of students in animated discussions and

wondered if, without knowing it, they were talking about him. At the administration building he paused to eye some billboard announcements of autumn events and class changes, chatting amiably with a couple of students. At a campus bookstore he made a few small purchases, including a map identifying the campus buildings and showing the walkways and street access.

It was all too pleasant and serene, Beringer thought, heading back to his car, all these fresh-faced kids in their designer jeans and Reeboks and button-down oxford shirts, thinking they had the world by the tail. What did they know about anything? Even Edie, pretty and pliant as she was, in the end was no better than a rubber doll. What did she think was the price of all those tedious classes when she stared up in agony at her tormentor?

He left the campus, smiling and satisfied.

Everything was falling into place.

LATER, CRUISING THE Lindstroms' neighborhood in the Buick LeSabre—having a second car at his disposal was like having a second mask to wear at a ball—he came unexpectedly upon Glenda Lindstrom in her green Dodge station wagon. Even from a half block away he recognized the car immediately, having seen it parked in the driveway over the past weekend. When the wagon turned into the drive, Beringer had a glimpse of Glenda's blond hair, cut shorter than he remembered it. His heart thudding, he drove on by without slowing or turning his head. Out of the corner of his eye he saw Glenda climbing the steps to the wide front porch. Still in shape, he noted, hadn't let herself go. Good. The little girl who had hopped out of the car and scrambled up the steps after her mother couldn't be more than five or six years old. *Their* kid. But where was Richie?

Thinking of the way Glenda moved as she went up those steps, Beringer parked well down the street but within sight of the front of the house. He felt a familiar rage, as comforting to his psyche as the touch of an old dog's head to his owner's hand. This wasn't the time. He wanted to play out the game with the Lindstroms as he had with Edie, only better. Let the trickle of fear become a river, then a flood. Give Lennie a chance to see what was coming if she was sharp enough, let it slowly dawn on her that there was nothing she could do to stop him, that neither the professor nor the police could save her.

A yellow school bus pulled up at the corner just down the street from the Lindstrom house. Two boys hopped out. One was a chunky kid with light brown hair and sturdy legs, the boy who had been at the beach on Sunday with his substitute father. He waved at the other kid and ran to the Lindstrom house, pounded up the steps without slowing and barged in the front door.

You ought to keep that door locked, Lennie, even when you're expecting the kid. You'll learn.

So Richie bussed to school. Glenda drove the little girl, Ellen, to school in the morning—must be in kindergarten or first grade— but Richie took a bus. After a moment spent in factoring this information, Beringer decided it was a bonus. There would be no problem getting Richie away from his home and his parents when the time came.

Follow the bus tomorrow, Beringer decided. See where it goes.

He started the Buick and drove away. On the north end of town he stopped at a public phone in the San Carlos Mall, where he dialed the Lindstrom home number he had memorized. The phone rang four times before an answering machine came on. Dave Lindstrom's voice. "Hello, you've reached the Lindstrom house. We're sorry no one—"

The message cut off as someone picked up the phone. Glenda, breathless as if she had been running, said, "Hello?"

Beringer listened to her breathing.

"Who is this?" she demanded. "Say something!"

Smiling to himself, Beringer hung up and walked back to his car. He was feeling fine, edgy fine, and when he passed a pair of teenage girls on the sidewalk he felt a sudden heat in his loins. Seeing Glenda, then hearing that catch in her throat, had excited him. It made him want to—

He ground his teeth. Images flashed through his mind. Edie Foster on the bed under him, the muffled cries becoming fainter, resistance seeping away, the firmness going out of her breasts as if the liquid of life was draining away. The need that seeing Glenda had aroused in him was powerful, but if he allowed himself to be diverted from the plan he would jeopardize everything. He had waited this long, he could wait a little longer. Take it a step at a time.

To ease the pressure, tonight he could dig out some of his hardcore videos, the ones he had picked up in Amsterdam. Or there was a porno film shop outside of San Carlos—he had noticed it driving in—he could stop there and pick up something new. Go back to the condo like the other commuters, he thought, kick back, have a beer, enjoy the show.

Think about the next one.

GLENDA DROPPED THE phone in its cradle as if it burned her fingers.

It was *him*. There was no doubt in her mind. How had he known exactly when to call? She hadn't been home more than a half hour. Was he watching—?

She ran upstairs and, standing to the side of the front windows of her bedroom, peered through the curtains down at the street. A man in a tan coverall with a Southern California Edison Company logo on his chest was coming down the side path from the Schneider house across the way. She watched him take a shortcut across the neighboring lawn and turn into the next yard. Was the meter reader an imposter? He was well built, Ralph's height . . .

Stop it!

She was becoming paranoid. It was absurd. The Edison truck was clearly visible at the end of the block where the meter reader always parked the van. The other cars parked along the street were also familiar. No one was sitting inside one of them, watching her house. Watching her turn into the drive with Elli, watching Richie alight from his bus . . .

This is what he wants, she thought, her lips tightening. He remembers how easy it was to make her fall apart. How quickly her confidence was shattered, her pride shredded, until she jumped at the sound of his voice as if it were a whip flaying her flesh.

He thinks I'm the same woman, and I'm not.

The self-assertion startled her. She stood very still, as if any movement might shatter the fragile truth she had uncovered.

She was scared, she couldn't deny that. When she remembered looking into Ralph's pale gray eyes, cold as Antarctic ice, what she recalled most vividly was that nothing human looked back at her— no sign of pity or remorse, no understanding of the pain he in- flicted. Because she knew what he was capable of, Ralph could still frighten her, but she was not reduced to jelly. If he expected to deal with the whimpering girl he had once tried to destroy, he was making a mistake. Maybe she could turn that against him.

But not alone.

Since Friday night she had avoided telling Dave all the ugly details about her first marriage. She couldn't put it off any longer. He had to be made to understand that Ralph Beringer was not an inconvenience from her past, he was dangerous.

Soon, she knew, Ralph would not be satisfied with harassing telephone calls.

But there were things she could do before talking to Dave. Basic precautions to take. Locking doors and windows, for instance.

The thought galvanized her. She went around the upstairs rooms first. All had older, double-hung windows in wooden frames. Although each had once been fitted with simple flip-out metal stop- pers, over time some of these basic security devices had broken or been removed. She closed the stoppers that were still in place, leav- ing two windows in Richie's room unsecured.

Downstairs was the same story. Several windows were frozen by layers of old paint. No intruder could pry them open easily. Stoppers were missing from several others, and Dave had never got around to installing the dead bolt he had purchased for the back door. What good was served by the dead bolt on the front door if someone could just open the back door with a stiff plastic credit card and walk in?

The two children were in the den. They were allowed an hour of television after school before Richie started on his homework.

Glenda would be glad when Elli was far enough along in school to have homework assignments. That might quiet the nightly protests over more television. Elli couldn't understand why *she* couldn't watch TV just because Richie had homework.

"Come on, guys, put on a sweater or a jacket. We're going to Home Depot." She shushed the instant protests. "I have to pick up a few things and you're not staying here alone, so there's no point in arguing."

"I got work to do," Richie complained.

"Well, you're not doing it right now, so you can come along. I may need you to watch Elli, and you can help me pick out some window locks."

"Whatta we need window locks for?"

The afternoon was turning cooler. The weather seemed to be in suspense since last week's fires, as if it couldn't decide what to do as an encore for October. Another high pressure system over Utah and Nevada might push hot, dry Santa Ana winds into the Southland, escalating another fire threat, or, if the high pressure dissipated, it would clear the way for long-needed Pacific storms to sweep in, bringing rain, cold, freeway accidents and mud slides in the fire-ravaged hills. If Southern California weather was frequently unpredictable, it still had its patterns.

So did people, Glenda thought.

She checked her side-and rear-view mirrors as she drove. She didn't spot a car that looked familiar, or one that stayed behind her when she made several turns to alter her normal route.

Home Depot's parking lot was crowded as usual and she had to park some distance from the entrance. She kept Richie and Elli in front of her while her gaze ranged back and forth along adjoining aisles. Would Ralph confront her in so public a place? Although she didn't think so, Ralph was even less predictable than the weather.

Richie's protests had been mild because he actually enjoyed wandering around the aisles packed with hardware and lumber and home improvement needs. Old-fashioned hardware stores had been more fun, as Glenda remembered them, but few of them remained. The Depot was about all that was left anymore.

She held Elli's hand as she hunted along a section displaying various door and window locks and security devices. Twice, when Richie started to wander off, she called him back. The third time she told him she needed his advice on what kind of stoppers to choose. Whether convinced by the ruse or not, Richie put his mind to the problem with typical intensity. He pointed out some easy-to-install devices for wood-frame windows that seemed more intruder-proof than those Glenda had had in mind.

As they walked out of Home Depot with their purchases, a fist of tension gripped Glenda's stomach. Her eyes searched the faces around her, jumping nervously back and forth to survey the parking lot. She felt Richie's curious gaze. Was she that obvious?

Driving home, she began to relax. At least she was doing something herself, not simply waiting for *him* to act. As soon as she could find the right moment she would talk to Dave—not only about what Ralph had done to her in the past, but about setting up some ground rules for now, especially for Richie and Elli.

Their wide, tree-shaded street seemed quiet and peaceful in the dappled late afternoon light. It was a street populated by ordinary, decent people, the kind Dave put his faith in. Trusting people. People who watched the TV news every night and were shocked by reports of drive-by shootings and carjackings, people who were horrified by lurid tales of the atrocities committed by the Jeffrey Dahmers, Hillside Stranglers and Night Stalkers, people who remained comfortably assured that such disasters could never happen to them.

Glenda was not naive enough to believe that hers was a Street of Dreams where, behind the clean lace curtains, there were no drunken rages, petty burglaries, divorces and betrayals and all the other conflicts and cancers that afflicted the human race. Overall, however, she had always felt the neighborhood to be what the local real-estate ads proclaimed—a nice place to raise your children, enjoy barbecues with your neighbors, go to church on Sunday.

Entering the quiet house, Glenda felt a momentary anxiety. The children's suddenly noisy contentiousness, along with a hasty perusal of the downstairs rooms, left her relieved and feeling a little foolish. She installed two of the new stoppers on the dining room windows, left the others for later, and started preparing dinner.

Time passed. Cars came and went along the street in the long autumn twilight. Glenda normally had dinner ready at six o'clock. Dave was almost always home before then, in time to have his ritual glass of wine—he had believed a *60 Minutes* story suggesting that Frenchmen lived longer because they drank red wine every day. Tonight, however, six o'clock came and went. She turned the oven temperature down to keep the chicken-and-rice casserole warm without having it shrivel up.

At six-thirty she called Dave's office at San Carlos College. She let the phone ring ten times before hanging up.

She had barely put the phone down when its strident ring made her jump. She snatched it from its cradle. "Dave? Where are you?"

Silence answered her. No, not total silence, she realized. The hand holding the phone began to shake.

"It won't do any good," a voice whispered, unrecognizable. "Nothing will, you know that, don't you?"

"Ralph?" Her cry was shrill. "Ralph, God damn you—"

The infuriating drone of a broken connection caused her to hurl the phone against the wall. The crash brought Richie running. He stopped, wide-eyed with wonder, in the kitchen doorway.

Fifteen

THE SAN CARLOS PD was a small department serving a college town with a population of 28,000 at the last census. Pranks, disturbances and petty thefts on the San Carlos College campus—the usual complaints—were generally left to the college's security office. The Investigation Unit at the SCPD handled more serious crimes. It consisted of a half-dozen ranked detectives and clerical support personnel. The busiest desk was Robbery-Burglary, manned by two investigators sharing a corner of the squad room with Tim Braden, whose desk was officially called Violent Crimes.

Nearby Los Angeles had recorded more than one thousand murders the previous year, or about three a day. San Carlos had had three murders on its books for the entire year. Two had been the result of family disputes, the other a shooting during an armed robbery.

Braden was at his desk Wednesday morning when a fairly tall, well-dressed woman entered the squad room, glancing around tentatively as if she were looking for someone. There was a suspension of activity in the room, an all-male bastion except for Lillian Peters in records and Linda Perez on the Domestic Complaints desk. The hush caught Braden's attention. Glancing up, he saw a blond woman in a dark blue suit saying something to Peters, who nodded toward Braden over her shoulder.

A half-dozen pairs of eyes watched the woman's progress across the room to Braden's corner, where his desk was back-to-back with the one shared by the two investigators in Robbery-Burglary. The woman was not skinny but in very solid shape, Braden thought. She wore the crisply tailored Ann Taylor suit over a powder blue blouse. Sensible walking shoes with low heels. Braden's appraisal didn't miss the trim calves and ankles.

"Detective Braden? I'm Agent Younger . . . from the FBI's Investigative Support Unit?"

Eastern seaboard accent, not unpleasant, the voice a little husky and well-modulated, gray eyes cool and contained. Braden's blank expression earned him a small frown.

"You didn't hear from Quantico? That I was coming?" She was obviously surprised. "You *are* Detective Braden?"

"Uh, yeah. Is everything a question with you?" He was thinking that he really liked the sound of her voice, but his flip comment came out as sarcasm.

A flat film dropped over the FBI agent's eyes, like shutters closing. "Not if I get an answer the first time, Detective."

Braden waited another moment. The truth was, she flustered him a little. Brisk, self-possesesed career women as attractive as this one tended to do that. Braden hesitated over a question as simple as whether or not he was supposed to stand up and shove a hand at her, something he would have done automatically if she were a male agent. What was an FBI agent doing here, anyway? And what was he supposed to have heard from Quantico, which was always on the line to him with the latest gossip?

He gestured toward a wooden chair beside his desk. "I'm Braden. What unit did you say that was?"

"Investigative Support. You've heard of it as the Behavioral Science Unit, maybe?"

"Maybe." That got under his skin a little. "Look, I'm kinda busy—"

"Let's understand each other, Detective Braden," she said pleasantly. "I know local law enforcement officers don't generally do handsprings when they hear anything with the word Fed in it. But we received your VICAP report . . . on the Edith Foster killing?" The questioning lilt again caught Braden's ear. "I'm here as a consultant and adviser, that's all."

"Well, I appreciate that, Ms. Younger, but the Foster killing isn't a federal case."

She hesitated, as if deciding how much to say to him. "There are factors that lead us to believe Foster may have been attacked by a repeat killer. We've done a great deal of work on psychological profiles of serial killers that may be of help—"

"I'd really like to sit down with you and talk about killer profiles and all that," Braden cut her off impatiently. "But like I said, I'm kinda busy here. I don't have a serial killer. What I've got is a single homicide, a nineteen-year-old girl stabbed and beaten to death, some wacko out there thinks he's got away with it. We can have our meeting later—"

"Don't patronize me, Detective."

Agent Younger didn't raise her voice but its edge cut through the background babble in the room. Faces turned toward them. Braden recognized the stiff-backed reaction he had seen before in women invading traditional male enclaves—female cops and district attorneys, for example. The agent's expression said she had been through this before. It had probably been the same in the Bureau when she started out. You had to prove yourself every step of the way, the look said, you couldn't back down an inch or show any weakness, you couldn't take any bullshit or *they* would just pile it higher.

She leaned forward over the corner of Braden's desk, speaking low enough so that only he could hear. "Like I told you, Detective Braden, I'm here to help, not to invade your precious territory. But if that's the way you want it, we can play it your way. I didn't fly out here just to get some California sunshine, which I haven't seen much of this morning anyway. If what I believe happened here in San Carlos holds up, there's a lot about this homicide of yours you don't know and apparently can't be bothered to find out. If it's too much trouble for you to work with me, as soon as I've had a chance to look into this case on my own, if what I think happened stands up I'll get on to Washington and let them take it from there. I believe there's a jurisdictional question here; the victim was found on U.S. government property and county detectives were first at the scene. The way it looks to me, Detective, you won't have to bother about the case at all for long. You won't have to worry about cooperation or civility or even being professional."

"Take it easy—"

"I *am* taking it easy. You want to see hard, Braden, just stick around."

A slow, hot flush crept up Braden's neck. He watched the FBI agent stalk out of the squad room, brushing past a startled uniform at the doorway. Even in that moment he was able to admire the way her hips swiveled when she walked off stiff-legged like that, tight calf muscles and trim ankles and rhythmic little jerks of her hips. Solid hips, Braden thought. His mother would have approved, thinking of grandchildren. What made him think of that? Did it make him a sexist pig in addition to being a jerk?

Across the room a detective started to clap, and others joined in. "Way to go, Timmy!"

The grins were not all supportive. Braden had never become Mr. Popularity in the SCPD squad room, in large part because he had vaulted over others in rank when he was brought in from the outside, but also because he had been touchy and aloof in the beginning. He had been variously viewed as (a) the Asshole Big City Detective who had come to show all the cops in the little hick town how it was done; (b) the Asshole Big City Detective who, having lost his head and his job in Los Angeles, had brought to the San Carlos PD a notoriety it didn't need; (c) the Asshole Big City Detective who was too good to mingle with the little people; or (d) the Asshole Big City Detective with an attitude.

Well, he had had an attitude all right, Braden grudgingly acknowledged. Bitter, feeling used, angry over the injustice of the hand he had been dealt, it had taken him a while to remember his father's sensible advice. "Play out the hand, son. You won't always like the cards you get, but look around the table. You won't see many happy smiles." An avid Saturday night poker player, Frank Braden had leaned heavily on gambler's clichés. "A royal flush is like winning the lottery. It's not something to count on." "Don't worry about a man's eyes, Tim, worry about his hands." There was an exception to the latter rule. "Unless they're dead eyes. You see a man at the table with dead eyes, real dead eyes, you better know you're good or find yourself another game."

Braden had begun to earn some respect in the squad room,

mostly by keeping his mouth shut and doing his job. But the Edith Foster case was his first tough challenge since joining the SCPD, and he knew there were some in the room who were waiting for him to trip and fall flat on his face.

Behind him a voice said, "Come in here, Braden."

It wasn't a request. Captain Hummel's tone was its usual roll of gravel down a chute. Braden rolled his eyes at the two suits from Robbery and followed the captain into the fishbowl.

"I got to hand it to you, Braden, you sure have a way with women."

"She had no call to—"

"You were brushing her off."

Braden sighed. "Come on, Captain . . . psychological profiling on this case? What's that all about?"

"I'm gonna let you off the hook this time, Detective, because I didn't get this memo over to you this morning. Goddam civilian review board meeting, how the hell are we supposed to get any work done?" Hummel pushed a piece of paper across his desk at Braden. It was a fax under the letterhead of the Federal Bureau of Investigation. Braden ran his eye quickly down the sheet. It told him pretty much what the female special agent had said, that she was being sent out to advise and consult.

It added something new. The FBI's computer had matched the details of the Edith Foster killing with a similar murder committed eight years ago—in Germany.

"Shit," Braden muttered. "The Bureau thinks this wasn't a onetime shot? That we have an international killer? How the hell could they get onto something like that so fast?"

"Maybe you should ask the lady," Hummel said. "Isn't that what VICAP's supposed to be all about? That is, you can ask her if you get another chance. Is any of this getting through to you, Braden?"

"I'm supposed to cooperate."

"You've got it."

"I'm open to new ideas. I don't roll my eyes anytime a Fed comes into the room."

"Better and better."

"She looks like Barbie on steroids, for Chrissake. Is there a Barbie FBI Agent doll with muscles?"

"I don't know. You look like Boris Karloff this morning, what do you care? You got somethin' against good-lookin' women? Is there somethin' you been wantin' to tell me, Detective?"

"Only that I have a homicide to look into. That's bad enough without a serial killer circus."

Hummel regarded him steadily. His eyes were small in a beefy red face. Braden had never been able to read the captain's eyes. They were so small and hard they gave Hummel an edge, Braden thought, if anyone had the balls to go eye-to-eye with him. "Let's pray to God it's just one homicide."

"Yeah."

As Braden turned to go, Hummel's voice stopped him with his hand on the doorknob. "And when Barb comes back, treat her with respect. Is that understood, Detective?"

"I wouldn't have it any other way."

"Good. You might even learn somethin'. Her name's Karen, by the way, not Barbie."

"Am I supposed to care?"

"You never know, Detective."

Sixteen

FBI SPECIAL AGENT Karen Younger was staying at a Red Roof Inn on the outskirts of San Carlos, just off the freeway on the east side. Braden dialed the motel's number from his car. When her room phone wasn't answered, he drove around aimlessly for a short time, feeling generally pissed off.

Then he had a hunch.

From the civic center he drove south through Old Town, past the San Carlos College campus and past the Alpha Beta shopping center where Edith Foster's 280Z had been found abandoned. A few minutes later he was out of the city, cruising between long, flat dunes on his right and the protected wetlands on the inland side of the highway.

He found Agent Younger where he had expected her to be: at the crime scene.

Braden parked behind the agent's rented Ford Contour and walked to the bridge where Younger leaned on the railing. She didn't look up as Braden stopped beside her. Her expression was as somber as the day, which remained overcast and cool. The offshore breeze blowing uninterrupted across the dunes had a cutting edge.

"Was any trace evidence found on this railing?" she asked after a moment.

Braden shook his head. "He was careful. Right about where you're standing the techs found scrapings from a plastic sheet she was wrapped in. This is where he dropped her over."

Little evidence of the crime scene was left, other than some yellow police tape flapping in the breeze where one end had pulled loose and, over beside the bike path, the remains of some candles and wilted flowers that had briefly memorialized the murdered girl.

Braden understood why Karen Younger had needed to visit the crime scene herself. Reading a report was no substitute for being there. Staring down at the creek bed, was she mentally sorting through the police photographs showing Edith Foster's body face-down in the mud? At the same time was she trying to fit inside the skin of the killer? Most investigators tried it, one time or another, with varying success. He wondered if Younger was good at it and that was why the Bureau had sent her. Irrelevantly he decided that her eyes were more gray than blue, as if they reflected the sky. He wondered if they would appear more blue than gray on a warm, sunny day.

"Where you from, Younger? That accent . . . New York?"

"I grew up in Philadelphia."

"Is that where you picked up that chip on your shoulder?"

"Part of that's inherited. My mom was the same way. Nobody gave her any lip."

"I suppose that means, if you hadn't met some kindly bene-factor who steered you along the right path, instead of being an upright FBI agent you could've ended up on the other side."

"A hit woman for the Mob," she agreed. "Or maybe a Phila-delphia waitress."

Another silence fell between them, but the tension had gone out of it.

"So what do your friends call you, Detective?"

"My really good friends call me Braden. Everyone else calls me Detective Braden."

"Cool," she said. "I'll bet your mother still calls you Timothy."

"Yeah, and my ex-wife called me Tim. You'll notice I said ex."

"You work hard at getting people to dislike you, don't you, Braden?"

"Hell, it ain't hard."

She studied him thoughtfully. Then she looked back down toward the creek. "Washing the body, wrapping her in plastic, dumping her out here . . . he's a very organized killer, Detective. And he's had a long time to plan this."

"You seem to know more than I do. How about we go somewhere out of the wind and talk?"

"Why the change of heart?"

"My captain and I had a little heart-to-heart. There's a diner back up the road. You want to follow my car?"

SHE FOLLOWED HIM along the highway to the Bright Spot. Walking toward the entrance, Braden pointed out the telephone from which Harry Malkowski had made his 911 call after discovering Edith Foster's body. The diner was nearly deserted. They sat at a window booth facing each other, with a view across the highway over the empty dunes.

Braden listened to the record on the jukebox. Otis Redding, "Dock of the Bay," he thought, pleased with himself. Karen Younger studied the collection of vintage car photographs on the walls. Iris, the leggy, frizzy-haired blond waitress who had been on duty when Braden interviewed Harry Malkowski, approached the booth, eyeing the FBI agent with curiosity. She took their orders for coffee, then said, "Catfish is good today. It's farm-raised."

The menu featured such old-fashioned comfort foods as hot beef and hot turkey sandwiches, macaroni and cheese, hamburgers and milk shakes. "I'll have coffee and the Philly Cheesesteak sandwich," Braden said.

"I'll have the same," the FBI agent said.

When they were alone they studied each other warily across the formica table. Braden had seen the admiration in the waitress's eyes when she looked Younger up and down. He decided the word Iris would have used was classy.

"If we're going to work together, Braden, there's something I have to know."

He stiffened, guessing what was coming. "If you have something to ask, ask it."

"That woman on the video, why'd you hit her?"

"To control her."

"Oh, come on, Braden, you were on camera, she—"

"The camera lied."

"Cameras don't lie, Detective."

"They do if what they show is selective. What you saw on that film—what the whole damned country thinks it saw—was a lie."

The scene flashed through his mind for perhaps the thousandth time. Filmed by the supposed victim's neighbor in blurry black-and-white, under poor light conditions, the video recorded what looked like a classic case of police brutality. There was Braden stepping through a doorway. Then a young black woman flying out the door, screaming at him. Braden turning away, the woman grabbing him, getting in his face, Braden pushing her off. The woman rushing after him again, but now Braden's body hid her partially from the camera's lens, and the world never saw what Braden did— the bottle opener with a spiral metal corkscrew in the woman's hands. She jabbed it at Braden's eyes. All the camera recorded was an image of this skinny black woman struggling with a much bigger, stronger white man, twisting free of his grip, appearing to try to slap him . . . and Braden either shoving or slapping her, sending her sprawling through the doorway. Then Braden, in a move that looked very bad on film, charged through the door after her. The camera stared at the empty doorway while the woman's screams rose higher, becoming a shrill plea for help.

Younger's eyes were noncommittal. Reserving judgment, Braden thought. She said, "What was it all about, anyway? The news stories glossed that over."

"It started as a typical domestic triangle—the woman, her husband and her lover. The husband had a knife but the lover had a gun, so guess who won? When we got there the husband was already down—he was DOA at the hospital. We were trying to arrest the second man and the soon-to-be-rich widow became hysterical, out of control. When she flew at me I tried to give her some space. I stepped outside but she came after me."

"With a corkscrew."

"Yeah."

"Which was never found."

"That's right," Braden said in a flat tone. "Somebody took it . . . someone who wanted to create problems for the police. It happens. Listen, if you knew all this, why did you ask?"

"I wanted to hear what you had to say. Hey, Detective, you have to admit it looked bad on video."

Braden himself had been shocked when he first saw the film footage. Rehashing it now, he felt the burden of the past year bearing down on him. The curiosity in the FBI agent's eyes was nothing new. When the corkscrew couldn't be found, Internal Affairs investigators were openly skeptical about Braden's story. The tabloid news media had a field day. In the eyes of a national television audience Braden was instantly proven guilty. Open and shut. The Corkscrew Cop, one reporter called him, and the name stuck. Even David Letterman joked on *The Late Show* about the difference between a cop being screwed and being bent.

Pending the departmental investigation of the incident, Braden was suspended. The widowed woman's lawyer quickly brought suit against Braden, the police department, the police chief and the city. Eventually the internal investigation cleared Braden. His partner at the scene and other witnesses supported his story about the woman going berserk and striking at Braden's face with some kind of weapon. The partner confirmed that Braden had followed procedure in doing everything possible to defuse the situation, walking away from the woman and ultimately slapping her only when she became violent.

In the end none of that mattered. Braden was reassigned to a desk in Parker Center, out of public view. The city, seeking to avoid the expense and notoriety of an inflammatory trial, settled with the bereaved widow out of court. An agreement with the police officers' union allowed Braden to transfer out of the LAPD to the San Carlos Police Department, a comparative backwater agency that had been trying to hire a qualified criminal investigator for more than six months.

The Incident followed Braden to San Carlos. Initially there were organized protests by students and some faculty members enraged over his hiring. The conservative mayor and city council, elected on law-and-order campaign platforms, refused to back

down. Protesters were reminded that there had been a rising inci-
dence of rape and assault on campus. Timothy Braden had a distinguished record, he had been cleared by his department, he was
a valuable asset for the SCPD, the college and the community.

Although there were cries of whitewash, the demonstrations
died away, especially when local TV stations lost interest; but the
memory of the Incident lingered on—even that insufferable nickname surfaced once in a while.

When Braden stopped talking there was a long silence. He
thought he detected a change in the FBI agent's attitude when she
spoke again. "Fair enough, Detective. I don't suppose that was
easy—"

"Cut the bullshit," Braden snapped back. "What are you, a
shrink?"

Karen Younger smiled. "As a matter of fact, Braden, I am."

The waitress had brought their Philly Cheesesteak sandwiches
while Braden talked, and the agent examined hers dubiously.

"Anything wrong?" Braden asked.

"They never saw this in Philadelphia."

"This is a Philly Cheesesteak sandwich California style. That's
probably watercress there, see?"

"I don't want to know."

They munched on their sandwiches quietly, Braden with more
enthusiasm than someone who had grown up eating real Philadelphia Cheesesteak sandwiches. When they had finished Iris brought
more coffee and whisked away their plates.

"Okay, Agent Younger, if this Feel-Good Hour is over, what
say we get back to why you're here."

"Tell me what you've learned so far, Detective. Besides what's
in the preliminary autopsy and the incident reports you faxed to
us."

"Edith Foster went out to meet someone Friday night—probably her latest boyfriend. She was seen between ten and eleven at
The Pelican, a coffeehouse downtown. At midnight she made some
purchases at a supermarket on the south side of town—you went
by it driving out here. Her car was found parked in the market's lot
Monday morning. It was parked around the side, but the assistant

manager remembers seeing it when he came to work on Sunday and again when he left that night. He thought it might have been there Saturday, too. He was gonna report it, he says, but he hadn't got around to it. Too busy."

"So you think she was abducted from the parking lot after midnight."

"Either that or she went off willingly in her boyfriend's car and never came back."

"Why did you call him her latest boyfriend before?"

"She was a popular girl. Between the lines, maybe she slept around a little more than was good for her."

"Mm."

"Whatever that means. The thing is . . . her latest is a mystery man. According to her roommate, Foster liked older men—including some of her professors. Supposedly, she had a crush on one of them last year. Then they broke up or something, or summer vacation got in the way, but the roomie thinks Foster was seeing him again. At any rate, she was seeing someone for the last four or five weeks and was very closemouthed about it."

"One of her teachers?"

"That'd be a good guess. There's some kind of rule against faculty and students doing their thing together."

"Delicately put."

"I thought so." Braden paused in his summary. "So you see, Younger, there's good reason to think we should be looking for our killer right here in San Carlos, not at something that happened in Germany eight years ago."

"The two don't necessarily rule each other out."

"Be easy to check, though. Get a list of the faculty, eliminate women and those who are too old or too young, and run the others, see if they were in Germany at the right time."

"That's worth doing, Detective. That's something I can do."

Braden nodded. It was the kind of thing the FBI was good at.

"This roommate . . . do you think she knows more than she's told you?"

"Sheri Kuttner? Yeah, she knows more, or thinks she does. I get the feeling she was a little jealous of Foster . . . or maybe she resented this guy coming between them. She and Edie were best friends."

"If he was an older, married man, Sheri would probably have disapproved. She might have believed Edie was being used."

"I don't know about Sheri disapproving of what Edie was doing—I don't get the impression these kids are very judgmental—but you're right, she didn't like what the professor was doing. Some of them do take advantage. I remember when I went to college, one of my professors had this regular revolving door for coeds, at least one every semester."

"I was thinking more of Sheri Kuttner's reliability."

"I know what you were saying. You want to know what this professor of mine taught?"

The FBI agent eyed him speculatively. "Psychology."

Braden grinned at her. "You've got it."

"I'd like to talk to Sheri. Maybe she'll open up more with a woman."

"Be my guest." Braden waved the attentive Iris off. "So what's this German angle? Where does a serial killer fit in . . . from the Bureau's point of view, that is."

"We don't have an ax to grind, Braden . . . and I wish to hell I didn't believe what I do. Eight years ago a similar murder occurred near Wiesbaden in what was then West Germany. That's near a major U.S. air base. The crime was never solved. The details were entered into VICAP's database several years ago as a control. The entry was never supposed to turn up a match in this country, but now it has."

Braden regarded her with a cop's flat, skeptical gaze. "Eight years ago?"

"That's right. The case was investigated by the FBI and the German *polizei*. There was a suspicion that the murderer might have been an American, but it was never proved. The girl was with another soldier the night she was killed."

"Another soldier?"

The agent's gray eyes looked past Braden's shoulder at some distant point. She described the bridge and the service platform where the girl's body was found. "The theory was that the girl and her soldier went down to the service platform for a little privacy, and the killer caught them there."

"Both of them?"

"The river deposited the boyfriend's body downstream two days later. He had some contusions about the face, suggesting he'd been hit, but he died from drowning."

Braden stared at her for a moment, then shook his head. "That's different from my case. I have only one body. Anyway, eight years is a lifetime between murders, and it's a long way from Wiesbaden to San Carlos."

"Not far enough, apparently."

"You seem pretty sure."

"If I weren't, I wouldn't be here. Believe me, Braden, you have a serial killer on the loose here."

"Why'd they send you?"

"Because I was there when this guy got his start. I was in Germany. It was my first year out of the FBI Academy, acting as a liaison with German authorities."

"You don't look old enough."

She didn't, he thought. When she first walked into the police station that morning he had thought someone's daughter was visiting. Now, in the fluorescent glare of the diner, she appeared definitely older, but still no more than thirty. There was also something in her face he hadn't seen at first, a toughness she neither affected nor tried to hide. Her gaze was direct, unflinching. She wouldn't give away anything to Captain Hummel in a staring contest, Braden thought.

"I still think it's a reach. What's the connection? Where's the link? Just because two women were beaten to death in similar ways, and a knife was used on each of them—"

"Do you really think I'd be here if that was all there was? Come on, Braden."

He felt heat at the back of his neck, irritated by the scolding tone. "Okay, spell it out for me. This better be good."

"Both women were beaten to death. In the first case the victim, Lisl Moeller, was cut up badly because he used his bare fists and he wears a wedding ring. He's had time to think about blood matching and tissue samples since then, so he wore gloves when he killed Edith Foster. But if the coroner is right, this time he had something hard under his gloves."

"Could've been holding a roll of quarters," Braden said.

"Whatever. He doesn't care what kind of damage he does. When he gets going he's a very angry man—also very strong. He handled these women easily, along with Moeller's soldier boyfriend. There were no defensive wounds in either case, and no blood or tissue under the women's fingernails to indicate they were able to scratch or hit back."

"He hits 'em like Foreman hit Moorer," Braden said thoughtfully. "One punch, the fight's over."

"I expect so, Detective."

"These defensive wounds—"

"Bruising or abrasions where she might have tried to ward off an attack. As you know, they usually show on the hands or arms. Lisl Moeller's wrists showed circular bruising, indicating he might have grabbed her wrists while she struggled, before he hit her. Edith Foster didn't even have that much of a chance."

"Go on."

"He rapes his women, probably both before and after. In Germany he left semen. Here in San Carlos he practiced safe sex—and denied us any blood or semen to match." Karen Younger's tone had become detached, clinical. "He uses a knife with a short, fairly dull blade, probably a pocketknife or Swiss Army knife. He probably carries it all the time. At least we can hope so."

"Our ME didn't specify a pocketknife—"

"He described a short, straight, dull-edged blade. The killer doesn't use it like a surgeon because it tears as much as it cuts. Moeller's cuts were postmortem; Foster's either perimortem or later. She might have been alive. He likes to hurt women, Braden. He's getting even."

Braden was beginning to feel uneasy as the index of similarities in the two murders lengthened. But the FBI agent's theory was still too farfetched, the incidents too far removed from each other in time and place, for him to give it credence.

"He cuts the woman's initial across her abdomen," Younger

continued in the same remote tone. "A single large letter—block, not script, because that kind of lettering is easier with a dull knife. Cutting into flesh isn't as easy as some people think." She paused again briefly. "He's right-handed. The horizontal strokes for the letters are made from left to right, which is natural for a right-hander."

In spite of himself Braden was listening closely now, not wanting to believe what he was hearing. Christ, eight years! Was it possible? If the agent was right, what would the creep have been doing for the past eight years? And why would his anger erupt again at this time? Why San Carlos?

"Then the killer has left a final message for us, in case we had any doubt. In each case he used the knife to make one more cut, extending an opening. She's only a cunt, he's telling us."

Braden stared in silence out of the streaked window of the Bright Spot. The day had turned bleaker. Why didn't it rain? At least that would lessen the fire hazard in the hills. After several moments he said, "Shit."

"He's here, Braden. The same man. He's starting again."

"Even supposing you're right, what set him off again? What brought him into my backyard?"

"I guess that's what we have to find out."

Seventeen

IT WAS WEDNESDAY before Glenda found the courage to talk to Dave at length about Ralph Beringer. By then he had given her even more reason.

Dave had come home that evening in a foul mood. For the second time in three days his car had been vandalized in the faculty parking lot. Monday the Nomex coat had been stolen from the back seat; today someone had slashed one of his tires. Senseless vandalism annoyed the hell out of him, he complained, and he couldn't imagine how young men or women, on the verge of adulthood, could think there was anything clever or amusing about slashing someone's tires.

Glenda had felt a chill, listening to him.

Dave had grumbled irritably through half their delayed meal before he realized that she was hardly paying attention. He waited until they were alone in the den after dinner before asking what was troubling her.

"He called again today."

"You talked to him? What did he—?"

"He hung up on me."

She knew instantly what Dave was thinking, that it was a wrong number. But the pinched frustration and anger in Glenda's face stopped him from saying it.

"That's the third call since last Friday. He's also been following me, spying on me and the kids."

"How do you know that?"

"One of Elli's teachers called me this afternoon. She wanted to know if we knew anyone with a large, dark blue sedan. It was parked near the school, and one of the children said the driver of the car was asking her questions about Elli."

The shock in Dave's eyes pleased her irrationally.

"Hey, I've seen that car." Richie stood in the doorway of the den. Glenda wondered how long he had been listening. "It's cool . . . a 1993 Buick LeSabre."

"You've seen it? Where?"

"It was parked up the street yesterday when I got off the bus." The boy's eyes were openly curious.

"You're sure about that?" Dave asked sharply.

Richie was not above dramatizing things. But the boy was crazy about cars. When he was younger he had built up a vast collection of small plastic copies of just about every make and model automobile. He still had most of them in a box in his closet. If he had seen the car, Glenda knew, and he said it was a '93 LeSabre, that's what it was.

"Sure I'm sure. I saw it again this morning. I think it was following my bus."

When Dave sent Richie up to his room to finish his homework, Glenda retreated into silence.

"Let's not jump to conclusions, honey," Dave said. "We don't know for sure—"

"It's him," she said bitterly. "He's doing it openly. He *wants* us to know. Why else would he ask that other girl about Elli? Why would he park where Richie was able to see his car?"

"Okay, but—"

"And who do you think stole your coat? Or slashed your tire?"

"Student pranksters—"

"When was the last time student pranksters sneaked into the faculty lot and slashed a faculty member's tires? They could get tossed out of school."

"But that's such a childish thing for Beringer to do, so . . . ." He fumbled for an explanation that would be less bizarre than hers.

"Malicious," Glenda said shortly.

"I can hardly believe he'd waste his time that way."

"Later, Dave." Glenda cocked her head, alerted to a small sound in the hallway.

"But—"

"Not now, Dave."

"IT STARTED ON our honeymoon," Glenda said.

She and Dave were in their upstairs bedroom, the kids both asleep now, or at least in their beds, the night silent beyond the windows. No sounds along the empty street. In the distance a siren pealed, so far away it didn't seem part of San Carlos, it belonged to that great troubled megalopolis to the north.

Glenda sat up in bed, pillows propped behind her against the headboard, as she talked quietly, her gaze avoiding his. "I thought he became very tired of me very quickly," she said. "I felt . . . inadequate. He'd make fun of me . . . my breasts, my hips, my butt— no, don't interrupt, I have to do this. When the abuse began to be physical, at first he acted as if it was all in fun. Things like twisting my nipples between his thumb and forefinger hard, or pinching the inside of my thighs—not playfully, but trying to hurt.

"He acted very jealous. I don't think he really cared what I did, but he would act as if he did. If I went to the store to pick up some groceries, he would question me afterward. *'You've been all this time picking out cereal?* I'm supposed to believe that? Who were you talkin' to in there?'

"The verbal abuse never stopped. He just kept after me. Nothing I did was right. The apartment was never clean enough, even if I scrubbed on hands and knees. The baby—Richie—was spoiled. I didn't know how to raise him. I was letting myself go, he was ashamed to take me anywhere, ashamed to admit I was his wife." She broke off, trembling. "I know this sounds petty, whining—"

"No, no—"

"—but that was only the beginning, the first six months or so. I really believe he thought he was being supertolerant. He'd compare me to his mother, how her home was always spotless, how she couldn't stand a slovenly housewife . . . but it's funny, that's the only time he ever mentioned his mother. I don't even know if she was dead or alive. He didn't have any pictures of her, any keepsakes from his childhood, anything to remember her by. If she was alive he never wrote her or called her on the phone or heard from her. It was as if he didn't have any family, no mother or father, no brothers or sisters or uncles or cousins. It was like he sprang into the world by himself."

"Maybe he was an orphan."

"No, I don't believe so. He grew up with his mother. I'm sure of it. If you want to know the truth, I think he hated her. He compared me to her unfavorably all the time, but I believe that was a lie. He was only building her up to tear me down."

"It sounds like a rotten marriage, honey. You're lucky you got out of it when you did."

She looked at him for a long moment in silence. "You don't understand yet, Dave. I haven't even started."

He seemed puzzled, and for a moment anger flashed in her. She took a deep breath. She folded her hands in her lap to hide the tremors. "I was an abused wife. Do you know what that means?"

"He hit you?"

"My God, you haven't been listening to anything I've said!"

"Of course I've been listening. He sounds like a real jerk, but—"

"He's not a jerk, Dave! Do you hear me? He's a monster!"

Dave looked as if she had slapped him. "You don't really mean that."

"Yes, I mean exactly that. He hurt me any way he wanted. At first it was the cruel pinching, the gripping and twisting. He loved to show how strong he was, how he could do anything at all he wanted with me and it was no use resisting. Then he started to slap me around . . ."

"Honey, you don't have to go on with this."

"Yes, I do. I've waited too long. I never should have hid it from you. I didn't want you to think less of me."

"I wouldn't have thought less of you. I don't . . ."

Hot tears stung her cheeks and she brushed at them with one

hand. Her words rushed on. She couldn't have stopped the out-pouring now if she had wanted to. "He drank a lot. Most military men do, it's part of their macho thing. When Ralph drank he be-came meaner, more abusive. He'd come home late, drunk, and he'd start accusing me of things, beating me for what I didn't do and beating me for denying doing them. He'd hit me or pinch me where it wouldn't show, but after a while he got careless about that. Our neighbors, friends, they started looking at me strangely, and I had to come up with a lot of excuses for running into doors or tripping on the stairs, to explain a black eye or why I was limping or couldn't lift my arm. I found out later Ralph told them I was drinking and hurting myself."

By this time Dave was pale, tight-lipped with anger. "Why didn't you leave him?"

"Why doesn't every woman leave a man like that? Don't you think I wanted to? I was afraid of him! He made it clear he'd find me if I tried to leave. He threatened to take Richie from me and I'd never see him again. I really believe if I'd tried to leave him then, he would've killed me."

"You can't really mean that."

"You don't know him. You don't believe there is real evil in this world. You don't want to see it, so you pretend it's not there."

"I'm not blind—"

"But you don't want to see the ugly side of things. You don't even like the graphic violence in the new movies. It sickens you."

"It's bad art," Dave retorted. "And it's self-defeating. Once you start down that road it's never enough—"

"No lectures, Dave, please. Not now."

He stopped, baffled. When he tried to take hold of her to comfort her she flinched involuntarily. After a moment he said, "You're still scared of him."

"He's angry and he's dangerous. He's bottled up the rage all these years, and now he's come after me. What do you think?"

"I think . . . I think maybe it's time to go to the police. Sign a complaint about harassment, threats. Maybe you can get a restrain-ing order."

"What good will that do? We don't even know where he is!

We can't even prove he's the one who's been making these phone calls, stealing your slicker, cutting your tire."

"If he did that—"

"Of course he did it! And that means he's been following you around, spying on you just the way he's been watching Elli and Richie and me. But if I told the police all that, they'd only brush me off. You know what they'd say? Even if it's Ralph doing this, he hasn't committed any crime. Calling up and wanting to talk to his son isn't a crime."

"Malicious mischief is."

"We can't prove he did any of it. Nobody saw him. He's too smart for that."

He wanted to take her in his arms, to comfort and reassure her, and this time when he put his arm around her she didn't pull away. Dave held her quietly, kissing the salty tears on her cheeks. Her body remained rigid, her eyes tense. She seemed fragile and vulnerable, as if the slightest touch might cause her to shatter like fine porcelain. He was more disturbed by her state of mind than by the threat of Ralph Beringer's escalating harassment.

"Feeling the way you did, how did you ever find the courage to leave him?"

"I didn't." Her expression shaded into something bleak and remote. "I waited until he was overseas. I was in therapy with a support group for battered army wives—there were quite a few of us. I was only able to get help after Ralph was gone. I didn't have the guts to leave him until he was far enough away that I could do it by mail." The words were harsh with self-disgust.

"You can't blame yourself for that—don't let him do that to you."

"He already did, Dave . . . a long time ago." She rolled away from him and swung her legs off the bed. "You want to know how he answered my letter? I'll show you."

She left the room. Dave heard her bare feet pad along the hallway to the spare room they used as an occasional guestroom and also for storage. Some dull thumps told him she was getting a box down from the stack in the closet. Waiting, he had the feeling of having stumbled into a nightmare, like someone in a fantasy film.

The kind of things Glenda described happened to other people, not to anyone he knew—certainly not to his family. But her experience with her first husband explained many things to Dave about their own relationship and the way he thought she had flowered during their six years together. He had taken pride in seeing the timid, hesitant, agonizingly self-critical young woman he had first met grow into someone mature and confident and open. He had never known what was behind her nervousness, her lack of self-esteem, her sudden tension when a car door would slam during the night somewhere up the street. A great deal was now clearer, and he wondered how he could have been so obtuse, so slow to comprehend a pattern that now seemed obvious.

Glenda returned carrying an ordinary letter-size envelope. The paper was old, somewhat yellowed. He could not read the faded cancellation stamp, but the stamps on the envelope were German. He raised his eyebrows questioningly.

"I received this about three months after I wrote Ralph in Germany to tell him I was leaving him."

Dave Lindstrom read the brief note. He glanced up at her. Then he read the message a second time. Its callous bluntness offended and angered him. He could readily understand why, under the circumstances, Glenda had been frightened by it. But that was, after all, a long time ago. Tempers cooled, wounds healed. Eight years was a long time.

"What are you trying to tell me, honey?"

"Ralph sent me that note as a warning. He likes to play those kinds of mind games, Dave. He likes to shake you up—scare you. Just like these phone calls we've been getting. He wanted to give me something to think about. And he was telling me in no uncertain terms that someday he would be back, and he wasn't finished with me."

"You're reading a lot into this note."

"No! I'm not exaggerating! I know him, Dave. He's something you don't even believe in outside of a movie screen. And he's come back for me . . . and for Richie."

Eighteen

RICHIE SAW THE Buick again Friday morning on the way to school.

Billy Dickerson had just dug an elbow into Richie's shoulder, laughing, and when Richie swung around to give Billy a knuckle shot on his bicep he saw the big blue sedan pulling out of a side street and falling in behind the school bus. He confirmed at a glance that it was a '93 LeSabre. The car fell back quickly. Richie had only a glimpse of the driver's face behind the wheel, but that glimpse made him a little dizzy with excitement.

The babble of the school bus whirled around him. This morning Richie felt removed from it, as if he were floating up around the roof of the bus, watching all the kids at their horseplay. His excitement gave way to the odd confusion he always felt about the stranger who was his real father. He remembered the rush of emotions a week ago when the man on the telephone made his stunning announcement. Richie had been assaulted by a bewildering compound of anger, resentment and excitement—and something deeper that he couldn't name, something that left him shaking, his heart hammering in his chest like a blind thing trapped in a cage.

He told himself that he might be wrong about the driver of the Buick. He might just be someone going to work. Richie peered out the back window. The Buick continued to follow the bus, staying one or two car lengths behind. Sometimes it would drop farther back, but even when traffic became heavier it stayed in sight, keeping pace.

It was him, Richie thought. Ralph Beringer.

His father.

Richie knew exactly what he looked like. Besides the one photograph his mother kept in a frame, showing her with Beringer and Richie as a baby, she had other pictures in a cardboard box in one of her dresser drawers. Several years ago Richie had found them. Seeing the unposed snapshots of the young, muscular soldier in his air force uniform, Richie had experienced that peculiar mingling of anxiety and excitement Beringer's image evoked in him. He took one of the photos, and for weeks afterward he waited in terror for his mom to announce that she had discovered the theft. She never did. Maybe she never looked at those old pictures anymore. Maybe she didn't care.

Richie hadn't been worried about physical punishment for taking the snapshot. Neither his mom nor his dad—Dave, that is, not his real father—believed in spanking. Mom exercised discipline in other ways. A sad disappointment in her voice ("Oh, Richie") was enough to bring tears to the boy's eyes. A cool distancing in her tone of voice, or a silent stare, were as effective as blows. Richie's feelings for his mother were not ambivalent, and he never wanted to disappoint her.

It was the same with Dad—Dave. He would lose patience sometimes, raise his voice, but he never threatened Richie. His way was to talk things over quietly. That was why Richie had been hurt and resentful the night Dave shoved him so hard he cracked his head against the door frame, the same night Ralph Beringer had telephoned.

His anger hadn't lasted, of course. He had been okay with Dave afterward, like when they went to the beach on Sunday. Richie had seen right away what his parents were up to that day. He wasn't stupid. There had been something warming and delicious about their mutual anxiety over him, Dave suggesting they go off together, Mom watching them go with that worried look she sometimes wore.

Ignoring the babble on the bus, Richie fished inside his jacket pocket for his wallet. He slid out a plastic sleeve and peeked at the snapshot. The man in the photo didn't look like a Ralph. Ralph seemed like a wimpy name, like the kid in Richie's class who was always out sick. The soldier—Richie's real father—was obviously no wimp, even though he wore glasses. You could see that right off. You could see how tough he was.

"Hey, Richie, lemme see. Whatcha got?"

Richie shoved the sleeve back into the wallet and the wallet into his pocket. Billy grabbed at it. "Come on, Richie, show us."

"Get lost."

"What is it? Dirty pictures?" Grinning, Billy raised his voice. "Whatcha holding out on us? Feelthy pictures?"

With no recognition of the fury he was unleashing, Billy danced in the aisle by Richie's seat, leading a taunting chant that was quickly picked up by others. "Dirty pictures! Dirty pictures!"

Gene Couzzens, the balding, potbellied bus driver who had grandchildren Richie's and Billy's age, became annoyed over the commotion. He called out, "Cool it back there. You, Billy, sit down!"

"Feelthy pic—"

All of the turmoil Richie had felt over the past week exploded. He hurled himself out of his seat at his tormentor. "I'll kill you!" he cried.

He punched the startled Billy Dickerson in the face. Blood spurted from Billy's nose. Then they were pummeling each other, wrestling more than hitting, their punches hampered and ineffective in the narrow aisle. The other boys on the bus jumped to their feet or stood on their seats, yelling gleeful encouragement. Some of the girls shrieked with exaggerated panic.

The bus pulled over to the curb. The usually amiable driver bulled his way along the aisle. He grabbed Richie by his shirt collar and forcefully pushed him into his seat. Then he did the same with Billy. "Cut it out! I'm reportin' both of you."

"He hit me first!" Billy complained tearfully. The tears came more from a sense of injustice than from his battle wound. He held a bloody tissue under his nose.

"You ast for it," Couzzens growled. "Now sit down, put your head back and keep it there. That'll help stop the bleeding. I don't want any more trouble from either one of you. And that goes for the rest of you."

Mocking cheers and applause followed the driver along the aisle to the front of the bus.

Richie sat rigid in his seat, eyes staring straight ahead. He was humiliated and angry out of all proportion to the incident, which had amounted to no more than everyday razzing from his friend Billy. *My real dad wouldn't take it*, Richie muttered to himself. *He wouldn't take any shit from anybody.*

Ignoring Billy Dickerson's glower, Richie swung around and stared out through the bus's back window. He was just in time to see the dark blue Buick make a left turn onto San Anselmo Drive, a wide street flanked by rows of condominiums and apartments.

Richie's first reaction was disappointment. Maybe he had been wrong about the driver's identity. Maybe it was only a coincidence, the Buick pulling out of a street near his house and following the bus.

But he didn't believe it. He had seen the Buick before. One of the teachers at Elli's school had seen it too.

Richie guessed that Ralph Beringer's presence in San Carlos had a lot to do with the way his mom had been acting lately. He didn't understand exactly what was happening, but one thing seemed very clear: His real father had come back into his life.

He wondered if Ralph Beringer was staying somewhere on San Anselmo Drive.

THAT AFTERNOON, ON the other side of town, Special Agent Karen Younger met Edith Foster's roommate in the dormitory room Sheri Kuttner had shared with the murdered girl. The room had already been searched without anything significant turning up—no tell-all diary or little black book of phone numbers, no packet of love letters pointing directly at the probable killer. Sheri had provided Detective Braden with a list of Edie's friends, teachers, and activities on and off campus, supplementing the class list Braden had obtained from the Dean of Women. The names of the faculty members and other college personnel had already been screened and forwarded to the FBI for comparison with military records.

Sheri sat on the edge of one of the two twin beds in the room, unable to keep from glancing at the other bed, which had been stripped down, sheets and a blanket neatly folded at the foot. The built-in shelf in the headboard, a student desk and a small chest of drawers used by Edie were all bare, the girl's effects having been released to her family.

Sheri Kuttner was more than a little in awe of the FBI agent. Sheri admired the woman's outfit—loose brown herringbone jacket over a yellow silk blouse and beige slacks—her somewhat full figure, short straight nose, the stylish cut of her short blond hair. Most of all, though, Sheri was impressed by the agent's intelligent gray eyes and the cool self-confidence in them. Sheri wondered if she would ever know that kind of composure.

"You've had time to think about things, Sheri," Karen Younger said quietly. "Is it okay if I call you Sheri?"

"Uh . . . sure."

"I'm Karen, okay?"

Sheri didn't think she would ever be able to call the FBI woman Karen.

"I told that detective everything I knew. And I gave him a list of Edie's professors and other stuff."

"I know, and we appreciate your help. We just thought you might have remembered something else . . . anything Edie might have said about who she was going to see that Friday night."

Sheri averted her gaze, thinking that those quietly observant gray eyes could peer right into her mind.

"You told Detective Braden—at least that was his impression—that Edie had been seeing a married man, perhaps one of her teachers."

Sheri was silent. She twisted a Kleenex between her fingers. "I don't know, maybe I said that, but . . . I don't know."

"I see." The agent studied Sheri speculatively for a moment. Then she said, "Did you and Edie take any of the same classes?"

"Well, not many. I mean, she was going for a BA, majoring in English. I'm in pre-med."

"You want to be a doctor?" There was approval in the agent's voice.

"Maybe. I don't know now . . . after visiting that morgue I'm not so sure."

"Don't let that stop you, Sheri, if that's what you want to be. You'll learn to handle that part of it."

"Will I?"

"I'm sure you will."

After a slight hesitation Sheri said, "We did take one class together last semester."

"What class was that?"

"Contemporary Film Studies. Everyone wants to take it."

Karen Younger smiled. "Why is that? Because it's easy? Or because you all like to watch movies?"

"Yeah, I guess. But the girls all like him . . . the professor."

"Who is that?" Karen glanced down the list of Edith Foster's teachers. "Dr. David Lindstrom?"

"Yes."

Something in Sheri Kuttner's tone caused Karen to glance up quickly from her notes. "What is it, Sheri? What do you know?"

"I never actually saw them together. Maybe I shouldn't say anything, but . . . I know how Edie felt last year when we were taking his class. We used to kid about all the excuses she made to stay after class or go to his office. I mean, Edie could be pretty obvious when she wanted to. She made sure we sat in the front row, and the way she would dress and all . . ."

"Making sure the entire package was on display?" The agent seemed more amused than disapproving.

Sheri giggled nervously. "Yeah, sort of . . . like that. Then she started going out at night without saying where she was going, and she was real closemouthed about it, and I used to wonder if he was, you know, the one she was seeing."

"Dr. Lindstrom?" Karen repeated the name quietly. "This is very important, Sheri."

"I know. Edie never actually *said* she was seeing him, but she was seeing *somebody* she wouldn't talk about. And I know she sometimes acted as if she thought Dr. Lindstrom was the Second Coming."

"Do you think she still felt that way? You're talking about last semester, but you told Detective Braden Edie was seeing someone over the past month or so."

Sheri frowned. The question was one she had asked herself without coming up with an answer. "I'm not sure," she said. "It's funny you should say that. I mean, I thought before summer vacation she'd begun to cool off about the guy she was seeing. Edie was like that."

"Is that why you hesitated? Because Edie was acting excited again this semester about who she was seeing, and you thought it had to be someone new for her to feel that way?"

"Well, you know, she wouldn't let anyone string her along. I mean, Edie didn't have to. There were plenty of others wanted to go out with her."

The agent studied her thoughtfully. "That's very astute, Sheri . . . very observant."

"Well, uh . . ." Sheri felt warmth in her cheeks at the unexpected praise. "I don't actually know for sure that Edie ever went out with Dr. Lindstrom. She hinted at it a couple of times, but sometimes she'd do that just to make you jealous."

"She knew you also liked Lindstrom?"

The perception startled Sheri. Her heart thudded. How could she have named Dr. Lindstrom? My God, what was she thinking? Just because Edie boasted how she could make any of her professors jump through hoops if she really wanted, and she knew how Sheri felt about Lindstrom . . .

"He's really nice," she blurted. "I mean, Dr. Lindstrom's not the kind . . ."

"No one is," the FBI agent said.

*   *   *

LATER THAT AFTERNOON Karen met Braden by prearrangement at The Pelican, the coffeehouse on the downtown promenade where Edith Foster had gone the night she disappeared. The place was not full at that hour, and Karen had to imagine what it would be like later that night for a poetry reading and a TGIF conclave of students celebrating the end of the week.

"One of Foster's friends saw her here that night," Braden said, bringing her up to date. "And the girl who read her poems that night knew Edie and recognized her. That was around eleven o'clock."

"Did either of them see anyone with Foster?"

"The poet was too busy doing her thing. The friend thought Edie might have been with someone but she isn't sure. It was crowded. The place is a zoo on weekends, she says, especially Friday night. People come and go, and there's a lot of mixing."

"Good place to meet someone if you don't want to draw attention."

"Exactly," Braden said. "You like this Viennese coffee?"

"It's delicious."

"I can't stand milk in my coffee."

They both fell silent, having quickly run out of small talk. They were on the Job, not a date. Braden was already impatient to return to the station. Still, Karen thought, he was bending a little . . . more than she had expected.

"So who does Sheri Kuttner think Edie was seeing?" the detective asked in his abrupt way. "Did she open up at all?"

"She's not sure who Foster was seeing this past month—she thinks it might have been someone new. But Sheri is fairly sure that last semester Edie was seeing one of her professors, a Dr. David Lindstrom. He teaches in the Film and Television Studies program."

"They give you college credit for watching movies and TV?"

"Maybe not just for watching, Detective."

"Lindstrom, huh . . . yeah, he's on the list." Braden frowned.

"He's a volunteer firefighter. Supposedly that's where he was last Friday."

"That kind of lets him out."

"Not necessarily. They got that fire under control late Friday. Maybe the volunteers were released early. Maybe in all that confusion it would've been easy for someone to slip away."

"It's possible," Karen said, not hiding her skepticism.

She studied Braden's profile as he sipped his coffee and gazed around the room, which was beginning to fill with college-age youngsters in pairs and groups. Braden wasn't half bad-looking, she thought, though he would probably look considerably better if he were getting more sleep. He was tough and stubborn, but less of a Neanderthal than some cops she had met. Watching him at work, she was inclined to accept his version of the events that had won him notoriety on television. After their initial abrasive encounter the SCPD detective had been cooperative, civil, even pleasant. She didn't know if he was humoring her because he had been ordered to, or if he had miraculously had his consciousness raised over the past few days.

"There's another reason Lindstrom isn't the one," she said.

"Now what would that be?"

"I've had a report from military archives on the faculty list I faxed back to Washington. No one on the list was in Germany eight years ago, or in military service at that time. There are several Vietnam vets on the faculty, and two army reservists who were called up during the Gulf War, but neither of those was sent to Germany."

"Yeah, well . . ." She recognized the stubborn denial in his eyes. "Maybe that just means your German killer was someone else. What we could have here is simpler—someone who knew Foster or was involved with her, someone like Lindstrom. Maybe Foster dumped him, or she wanted him to dump his wife and threatened him, and he lost control. Bye-bye, Edie."

"It could just as easily be someone who didn't know her at all. Do you always have to act like you don't give a damn, Detective?"

"Who said it was an act?"

"I do," Karen snapped. "And you're wrong about Lindstrom."

"I like him," Braden said, unwilling to back off.

"I think Edith Foster's killer was more than a jealous or angry or frightened lover. He's a serial killer who's let the genie out of the bottle. It's been a week already, Braden. I think he'll kill again, and we're running out of time."

Nineteen

AFTER SHE HAD a hamburger at Burger King that Friday evening, eating by herself, Natalie Rothleder returned to the San Carlos College campus and spent two hours in the library working on a research assignment, a term paper for her Lit class on the English Romantic Poets. Two hours with Wordsworth and Coleridge, Byron and Shelley were her idea of a neat way to usher in the weekend. Something of a loner, Natalie didn't mind being alone with her favorite poets.

San Carlos College, which had built its academic reputation on its Liberal Arts program, was not exactly a liberal bastion. From Natalie's viewpoint it was a WASP school with a sprinkling of token minorities—blacks, Asians and Hispanics. Natalie regarded herself as the token Jew in her class. She was attending the school on what she called a free pass—in reality, a hard-won scholarship. She felt like an outsider. She had suffered enough casual slights and rebuffs to make her defensive, touchy, a little arrogant and fiercely independent.

Which explained why she was not living in one of the dormitories or sorority houses but in a boardinghouse a block from the edge of the campus, in one of the old Victorian houses on Cypress Street that had been converted into rooms for students.

It also explained why she was studying alone on a Friday evening at the library, and why she planned on walking home alone. Because of the recent murder of a coed, Edith Foster, there had been a fluttering of unease among female students on campus. Many were reluctant to go out alone, especially after dark. Natalie was scornful. No perverted sex maniac was going to manipulate her life. Just let him try something with her.

Natalie had taken a course in self-defense at the local YWCA, in which she had been counseled, in the event she were ever attacked, to do two things: fight back as hard as she could, and scream as loud as she could. She also carried a can of pepper spray in her purse, and she wouldn't hesitate to use it.

Natalie suspected that her independence was one of the reasons she didn't have a date that weekend—or any weekend since the fall semester had started. That and her brains. That's what her mother told her. "You scare boys off, Nat. It's not always smart to be too smart."

"If a woman having any intelligence scares them off, that's their problem," Natalie had retorted. "Let them find a bimbo."

It wasn't that she was ugly. She wasn't really what you would call pretty, she knew, but she was arresting. Interesting-looking, she thought. "You could be exotic if you'd make half an effort," her mother said. "Men play up to fairy tale princesses, but they like exotic better. You listen to your mother. I know."

Her mother thought *she* was exotic.

Natalie was five feet four, a hundred and twenty. She had lustrous black hair that fell halfway down her back when she let it out, though she usually wore it in a ponytail tied with a ribbon or piled up high in back. She had rather full black eyebrows she didn't much care for but refused to pluck, huge brown eyes, a Streisand nose and a wide, generous mouth her mother said was just like Julia Roberts's mouth. Her mother had also tentatively suggested that Natalie's father was willing to pay for having her nose fixed. "Just a little. It would make those exotic eyes of yours even more exotic, and your lips would look fuller."

"My mouth is already big enough," Natalie had said. "So is Julia Roberts's."

She also liked her nose the way it was, like Barbra's nose.

At nine o'clock she set aside the reference books she had been consulting. The librarians insisted that you leave them on the table rather than returning them to the stacks yourself, as if any dodo couldn't figure out the decimal system and put books back in the right place. Natalie was considering majoring in Library Science. She gathered up her Romantic Poets textbook and her notebook, dropped them into the canvas Bookstar tote, and walked toward the exit, looking exotic in snug-fitting jeans, dirty Reeboks and a Sierra Club wildlife sweatshirt with a dramatic sketch of an eagle on the front, hook-nosed and fierce.

"Good night, Natalie," one of the assistant librarians called out. Connie Osborne was a senior, a Library Science major, neither pretty nor exotic.

"G'night."

Out of the corner of her eye Natalie saw the tall, sandy-haired man rising from a nearby table piled with periodicals. She had noticed him earlier, covertly glancing his way when he was absorbed in a magazine. *Good-looking WASP* had flashed through her mind. Though she passed him on the way to the exit, she wouldn't give him the satisfaction of looking directly at him. Too old to be a student, she thought, unless he was one of those semipermanent grad students living off dad's allowance. Hair a little too long, allowed to grow over his ears and collar, but clean. A professor? Maybe in the engineering school. Outdoorsy look, with a deep tan and muscles under his polo shirt. Maybe he built bridges.

She was outside on the wide library steps, a little annoyed with herself and her schoolgirl speculations, when she heard the scrape of a footstep behind her. A quiet, pleasant male voice said, "Excuse me, Natalie . . . would you like some company?"

Her large brown eyes challenged him boldly. "I beg your pardon?"

He smiled, completely at ease with her icy challenge, not like the dweebs who occasionally found the nerve to ask her for a date. And up close he was overpoweringly a male animal. She felt a catch in her throat and a fluttering in her stomach.

"All I meant was, there's been some concern on campus this week about girls walking alone, especially after dark. I'd be glad to tag along—"

"Oh, for God's sake, I don't need an escort."

"Do you live in one of the dorms?" His glance flicked out across the darkness of the campus. "It's no trouble . . ."

"I'm not a girl, and I'm not scared to be out after dark," Natalie said disdainfully, tossing her long ponytail and starting down the steps. "I don't live in a dorm, but my place is only a block off campus."

Why did she have to add that? He had flustered her. She found herself wishing that she hadn't come on so strong. So what if he was a WASP? He was a hunk. Like one of those models in the Barely Buns calendar one of the women at the boardinghouse had put up on the bulletin board in the hallway . . .

"Well, just be careful, Brown Eyes," the stranger called after her.

By the time she permitted herself a single glance over her shoulder the library steps were empty. He was gone. She felt a surprisingly keen disappointment. Probably if she had had the nose job he would've followed her.

He called you Brown Eyes.

Huh!

She straightened her shoulders and strode off briskly. Sniffed in scorn at the notion of allowing a tennis pro or ski instructor or whatever he was to pick her up at the library, which was reputed to be among the top three pickup places on campus. He had probably been reading a stack of Sports Illustrated magazines, not Engineering Digest.

Something flickered at the edge of her consciousness, like her mother's voice warning her to be careful. But Mr. Golf Pro wasn't one of those creepy losers who needed to prey on helpless women to get his rocks off. He could sell tickets. He could walk into any of her classes and hand out tickets. Take a number, get in line, wait your turn.

Called her Brown Eyes.

Natalie sniffed again, less convincingly, tossing her ponytail in an unconscious gesture of dismissal.

The path she followed went past a couple of administration buildings and down another short flight of steps, where it came to a fork. Natalie turned left. Her route carried her past the Science Building to a circle surrounding a modern sculpture, one of those oversize creations, welded together out of pieces of scrap metal, that pointed toward the sky and was therefore considered to be an optimistic statement about the Human Condition.

Natalie sniffed at it, swinging her ponytail.

Some students were gathered along another wide flight of steps lit on either side by the gas lamps that were intended to integrate the college with the character of the surrounding Victorian neighborhood. She wondered what school of design taught that ploy.

Now the path led toward the southwest corner of the campus where it intersected with the corner of Cypress and Princeton streets. North and south streets in the area were named after trees—Oak, Cypress, Cedar, Pine—while east and west streets were named after Ivy League universities. Apparently no one taught city planners or developers a course in Street Names.

With an abruptness that was unexpectedly unnerving, Natalie found herself walking in semidarkness. The curving path was crowded on the left by bushes and on the right by a grove of eucalyptus trees, the latter fragrant in the night air, a lemon scent. The gaslights infrequently spaced along the path were atmospheric, but the streetlights on Cypress, glimpsed through the trees, were much brighter. The gas lamps flickered in the shadows, their light seeping outward only a short distance rather than casting a bright glow along the walkway.

Natalie's footsteps quickened. She listened to the squeak of her Reeboks on the cement. A rustling in the brush to her left caused her stomach to clench. In spite of her earlier bravado she walked faster, her heart racing ahead of her steps. There was another sound like leaves crackling, and her gaze darted into the shadows of the eucalyptus grove.

She passed under one of the gas lamps, momentarily relieved by the security of its feeble glow, then plunged into another patch of darkness. She could hear the wind now, the wind that explained the rustling in the bushes and the stirring of the leaves on the ground and the sighing high overhead in the eucalpytus branches.

She was nearly to the street intersection, close enough to begin to feel foolish over her nervousness. They really ought to change the damned lights. What would it be like at the end of the month when the clocks had to be set back an hour and it started getting dark on campus at five o'clock? Talk about hearts aflutter—

Her own heart seemed to stop.

A figure stepped onto the path in front of her, just this side of the street corner, blocking her way. She hadn't noticed before how the tall trees cut off the light from the street lamp on the north side of the intersection, leaving her and the intruder standing in a pool of shadows. She started to wheeze, gasping for breath, like her sister Ruth having one of her asthma attacks.

Then a chuckle reached her out of the darkness, "Hey, Brown Eyes . . . just wanted to make sure you got home safely."

Her reaction left her weak, her knees quivering. A giggle born of anxiety and relief escaped her open mouth, and her cheeks flamed at the sound.

He took a step toward her and she was struck by how he moved, flowing like an athlete. In the same moment, as she tried to find her tongue to say something witty or intelligent, wary questions lit her brain. How did he know which way she was going when she left the library? She hadn't said what street her boardinghouse was on. And how had he got here ahead of her? She had practically been running part of the way.

"I really wanted to see you again, Natalie. Do you know why?"

His voice was disarming, pleasant, but now she felt an unspoken menace charging the night air with an electricity she had not felt before.

"It was your name," he said mysteriously.

Natalie bolted. Galvanized by fear of that mesmerizing voice, she leaped toward the screen of trees to her right. The man was quicker. She spun away from him, ducking under a branch. Her foot slipped on a pile of leaves.

She felt his hand on her shoulder, plucking her up as if she were lint on a sweater, turning and lifting her. She was close enough to see his eyes glint behind the lenses of his glasses. She opened her mouth to scream and he hit her in the chest.

She had never known such hard and massive pain. Her mouth was open but no scream came. She couldn't breathe. Her lungs were on fire. He clubbed her on the back of the head and she collapsed at his feet, dazed, helpless, only semiconscious as he lifted her easily into his arms.

From a long way off she heard him say, "We're going to have fun, Natalie," before she drifted off.

She had never had a chance to knee him in the groin. She had been unable to scream. And she had completely forgotten the pepper spray in her purse.

Twenty

SHORTLY AFTER MIDNIGHT the San Carlos police dispatcher awakened Karen at her motel. She met Braden near the edge of the San Carlos College campus. Yellow crime scene tape stretched around a paved area centered on a large Dumpster set against a ten-foot high concrete block wall. One of the classroom buildings loomed to the right. The secluded area behind the building was accessed by a service road running along the southwest perimeter of the campus off Princeton Street.

The coroner's technician, Ted Nakashimi, was already there along with a half-dozen uniformed San Carlos police. Clusters of students hovered in the background. The presence of a number of police and official cars, their red and blue lights flashing, gave the late-night scene the aspect of a miniature circus with its center ring, spotlights and hushed spectators.

Karen followed a string of trouble lights to the Dumpster. The ME squatted on his heels inside the large metal container. Apparently the Dumpster had recently been emptied because there was only a small pile of paper trash in one corner. The only other object in the container was the body of a young woman. She was naked except for torn panties tangled around her right ankle, short white socks and Reebocks. Karen saw long black hair in a ponytail, a dark triangle of pubic hair, bloody wounds . . .

"Trash," she murmured. "That's how he thought of her."

"What?" Braden was scowling. There was an intensity about him she hadn't observed before. "Oh, yeah . . . her name's Natalie Rothleder. Was."

The victim had been battered ruthlessly around the face and chest. One blow had nearly ripped the nipple from her left breast. Her face was unrecognizable, and Karen wondered how she had been identified so quickly. The familiar crudely slashed initial mutilated her belly. Karen craned her neck to peer past Nakashimi's shoulder. Two vertical lines were connected by a slash from top to bottom. N, she thought.

N for Natalie.

"How did you identify her?"

"Some students coming back from a late movie saw a bloody white sweatshirt in the brush off one of the footpaths. It had her name tag sewn inside. Campus security was able to track her for us through school records."

"What was she doing out alone?" Karen felt a kind of despair as she asked the question.

"She lived in a boardinghouse on Cypress, about a block from the campus. She was at the library up until about nine o'clock, then left. Presumably walking back to her room. They've started a buddy system on campus since the Foster thing, but Rothleder didn't take advantage of it."

"How was she found?"

"The students took the sweatshirt to the security office. That set up a search of the campus by the security officers and some student volunteers. A security guy—that's him over there with his head between his knees, Walker's his name—remembered hearing a car in this area around eleven, so he checked it out. There's a possibility he just missed the killer. When he searched this area he spotted blood on the ground there, and some more on the Dumpster."

"She was killed somewhere else." It was a statement, not a question.

"Yeah, same pattern as before. I figure the killer grabbed her on the path she took from the library to get to her boardinghouse. Some of it's fairly dark and isolated. He dragged her to his car or someplace safe. He raped her in every opening he could find, beat her to death, did his number with the knife, then drove around looking for a place to dump the body. Or he had this place already picked out."

"She wasn't gagged or tied up?"

"Not unless the ME finds something I missed. I figure she was knocked cold. Nobody heard any screams."

Ted Nakashimi climbed out of the dumpster, dropping lightly to his feet on the pavement. He signaled for two ambulance attendants waiting with a body bag to transport the body to the county morgue. He nodded at Braden and the FBI agent.

"How long has she been dead?" Karen asked.

"About two hours, give or take. Rigor's just starting, and the body temp has cooled only a few degrees from normal. I'd guess she died between ten and eleven, somewhere in there."

"Any defense wounds?"

"Nothing obvious. I'll have to examine her on the table," the ME said cautiously.

No one asked him the cause of death, although the question was technically open.

When Nakashimi moved off, Braden and Karen stood alone for a long minute in silence, watching the activity around the Dumpster. Finally Karen said, "He took more risks this time."

"It was quick and dirty," Braden agreed. "So maybe he missed something, made a mistake. We'll search the campus as soon as it's light—maybe we can find out exactly where he grabbed her."

"Why did he pick her? Just because she was alone and vulnerable?"

"Maybe." He paused as the attendants walked by carrying the body bag by its wide straps. Beyond the paved area, at the fringe of the light, there was a whisper of sound, like a collective gasp, from the audience of students. "She made herself a target."

"Are you saying—"

"I'm only saying she gave him the opportunity. I doubt we'll have any more women walking this campus at night alone anytime soon."

Karen shivered, suddenly aware of the cold. She hadn't expected Southern California nights to be this chilly in early October, and she had rushed out wearing only a light jacket.

After a moment's brooding Braden said, "My captain has been on the horn making noises about a special joint task force with the sheriff and the FBI. You know anything about that?"

"It's news to me." Buddy Cochrane wouldn't necessarily brief her ahead of time, she thought.

"We'll have people tripping over each other. And the media won't be long putting one and one together to make two, so from here on out it's gonna be like living inside Hard Copy. We have to catch this bastard."

Karen frowned, wishing as usual that there was some way to reconcile the rights of a free press that had abandoned all the rules with the needs of a murder investigation.

"What I'm saying is, we don't have time to waste. You awake enough to talk about that profile of yours?"

Karen nodded, surprised, thinking that it was an extraordinary concession for Braden to make, and confirming to herself that there was a new edge to the detective. A second murder on his doorstep would do it, she thought.

"I wouldn't be able to sleep now if I tried," she said.

TO HER SURPRISE, Braden picked a bar rather than an all-night coffee shop or his corner of the squad room at the police station. The place was dark and smelled of beer and stale smoke. He nodded at a couple of men sitting at the mahogany bar as he led Karen to a booth in the back of the room. The men at the bar watched them with cops' eyes.

"It's a hangout away from the Job," Braden said. "We won't be bothered back here."

Karen wondered aloud if smoking was still allowed in bars in California.

"Yeah, you can smoke," Braden answered the question. "It's only restaurants and offices where you can't."

"I don't smoke, I just wondered."

"You mind if I do?"

They both ordered coffee and Braden lit a cigarette. Karen

wished he hadn't but decided to say nothing. He hadn't smoked before in her presence. She wondered if the need reflected the new intensity she sensed in him.

"What he did to this girl tonight . . . there's a lot of rage there, Agent Younger."

"Call me Karen, for God's sake. And yes, there's a great deal of anger being expressed."

"Toward who? His mother? Isn't that the usual excuse?"

"As a matter of fact, it is. Not an excuse but a common factor."

"So what else does this profile of yours suggest . . . if you've got far enough along to say?"

She took a moment to organize her thoughts, feeling suddenly pressured. She heard Buddy Cochrane's voice. *Don't be afraid of guessing wrong. Trust your instincts.*

"We know he's a white male," she said, "who has a reason, real or fancied, to hate women."

"How do we know he's white?"

"His victims—all three of them—were young white women, and he was not threatening to them. Otherwise he wouldn't have been able to get so close without alarming them to the point where they would normally have tried to run or to defend themselves. So he's a white male, in his thirties, presentable-looking—"

"Whoa, wait a minute, slow down."

"A few of these people start in their teens," Karen said, riding over his protest, "but not many, and they're never this organized that young. Our killer is mature. He's very much in control. He's stronger than average, and he moves well. He's in good shape. He can function just like Mr. Average Citizen. He can do all the things that ordinary people do every day. He may even be married, have a family. He isn't crazy, and what's more important, he doesn't *look* crazy. He's been around this past week, Braden, watching us, but no one has noticed him. Some women might think he's handsome, to others he looks ordinary. He could be their accountant or insurance salesman. That's why he's invisible. If he looked like a monster, one of these women would have been screaming and fighting back. The only way he's different from the people you see on the street or in the office, or even in church, is that he is killing women, brutally expressing a deep-seated rage against them, and he doesn't feel any guilt or remorse or fear of going to hell for what he's doing. He feels only the pleasure he gets from doing it, and that, God help us, is getting better and better."

Karen paused, taking a deep breath to slow the rush of words. Without thinking, she waved at the smoke clouding the booth. Noticing the gesture, Braden stubbed out his cigarette. Her jacket would smell of smoke, Karen thought. She recognized that, in focusing on such everyday concerns as the smell of secondhand smoke on her clothes, she was clinging to a cozy familiarity. The exercise helped her to continue talking about an act of savagery that mocked humanity's triumphant crawl out of primeval slime.

"He's not Superman," Braden growled,

"No, he's not Superman, but he's probably beginning to think he is. He's getting better at this, Detective. He likes it. He's getting off on the power trip, the sexual dominance to start with, but also the fact that he's got the police jumping through hoops. He's becoming an expert at killing in the most brutal, basic way. He's beginning to think he's invincible . . . that no one can stop him."

"And he's not crazy."

"He's a sociopath, but he's not crazy. He hasn't lost his sense of reality. He knows what he's doing."

Braden sipped his coffee, stared toward the men talking in low voices at the bar, started to reach in his pocket for another cigarette and changed his mind. His gaze returned to Karen. His eyes felt hot on her skin.

"You said he's organized. I know that dichotomy—"

"Don't try to trick me with big words, Braden," she said with a wry smile. "I know you think most of this is voodoo."

"I didn't say that."

"You didn't have to. Anyway, give me some time on the organized-versus-disorganized part of the profile. I'd like more time to think about it after seeing Natalie Rothleder. I'd rather talk about some other things that puzzle me."

"Such as?"

"This guy is different. He's not acting like most serial killers, and I can't even put my finger on why I say that. Also . . . how does he choose his victims? Does he know them? Or does he just know this is the one he's been waiting for when he spots them?"

"They were both coeds. Both young, one blonde and one brunette—"

"Two blondes," Karen said firmly.

"You're still sticking to the German connection?"

"There's no question about it."

"Mm. One thing about that really bothers me . . . that he could wait eight years or more."

"Jeffrey Dahmer waited nine years between his first and second killings," she said, clearly surprising him. The story of the serial killer who had murdered and mutilated at least seventeen victims in Milwaukee, Wisconsin, in the late 1980s and early '90s, practicing cannibalism and necrophilia upon their bodies, had shocked even the most hardened law enforcement officer, but little attention had been paid to the time lag. "He killed his first victim in 1978, and he didn't kill again until 1987. After that the killings escalated—one a year, then two, on up to at least eight known victims in 1991. It's unusual, Detective, but it happens."

Braden was frowning. "You're good at this, Younger."

"Karen," she reminded him.

"Yeah, Karen. So humor me. Give me your scenarios for how he worked it. I mean the two killings here in San Carlos. Start with Edie Foster."

She tried to put herself inside the killer's head, feeling uncomfortable but determined. She thought of Foster, picturing the beautiful girl not as she lay facedown in the creek bed in the photos Karen had viewed, but as she was when still alive, dressed in her saucy T-shirt and miniskirt, strolling along the downtown promenade and joining the noisy Friday night celebration at The Pelican.

"We think she was with someone at the coffeehouse that night—they probably drove there together—but he's not the killer. The killer spotted her when she came out of The Pelican around eleven, eleven-thirty. Her friend joined her outside and they went to the car they were using. They drove back to the Alpha Beta, where they'd left the other car. They talked but the friend didn't stay—maybe they had an argument. He drove off and she went into the market. The killer saw she was alone now, so he pulled his car over close to hers. When she came out she had a good look at him but he didn't frighten her. While she was unlocking her door he grabbed her."

"No groceries on the ground or in her car."

"He was careful. He overpowered her, threw her into his own car, taped her up and drove her to his pad. I don't think he kept her in his car for four or five hours. He had someplace to take her, an apartment or a motel room. When he was finished with her it was almost morning. He drove out along the coastal road, made a couple of passes until there were no other cars in sight, then he stopped and dumped her."

"Before which he bathed her to remove any trace evidence, wrapped her in a painter's plastic dropcloth and left us nothing to go on. We're canvassing the motels," he added.

Karen felt uneasily close to the man she was describing. She thought of him sitting in another booth nearby, listening, smiling to himself.

"What about Natalie? What's your second scenario?"

She took another deep breath. She stared at the stub of Braden's cigarette in the ashtray. She could still smell it. She had never smoked, but she wondered if a cigarette would have helped her now.

"He was looking for number two. It had been a week, he had to have that feeling again. He was patient following Edie Foster, working it all out so he wouldn't make any mistakes, and he took his time with her after he had her. But tonight he was more aggressive. I think he was in the library when she was there, or he was outside watching. He didn't go there to read a book. He saw Natalie leaving alone, followed her and saw where she was heading. He took a shortcut across campus to get ahead of her. He jumped her somewhere along the way. He had a car close by, or else he hid her in the bushes while he went to get his car. He probably wanted to have her all night, like the other one, but he couldn't wait." She paused, briefly reviewing her scenarios and accepting them for what they were—educated guesses. She might be way off the mark. "He took risks both times, Braden, but they were acceptable risks. It was dark, no one else was around, the women didn't have a chance."

"Yeah," Braden said sourly.

"Both times the victims were strangers. He chose them because something about them triggered his anger. He saw something in them, even though they didn't really look alike, weren't friends or otherwise connected."

"We don't know that yet."

"But they were random choices. They happened to be in the wrong place at the wrong time."

"Maybe. I have a couple other scenarios."

Karen Younger waited.

"He knew both of them," said Braden, "and they knew him. That's why they weren't scared when he approached one of them late at night in a parking lot, or the other one after she left the library. He also knew his way around the campus. That's how he got ahead of Natalie Rothleder. He's not a stranger here."

"It's possible," Karen admitted grudgingly. "I don't know, Braden, it doesn't fit . . ."

"It doesn't fit because you don't want it to. It leaves your German girl out of the picture."

"All right, tell me something else. Why the initials? Is he telling us something?" She leaned closer to Braden, her face flushed. "*Is he picking them by name?*"

"That's too goofy," Braden said, taken aback. "You say he's not crazy. That's crazy."

"Unless he's telling us something."

"If he is, I don't know what the hell it is." He scowled. "He worked it so he could have Edie for hours, but you say he had to have Natalie right here and now. If he's still in control, how come he changed his approach?"

"I think he lost it a little bit this time, but he's capable of improvising. He's learning by doing."

"On-the-job training."

"Sort of. He's smart, and he's been thinking about this for a long time, fantasizing about it. Maybe in the beginning it was only a *what-if* kind of thing, but he's been thinking about it ever since that night he killed Lisl Moeller, remembering what it was like, fantasizing about doing it again. He's had a lot of time to plan how to do it without getting caught. He knows about blood and semen, trace evidence and fingerprints. He knew enough to wash Edie thoroughly. He wasn't able to do that with Natalie, but I'll bet the ME won't find much."

"You think he could be some kind of cop? Maybe an MP, if he was in the service?"

"It's possible but not necessary. Hell, Braden, the whole country watched the O. J. hearings and trial. Everyone's a forensic expert now."

Braden brooded in silence for a time, examining the FBI woman's comments and taking what he wanted from them. Then he said, "You mentioned problems with the mother being a common denominator with serial killers. What about the father?"

"The lack of a positive father figure is almost universal among these people. Either there's no father, an abusive one, or he was missing very early on. That left the mother alone to give him love, nurturing, compassion, a sense of morality. And if, instead, she gave him abuse, neglect, hatred, betrayal . . ."

"How could a mother betray him?"

"If she was a prostitute, for example, or acted like one, at least in the child's eyes that could mean betrayal. Or if she was simply someone who couldn't—and didn't—love him. What greater betrayal than that can there be?" Karen sighed. "For some women a child isn't a gift but a burden . . . a form of punishment . . . a constant reminder of her failures."

Suddenly Karen felt the dark presence of the man she was hunting. The smells and the smoke of the bar closed in on her. She slid out of the booth. Her movements were jerky and distracted. "Sorry, Detective, I've got to get out of here. I need to do some more thinking. We need more than we've learned so far. Maybe forensics will turn up something useful."

Braden fumbled for a couple of bills, tossing them on the table with the check. "I'll come with you."

"No," she said, an audible tension threading her voice. "I need to be by myself." Seeing Braden's surprise, she added, "I've been fantasizing about this bastard for eight years myself, Braden. I never really thought I'd meet him again, but the fantasy was always there. And I always caught him. You know what I'm saying?"

"I think so."

"It's not a fantasy anymore. That's what scares me. I'm afraid I won't catch him."

She turned and walked away quickly, leaving Braden staring after her.

Twenty-One

BECAUSE OF ITS location on the highway en route to the beach, the Bright Spot diner always did a pretty good Sunday breakfast business. Since a murdered coed was found under the bridge just up the road, and the cafe was identified on television as the site of a 911 call about the girl, business had been up fifty percent. On Sunday, with local newspaper headlines screaming about a second killing, the trend continued.

There weren't as many just plain gawkers, Iris Whatley decided. She had been working as a waitress at the diner for the past four years, and she thought she knew her customers. The sensation-seekers had been largely replaced by another group dedicated to remembering Edith Foster. They had made the site under the bridge where the girl was found a sort of shrine, placing bouquets of flowers, crosses and notes that read "We loved you, Edie" and "God bless you." These pilgrims also had to have Sunday breakfast out, like many other Southern Californians, and the Bright Spot was on the way.

The crush eased off around one o'clock, and Iris had a chance to take a deep breath for the first time in four or five hours. She had hardly sat down at the counter to take a break for coffee when her brother-in-law, Jerry Boyarchek, came in with one of his golfing buddies and slid onto a stool next to her.

Jerry's buddy, Floyd something-or-other, headed for the john in back, giving Iris a lecherous appraisal over his shoulder. Iris probably had more to do with the Bright Spot's regular breakfast and luncheon business than the food or the diner's nostalgic atmosphere. She had a great figure and legs for the T-shirts and short skirts the waitresses all had to wear, plus that lush tangle of blond hair and the complexion of an English milkmaid. Besides, she was friendly and good-natured with the customers.

"He likes you," Jerry said with a grin, cocking the visor of his golf cap in the direction Floyd had taken.

"Please, don't get me all excited."

"Hey, look who's bein' choosy. Floyd's a good guy, you could do a lot worse."

"Have you been telling stories about me, Jer? Maybe embellishing things a little to get old Floyd interested?"

"So what's wrong with that? It's not like you're gettin' any younger, hon. Susie and me, we worry about you."

Stung, Iris glared at him. She knew a lot better than Jerry Boyarchek that she wasn't getting any younger. In her own mind thirty-five and unmarried was approaching some sort of deadline, like a warning flag in a race that had only a limited number of laps to go. But she was also aware that her looks, even including the weariness about her eyes suggesting she had been around the block but was still on her feet, attracted more men than were put off.

"Let me do the worrying, Jer, okay? I'm good at it. I don't need any help."

Jerry put his hand on her arm and kept it there. "Hey, don't get me wrong, Iris, I'm not knockin' the merchandise."

Iris stared at him. Jerry was so transparent it was laughable. "Give me two weeks and I could have your friend Floyd doing dog tricks on command," she said coolly.

"Come on, I didn't mean anythin'—"

"You too, Jer, only I wouldn't need two weeks." She leaned toward him deliberately, just enough to let him feel the slight pressure of a firm breast against his arm. "What do you say? If I made you the right offer right now . . . would you sit up and beg for it?"

She saw the light change in his eyes. He licked his lips, his gaze suddenly evasive. Any second he would start hyperventilating, she thought.

"Yeah, I thought so," she said dryly. Out of the corner of her eye she saw Floyd returning from the restroom, passing another man who had taken a seat at the counter. "Guess I oughta have a little talk with sister Susie."

"For God's sake, Iris, don't even joke about that. You know how Susie is."

"I know how Susie is. And you too, Jer. Just keep it in mind."

She rose from her stool, nodding indifferently at Floyd as she passed him on her way behind the counter. She picked up a fresh pot of coffee and carried it down to the end where the stranger was patiently sitting by himself. It did not occur to her immediately that he was the reason she had shortened her break, rather than irritation with her brother-in-law.

"Coffee?"

"Yes, thanks, black." He had a quiet, self-assured voice and a tan that hadn't come from a lamp. She put a lot of stock in her ability to read men's eyes, but his were obscured by tinted blue lenses set in gold-framed aviator glasses.

"Would you like to see a menu?"

He smiled. "What would you recommend? I'm not very hungry."

"The pecan pie's good. Our pies are fresh, we bake 'em ourselves." Which wasn't exactly true, but the pies *were* baked fresh by a local bakery that supplied several restaurants in the area.

"Let's try the pecan pie then."

Iris grinned. Walking away, ignoring Jerry Boyarchek's stare, she told herself, *For Chrissake, honey, don't drop the pot.*

She had seen the sandy-haired man before. He had stopped at the diner at least once during the past week for lunch, and another time for dinner. Each time he had been alone. She noticed that he wore a wedding ring, but he was eating out alone regularly, so what did that mean? A salesman on the road? He didn't seem like the type.

He was . . . She groped unsuccessfully for the right word. It came to her when she brought him his wedge of pecan pie and he glanced up with his easy smile. Not Floyd's leer or Jerry's smirk, just a normal smile, as if they were already friends. *Fit* was the word. About as fit as a man could be.

Iris herself worked out at a beach area club. She punished her body to keep it leaner, firmer and, let's face it, shapelier. For that very good reason she appreciated a man who took care of himself. This customer wasn't handsome, not really, just a guy to glance at, with nothing broken or ugly. But the hands surrounding his coffee mug were large and strong, and she remembered now the way he had moved when he entered the diner and walked toward the counter or a booth. Thinking of it, she pictured a tight, hard ass, flat stomach, big hairy chest with swelling pecs. He moved like a goddam big cat, Iris thought.

She was busy for a while, working both the counter and the front window booths. By the time she scooped up the coffeepot again and started along the counter filling up half-empty mugs, Jerry and Floyd were leaving. Iris gave Jerry only a nod and Floyd the cold shoulder. The sandy-haired man pushed his coffee mug forward as she approached.

"How was the pie?" Iris asked brightly.

"Terrific." Without taking his eyes off hers, he jerked his head toward the cash register, where Jerry, just turning away, glanced toward them as he headed for the door. "Friend of yours?"

"Not hardly." Iris offered a sardonic grin. "My brother-in-law."

"Ah, the brother-in-law," the stranger answered, as if they shared some secret knowledge about brothers-in-law.

For a moment his eyes continued to hold hers, light gray eyes behind the blue lenses, and she felt her heartbeat actually quicken.

Flustered, Iris kept busy for the next few minutes. When she looked up once more, the stranger was standing by the cash register. She took his check and changed a five-dollar bill. While she counted the change he said, "Thanks for the tip on the pie . . . Iris." His glance lingered on the name tag on her T-shirt. She didn't mind at all having him stare at her chest. He smiled. "See you again."

He walked out. His khaki pants fit snugly across his buttocks.

THE RAIDERS WERE playing the Dallas Cowboys on TV that Sunday. By the time Ralph Beringer returned to his sublet apartment from the diner he had missed most of the first half. He clicked on the television, retrieved a cold beer and a bag of nachos from the kitchen, and eased back in the La-Z-Boy recliner in the living room.

He remembered other times, sitting in a chair with broken springs, Saturday and Sunday afternoons when a game was on TV, his feet up on a dirty ottoman, and having them summarily pushed off the ottoman. *"Are you gonna sit there all day? There's work to be done around here."*

But it wasn't work she had in mind. It was sending him out of the room because one of her "callers" was expected soon or already drooling at the door.

"And don't come back till I tell you."

Just before halftime Troy Aikman hit Michael Irvin for a TD on a crossing pattern, putting Dallas ahead by seven points. Beringer liked the Raider's bad boy image, but he was even more impressed by the Cowboy's cool professionalism. Trash talk, shirttails hanging out and late hits didn't get it done against the real pros.

Talk was cheap. Threats and intimidation went only so far. The time was coming for sweet little Glenda and her shack-up, Lindstrom, to find that out. As far as Beringer was concerned, Lindstrom was not Glenda's husband. The divorce was an aberration he had never accepted.

Watching the rest of the game and working his way through a six-pack of beer, he missed whole sections of the action when his mind strayed off. Instant replays of another kind. He keenly regretted not having had more time with Natalie, under better conditions.

She had got him hot, just watching her there in the library. It was not only her sensual looks. He was struck by her haughty, superior air. Slyly observing her, he had felt the desire to take her down a peg. The desire had become an imperative when he heard her name called out. The name was like the quarterback's play-calling signal: *Hut, hut . . . go for it!*

He could have blown everything. He knew he should have circled around her if only for a day or two, biding his time, watching and waiting for the right moment. Instead he had plunged recklessly ahead. Pure luck that it had worked out so well. She had fought him for a bit, as he had expected, and he would have enjoyed playing out that scene with her at length, but he couldn't take the risk. She might have started to make noise. After a couple of solid punches with the sleeve of steel balls in his fist, the resistance had gone out of her. He remembered dragging the sweatshirt over her head, and a flash of naked breasts, the dark nipples staring up at him.

He had hidden her behind the brush well away from the footpath while he brought his car around. The Taurus this time. Then into the hills, where he found a deserted spot and parked. He really didn't remember much after that. When he started to hit them, to give them what they'd asked for, everything blurred behind a red film. It had been different with Edie because he had had plenty of time, time to enjoy her and to relish her terror. Too bad it had to be so quick with Natalie. She had deserved better from him.

Next time, Beringer thought.

Iris.

Not yet, he thought. It was tempting to make her next in line. The waitress had a body that wouldn't quit; she was a genuine bitch, pushing her boobs in his face like that, and she had the right name. The name excited him.

But he had to be more careful. He couldn't let himself spin out of control again. Not after all his years of waiting and planning for this time. Cool it for a few days. Iris could wait her turn, she wasn't going anywhere. And he still had to find one more of the chosen. In the meantime he could ratchet up the pressure.

Did Glenda have a clue yet? Did she even remember that promise he had sent her from Germany? (A mistake; he never should have mailed the note in his own handwriting, but nothing could be done about that now.) Did she have any inkling at all that the coeds were for her?

Late in the fourth quarter, the Raiders down by ten, they kicked a field goal to narrow the gap to one touchdown. As they lined up to try the obvious onside kick, Beringer watched without emotion. Desperation time, 100-to-1 shot. You should never let it come down to that, where you had to trust to a lucky bounce.

Stick with the game plan. Should he go afield for the next one? It was tempting. There would certainly be less risk. After two killings security on the college campus would be tight, making it harder to isolate another college queen, especially one who had to bring a singular gift to the game.

But the added risk gave a brighter edge to the fantasy Beringer was playing out. As a participant in the great game of Life and Death, he was now calling the plays. Besides, he had established a campus link to Dave Lindstrom, and he had something else in mind for the professor . . .

The onside kick failed, as Beringer had known it would. He watched the Cowboys run out the clock. Aikman, cool and efficient, went down on his knee for the last two meaningless plays as the seconds ran down. Watching the quarterback, Beringer reviewed his own actions over the past ten days. Not always retaining his cool, nevertheless he had made no serious mistakes. He had gotten away with grabbing Natalie impetuously. No one had seen him.

What about the car? Was there any chance the Taurus had been noticed where he had it parked near the campus? Maybe he ought to stay with the Buick for the next week. When he had signed the sublease agreement for the apartment he had not used his real name. Not that he expected the car to be traced back, but even if it was, all he had to do was disappear. Mr. No Name. The mystery man.

Beringer was still sitting there in the La-Z-Boy recliner when the first edition of the nightly news came on. For the second night in a row the lead story was the shocking discovery of a second murdered San Carlos College coed. A reporter was shown standing in the paved service area, with the dumpster in the background, reporting live although there was little to be seen other than the familiar yellow police tape defining the crime scene. The camera cut to a shot from the previous morning. Beringer's reaction quickened with interest when one of the investigating homicide detectives was shown arriving at the scene, warding off reporters' questions. Braden was his name. Brushed past the media vultures like a tugboat plowing through a flock of squawking seagulls. Tough-looking son of a bitch, Beringer thought with a grin.

Maybe he ought to give the homicide guy a little push in the right direction?

No, Beringer decided after a moment's thought. That wasn't necessary. He'd get there on his own . . . right where Ralph wanted him to go.

Twenty-Two

EDWARD BATCHELOR PRENTISS walked the length of the block past the civic center, studiously avoiding a glance at the police station, as if his errand were taking him to the public library in the next block, or to city hall to pay his water bill. He was a middle-aged man wearing well-tailored gray worsted slacks and a white cableknit sweater. His hair was full, longer than the current fashion, silvery gray and brushed back from his temples. Rather distinguished, a fact of which Prentiss was usually aware.

Today his thoughts were less vain, less fixed upon the figure he cut than upon his anxiety. And his dilemma. A full professor with tenure at San Carlos College, in line to become chairman of the history department, respected and even admired by his colleagues, he was suddenly facing the possibility of a career disintegrating in ruins.

At the corner he hesitated, then crossed the street and started back. In the little park directly across from city hall he paused, watching the birds flutter around an old man on a bench who doled out seed from a plastic bag.

A police car pulled out of the parking lot behind the police station and drove past him. Prentiss watched it go by, aware of cold cop scrutiny.

What would such men think of him? He shivered, touched by a nameless chill. He knew little of them, and they knew even less of a man like him. What would he say to them?

I knew Edith Foster. She was in one of my classes. She flaunted herself, made it clear she was available. You have to understand, I'm

a married man, a respectable man, a husband and father, but she was
unbelievably sexy, beautiful, she made me a little crazy.

I see. Were you with her that Friday night, Dr. Prentiss?

Well, yes, we met at The Pelican, but . . . we didn't go anywhere.
Before that, four or five times, we went to a motel in Santa Ana. It's
not that far, and no one would see us there. But it was over between
us, you see. That's what Edie wanted to tell me that night. I think
she was . . . growing tired of me. After only a month.

Did you become angry, Doctor? Is that why you attacked her?

Impossible! Prentiss told himself. He could never subject himself to that sort of inquisition.

When the news of Edith Foster's death broke a week ago,
Prentiss had been stunned, initially disbelieving. Then he became
terrified. What if someone had seen him talking to Edie that night
at the coffeehouse, or leaving with her? They had been circumspect
whenever they met in public, but what if she had talked to one of
her friends about him—named him? His life would be destroyed.
His marriage . . . Martha would never tolerate the public scandal.
He suspected that Martha knew of his occasional—quite infre-
quent, really—dalliances with twenty-year-old students, but nothing had ever been said. She had sensibly looked the other way. But
this . . . she wouldn't be able to ignore it.

Nor would the school administration. He would be disgraced.
He would lose everything. And the point was, he had done nothing!
He was innocent of the girl's murder—knew nothing about it.

It must have happened after he left her at the Alpha Beta
parking lot. Angry, yes, mortified that the little tart had tired of
him before he grew weary of her . . . while he was still besotted over
her, in fact. But she had been alive and well when he left her. He
had driven straight home, poured himself a large glass of Glenlivet,
closeted himself in his den until he was able to deal with his humiliation, anger and, yes, grief . . .

The killer must have picked her up there in the parking lot, or
followed her when she left. Or—he wouldn't put it past her—Edie
had picked *him* up, whoever he was, and got more than she bar-
gained for.

That last thought was uncharitable. Nettled with himself, Prentiss turned away from the bird man and his flock. He continued along the street past the police station. The point was—he adjusted his thoughts—he had absolutely nothing to do with the poor girl's murder. He couldn't help the police find her killer. What was he supposed to do—destroy his reputation, his position, his *life* in a quixotic gesture? All to no purpose?

After a week of torment Edward Prentiss had determined to remain silent. If anyone had known he was fucking Edith Foster, they obviously would have come forward or the police would have come knocking at his door. He was out of it. It had nothing to do with him.

Then came the second killing.

He didn't know the girl, Natalie Rothleder. As far as he could recall, she had never been in any of his classes. But her death shook him badly, almost as much as Edie's murder. Prentiss regarded himself as a respectable citizen. He was vociferously Republican, in favor of the death penalty and the three-strikes law, strongly opposed to the progressive criminalization of American society under the liberals. How could he then remain silent? If he had any knowledge whatever of Edie Foster that would help the police to find the murderer of two young women, surely it was encumbent upon him to come forward.

That realization had brought him downtown this morning. Now, at the end of the long block across the way from the civic center, Prentiss stood irresolute. One hand nervously combed his silver hair back from his temples.

If he didn't come forward, he thought, and he was eventually linked with Edie, serious questions would be raised. But after more than a week that risk seemed diminished. And didn't a second and similar murder, strongly indicating the hand of a serial killer, prove that what had happened to Edie had nothing to do with him?

He couldn't do it. Couldn't make his legs carry him across the street to the police station. Couldn't give himself up in the vague hope that something he said might help find the killer.

It wasn't that he was cold or indifferent to the fate of those two innocent young women. God in heaven, he had cared for Edie! He couldn't think of her, that firm, nubile body, the unblemished texture of her skin, those exquisite long legs, without breaking out in a sweat. But she was dead. Nothing he could do would bring her back.

She had chosen her own fate. All he could do was go on.

He glanced at his watch. He had a lecture to give in less than an hour. As he shot the sleeve of his jacket and looked up, a couple climbed out of a station wagon across the way in the public parking area in front of the police station. The man, tall and slender, looked familiar. He said something to the woman, whose body language was stiff, angry and determined. Prentiss watched her with a certain admiration as she stormed up the steps as if leading a charge, the man hurrying to keep up even with his longer strides.

Prentiss did so admire a handsome woman!

His car, a silver Lexus, was parked in a city lot another block away. He walked there briskly, not looking back, feeling almost lightheaded with the release of his burden of guilt. His distinctive good looks drew more than one approving glance.

DETECTIVE LINDA PEREZ, promoted to Detective/Third less than four months ago, handled most domestic complaints investigations that came to the attention of the San Carlos PD. It often seemed to her that her role was more that of a marriage counselor than a policewoman. And at age twenty-nine, once divorced, survivor of three more or less disastrous love affairs interspersed between long stretches when she might as well have been living in a convent, she didn't exactly consider herself overqualified to give advice on domestic relations.

The fights she could handle. The reports of abuse she met head-on, always giving the woman the same advice: Get out while you can. Run. Don't even look back. Few of the victims ever listened.

The couple seated across from Linda's desk this morning had a different complaint. The husband was lean, quiet, soft-spoken— a gentle man more worried about his wife than about the problem that had brought them to the station house. If Linda knew anything at all about couples, this man was not an abuser . . . but apparently the wife's first husband had been.

Linda glanced down at the Incident Report. Ralph Beringer, she had written on the form. Sandy hair. Six feet, two hundred pounds. Mid-thirties. Might be wearing an air force uniform. His ex-wife—now Glenda Lindstrom—had not seen him in eight years, so he might have changed some. Always wore glasses and favored tinted lenses. No known scars or distinguishing marks.

"What can you do?" the woman asked.

Linda read the tension in her posture and around her eyes. She was still in control but she was being pushed toward the edge.

"The truth is, Mrs. Lindstrom . . . until he actually does something, there is nothing we can do."

"He's threatened us! He's made harassing phone calls. He's stalked my children!"

"According to what you've told me, he hasn't made any direct threats. And these phone calls . . . except for the first one, when he spoke to his son, the caller has not actually identified himself."

"What are you trying to say?"

"That you can't say for certain who's been making these calls," Linda explained patiently.

"That's ridiculous!" Glenda Lindstrom retorted. "I'm telling you, I know it's him. He's angry because I remarried. He's hurt me before and he'll do it again. He's vindictive and he's dangerous."

"Take it easy, honey," Dave Lindstrom said.

Linda Perez suppressed her irritation. The truth was, she was having a hard time taking the Lindstroms' problem seriously. Rumors had floated around the squad room all morning that a task force was being formed to work on the Foster–Rothleder killings, the biggest case the San Carlos PD had ever handled. Captain Hummel had Detective Braden in the fishbowl, and the two of them kept glancing out at the squad room as if counting noses. Hummel's glance had touched briefly on Linda and the couple at her desk before moving on.

Linda felt a sharp disappointment. Not only was the hunt for a serial killer the department's biggest case in memory, but Tim Braden was heading up the investigation . . . and Linda, in her own phrase, had a thing for Braden. If she were working with him on a major case he would have to notice her. Fat chance, maybe, with that elegant Feeb in the wings, but a fat chance was better than none at all. Maybe Linda would have been the one to find something on the wacko they were hunting . . .

Linda had carefully avoided telling the department's consultant shrink about Braden during her regular sessions, afraid that word would leak out and the other cops would have something on her. Not that she cared what the rest of those jerks thought, but it would inevitably get back to Braden and she couldn't bear the thought of that.

"Perhaps you could talk to Beringer," the man was saying.

Linda pulled her thoughts back to the problem before her. "Talk to him?"

"I think it might help if he were put on notice that the police are aware of him and his attempts to harass our family."

"That might not be so easy," Linda said, something of her impatience creeping into her voice, "since no one has actually seen him or knows where he is."

"You haven't been listening!" Glenda Lindstrom said hotly. "I saw him at least once, following us. One of our daughter's teachers saw him outside her school. Our son Richie saw him following his school bus."

"When you saw him"—Linda glanced at her notes—"he was in a gray Taurus. The man Richie said he saw was driving a dark blue Buick. Is that correct?"

"What difference does that make?"

Linda remained silent, giving the situation a moment to cool down. She was accustomed to dealing with couples, married and unmarried, young and old, whose emotions ran at white heat. A period of quiet was often as effective as a cold shower.

Glenda Lindstrom turned to her husband. "Let's get out of here. They're not going to do anything."

"Just a minute, Mrs. Lindstrom, that's not true. But you must understand there are limits to what the police can do in a case like this. We have to work within the law just as the average citizen must."

The woman was on her feet. She leaned forward, palms straddling the corner of Linda's desk. "But not *him*, Detective. He doesn't have to obey any laws. He doesn't care about the law. That man abused me once. He terrorized his own son. He's followed me here to San Carlos for one reason only—to punish me for divorcing him eight years ago. If you won't do anything to stop him, we'll have to do it ourselves."

"That wouldn't be wise, Mrs. Lindstrom—"

"No? What's your best advice, then? Just sit back and wait for him to harm my children? To do to me whatever it is he's been planning for the past eight years?"

"Mrs. Lindstrom," Linda said sharply, "*you* haven't been listening. Ralph Beringer—if he is, in fact, here in San Carlos—has committed no crime. I'll try to find him—if he's staying in a motel, for instance, he would be registered—but he could be anywhere. If you learn where he's staying, notify me immediately and I'll talk to him. If you do hear from Beringer again—if he makes any overt threats or harasses you in any way—call me. In the meantime, all I can advise you to do is to exercise reasonable precautions. I'd suggest you start recording all incoming calls on your answering machine if you have one—"

"We do," Dave Lindstrom said.

"Don't answer any calls until you hear who it is. When you go out, be more aware than usual of your surroundings. Talk to your children about doing the same." She paused, looking the angry woman in the eye. "And don't do anything foolish."

"I've already done that," Glenda Lindstrom said coolly. "I came in here."

Linda Perez's cheeks burned as she watched the couple leave the squad room and start down the stairs toward the lobby. She tried to think of a zinger to hurl after the complainants. *Maybe your ex just came to see his kid! Have you considered that?*

The zinger, she thought, didn't have much zing.

ON THEIR WAY home Dave was thoughtful, preoccupied. Finally he said, "What was that about Beringer terrorizing Richie?"

She remained silent, staring away from him out the side window.

"You told me about him abusing you. What did he do to Richie?"

"He . . . abused him too."

"How? Do you mean spanking? Yelling at him? What?"

He had raised his voice. Watching her, he failed to see the car directly in front of him stop quickly as a traffic light changed. Dave had to slam on the brakes and swerve sharply to avoid a tail-end collision.

Waiting for the light to change, he gripped the wheel and stared straight ahead. Finally Glenda said, "He used to slap Richie around. Hard slaps. Shake him and threaten him with more until Richie screamed."

"My God, the boy wasn't two years old!"

"Once he burned Richie with the tip of his cigarette. He claimed it was an accident. I think Richie's reaction was so extreme that time it sobered Ralph up. He made a big show of treating the burn, putting salve on, telling Richie it was an accident. But it was deliberate. I knew that."

"Did you report any of these things to the police? Or to someone with the air force?"

"You think I haven't blamed myself over and over for allowing it to happen? But Ralph swore if I told anyone he would really hurt Richie. Not just me, but Richie. It wasn't an idle threat, Dave. He meant it."

"You make him sound like . . ." He didn't finish the sentence. A *psychotic*, he thought.

"He is," Glenda said bitterly.

Twenty-Three

THE SMALL CONFERENCE room, more frequently used for staff meetings and Christmas or birthday parties, was crowded. There were a dozen folding chairs in three rows, not enough for the half-dozen SCPD uniforms, three detectives pulled from other assignments, and five sheriff's deputies who were to be part of the task force, in addition to Tim Braden and Karen Younger. To the right at the front of the room was an oak table and one chair, to the left a white markerboard on a pedestal.

Captain Hummel planted a heavy hip on one corner of the table. "All right, cool it!" His gravel voice carved a clear path through the buzz of talk. "You all know why you're here. We have a repeat killer shoving it to us, and it's the decision of the chief and the county sheriff that we organize a multijurisdictional investigative effort. Detective Braden caught the first case and he's still in charge of this investigation, but the sheriff is lending us some manpower, which as you all know we badly need." He paused. "We're also going to have the cooperation and assistance of the FBI."

"Whoopee," a cop leaning against the back wall muttered.

"You got somethin' to say, Janowicz?"

"Surely not, Captain."

"That's good, because I wouldn't want to think you were askin' to be booted off this team and assigned to security for the Junior League meetings." The captain glowered a moment to let his warning sink in. "If experience tells us anything, the FBI will probably run its own show. No offense intended, ma'am," he added, with a glance toward Karen Younger.

"None taken."

"As far as the rest of you are concerned, Detective Braden heads up this task force, and he'll be reportin' directly to me. If God had meant it to be any other way, he would've made one of you captain. Everyone clear on this?"

There was a chorus of "Yo," "Amen" and "Hear hear."

Hummel turned the meeting over to Braden, who stood unsmiling by the markerboard until the bantering subsided. He ran through the details of the investigations into the deaths of Edith Foster and Natalie Rothleder. Using the board and a black marker, he listed the few dissimilarities, which included the length of time the perpetrator had had the victims and the locations and circumstances in which the bodies were found. The parallels between the two killings made a much longer list on the board. The killer had beaten both victims with a weighted, gloved fist; had sexually assaulted them, causing both vaginal and anal tearing, in each case using a condom and leaving no semen or blood; had cut each victim's initial across her abdomen with a bladed instrument, and had used the same blade to sexually mutilate the women. Both attacks had occurred at night without witnesses. Both victims were young white women, students at San Carlos College.

"These attacks were very quick and overpowering," Braden said in concluding his summary. "There was no outcry, no evidence of a struggle. This guy is vicious, he's strong, and when he attacks he means business."

"Could he be a fighter?" one of the uniformed officers called out. "He punches these women out. It ain't always so easy. I mean, he puts 'em down so there's no fuss or muss. Nobody hears nothin', nobody sees nothin'."

"How about the martial arts freaks?" one of the sheriff's deputies asked.

"Would a martial arts expert carry lead in his fist?" Braden countered.

"Only if he was cheatin'," the deputy answered, provoking laughter.

"The boxer idea is a long shot but it's worth checking out."

Braden addressed the cop who had raised the question. "Run with it."

"When does he cut them?" asked one of the older investigators, normally on robbery detail. "Before or after they're dead?"

"According to the ME reports, the cutting is perimortem—around the time of death. She might still be alive after the beating, but not for long. Most likely she's not conscious when he cuts her, if that's any consolation. There's very little bleeding in the tissues around the knife wounds, which there would be if the wounds occurred earlier in the attack."

After a few more routine questions Braden held up his hands, palms out, for silence. "You'll all be given specific assignments. We have to find this guy. He likes killing, and he may just be getting started. That means no leaves, no sick days, and twelve-hour shifts. You'll log plenty of overtime while you're working with the task force." He glanced toward the FBI agent, who was seated at the end of the first row of chairs. "It also means we need all the help we can get. We've requested help from the FBI's Investigative Support Unit out of Quantico. As you know, one of the things that unit does is analyze violent crimes and develop profiles of the perpetrators. They've had some very exceptional successes in describing serial killers that have led to arrests and convictions. Special Agent Younger is with that unit, and she's been here working the case since last Wednesday. She already has some thoughts on our killer."

There was a stirring of interest as Karen took Braden's place at the front of the room. She was wearing a tan corduroy blazer, brown slacks and shoes, and a pale beige turtleneck sweater. The outfit was more casual than the Bureau's button-down image, and Braden wondered if the choice had been calculated. He thought she looked terrific.

"Good morning," she said. "I'm going to get right into the profile, but first I'd like to add something to what Detective Braden has told you." Her gaze moved across her audience, making eye contact, pulling them into her orbit. "It's my belief that the two murders here in San Carlos are not the killer's first. Eight years ago, near Wiesbaden, Germany, a German girl and her American soldier lover were both murdered. The details of the girl's death precisely match those of the two recent killings." She waited for the exclamations of surprise and disbelief to die away. "The German girl was raped repeatedly and violently. She was beaten to death by her assailant's fists. The actual cause of death was a blow that crushed her larynx. Before he left her, the killer carved her first initial on her belly with a small knife blade or similar instrument, and her vaginal opening was mutilated with the same blade."

This time she had to wait longer for the reaction to subside. Then one of the plainclothes cops said, "How do you connect Wiesbaden with San Carlos?"

"We're not sure, but it was suspected by German authorities that the murderer of the German girl might have been an American soldier. If so, it's not unreasonable to assume the same man would eventually return to the States."

"Jesus H. Christ!" the detective swore. Then a thought occurred simultaneously to him and several others, all of whom tried to ask similar questions. Had anything been done to track recently discharged soldiers in the area? Did someone stationed in Germany eight years ago come from San Carlos? Or from anywhere in Southern California?

"All right, listen up!" Karen stopped the babble with a surprising ring of authority. "We started from another direction, running the names of all current male staff and faculty members at San Carlos College through NCIC computers and military archives. We've since expanded that search to include maintenance and other employees of the college. We've come up with several Vietnam veterans, one who served in Korea, two from the Gulf War. None were stationed in Germany at any time, or even in Europe." She smiled. "One has an outstanding warrant—for unpaid traffic tickets. I needn't tell you the college administration isn't happy about the implications of our search."

"You're saying someone at the college is murdering coeds?"

"It's a possibility we had to look at. Obviously, though, the killer could be anyone in the San Carlos area. He needn't have come from here. Going back to the earlier question from Detective . . . ?"

"Tomczak."

"Your suggestion about going at this search from the opposite direction has also occurred to us. Instead of looking at people we know are here in San Carlos and trying to track one of them back to the first killing in Germany, we have begun tracking servicemen stationed there eight years ago who have recently been discharged or returned home on leave. That is, of course, a much wider search."

"Could be thousands of guys."

"We're trying to narrow it down. If anything turns up, you'll know it. In the meantime, I think I can tell you some things about the killer that may help."

For the next fifteen minutes Karen ran briskly through the details of a sociopath's profile. She quickly sketched the most significant differences between organized and disorganized serial killers. The latter, she said, were seriously psychotic, usually poorly educated, unprepossessing in appearance, often incapable of holding anything but the most menial jobs. They acted impulsively, selecting victims at random. The attacks were often wild, blitz assaults. They were always sexual crimes, but the killer was frequently unable to complete his sexual assault, at least while his victim was still alive. Such killers were seriously dysfunctional sexually.

"You're sayin' that's not our guy," Janowicz rumbled impatiently.

"Correct. The killer of Edith Foster and Natalie Rothleder—and, I believe, Lisl Moeller in Germany eight years ago—is very organized, very much in control most of the time. He is almost certainly older than the typical disorganized killer, who is usually caught long before he's twenty-five. This man is probably in his thirties. He's presentable in appearance, so he doesn't immediately frighten his potential victims. His clothes are fashionable, his hair is clean, he's not dirty or smelly. He may even be physically attractive to these women. As a soldier, he was able to function in an organization that demands control, discipline, order." As she talked, Karen listed these characteristics on the board, putting a check mark in front of each item. Some of the physical details provoked a skeptical exchange of glances and eyebrow-raising among the task force members. "He's mobile, which means he has a dependable car. He's too careful to trust an older, unreliable car. Although he's made no attempt to bury or hide the bodies—he apparently wants them to be found—he's been very careful not to leave anything behind that might identify him, which is the clearest indication of an organized killer. Also, he's not sexually dysfunctional. He has apparently had no trouble completing multiple sex acts with his victims while they were still alive. The fact that he kept Edie Foster four or five hours suggests that, like most organized killers, he enjoys exercising power and control over his victims. If they resist, he probably becomes more violent. I don't suppose I need to emphasize that, although these are sex crimes, sex really has very little to do with it. They're hate crimes. The killer is expressing a deep-seated anger and hatred for women."

Karen paused, staring at the list she had made on the white board, describing the man who had haunted her dreams for eight years. "You won't be able to recognize him by looking at him," she said in a low voice, as if to herself, "but he'll know you. He's probably watching us closely, following our progress, laughing at us. He's very confident . . . and he's on some kind of fantasy trip that has brought him to San Carlos." She swung around, once again commanding the full attention of the tough, seasoned cops watching her, even though most of them were older and more experienced on the Job. "He's going to kill again, and soon. If I'm right and he's waited eight years for this, he probably planned what he was going to do, or fantasized it often enough that he was able to work out how to do it without being caught. I don't think events have changed his plans, but *he's* changed. Having the Foster woman was so exciting, so satisfying, that he kept her through the night, but he may be past that now. He didn't keep Natalie Rothleder alive for long. And I don't think he can wait very long for the next one."

"How long?" someone asked quietly.

"He waited a week between Foster and Rothleder. I doubt very much he'll be able to wait longer than that."

"Shit," an officer muttered.

"This week," Karen said with conviction. "He'll strike again before the week is out."

*   *   *

WINDING UP THE meeting, Captain Hummel's words were harsh and emphatic. "The official line is, we got two murders, okay? The German connection so far is a theory. Maybe it's a good one and it'll help us catch this bastard. But officially, and I want every one of you to hear me good, we have two women who've been beaten and stabbed. That's all. Nothin' goes out about Germany, and nothin' about carvin' their initials on the victims' bodies. We're holding onto that as long as we can. If it gets out, I'll know it was one of you and I'll find out who. Do I have to repeat that? Nothin' gets out that we don't want released."

Nobody laughed.

Twenty-Four

"ELLI?"

The man who called out her name was smiling. The little girl wasn't worried or concerned, because the man had a pleasing manner and appearance, and he knew her name.

"That's your name, isn't it? Ellen Lindstrom, but they call you Elli, right?"

She nodded, unaccountably shy. Normally she talked a mile a minute, or at least that was what her daddy said, but there was something insistent in the man's tone that made her uncomfortable. Instinctively she took a step backward.

"I bet your mom told you not to talk to strangers, am I right? That's good, Elli, your mom is right. I'll bet Mrs. Drummond has told you the same thing, hasn't she?"

Elli nodded, relaxing a little. A bad stranger wouldn't talk to her about her mother and Mrs. Drummond, her teacher. Nevertheless, she glanced over her shoulder toward the swing she had vacated a moment earlier. Another girl had grabbed the swing. Behind her, a group of boys and girls were climbing over a large pink dinosaur with crawl holes in the middle and a small slide for a tail.

"I saw you on the swing. You were going pretty good there, Elli, all by yourself."

"I can swing by myself."

"I bet you can. I know you can."

"I can climb the dinosaur, too. I did it yesterday but I fell down and skinned my knee. See there? It bled, too, but I didn't cry, except for a minute. It's better now, but Mom says I'll have a scab and I mustn't pick at it or I'll have a scar."

"You listen to your mom."

"Do you know Mommy? Do you know Daddy, too?"

But the stranger was no longer listening to her. He was staring across the playground toward the school building, where Mrs. Drummond had just come out and was looking around. The teacher looked straight at them.

"I know your mommy. You tell her you saw me today, okay? And I'll see you again, Elli. Real soon."

Mrs. Drummond was hurrying toward them across the yard, walking very fast, but the stranger turned away, not waiting for the teacher. Mrs. Drummond kept staring after him as she hurried toward Elli. Maybe Mrs. Drummond liked him, the girl thought. Maybe she also thought he was a nice man.

"I was only out of the yard for a minute, Mrs. Lindstrom . . . not even that long. I went inside the school with one of the girls who was upset—not all of the girls are as well adjusted socially as Elli is."

"I didn't send her to this school so she could be adjusted to strange men!" Glenda heard the edge of panic in her voice. Her heart was still racing from her reaction when Helen Drummond told her about the man she had seen talking to Elli.

"I'm really sorry. As soon as I saw him with her, I hurried over. But he was already leaving. It was the same man I saw last week, I'm sure. He drove off in that same car."

"A blue Buick?"

"Yes, I think so. Those cars, they all look so much alike."

Glenda tried to curb her anger. Drummond knew better, for God's sake, but haranguing her wasn't going to help the situation. "Can you . . . can you tell me what he looked like?"

"Well, he . . . that's sort of funny, Mrs. Lindstrom, but he's hard to describe. I mean, he was presentable, not at all rough-looking, but there was nothing really distinctive about him to make you notice. Except maybe ... yes, he was wearing tinted glasses. Not sunglasses, not as dark as that, but I know they were tinted."

Ralph!

Glenda was gripping Elli's hand as she talked to the teacher, and she squeezed so tightly that the girl looked up at her, suddenly anxious. Glenda tried to smile reassuringly.

"Do you know him, Mrs. Lindstrom?" Helen Drummond asked. She was also anxious.

"I don't want him near Elli," Glenda said. "If you see him near her, call me. And call the police at once."

The teacher paled visibly. "Oh, dear," she said.

In the car Elli watched her mother. She was sensitive enough to the angry tension in her mother that she was close to crying. "Did I do something wrong?" she asked, her voice small and tremulous.

"No, honey," Glenda whispered. Then she corrected herself. "Well, you know what I've told you about talking to strangers."

"He didn't act like a stranger," Elli said, her lower lip trembling.

They never do, Glenda thought.

"I know, it's not your fault. It's just that ... if you see him again, I want you to go straight inside the school, or straight to Mrs. Drummond if she's outside with you. Okay?"

"Okay." The girl was silent a moment. The car's tires made thumping noises as they went over cracks in the pavement. She remembered the funny shy feeling she had had when the strange man first spoke to her. "Is he a bad man, Mommy?"

Her mother looked at her quickly, then away. How much could she tell her daughter without sowing seeds of fear and anxiety that would ripen when Elli was older? Bad men don't always look like bad men, she wanted to say; sometimes they look and act and talk like nice men.

She forced a smile. "Let's forget about him for now, okay?"

Elli nodded, relieved. After a moment she said, "You hurt my hand."

"Oh, honey, I'm sorry. You mean when I squeezed it? That was like a little hug. You know how it is when we hug sometimes really hard? So hard it almost hurts? Well, that was a hand hug."

Elli grinned happily at this explanation. "I wish my hand was bigger."

"So you could squeeze back?"

"I'd give Richie a hand hug!"

ONLY WHEN SHE reached home and Elli had gone cheerfully off to watch television did Glenda's icy calm begin to shatter. She felt as if she were breaking up into slivers, that at any moment she would fly apart. She began to tremble, a quaking from within like the earth's own tremors that had become so familiar since she'd been living in California.

An earthquake was the result of a deep, invisible fault line. She saw herself that way—flawed, concealing a massive fault beneath a calm, ordinary facade.

She heard Elli's piping laughter from the den, and the sound pierced her heart like shards of glass.

I won't let him do it . . . not to her.

She knew what Ralph was attempting. He wanted to terrorize her, to turn her back into the frightened, demoralized rabbit he had used and abused more than eight years ago, finding her weak and contemptible. She wouldn't—she couldn't—go back to that. She would not be that woman again, reduced to begging, pleading not for herself but for her child . . . that haunted, pitful creature with the darkly shadowed eyes and purple-yellow bruises, hiding in her own house. Literally jumping when she heard his voice. *Where have you been? What took you so long? You think I don't know what you're up to? How long does it take to buy a jar of spaghetti sauce?*

Forever, she thought. Staring at the different jars and labels, so many of them, each so expensive. What if she picked the wrong one?

Why did you buy that? Do you expect us to eat that crap? What did you do with the rest of the money? Do you think I'm made of money, for Chrissakes? Is that why you married me?

Glenda put her hands to her head as if to shut off the torrent of questions. She didn't know how long she stood there, paralyzed. When she came out of a kind of trance she found herself standing in the kitchen, aftershocks still sending quivers through her body.

"I won't go back to that," she whispered.

"Mommy?" Elli was standing in the kitchen doorway, holding her favorite doll, a soft, pug-nosed country doll with yellow braids and a blue gingham dress. "Is something wrong?"

"No, no, honey . . ." Glenda squatted on her heels to bring herself to eye level with the little girl. She held out her arms as Elli came to her, uncharacteristically tentative.

"Why are you crying?"

Glenda wiped at her cheeks with the heel of her palm, astonished to find them wet. "I was just remembering something sad, that's all . . . something from a long time ago."

"I don't want you to be sad."

The five-year-old sounded so grave that Glenda suppressed an absurd impulse to giggle. She swept Elli closer, hugging her tightly. "Tell me if I hug you too hard," she whispered. "Like that hand hug I gave you, okay?"

"It doesn't hurt," Elli said, hugging her back.

Elli was being affected already, Glenda thought. Both Elli and Richie.

Ralph wanted each of them to suffer.

He wouldn't stop until he had destroyed them all.

T HE INCIDENT IN the schoolyard with Glenda's daughter had put Beringer in good spirits. After leaving Elli and her worried schoolteacher behind, Ralph drove south across town toward the San Carlos College campus, humming to himself while listening to SportsTalk on his car radio.

He didn't plan on venturing onto the campus again. His presence there, without a logical explanation to account for it, would

be not merely reckless but stupid. Police and campus security officers were on the lookout for the mad-dog killer (no reporter had
come up with a suitable name for him as yet, something catchy like
Son of Sam or the Midnight Stalker). Almost certainly he would
be stopped, and he couldn't afford close scrutiny.

He had decided it was safe enough, however, to have Eggs
McMuffin for breakfast at the McDonald's across from the north-
west corner of the campus, which he had done earlier that morning,
or lunch at one of the other student hangouts in the immediate
area. He had been doing that each day, drinking enough coffee to
keep the *Titanic* afloat and his brain on red alert. These stops had
enabled him to pick up talk about the beefed-up security on campus, the escort and "buddy" programs and other measures, none of
them very original or intimidating to someone as resourceful as
Ralph.

Today for lunch he chose a Mexican restaurant popular with
students, less than a block from the edge of the campus. Rosie's
specialized in tacos and burritos and inexpensive platters. Beringer
sat at one of the small tables surrounded by chattering students.
He ordered a beef enchilada platter and a Carta Blanca, a light
Mexican beer.

He was halfway through his lunch when he spotted the girl.

She had just come into the cafe and was standing poised at
the entrance, as if she were looking for someone. She was tall and
lanky, nearly as tall as Beringer himself. Five-ten, he guessed. Short
skirt, legs from here to Hawaii. Auburn hair cascading down her
back like a waterfall. A big, wide, generous mouth, like a model's.
Beringer felt his blood quicken. He had to force himself not to stare.

He had seen her before. He was sure of it.

With a crowd of students earlier that week, leaving one of
David Lindstrom's classes.

The girl's immediate sexual appeal and the link to Lindstrom
were not enough, of course. Another student sealed the girl's fate
when he called out to her. "Hey, Nan! Nancy! Over here!"

Hunched over his table, Beringer felt the shot of adrenalin as
if he had been punched. He took a swig of beer to cover his reaction. Out of the corner of his eye he saw Nancy slide into a booth

to join three other students, two boys and a girl. (Beringer thought of them as pretty children, not adults.) He noticed that the group automatically paired off into two couples. Nancy joined the student who had called out.

Beringer pushed his half-eaten platter away, no longer hungry. Reining in the wild excitement was like trying to control an unruly horse.

He ordered another beer, not wanting to leave while Nancy was there. The group talked animatedly, not holding their voices down, and Beringer was able to pick up some of the conversation about the two recent killings. The students exchanged ghoulish speculations and nervous jokes about locking their doors and looking under the beds at night. Nancy said she wasn't going anywhere without Mark, especially at night. Mark grinned.

Beringer wondered where she lived. On campus or off? Did she have a car? Was Mark, the long-haired jerk sitting with her, the girl's one-and-only? Where did she go after classes? Any of the answers to these questions might put the girl safely out of Beringer's reach, forcing him to search elsewhere.

But he didn't believe it. He had a hunch about Nancy. He felt the same immediate kinship with her that he had felt for Edie and Natalie, and still felt for Iris. Like the others, Nancy had been presented to him with minimal effort on his part, as if the gods themselves were conspiring to make everything possible for him, exactly as he had fantasized it for the past eight years.

The quartet of students left the Mexican restaurant together a half hour later. At the edge of the campus they separated, Nancy and her boyfriend returning to afternoon classes, the other couple going off on their own. From across the street Beringer studied pictures of listings in a real-estate agent's window, suppressing his frustration. He couldn't follow Nancy onto the campus. How was he going to find her again?

Then he heard the girl's voice raised. It had a light, schoolgirlish sound that Beringer found enormously attractive, though it seemed much younger than her ripe woman's body. "We'll see you at the powwow!" Nancy called after the departing couple.

Beringer stared after her. The long hair was evidently a proud feature. Loose and wavy, the color of dark red Washington apples, spilling halfway down her back. She kept tossing it as she walked away with her boyfriend, unconsciously reaching back to let the heavy mane cascade through her fingers.

Beringer felt the familiar heat. She was the one.

What the hell was a powwow?

Twenty-Five

RICHIE LINDSTROM MISSED the bus after school.

The miss was intentional. After his last class of the day he slipped into the locker room and waited until the room emptied out. Some older kids were playing basketball in the adjoining gym, the thump-thump of a dribbling basketball keeping pace with Richie's heartbeat.

When he finally came outside the bus was gone.

The day was warm for October, the temperature in the mid-seventies under a partly cloudy sky. It was also smog season, and the prevailing yellow haze was visible to the north over the Los Angeles basin. Another Santa Ana was brewing, and even higher temperatures were forecast for the weekend ahead. Richie wasn't sure exactly what a Santa Ana wind was, although he had heard the term at least a thousand million times on TV. He had a vague notion it had something to do with the city of Santa Ana. The only thing he knew for certain was that it meant hot desert winds and cool dry nights. Great beach weather.

Richie wondered if his real father liked going to the beach. He wondered if Sergeant Ralph Beringer had felt the hot desert winds of the Middle East during the Gulf War. He was a soldier, he must have been there. Richie actually knew very little about his father.

He thought about these things as he walked, following the route the school bus had taken without him. Richie didn't mind walking, and he figured it was less than two miles to San Anselmo Drive where it crossed Washington Boulevard. From there he had enough change saved from his lunch allowance to catch a city bus that stopped only three blocks from his house.

The sun felt good as he walked, but the closer he came to San Anselmo the more jittery he began to feel. Mixed with his excitement and anticipation was another emotion, one that caused his scalp to tingle and his throat to go dry. He cut across the huge parking surface of the San Carlos Mall with its Penney's, Sears, Robinson's-May and about a thousand other stores. Just beyond the parking lot he could see the tops of the old date palms along the center divider that defined San Anselmo Drive.

For the four blocks extending north of the shopping mall toward the foothills the street was a wide boulevard. Once older estate homes on huge properties had faced each other across the boulevard; now only a few of these three-story Victorian piles remained, converted to law offices and insurance offices. The rest had been torn down to make room for apartment houses and condominium complexes—Mediterranean style buildings in pink stucco with tile roofs, sleek modern structures of glass and steel, imitation Cape Cod designs painted in gray or blue and white, a few older apartment houses with tropical motifs and plantings. Walking slowly up the street, Richie realized with dismay that these large buildings contained hundreds of apartments and condominiums. By the time he reached the last of the four long blocks with the palm tree center islands, Richie's excitement had faded. At the end of the last block the street narrowed to two lanes where it climbed into the hills. On these curving hillside streets San Carlos's wealthier citizens had built secluded estates when they fled the mall-dominated flats below.

Richie guessed that his father wasn't living in the hills. He had come to San Carlos only recently. It made more sense that he might be staying in one of the many apartments along the boulevard, but how was Richie to find him? Maybe he didn't even live on this street. Maybe he had only turned this way on the day Richie spotted him because he was going to the mall.

Richie's disappointment was not as sharp as he had expected. There was also an odd relief, a lifting of tension, taking away the nervous edge to his anticipation.

Crossing the street, he started back along the opposite side, peering at the buildings and what he could see of the subterranean parking areas. There were cars parked all along both sides of the street, but the gated underground parking caught his eye. Although, like many youngsters, he saw gates and barriers as more of a challenge than a deterrent, he recognized the futility of trying to sneak into every one of the garages in the hope of recognizing a dark blue 1993 Buick LeSabre. The multiunit buildings also had many entrances, each with banks of mailboxes. The chance of finding one with Ralph Beringer's name on it seemed remote.

Richie had no sooner accepted this depressing conclusion than he saw the car.

In the middle of the next block, a dark blue car emerged from an underground parking garage and paused before entering the street. It was a late model Buick, immaculately maintained, its glossy paint glittering in the sun. Richie started to run. The Buick suddenly shot out into the street.

A break in the center island strips allowed the car to cross through and turn left without pausing. Richie shouted and waved. His legs pumped furiously, his heart thudding, the quivery excitement building with each stride. "Dad! Dad! Wait for me!"

But his father didn't see him. The Buick pulled smoothly away, slowed at the next corner, then accelerated down the street.

Richie pulled up on the sidewalk, panting heavily. Tears stung his eyes. He felt a weight as heavy as despair, out of all proportion to what had happened. His dad hadn't seen him, that's all. He hadn't run away.

Besides, now you know where he lives.

The realization cut through Richie's anguish. He blinked back the tears and scrubbed at his eyes with his knuckles. His gaze turned away from the boulevard where the Buick had vanished toward the building it had come out of.

The apartment complex was called Vista Valencia. Mature evergreen plantings surrounded the walled patios of the front units. Masses of bougainvillea, hyacinth and geraniums lent their colors to the beige stucco buildings. All of the units, Richie noticed, had either small balconies or private patios. The shrubbery next to the patios was tall and thick enough to hide someone in their shadows, especially at night.

The long row of units had three entrances but only one drive-way leading down to the lower level garage, which was secured by a grilled barrier. The entrances had locked gates. Just inside were stacks of brass mailboxes set into a side wall.

Richie peered through the wrought-iron grille of one of the entries at the narrow name slots above each box. By squinting he could make out most of the names.

There was no name tag for a Ralph Beringer.

Richie repeated the process at the remaining two building en-tries with the same disappointing results. Then he returned to the central entrance, next to the driveway. A car had stopped on the ramp just below Richie—a silver Honda Accord. At that moment, with a heavy rumbling, the barrier at the front of the garage began to lift.

Instantly Richie realized what was happening. The driver of the Honda had activated the barrier by punching a button on the remote control he carried in his car. As the small car drove through the opening, Richie slid down a short incline, jumped to the pave-ment, and darted into the gloom of the garage before the slow-moving gate could close.

Quickly he slipped to the side, away from the entrance. Half-way down a long row of stalls the Honda slid into a parking space. Richie heard a car door slam and the blip of an electronic lock. He crouched between two cars. The footsteps of the Honda's driver came toward him, echoing hollowly through the garage. But at the last moment the driver turned away toward a back wall. Peering after him, Richie saw lighted signs over a stairway and an elevator. The Honda driver summoned the elevator with the push of a but-ton and stepped inside.

Richie waited. Silence settled over the vast wilderness of con-crete and metal where he crouched. Emboldened by the silence, Richie stepped out of his hiding place and walked along the center aisle he found himself in, looking at the parked cars on either side. He returned along the next aisle. More than half of the parking slots were empty. The people who used them were probably at work, Richie thought, or shopping at the mall.

The Buick was gone, of course, so Richie didn't know exactly what he hoped to find. The spaces were identified by numbers, not names. He guessed the numbers would be the same as their owners' apartment numbers. Richie had no way of knowing the number of the unit where Beringer was staying.

He stopped next to a gray Ford Taurus, parked in slot 110. His heart gave a little jump, like a blip on a TV screen.

More than a week ago, the Sunday he went to the beach with his fa—with his stepfather—he had seen a car just like this one. Later, when he spotted the blue Buick near his house and following his school bus, Richie had concluded he was wrong about seeing the Taurus more than once that Sunday. But it had been a Hertz rental car. So was this one.

Richie didn't know why, if he had only recently come to San Carlos, Ralph Beringer would need two cars. But he had no doubt whatever that this was where his father was staying.

Vista Valencia. Apartment 110.

Twenty-Six

AT FIRST DAVE Lindstrom thought the detective on the phone wanted to talk to him about the harassment complaint against Ralph Beringer. Then the caller, whose name was Braden, identified himself as a homicide investigator looking into the recent deaths of two San Carlos College coeds.

"We're all shocked," Dave said. "Nothing like this has ever happened here before. As campuses go, ours has had a better record than most. But I don't see how I can help you."

"It's my understanding you had both of these young women in your classes. I thought maybe you could tell me something about them."

"Well, I'll try."

They made an appointment for three o'clock, after Dave's last class of the day. Waiting for the detective to arrive, Dave thought about the two murdered girls. He recalled Edith Foster more clearly than the Rothleder girl because Foster had made a point of being noticed. It wasn't the first time Dave had had a student show off her legs or excess cleavage, but he had never had any trouble turning down the invitations, spoken or implied. Foster had been more persistent than most, and her roommate had implied knowledge of something more than flirtation between them. Had she told the detective as much? Was that why he wanted to talk to Dave? The question left him feeling uneasy.

Detective Braden arrived at precisely three o'clock. Dave waved the cop to the only extra chair in his small office, an oak chair by the window that was usually occupied by a worried student. Every inch of space in the room was taken. One whole wall was filled with bookshelves. Crowded freestanding bookcases stood against two other walls, one of them devoted entirely to videos of movies, sandwiching a four-drawer file cabinet and stacks of cardboard file boxes. Dave's desk was piled with folders, correspondence trays and heaps of papers and periodicals. The one small open wall space was filled by a poster from the early 1940s of Bette Davis in *In This Our Life*.

"Would you like some coffee, Detective? We have a large coffeemaker in our conference room. It's just down the hall."

"Thanks. I'm coffeed out."

The detective had a blunt, no-nonsense manner. His face was all hard planes with weary eyes and a tight mouth that reminded Dave of a line in Thomas Hardy's *Return of the Native* describing the rural peasants as having lips that met like the two halves of a muffin.

He wasn't sure exactly what he had expected. His adolescent and adult life had been circumscribed by movies, as fan and scholar. In college he had been an actor and even a neophyte moviemaker; in real life, as he put it, he had ended up as a critic, analyst and teacher of the medium he loved. Over all those years of watching movies he had observed thousands of cops on screen, but he suspected that the reality of homicide investigation had rarely if ever been captured. The movies preferred lone knights-errant—private eyes, courageous reporters, angry survivors—to the dogged, weary investigators who solved real crimes. He wondered if Braden had ever been involved in a lethal car chase, a confrontation in a dark abandoned warehouse or a silent stalking in the woods.

"How can I help you?" Breaking the silence, Dave realized that the detective was quite content to let it linger.

"You don't mind if I tape this conversation?" Braden produced a small tape recorder and set it on a corner of the desk.

Dave stared at it, surprised. "No . . . of course not."

"Good. Saves a lot of paperwork." He pushed the record button and the tape began to wind. "This is an ongoing investigation into the deaths of Edith Foster and Natalie Rothleder . . ."

Braden gave the date, time and place of the interview before recording Dave's name, address, home and office phone numbers and his occupation as an assistant professor of film studies at San Carlos College. Then he said, "You knew the two students whose names I just gave."

"Yes . . . I told you that on the phone."

"What can you tell me about them?" Movie cops spoke more harshly and aggressively, Dave thought. Barton MacLane was the prototype in the film noir of the forties.

Dave reviewed his mental portraits of the two students. "They weren't kids, Detective. They were young women, mature in different ways."

"How's that?"

"Edie Foster was . . . sexually mature. Outgoing, very self-confident, popular. A very attractive young woman, perhaps a bit spoiled, like a pretty girl who's always had her own way because she was so pretty. Not an especially good student, because she only worked at what interested her."

"Did you give her a good grade, Doctor?"

"A 'C,' I believe. Passing grade, average performance. She could have done better." Dave frowned, wondering about the significance of the question. Wondering what the detective was looking for from him. "Natalie Rothleder was quite different. Brilliant student, hardworking, intense, ambitious—partly, I think, because she had much lower self-esteem than Edith Foster."

"Attractive, too, was she?"

"Yes, very. More than she realized, I think." Dave paused, watching the slow unreeling of the tape in the small recorder. "What are you getting at, Detective Braden? You know these were both attractive young women, inviting targets for a sexual psychopath."

"That who you think killed them?"

"I'm not a detective," Dave answered quietly. The detective's cryptic style was becoming irritating. "I understand both women were raped and brutalized. Sexual psychopathy seems to be a fairly obvious assumption."

Braden nodded without apparent interest. "Do you ever go out with your students, Dr. Lindstrom?"

Dave stiffened, suddenly wary. After a moment he said, "No. Aside from the fact that I'm happily married and it's against this college's faculty rules, I wouldn't put myself into that kind of awkward and compromising situation."

"We all have good intentions, Doctor. Sometimes we don't always live up to them."

"I don't know what you've heard, Detective, but I never went out with Edith Foster or Natalie Rothleder. I never met either of them outside the normal college setting." He flashed again on the Foster girl sitting in the front row, crossing her legs, smiling when the movement caught his eye. "Sometimes students fantasize about their teachers. It's normal. I've never taken advantage of that."

"Very commendable," Braden said dryly. Abruptly changing direction, he asked, "You're a volunteer firefighter?"

"That's right."

"You were involved in fighting that fire in the hills a couple weeks ago? Specifically, the Friday night the Foster girl was killed?"

"Yes, I was. So I couldn't possibly have had anything to do with her murder, could I?" Dave hated hearing the quiver in his voice, hated even more to have the homicide detective hear it—or the tape machine record it.

"You were relieved for part of that evening."

The recognition that the detective's questions were more than casual—that he had actually been investigating Dave's movements that night—chilled him like an icy wind.

"I went home for a few hours to rest, be with my family. I was back on the lines a little after midnight."

"Uh-huh. No one remembers actually seeing you on the lines after midnight Friday, Doctor, or even on Saturday."

"That's ridiculous. Ask one of the fire captains. I know there was a lot of confusion that night, but . . . our crew boss would remember me. I was working with him late Friday night and all Saturday morning, cleaning up some hot spots."

"What's his name?"

"Jim Roget. He's a Navajo Indian."

Braden glanced at him curiously. "An Indian?"

"He's probably gone back to Arizona. There were about a dozen Navajo firefighters came over that week. He'll confirm what I've told you."

"That's fine, Doctor, that'll help a lot." Braden smiled for the first time during the interview. It was not a friendly smile, Dave thought. Polite, nothing more. "I guess that's all for now. Oh, by the way, you were teaching a class this past Friday night? The night the Rothleder girl was hit?"

Dave's momentary relief dissolved like steam on a heated windshield. "It was a graduate school seminar in cinematography."

"What time was that, Doctor?"

"From seven to nine." Dave's angry defensiveness was gone, replaced by bewilderment. "It was over about a quarter to."

"Yeah, that's what I was told."

Braden punched a button, stopping the tape. Both men stared at the recorder for a moment, as if it exercised a special fascination. Then Braden picked it up. "Thanks for your cooperation, Dr. Lindstrom. I'm sure I'll be talking to you again."

"For God's sake!" Dave burst out. "You can't really suspect me of doing these things. Whatever gave you that crazy idea?"

Braden's skeptical brown eyes didn't waver. "We have to look at everything, Doctor. It's routine. We may have a serial killer on this campus of yours. I can't worry about hurting someone's feelings."

He surveyed the organized chaos of Dave's small office, as if it might reveal its occupant's potential as a serial murderer. Then, as if it were an afterthought, he murmured, "Were you in the service, Lindstrom?"

"No," Dave said curtly, adding, "I was fifteen when the Vietnam War ended. I was lucky."

"Ever been to Europe?"

Once again the change of direction left Dave bewildered. "No. We hope to go someday."

"Yeah," Braden said, preparing to leave. "Don't we all?"

*   *   *

"I DON'T BELIEVE it!" Glenda exclaimed.

"He was serious."

"But that's ridiculous! Where did he get such an idea? Just because you had both of those students in your classes . . . my God, are they interviewing all of those girls' teachers?"

"I don't know. He said it was just routine."

Glenda stared at him. She checked the meat loaf in the oven, turned the temperature down and went to the stove to stir the gravy. For the moment she and Dave were alone in the kitchen. She had sensed that something was troubling him the moment he came home. Although he was a quiet man, there were nuances in his silences. She supposed that sensing such moods was part of what being married meant. "But you didn't think it was."

"No," Dave frowned. "The Foster girl . . . she made kind of a play for me."

"And did you play?"

"No," he answered quietly, meeting the inquiry in her eyes. "Never. Not once. Not Edie Foster or anyone else."

"Edie?"

"That's what everyone called her."

"I'm sorry," Glenda said, contrite. She shivered. "That's the way it works, isn't it? That's the way the police think. Someone must have told that detective about Foster liking you, and he immediately put the worst possible twist on it."

"As long as *you* don't," Dave said. "Once he talks to Jim Roget, the whole question becomes moot."

He wasn't quite sure why that prospect was not as reassuring as it should have been.

THE KITCHEN WAS the room Dave and Glenda liked best in their early California house. It was large, bright and spacious, with ample space for the antique harvest table Glenda had found at the antique swap meet in Long Beach five years ago. Long before developers came up with the idea of a "family room," the old-fashioned large kitchen was a gathering place, a debating forum, a place for snacking, doing homework, carrying out projects, playing *Hearts* or *Monopoly*, or sitting quietly over a cup of tea. This kitchen was that kind of room.

On this Thursday night the usual warm family atmosphere was missing. Both parents were preoccupied. Richie ate in silence and picked at his food, even though meat loaf with mashed potatoes and gravy was one of his favorites. Only Elli seemed oblivious of the tension that made the air seem heavy, ready to hum and crackle if someone struck a spark.

Someone did.

Toward the end of the meal Richie put down his knife and fork and stared at his half-eaten dinner. He poked at the last of his meat loaf. The gravy on his plate was getting cold, congealing around some uneaten carrot slices, which sat in the gravy like orange lily pads in a muddy pool. Richie looked up at his parents, who sat across from him at the long table.

"I wanta go see my dad," he blurted out.

His parents stared at him, their expressions frozen. He might as well have shouted "Shit!" at the top of his voice, Richie thought. He was nervous about their reaction, but now that the words were out he was stubbornly determined.

"What's he mean, Daddy?" Elli asked. "I can see you."

"He means . . ." Glenda faltered. "Oh, Richie, you don't know what you're asking."

"He's my dad, isn't he? I mean . . . my real father." Richie avoided Dave Lindstrom's eyes. "He's come back to see me—he said so."

"It's not possible," Glenda whispered. Her face was pale. Even her lips had lost their color.

"Why not? What's wrong with my seeing him? He's been overseas. He's a soldier, it's not his fault he's been gone all this time." His hot eyes accused his mother. "You never talk about him, you never tell me anything about him."

Richie's emotions were in turmoil. He was aware of Elli's wide-eyed wonder, his stepfather's scowl, his mother's stricken eyes. What was so wrong about everything? Why did he suddenly feel as if he couldn't breathe? Why did his heart hammer in its cage like a frantic hamster clawing to get out?

"You heard your mother," Dave said in a grim, uncompromising tone Richie had rarely heard from him. "You can't see him."

"Why not?"

"Richie, please . . . don't shout," his mother pleaded. "Think about what you're saying. We don't even know where your . . . where Ralph Beringer is staying. If he really wanted to see you, all he has to do is tell us where he is and we could talk about it." She paused. "And don't call him your *real* father. Your real father is the man sitting across the table from you, the one who's been there for you all the years while you were growing up, who's loved you and cared for you."

Richie's face burned. He didn't want to hurt his mother or stepfather. He was drawn toward his real father by a fascination he didn't completely understand, a pull as mysterious and powerful as gravity.

"You don't care about me!" he cried. "You hate him! You've always hated him."

"That's enough, Richie!" Dave said sharply.

"I'm gonna see him—" Richie choked up. He had almost let it slip out—that he knew where his father was staying. "You can't stop me!"

"Oh my God," his mother whispered.

"Now you listen to me," Dave said. "What you're feeling right now is natural. Maybe it's even the way you should feel—but not with the way your . . . your father has been acting. He's been following you and Elli behind your mother's back . . . making phone calls that have scared and upset her. He's playing nasty tricks with us, Richie, and as long as he keeps that up there will be no father–son meetings, is that clear? If he wants to start *acting* like a real father, then we'll see. But not until then. It's all up to . . . Are you listening to me, Richie?"

Richie clambered off the bench seat so hastily that his leg

jarred the table, upsetting a glass of water. He saw his mother reach for the glass too late. Elli gasped aloud. The confusion and anxiety that had been building within him swelled into a bubble that burst, spilling across the table like the water from the overturned glass. "I *will* see him! You can't stop me! It's not right—you're not my father! It's not right!"

"Richie!"

The boy raced from the kitchen, escaping his mother's anguished cry, fleeing from the awful sense that his life had changed forever in these past few minutes, that nothing would ever be the same again.

In his room he slammed the door and threw himself on his bed. He lay on his stomach, his body wrenched by sobs.

IN THE KITCHEN the silence was so complete that Dave could hear the kettle gurgling even though Glenda had turned it off moments earlier. Elli watched her parents with exaggerated curiosity.

"Why don't you go in and watch TV, honey," Glenda told her.

"I aweady watched an hour before dinner."

"That's all right, you can have an extra half hour tonight, okay? Go on."

When they were alone, Glenda said, "When was the last time you heard Elli complain about watching too much TV?"

"The show's better in here."

"You only said what you had to, Dave."

"Did I? I'm not sure. I mean, doesn't Richie have a right to see his father if he wants to? Do I have the right to tell him he can't?"

"Dammit, *you're* his father!"

"I guess not in his eyes, not now."

"Well, I'm his mother," Glenda retorted, "and I can say whether or not Ralph can come crashing back into our lives like this, harassing and intimidating us. You were dead right in what you said. Until Ralph stops playing nasty head games, any meeting is off limits. Period." She paused, white lines around her mouth. "I don't want him anywhere near Richie."

"Is there anything else you haven't told me?"

"I've told you enough."

The grim silence returned to the big warm kitchen. Ralph was accomplishing just what he had set out to do, Glenda thought. Turning us inside out. Playing on Richie's confusion. Making us jump at our own shadows. And Dave certainly didn't need this anxiety on top of what was happening in the college community. The idea that the homicide detective who had questioned Dave actually might suspect him of murder outraged her. He was the last man on earth who would harm those young women—it was absurd! The police didn't have time to listen to complaints about a real psychopath, but they had time to hassle a decent, caring man like Dave.

Glenda felt the world shift somehow. She had caught a glimpse of something so terrible as to be unimaginable, as if the monstrous terror that gripped San Carlos was psychically linked to her family's private horror. The perception—gone as quickly as it came—was like the first seconds of an earthquake, the ground moving beneath her feet, the sense of disorientation, the subliminal awareness of hovering at the edge of something unknown and unfathomable, over which she had no control. She could only wait helplessly for whatever was going to overtake her . . .

"What's wrong, honey?" Dave's voice, calling her back from the abyss.

"I . . . I don't know. Something . . . My God, Dave, what's happening to us? What did we do wrong?"

Twenty-Seven

THE HARASSMENT COMPLAINT made by the Lindstroms on Monday was still on Linda Perez's desk Friday morning. It didn't have a very high priority. After all, the woman's ex hadn't actually done anything illegal or harmful, and there had been no further complaints during the week. Glenda Lindstrom hadn't acted like your typical hysterical woman, Linda thought, but it wouldn't be the first time in her experience that a complainant conjured up some high drama to grab attention. Maybe the present husband was straying. Who knew?

Meanwhile, since Monday, Linda had had two new cases of spousal battery, supported by trips to Our Little Company of Mary Hospital, that she had to follow up on. Thank God the district attorney's office wasn't brushing these cases aside the way they used to.

Linda managed to complete a report later that morning on the Lindstrom complaint. A waste of time, another contribution to the mountain of paperwork that was part of the Job, but what else was new?

She had just dropped it into the Outgoing bin on the right corner of her desk when the FBI woman entered the squad room, who nodded pleasantly at Linda as she passed by, heading for Braden's corner.

Braden was on his feet. For Chrissake, was he going to hold her chair? No, Linda observed, but from her point of view what happened next was just as bad. Braden glanced at Captain Hummel's office, saw that it was empty, and led the Feeb into the office, closing the door behind them.

Linda Perez tried to observe them without staring. What was going on with those two? she wondered.

All work and no play?

"I READ YOUR report on Lindstrom," Karen Younger said.

"And?"

"Interesting."

"So did you run him through the Bureau's computers?"

"Of course I ran him. And got just what I expected. Nothing. He was never in Germany or the service, just as he told you. As far as I could learn, he's never even had a speeding ticket."

Braden stared out of the captain's fishbowl. He saw Linda Perez glance toward him, then look away quickly. He said, "It's Friday. Our guy's been out hunting the last two Fridays. Do you suppose he has a thing about the end of the week?"

"Maybe it has something to do with his normal schedule—his work schedule, for instance."

"Instead of getting drunk Friday night, he rapes and kills a woman. Was the German girl killed on a Friday?"

Karen frowned, her gaze suddenly distant. "No, it was a Saturday night. I remember, because I was called out Sunday morning after the girl was found."

Braden didn't know whether to be relieved or concerned. If Friday was significant, and the killer struck again, the media frenzy would make the last two weeks seem like a pep rally. "You talk to your bosses back in D.C.?" he asked.

The FBI agent hesitated briefly. "I talked to Buddy Cochrane—my boss—about what your captain said about bringing in an FBI task force. They want to help, Braden. They're not trying to ace you out."

"Uh-huh. You working for them or for us now?"

"I'm assigned here as a consultant for you and your people. If special agents ask me anything, I'll tell them. We're not competing, Detective—we're all after the same thing."

Braden turned away from the glass wall, putting his back to the squad room. The agent looked a little flustered, he thought, as if she herself realized that her assertion the FBI wasn't trying to take over the case was weak.

"What's your worst possible scenario?" he asked.

"The worst possible?" She considered the question seriously. "The worst is . . . he doesn't hit again. Not here. He moves on and disappears."

"And?"

"Six months from now, a year, three years, who knows? He's in St. Louis or Miami . . . he starts again."

They both brooded on this possibility, which Braden knew was not put out casually. The FBI had studied hundreds of serial killers. Karen Younger would know that some of them did exactly what she had suggested.

After a moment Braden said, "I don't think he's going anywhere. And I don't think he's the same guy you have in your files from eight years ago."

"You said that before. Where's it taking us now?"

"To David Lindstrom." When she started to shake her head in denial Braden pressed ahead, using his thumb to tick off his reasons against the tips of his fingers. "Sheri Kuttner pointed us at him—you did a good job getting her to open up. He wasn't in Germany, but he's the first real link between the two San Carlos victims. Both were his students. Sheri thought Edie was having a fling with Lindstrom. Maybe Natalie was next in line. Maybe he's one of those professors who has a new favorite each semester."

"So why does he suddenly start killing them?"

Braden shrugged. "Edie pushed too hard. We don't really have to know why or how. She didn't like being dumped for the new girl? Or it could have been the other way around, and she was brushing *him* off. Either way, they quarreled, he lost his temper and hit her. Then it got out of hand."

"He was packing weights in his fist when he hit her," Karen

pointed out. "Does that sound like a crime of passion to you, or something premeditated?"

"We're just guessing why he did it," Braden admitted. "But if she had threatened him in some way, that would explain it. He was vulnerable, a professor breaking the rules. Also, he's a married man, kids . . . he panicked."

"And Rothleder?"

"She knew about Foster," Braden said slowly, liking the sound of it.

Karen Younger shook her head emphatically. "You've got nothing but guesses, Detective. And Lindstrom doesn't fit the profile."

"The profile—"

"—isn't all bullshit. It's fact, Braden. From what I've learned, David Lindstrom is easygoing, affable, decent, well-liked. Nothing in his background points toward instability. Also, he's not physical enough."

"He's in good shape," Braden argued. "Jogs regularly. Fights fires in his spare time."

"The man we're looking for grew up a bully and he's still a bully. He's seething inside. He could never play a mild-mannered professor for as long as Lindstrom has."

"I'm not finished," Braden said stubbornly. "Lindstrom is a volunteer firefighter. He was on duty on the fire lines the Friday night Edie Foster was kidnapped, but he and his crew were given a few hours off to go home, grab a hot meal and a few hours sleep. They were supposed to be back on duty at midnight. Trouble is, there was so much confusion on the lines that night nobody can remember whether all the volunteers came back or what time."

Braden paused, reading the skepticism in the FBI agent's eyes. Trying not to stare too obviously at the way her teal green cashmere sweater molded her breasts. It seemed to him that Younger's edges had visibly softened since she had arrived in San Carlos, reflected in the way she dressed. Maybe it was getting away from Quantico, he thought, all those starched shirts and ties inside, all those Marines drilling outside . . .

"The absence of someone like Lindstrom could easily have

gone unnoticed. He could've grabbed Edie, kept her until it was getting light, then dumped her and showed up back on the fire lines, with no one able to say for sure he wasn't there all along."

"Someone would know. He mentioned a crew boss."

"Yeah. Supposedly he worked with this Navajo Indian all night. Trouble is, the Indian can't be found. He's from the reservation over there in Arizona. He took off last week for the back country, some religious thing. No one knows where he is or when he'll be back."

"All you have is speculation, Braden. Our killer is more careful than the man you just described. He also had to be in a position to follow Foster that night after she left the coffee shop."

"Unless he gave her a call, said honey I'm free, meet me at the regular place by the Alpha Beta."

"If this is all you've got . . ."

"There's more. The night Natalie Rothleder was killed, Lindstrom had an evening class, seven to nine. It let out a little early . . . about a quarter to nine." Braden offered her a thin smile. "Time and opportunity."

Karen Younger didn't hesitate. "He's your suspect, Braden. Not mine."

"You're pretty damned sure of yourself," Braden said testily. "What do you need us ordinary cops for?"

"Because I'm gonna catch the son of a bitch, Detective. And when I do, I don't want to be alone."

3RD ANNUAL SAN CARLOS Powwow, the poster read. Fri. 7–9 PM, Sat. & Sun. 11–8. Native American Dancers, Gifts & Crafts.

Staring at the poster taped to the coffee shop window, Ralph Beringer felt the hand of fate like a warm, caressing touch, guiding him unerringly. Not like a mother's hand—not for him. For Beringer that had been a thin, bony hand, one moment hot and demanding, the next cracking across his face or biting into the flesh of his arm with fingers like claws, always accompanied by the lacerating voice that peeled away his feeble child's defenses and left him exposed, trembling with fear.

He didn't know exactly what a powwow was, but it wasn't hard to figure. There would be Indian dances, booths hawking beads and turquoise jewelry and T-shirts, other vendors selling squaw bread, hot dogs and hamburgers. And there would be lots of students coming and going, or milling around in the darkness away from the action . . .

Including Nancy Showalter, with that healthy spill of dark red hair and the long legs and the big wet mouth . . .

Her boyfriend, too, but Beringer wasn't worried about him.

After learning the girl's name, he had discovered that Nancy lived in one of the on-campus dormitories. While that put her, for the moment, out of his reach, buffered by student patrols and a heightened security officer presence, the Friday night powwow on campus did not merely open a crack in that security, it threw the door wide open. Nancy would be there, and no one would question Beringer's presence. He would be invisible, just one of the crowd.

He could feel the drumbeat in his blood, like distant Indian drums the night before a battle, filling the air with promise.

Twenty-Eight

THAT SAME FRIDAY morning, after dropping Elli off at school and driving to the bookstore where she worked part-time, Glenda Lindstrom had asked Richard Alvarez, the store manager, if she could leave an hour early. Since she was always on time for work and accomplished as much on her short shift as many of his full-time employees managed in a day, Alvarez readily agreed. "Is everything okay?" he asked.

"Sure, fine . . . why?"

"Well, you've been looking . . . I don't know . . . worried."

Her smile was too bright. "When did you meet a mother who wasn't a worrier?"

Normally she worked from nine to twelve, coming in an hour before the store opened and leaving in time to pick Elli up at school at twelve-thirty. The three hours gave Glenda time to complete her daily bookkeeping and to update a running stock inventory—a task she had volunteered for when she saw the need.

She left the store at five minutes past eleven. After the previous incident at the school, under no circumstances would she be late, but she had more than an hour to spare.

Full Bore, the gun store whose newspaper ads she had often seen, was on the west side of town. She had always disapproved of gun stores in general. There were far too many weapons on the streets without encouraging the sale of more. The National Rifle Association's strident arguments about the right to own automatic assault weapons to shoot ducks or defend their homes against Communist hordes had always offended her with their blatant hypocrisy.

Who's being hypocritical now? she asked herself as she parked the station wagon outside the shop. She glanced around with a vague feeling of guilt, thinking of Dave. He felt even more strongly about guns than she did. She knew what he would have said if she had told him she wanted a gun to protect Elli and Richie. *"You can't really believe he means them any harm."*

Well-meaning people like Dave didn't want to believe there were real monsters in enlightened America at the end of the twentieth century. In the movies he watched, Dave readily accepted Freddy Krueger and Frankenstein's monster, wolfmen, vampires, even a Hannibal Lector, but offscreen he preferred not to recognize the existence of parents who dumped children in trash cans, men who brutalized their wives out of plain meanness, monsters who drank human blood and cannibalized their victims. Like this serial killer in San Carlos, she thought, though the police were cautiously refusing to label him as such.

A bell over the door rang when she stepped inside. She was immediately struck by the strong smells of oil and metal and leather. Everywhere she looked were guns, knives, holsters and accessories, bows and arrows. Racks of rifles and shotguns filled one whole end of the store. Handguns were displayed in glass cases under the long main counter. The salesman, a man in his sixties with thinning white hair combed straight back over a pink scalp pocked with incipient skin cancers, beamed at her. "Mornin', ma'am, what can I do for you?"

He reminded her of her grandfather. They would have had a lot to talk about, she supposed. Her grandfather, who had lived near Rhinelander, Wisconsin, had hunted pheasant and ducks and deer in their seasons. In Wisconsin, hunting was a way of life.

Her father had taught each of his girls to shoot, using a 9mm Beretta automatic. When she asked to see a similar weapon, the black handgun the salesman produced felt heavier than she remembered. It was also larger. How could she carry such a gun around without being obvious?

"It's a fine choice," the grandfatherly salesman assured her. "If you can handle it, that is. The slide mechanism needs a firm, hard pull. Some women have trouble with it, but you look to me like you got strong hands."

He showed her two similar guns, a Walther PPK/S 9mm, whose sleek design lived up to its quality reputation, and a Glock 17, a semiautomatic with a very smooth action and plastic grips that made the weapon lighter. She went back to the familiar feel of the Beretta. She had a large black leather purse she rarely carried. It was roomy enough to hide the Beretta.

When she tried to purchase the gun, however, she was reminded of the two-week waiting period. All handguns had to be registered and a permit had to be issued.

"Oh . . . I forgot." Her disappointment was transparent.

"There's no waitin' on a hunting rifle . . . or a shotgun, if you can handle one."

"I'm sorry, I . . ."

The elderly man studied her, reading her anxiety. Did he also see the fault line? Was it that obvious?

"You all right, lady?" He gave a soft chuckle. "Who was you figgerin' to shoot? Havin' a little trouble at home?"

"No," Glenda said quickly. Then she added, "I just want to protect my children."

The salesman stared at her. He walked away a short distance, peering toward the back of the store, where Glenda glimpsed a man at a desk talking on the phone. Returning, the balding old man spoke in a low voice, his manner conspiratorial. "I prob'ly shouldn't be doin' this, but you look like a decent woman wouldn't do nothin' foolish. If you really can't wait, I know someone you can talk to might be able to help."

He scribbled an address on a notepad and tore off the sheet, which he folded carefully before handing it to her. "I'll give him a call, let him know you're comin'."

"How far is it? I don't have much time . . ."

"Hey, it's four, five blocks. Off the highway, maybe you've seen it? Ed's Garage? And listen, ma'am . . . you take care."

"Yes . . . yes, thank you." She wanted to get out quickly, to escape the smells and the arsenal of death and the sharp scrutiny of the old eyes that surely saw through her motives and found her guilt. "Ed's Garage . . ."

"You can't miss it. And you come back now, y'hear?"

Eᴅ's Gᴀʀᴀɢᴇ ʜᴀᴅ a half-dozen older cars parked outside and two up on racks inside the service area of what had once been a working gas station and was now that rarity, an old-fashioned auto repair shop. One mechanic was down in a pit servicing a Ford LTD that reminded Glenda of the one they had traded in on the used Dodge wagon three years ago. A second man, Ed Portis, was the one whose name was on Glenda's scribbled note. He came toward her wiping his hands on a rag, glanced at the note and without a word led her out back of the garage. He unlocked a storage room and stepped inside, pulling the chain on a bare overhead bulb. When Glenda hesitated he gestured impatiently. The space she entered was not much bigger than a walk-in closet.

Without preamble Ed Portis unlocked a metal storage cabinet about the size of a school locker. "You want something small, not too heavy, that will do the job, am I right?"

"Yes . . ."

"You prob'ly been lookin' at automatics, am I right? This here's a revolver. Smith & Wesson .38 Special, two-inch barrel. It's the kind of gun cops use today as a hideout or backup, now they've stepped up to .44's and .45's to try to keep up with the bad guys. It's double-action, you just squeeze the trigger. Easy to use. There's some recoil you don't get with an automatic, but not too bad."

The six-shooter had a polished steel frame and barrel with wooden grips. It felt businesslike in her hand. And it was lighter and more compact than the 9mm automatics she had been shown.

"It's very nice," she said, cringing a little inside.

"But you'd like to see something else, am I right?"

He took the Smith & Wesson from her, returned it to the locker and produced a small stainless-steel automatic that was almost lost in his large hand. "This here's an AMT .380 Kurz Backup.

Made right here in Orange County. This one's used, but it's never been registered," Ed explained mysteriously. "Not as fancy as some, but it'll do the job. Uses these plastic-tipped short 9mm bullets."

"They look small," Glenda said, more for something to say than because she was concerned about the size of the bullets.

"Hey, I saw a demo with these little babies. Fired through a steel filing cabinet with a watermelon inside. Made a hole the same size goin' in on one side and comin' out the other. But the watermelon was spread over the inside of that cabinet like a spray paint. It's that little plastic tip there, it expands like a flower."

"I see," Glenda said weakly. But she knew the gun was what she had been looking for. It was very compact. It would fit easily into her purse. And it was not a toy.

"You want a gun small enough to carry and still have stopping power," the mechanic said, seeing the answer in her eyes. "At two hundred fifty bucks it's a bargain."

She wondered what Ed thought she wanted to stop with the gun.

It didn't seem to matter.

FROM THE GARAGE she drove directly to Elli's school, arriving ten minutes before Elli bounded out of the building. They stopped at a McDonald's for lunch, an indulgence Glenda agreed to only occasionally. Then they drove home to wait for Richie. These days Glenda didn't relax until both of her children were safe at home. Richie's behavior the night before increased her tension as she waited. She tried to keep busy by helping Elli with some finger painting at the kitchen table.

At three o'clock she went out on the porch. The sun was in her eyes as she gazed up the street. When the yellow school bus pulled around a corner and stopped she felt her pulse quicken.

One boy hopped down off the bus, turning to wave at someone inside. Then the bus pulled away.

Glenda stared up the street in disbelief. Richie wasn't there.

＊   ＊   ＊

He PROWLED THE mall until it was dark. Sat in the Food Court for a while, nursing a Slurpy and watching people eat all around him. He began to feel hungry. He left the area and, with the late afternoon crowds thinning out, walked to the end of the mall and stepped outside. Beyond the intervening hills the sun was setting out over the ocean, the horizon a wide canvas across which a careless painter had spilled buckets of pink and orange and lavender.

Returning to the mall, Richie killed another half hour in the Radio Shack store. The next time he emerged the sky was gray with only a narrow ribbon of red at its western fringe. At this time of the year twilight was brief, and by the time Richie made his way along San Anselmo Drive the shadows were already deepening between the buildings and in the thick foliage in front of many of the older units.

Apartment 110 at Vista Valencia was a front unit with a walled patio protected by established evergreens nearly as high as the wall and a mass of bougainvillea that spilled across one end. Numbered tiles mounted in a wooden frame beside the door identified the apartment, whose entrance was just beyond the locked gate, on the left side of an entry passageway to an inner courtyard. From the street Richie could see sliding glass doors leading from the apartment to the patio.

There was no light inside.

Richie stood irresolute on the sidewalk. He had counted on his father being there. A woman walking a small white dog on a leash glanced at him curiously as she passed, pulling on the dog's leash as it tried to sniff Richie's feet.

Slowly he approached the front of the apartment building. When he was within the shadows of the entry he looked back over his shoulder. The shrubbery around the front patio screened him from the woman walking her dog. After a moment's hesitation Richie slipped behind the evergreen bushes, crouching below branches that raked at his face. At the far end of the short wall the thicket of bougainvillea loomed. Richie knew better than to try to climb there—the bougainvillea over one end of the porch at home had sharp thorns—but the dense growth prevented anyone seeing him from that direction.

In the few minutes he had been there the shadows had thickened. He peered through the shrubbery toward the street. A car drifted by, but no one was in sight along the sidewalk.

Until that moment he had not been certain what he meant to do. Now he turned to study the stucco wall surrounding the small patio. It was less than six feet high. He was able to place both hands on top of the wall and, with a little jump, he planted his elbows over the top. The first time he tried to swing one leg up he lost his grip and fell back. He crouched behind the bushes, waiting for an outcry that would mean someone had seen or heard him. All he heard was a thin burst of laughter from a television set nearby.

On the next attempt Richie got his arms and one leg over the top of the wall. He perched there for an instant, struggling to keep his balance, then spilled over the wall and dropped inside.

He crouched in the darkness on all fours, his heart thudding. The patio, about twelve feet wide and five feet deep, contained several hanging plants badly in need of water. There was a webbed chaise and two white plastic chairs flanking a small matching table. Less than five feet away, a sliding glass wall faced the living room of the apartment.

As Richie tried to peer into the room, a light went on.

Twenty-Nine

"THEY'RE ON INDIAN time," someone joked.

Ralph Beringer didn't laugh. By eight o'clock—two hours after the powwow was supposed to have started—nothing much had happened. The Indians didn't seem to mind. He had seen several of them in the parking lot when he arrived at six, donning their dancers' regalia. More than an hour passed before the first of the dancers showed up at the arena.

The centerpiece of the powwow was a roughly circular arena in one of the college's open grass quadrangles. Chairs and shaded covers for the Native American participants surrounded the area, with many spectators bringing their own chairs, standing, or sitting on blankets on the grass. In the center of the arena a smaller circle of Native American drummers were grouped around a large drum. They had started singing to the beat of the drum about seven o'clock and had kept it up for the next hour in what was called the Gourd Song. A few dancers had drifted into the arena, men and women wearing traditional outfits, shuffling to the drumbeat while they kept time with gourd or metal shakers decorated with beads and feathers. Beringer had quickly found the chanting monotonous. It followed him remorselessly as he mingled with the crowds, young and old, that thronged the aisles fanning out from the arena. Here vendors had set up their stalls displaying bead and turquoise jewelry, T-shirts, pottery, baseball caps and other souvenirs. Beringer hoped to find Nancy Showalter among these stalls, joining all the other college girls teasing their boyfriends into buying them a trinket.

Over a loudspeaker he heard the master of ceremonies calling. "First call for the Grand Entry! Dancers, get ready . . ."

First call, Beringer thought, reflecting more disgust than impatience. That probably meant a few more dancers would straggle into the arena in thirty minutes or so. *Indian time . . .*

Two hours prowling and no sign of Nancy. Had she changed her mind about the powwow?

He stopped at a stall that sold Indian fry bread, dusted with powdered sugar and sweetened with honey. Beringer studied the crowds while he tore off pieces of the bread, which was surprisingly delicious. A man with a thick neck, hard eyes and a beer belly pushed past him. Nearby, a younger man with a buzz haircut moved along another aisle with the same alert air and roving gaze, hardly glancing at the goods on display. Both were plainclothes cops, Beringer thought.

He had expected them.

When he returned to the arena there was increased activity. The gourd dancers were finally finishing their last set, the drumming and chanting livelier than before. It built to a climax and stopped abruptly. Over the loudspeaker the announcer called out, "Dancers, get ready for the Grand Entry!"

Finally, Beringer thought, the real show was getting under way. Maybe that was what Nancy and her friends had been waiting for. Maybe they knew about Indian time.

The Grand Entry began with three groups of singer-drummers spaced around the arena. Slowly the circle filled with dancers, dressed in all manner of colorful shawls and scarves, feather headdresses and hair roaches, beaded shirts and leggings and moccasins. Some of the male dancers were as handsome as warriors in old paintings, and the women, especially the younger ones, were stunning. As the dancers slowly circled the arena, passing before Beringer, his eye was drawn to a slender girl in a white deerskin dress, fringed and decorated with elaborate beadwork. Her long, glossy black hair had been plaited into two braids, adorned with silver conches. She had a pretty face with small features and the black eyes of a fawn. She moved, like all of the female dancers, with remarkable grace to the beat of the drums, her moccasined feet hardly seeming to move while her slender figure rose and fell in perfect rhythm to the dance.

Beringer felt a familiar heat.

Crazy even to think about it. An Indian maiden was not part of the plan. Besides, the chances of her name being right for his purpose were slim to none. And it would be difficult to get her alone. Many of the Indians seemed to have come to the powwow in large family groups.

The announcer was explaining the meaning of the powwow as the dancers filled the arena, how it celebrated the gathering of friends and relatives, celebrated their traditions and customs and heritage as a people. "It is a time when we greet all of our brothers, the Sioux and the Cheyenne, the Kiowa and Omaha, the Navajo and Apache, Choctaw and Osage, in peace and love . . ."

Beringer stopped listening.

Across the arena, beyond the Indian girl in the white deerskin dress, Nancy had arrived. She stood several inches taller than her friend Mark, who stood beside her. She was wearing a short black skirt over a skin-hugging black body stocking—everything on parade, Beringer thought. She watched the dancers with animated delight, talking and gesturing.

Though agitated, Beringer did not move. He couldn't follow Nancy around, at least not closely. The beady-eyed cops and security guards would be alert for any solitary man stalking a young woman. He would simply have to wait.

She was his. She would not have been brought to his attention otherwise. Beringer, who had no faith, had come to believe in his destiny.

DAVE LINDSTROM CRUISED past the campus around eight-thirty, saw the crowds and a sign that read, POWWOW PARKING, with an arrow pointing toward one of the campus parking lots.

Dave remembered talking about the tribal gathering earlier that week at the dinner table, contemplating a family outing this Saturday. Would Richie have come here on his own? Angry over

the quarrel about his father, might he have sought out crowds and
activity?

Parking in the designated lot, Dave wandered along aisles of
stalls to the main arena. An elderly, dignified Native American was
giving an invocation, talking about Mother Earth, turning cere-
moniously to face all four directions as he acknowledged the rev-
erence his people had for the natural elements of life. The arena
was crowded with Indians in colorful dress. Dave wished he could
stay longer. He wished the family outing he had planned had
brought him here, not his frustrated, aimless search for his missing
son.

Walking slowly along the aisles past tented stalls, he replayed
the scene at the dinner table the night before. Could he have handled it better? Had he let Richie down in some way he had not
recognized or understood? Or was Glenda right in thinking that
Ralph Beringer was manipulating all of them, including Richie?

The futility of wandering the aisles overcame him. He turned
abruptly between two stalls, cut across another aisle and escaped
from the area. A shortcut between nearby buildings took him to
the back of the parking lot where he had left his car.

Moments later he was back on the streets of the city, asking
himself where Richie might have gone. Where did the boy plan to
spend the night? Was he with his father? Anger mixed with Dave's
frustration. Dammit, Richie knew how his mother would worry if
he stayed out all night? Was this his way of punishing her? Punishing both of them?

The mall, he thought. Richie was old enough to enjoy wandering along the mall, looking in display windows or exploring some
of the shops. It was worth a shot anyway. Dave couldn't think of
anything better.

He was running out of ideas. Reluctant to abandon the search,
he was also convinced that he shouldn't leave Glenda alone much
longer.

Most of the mall stores, he remembered, closed at nine. Soon
after that a ten-year-old boy on his own would catch the attention
of mall security officers. Grasping the possibility with a feeling that
he recognized as desperation, Dave headed for the north end of

town and the huge shopping complex that had come to dominate the lives of so many San Carlos citizens.

"WHAT THE HELL do you mean, you lost him?" Braden shouted into the phone.

"Well, uh . . . he was just browsing these stalls, that's all. I took my eye off him for a coupla seconds and he was gone." Deputy Pritkin spoke in the tone of one who would rather have faced a firing squad than make his report.

"How long since you missed him?"

"Ten—fifteen minutes or so. Uh . . . do you think he spotted me?"

"If he did, that means he deliberately gave you the slip." It seemed unlikely, Braden thought. Pritkin had been drafted into plainclothes for the assignment, but even if Lindstrom had recognized him as a cop, the professor would have had no reason to duck him . . . unless he had something to hide. "What about his ride? Did you check it?"

"Yeah. I mean, that's where I am now—in the parking lot. His car's gone."

Braden swore. What was Lindstrom doing roaming the streets alone at night? If he didn't have a class to teach, why wasn't he home with his family?

"You want me to keep looking for him, sir?"

Christ almighty, Braden thought. *Sir.*

"He's probably on his way home," he told the deputy. "Go and see. If his car isn't there, wait for him. I want to know when he gets home."

BERINGER'S MOMENT CAME unexpectedly two hours after the Grand Entry began in the lengthy powwow. A long session of intertribal dances was ending. His attention was distracted by another slim Indian girl in a jingle dress—her entire skirt was covered with silver baubles that jingled as she danced—when he noticed that Nancy was missing from her vantage point on the far side of the arena. The boyfriend was still there, Beringer saw with relief, but where was the girl?

He walked around the arena, forcing himself not to hurry. On impulse he took the aisle nearest to where Nancy had been sitting on the grass in her skintight outfit, like a whore on a picnic. As he walked between two ranks of facing stalls, Beringer took off his glasses and polished the lenses with the soft linen handkerchief he always carried. Business for the vendors was much lighter than it had been earlier in the evening. One seller was even putting some of his jewelry away, ready to shut down. Beringer felt the first twinge of panic. Surely the powwow still had a couple hours to go. Nancy wouldn't be bailing out this soon. Where—?

Then he saw her.

At the end of the aisle in which Beringer stood, Nancy Showalter paused to look around her. Apparently spotting what she was searching for, she started off purposefully to her right. By the time Beringer reached the end of the aisle, still compelling himself to stroll like a man with nothing on his mind, the tall girl was thirty yards off to his right, near the end of the quadrangle. There, beyond a screen of trees, Beringer saw what she was heading for: a row of portable privies set up to accommodate the needs of the powwow crowds.

Beringer no longer worried about suspicious eyes as he ambled toward the line of privies. What could be more natural and innocent?

Nancy had disappeared into the last cubicle in the row. As he neared it Beringer stopped, casually taking his time as he lit a cigarette. Exhaling, he glanced over his shoulder. A man in jeans and a cowboy hat was hurrying toward one of the privies, too preoccupied to look around. The expanse of lawn was surprisingly deserted.

He heard the rattle of the latch on the end privy as Nancy fumbled with the door. When she stepped out her eyes widened a little as she saw him standing there.

"Miss Showalter? I'm sorry, there's been an accident."

"What? What do you mean?"

"You'll have to come with me." He took her by the arm and started walking briskly, leading her behind the row of privies toward the nearby academic buildings.

"Is it . . . is it Mark? Has something happened?"

"No, your friend is fine." Beringer smiled reassuringly at her, still walking quickly, forcing her to break into a trot to keep up, not giving her time to think.

"I don't understand. Who . . . what—?" He felt the first tug of resistance.

Beringer pulled her into a shadowed lane between two buildings. Suddenly they were cut off from the crowded arena and the busy aisles of stalls. They were isolated, out of sight. One of Beringer's hands bit into the soft flesh of Nancy's arm. The other flicked open the blade of his Swiss knife. He held it close to the cringing girl's face, moving it slowly back and forth as her eyes followed it. The blade seemed to catch all of the light in the dark passageway.

"I don't want to have to cut you," Beringer said with terrifying calm. "We're gonna walk out of here to my car. Be a good girl, don't make me cut that pretty face."

"Please," she whimpered, "don't hurt me."

When he pulled her by the arm, she didn't resist. "Why would I want to hurt you?" he said. "This isn't about hurting you, don't you know that? This is about . . . love."

Among the cars in the parking lot, stumbling through the shadows, Nancy whispered, as if clinging to a last forlorn hope, "Was there really an accident?"

Beringer didn't answer.

Thirty

RICHIE HAD DOZED off. When he woke, stiff and cold, he was momentarily disoriented. He lay curled up on a plastic webbed chaise in a tiny enclosed patio. He sat up in alarm. Staring through a sliding glass door into a strange living room, he suddenly remembered lights coming on inside—remembered being scared. But no one had appeared, and he had figured out that a lamp in the living room and another in a bedroom were on automatic timers, set to turn on at a designated hour or when it became dark, creating the illusion that someone was at home.

He was at his father's place. How long had he been asleep? Richie didn't have a watch and he could not see a clock in the living room of the apartment. Had to be at least ten o'clock, he decided, maybe later. He was chilled and very hungry. Should have worn a sweatshirt or something warmer. He hadn't expected to spend the night outside in the cold.

Everything had seemed so simple, really. His father had obviously come to San Carlos to see him. Well, if he wouldn't come around to the house, Richie had to go find him.

He was suddenly seized with excitement. There was movement inside the apartment—someone was there. Richie saw the shadow of a man before the figure appeared, entering the living room from a small foyer. A tall, powerfully built man in jeans and a denim shirt crossed the room quickly, not glancing around, and disappeared down a hallway. Another light flared—the bathroom, Richie guessed.

His heart raced. The brief glimpse had been enough for him

to recognize Ralph Beringer, the soldier in the photograph he carried in his wallet. His father.

Black gloves, Richie thought. Their image stuck in his mind, probably because it was so unusual to see someone wearing gloves in warm weather. Maybe they were driving gloves.

Easing off the chaise, he moved into the shadows to the left of the sliding glass doors, suddenly apprehensive of his father's reaction, less certain of his reasons for being here.

Minutes ticked by. He wondered if he should knock on the glass door. He wondered if he should have come here at all against his mother's wishes. What had seemed so clear-cut earlier was now murky, an emotional tangle. He didn't want—

An arm shot into view. A hand slapped at the latch of the sliding door. The door skidded to the side, rumbling in its track. Richie stumbled backward, his heart in his throat. The big man grabbed his shirtfront, slamming him against the block wall of the patio. "What the hell do you think you're doing? Who—?"

Ralph Beringer's angry challenge broke off. He stared at the boy he had pinned against the wall. His grip loosened. "Shit, it's you!" he said.

"I . . . I'm Richie."

"Well, I'll be damned!"

His father stared down at him for a long moment in silence. Then, to Richie's surprise and intense relief, he began to laugh.

"How did you find me?" Ralph Beringer asked curiously after they were inside the apartment.

"I saw you following my school bus. I saw you a couple times, you were driving the Buick. Then I saw you turn off on this street, San Anselmo Drive, so that's where I came looking for you."

"You were looking for me?"

Richie nodded.

"That still doesn't tell me how you found this apartment." Beringer was frowning now.

"I didn't at first. It was just luck I saw you. It was yesterday afternoon, you were just leaving. I was up the street and I saw you drive out of the garage. I shouted but you didn't hear me."

"So how did you—?"

"I came back today after school. I knew where you drove out, so I snuck into the garage when somebody opened the gate. I was looking for the LeSabre but I saw your other car."

Beringer reacted sharply. "My other car?"

"Yeah, the Taurus." Richie grinned. "I'm really good with cars. You were driving the Taurus the first time I saw you. You followed us to the beach Sunday a week ago, didn't you?"

"Pretty smart kid," his father said, but he didn't sound very happy that Richie had seen him in two different cars.

They talked for a long time. Once he got started Richie couldn't stop talking. Beringer asked him a great many questions about his mom and Dave and Elli. He seemed to want to know all about them. Talking about them felt awkward, but Beringer did not appear to notice. Frequently, in fact, he seemed to stop listening, as if his mind had suddenly drifted off somewhere else. It was only after they had been together for some time, talking, that Richie realized his father was agitated about something. He couldn't seem to stop moving about the room as they talked. He had two whiskeys, one right after the other, and then a can of beer from the refrigerator.

He pressed Richie closely about his decision to come looking for his father on his own. Was he certain that no one else knew? He hadn't told anyone where he was going?

Finally—the digital clock on the VCR showed that it was after 11:00 P.M.—Richie asked tentatively if there was anything to eat in the fridge.

His father stared at him. "You're hungry?" he asked, as if the idea had never occurred to him.

"Uh, yeah . . . and I need to use the bathroom. I was waiting out there on the patio for hours."

Beringer went down the hallway ahead of Richie and peered into the bathroom. Then he stepped aside and nodded. "Go ahead, kid. And make it snappy. We'll go get a hamburger."

Oddly self-conscious, Richie closed the door before he let loose the flood he had been holding back. While he stood there, tremendously relieved, he glanced around the bright, blue-tiled room. It was just a bathroom, nothing special. The only thing different about it was the absence of a window. A vent fan went on when a switch next to the light switch was flipped.

When he washed his hands Richie noticed that the blue porcelain sink wasn't even very clean. There were small spots that looked like rust.

Drying his hands, Richie opened the shower door out of curiosity and peered inside. There was a wet towel on the tile floor in one corner, folded as if wrapped around something. Richie saw an edge of black peeking out of the folds. He thought immediately of the black gloves. Why—?

"Hurry it up, kid!" his father called. "Let's get going."

Richie eased the shower door closed and turned away as his father pushed the bathroom door open. "I'm ready," Richie said, hanging up the towel on which he had dried his hands. He started to ask about what was in the shower but changed his mind. "I could eat a cow," he said.

Beringer chuckled. "Whatever you say. And after that, son . . . I think we'll just give your mom a call so she won't worry."

He smiled, but there was something strange and unsettling about the smile, as if his eyes and his mouth were sending different signals.

GLENDA SLOWLY PUT down the phone. "He's got Richie," she said.

"Beringer? Goddammit, that's kidnapping!"

"A father can't kidnap his own son. Besides, he says Richie came looking for him."

"And you believe him?"

"You heard Richie last night. It doesn't surprise me." Suddenly she buried her face in her hands, her shoulders shaking. "Oh my God . . ."

Her despair welled up, and the tears she had been holding back overflowed. Dave held her in his arms until, gradually, the convulsive shudders tapered off and she was still.

After a while she pushed off and turned away. "I need a tissue. I'm a mess."

"You're not a mess. You couldn't be a mess if you tried."

They went into the den. Elli was asleep upstairs, and the house seemed unnaturally quiet. You almost forgot how much noise two children made in a house, Glenda thought. They sat in silence for several minutes before she said, "It never ends, does it?"

"This will. I promise you."

"You think you've buried the past, but it's always there, waiting for you. It's like you're going in circles. Didn't Einstein say something about time possibly being a circular track, and that opened the possibility of getting on or off at different times?"

"I don't know," Dave said, trying for a light, bantering tone. "I could never figure that guy out."

"You know all those cases you hear about child abuse, about abused children growing up to be abusive parents—or worse? It never stops. What Ralph started when he began beating me . . . it's not over, Dave. It's affected all of us. I was changed, Richie . . . and now you and Elli."

"Take it easy, honey. If he intended to harm Richie in any way, he would hardly have telephoned to let us know Richie's with him."

"Wouldn't he?"

"It would make no sense."

Glenda was not reassured. She looked away. The backyard was dark and she saw her face reflected in the window. Over the past two weeks, since Ralph's return, she had lost weight. The hollows of her cheeks and under her eyes were more pronounced. Ironically, the shadowed features made her familiar face, which she did not regard as beautiful in any way, more interesting, giving it a haunted quality. She looked a little like one of Dave's favorite actresses from the forties, the one who played Laura. Gene Tierney, she thought, in a blond wig, staring back at her.

Dave said, "What Beringer is doing will count against him

when it comes to custody, let's not forget that. It's irrational and irresponsible."

Dave still didn't get it, Glenda thought. This wasn't about custody. Ralph didn't want to be saddled with a ten-year-old. Richie would drive him crazy in a week. This was about revenge. Punishment. What Ralph thought of as payback time.

In that moment she had a sense of the answer to Ralph's scheming being right there in front of her, if only she were smart enough to see it. But before she could pursue the question Dave said, "We'll find them. I'll stay out all day tomorrow looking for them if I have to. This town isn't that big."

"I have this terrible feeling that we're missing something. I told you Ralph knows exactly what he's doing, but why has he waited this long? Why call up out of the blue and then avoid us? Is he just trying to drive me crazy?" She laughed harshly. "If that's it, well, it's working, Ralph, you son of a bitch. God damn you all to hell!"

"Take it easy," Dave said again, the words thick with restrained emotion. "Tomorrow morning we'll go straight to the police before I go out looking. This time they'll have to do something."

Glenda stared at him in silence. When she spoke her tone was bleak. "Ralph has that all figured out, too. They won't do anything." An image of the small automatic pistol in her purse flashed before her. Dave didn't know about the gun. "Whatever's to be done, no one else is going to do it for us. We're on our own."

Thirty-One

ON SATURDAY RICHIE'S newly discovered father took him to the beach. He insisted on it. A warming Santa Ana condition was building. The sky was a clear blue except for scattered white fluffy clouds running on the desert winds, and the temperature rose into the high seventies. As a result the beach was crowded, parking lots nearly full. Crawling along in the Buick LeSabre, Ralph Beringer saw a family in a Dodge Caravan waiting for another car to back out of a parking space. The car backed toward the waiting van, preventing it from reaching the spot. Beringer raced forward and, just as the car drove away, swung neatly into the vacated space, cutting off the van. He grinned broadly.

The driver of the Caravan honked his horn and shouted, shaking his fist as he leaned out the window. Beringer held up his middle finger. Seeing Richie's unease, he laughed. "Hey, you gotta grab what's there, kid. Nobody's gonna give you anything in this world. Take it from your dad."

They found an open patch of sand and spread out a blanket. Even though the water was very cold in spite of the warmth of the day, raising gooseflesh all over him, Richie ventured into the light surf. Beringer, wearing khaki shorts rather than a swimsuit, relaxed on the blanket, a cooler beside him holding a six-pack of beer. His father looked very muscular and strong, Richie thought with boyish pride—like an athlete. He had a scar under one knee, white against his healthy tan, and another on his back. Richie wondered if they were battle wounds.

Surfacing after plunging through a wave, Richie saw his father staring after a trio of young girls strolling along the beach in string bikinis. That was okay, Richie thought with a trace of defensiveness; Beringer was divorced, wasn't he? Why would Mom care? The question was confusing.

They spent two hours at the beach, Richie in and out of the water, his father working his way through the six-pack. When they left they stopped for lunch at the Bright Spot, where this neat blond waitress named Iris made a big fuss over them. She seemed to know his dad, kidding around with him, and she acted as if she were really glad he had brought Richie along with him to the diner. Beringer explained that he was divorced and Richie had been living with his mother. He didn't say that he hadn't seen Richie in eight years.

The boy had trouble keeping his eyes off Iris. She smiled whenever she went by carrying platters of food or the coffee carafe. Once, after pouring Beringer more coffee, she reached out and playfully ruffled Richie's hair.

"She's nice," Richie said afterward in the car.

"Yeah," his father replied thoughtfully. "Real nice. Which don't mean you can trust her around the corner," he added with a chuckle. "She's a woman, right?"

Unlike his mood the previous evening, Beringer had been relaxed all morning. That afternoon, however, back at the apartment, his edginess returned. They watched a football game on TV—Nebraska against Oklahoma—but once, late in the game when Richie happened to glanced at his father, he was startled by what he saw. Beringer was sweating and there was a strange glitter in his eyes. He didn't seem to be focused on the game at all. Richie started to ask if anything was wrong. A sense of caution stopped him—he wasn't sure why.

For dinner Beringer sent out to Pizza Hut, ordering a large with everything—Richie's choice. While they waited Beringer turned on the evening news, watching intently. When Richie tried to talk his father told him to shut up.

It was the first time Beringer had spoken harshly since their encounter on the patio Friday night.

Richie thought the news was boring. Nothing really exciting

was happening, and he was glad when the Pizza Hut delivery arrived. While they ate, his father became jovial once more, laughing loudly and often. He had been drinking steadily all afternoon, and he had two more beers with the pizza. Richie had the impression that Beringer wasn't having that good a time, that the laughter and joking around were forced. It made him uncomfortable.

Like most youngsters, Richie was more sensitive to nuances than adults realized. He knew how adults acted around kids when they didn't really like them. The euphoria he had felt starting out this first full day in his father's company trickled away, leaving an emptiness in his stomach that the pizza couldn't fill.

He thought of his mother. Of Dad—Dave, that is. He wondered what they were doing and if they were worried about him. He even wondered about Elli. Would his little sister be asking about him, curious because he hadn't come home?

Beringer was staring at him. "What are you thinkin' about, kid?"

I'm Richie, he thought. But he didn't say that, of course. Instead he said, "I was thinking about my sister Elli. She's just a kid, but . . ."

"You miss her?"

"Well, uh . . . yeah, I guess."

"You're too soft. That's somethin' you gotta learn. You start feeling soft for other people—it don't matter who they are—you know what's gonna happen? They'll walk all over you. You're old enough you got to start thinkin' about yourself."

Richie decided he wouldn't ask if he could call home. Without asking, he knew what would happen. There would be this shift in his father's eyes, as if someone else were peering out. It was really weird . . .

An uneasy silence fell between them. The noise from the TV set—a sitcom Richie never watched—filled the vacuum. The wail of a fire engine pierced the night and faded away, causing Richie to think again of his stepfather in his fire-retardant clothes, blackened with soot.

He broke the silence. "I was wondering, uh . . . maybe we could go to a movie. The mall is just down the street, they've got these six theaters—"

"Shit, you expect to be entertained all the time, is that it? Is that the way it is at home? Everybody's jumpin' all over themselves to keep Richie entertained?"

"No. I . . . I didn't mean . . ."

Tears stung his eyes. Ralph Beringer turned away in disgust. "Shit," he muttered again as he went to the kitchen for another beer. The snap of the top on the can made Richie jump slightly in his chair.

Returning to the living room, Beringer stared down at him. Finally he said, "I know just what you need, kid. And so does your old man."

He went down the hall to the bedroom. When he returned several minutes later he was carrying a stack of videos. "You're old enough to start your real education, kid, and tonight's as good a time as any."

Richie sat erect, his tears forgotten, watching curiously as his father began to set up the VCR.

STANDING ON THE balcony outside her room at the Red Roof Inn, after watching the sun set in another gorgeous flameout, Karen Younger reflected that murder and mayhem seemed more terrible in this bright, sunny place, as if the very acts were more suited to cold and darkness, to chilling rain and crashing thunder. You seldom heard thunder in Southern California, she had been told. Only if a Southern Pacific storm strayed this far north, a product of *El Niño*, whatever that was. Murder preferred the shadows. It seemed more bizarre where there was so much color and light.

Where, in mid-October, she had been too warm in her jogging sweats even at six in the evening. It was seductive, no question about that, but she wasn't sure if she could deal with life as well in so beguiling a climate. Once needed reminders of nature's harshness. You were going to face it sooner or later. Best if it didn't come as a total shock.

She smiled at her thoughts. After a while the air became cool enough to drive her back into her room. She took a quick shower, changed into sweater and slacks and went out to a solitary dinner at a nearby Coco's, an upscale coffee shop. She returned reluctantly to her room, whose bland contemporary decor had, like her solitary meals, become overly familiar in the past ten days. With a wry smile she wondered which she feared most about going into the field as a profiler—the monsters she had come to find, or the rooms in which she would have to wait for them.

Propped up on the bed with a couple of pillows behind her, she thought about her parents, who had moved from Philadelphia to a retirement community near Reading, Pennsylvania. This weekend they would probably go for a drive, delighting in the autumn foliage, maybe take in a fall craft festival or drive in to Reading to shop at the big outlets—her father hated them but her mother loved browsing and he could never refuse to indulge her. Poor family conditioning, Karen thought, for what she would find in her work.

She glanced at the telephone across the room, wanting to call them, to hear their familiar voices, answer the familiar questions. She was fine. No, no one new in her life. Yes, she knew it was getting late, her biological clock was ticking . . .

For a number of reasons, she never called when she was in the field. Someone in the Bureau was sure to complain of a potential security lapse. Someone in accounting would scream about unauthorized long-distance calls on the motel bill. Karen herself—the real reason—would feel that she was making herself vulnerable, exposing too much of herself to the monsters she hunted. In the field she built a wall between her personal life and her job. She couldn't let it be breeched.

She thought of Tim Braden and her mother's query about someone new. *Yes, Mom, I've met someone interesting. Unfortunately, he's a cop.*

Suddenly restless, she drew her briefcase onto the bed beside her and pulled out her case notes. Something there was teasing her, but it had stayed just around a corner out of sight. She scanned the accumulating copies of reports she had obtained from Braden, the coroner and the FBI's lab relating to both Edith Foster and Natalie Rothleder. Nothing jumped out at her. Factoring Lisl Moeller into the mix didn't help. Still nothing.

Her thoughts strayed back to Detective Braden. Not exactly what she had expected, but then her record on reading men was not something to hang from the rafters. Braden was stubborn, dogged, honest; what you see is what you get, she thought. She believed she understood what had happened to him that night he earned his fifteen minutes of celebrity. His reaction to the woman striking at him with a corkscrew had been a cop's reflex. *You swing an arm at me and I'm going to grab it. Not tentatively, but quick and hard, and ask questions later. That way I'll keep all my teeth, and stay alive.* The media had made it something else.

Braden had brooded in this quiet backwater for a year, Karen reflected, until the Foster–Rothleder killings galvanized him. He felt like a cop again. She wondered how much sleep he had had these past two weeks.

Stubborn, she thought again. He was unwilling to accept the fact—self-evident to her—that the San Carlos killer was the same one whose work Karen had encountered eight years ago in Germany. He—

The telephone startled her. She glanced at the digital bedside clock: 11:14 P.M. at Quantico, and Buddy Cochrane was still at work. She wondered when he was going to slow down.

"You're working late on a Saturday," she observed.

"I just got back from testifying before the grand jury in Tuscaloosa. We're getting an indictment there."

"The serial killings?"

"Seventeen bodies uncovered so far. I suspect there may be more, but he's had a change of heart and stopped talking. For a while, once he knew we had him, he was trying to save his soul, and he gave us some places to dig. Then he got scared, I guess."

"He's that rational?"

"He knew what he was doing," Cochrane said after a brief pause. "How about your case? I hear you have another missing girl."

"Yes . . . she disappeared from a Native American Indian festival at the local college last night . . . what they call a *powow.*"

"Friday again."

"I know."

"Our lab been any help? Franken in Hairs and Fibers said something about a match on the gloves your killer wears."

"Yes, we have a make on the gloves. He left traces of leather between two of Natalie Rothleder's teeth. They're unusual—fine goatskin gloves, usually sold to gardeners. But they're expensive. You can get them from Smith & Hawken, for example."

"Then there shouldn't be too many places to check," Cochrane suggested hopefully.

"There's a problem. The gloves are made in England, and they're sold there and in Europe. The killer could have acquired them there—especially if, as I believe, he first started killing in Europe."

Cochrane digested this in silence for a moment. Then he said, "What about the evidence he's deliberately given you?"

"What would that be?"

"The initials."

Karen was silent a moment. "I've played with them, tried to find a name or an acronym. LEN is a man's name. Or NEL, for Nell. Do you think he could be spelling out a name?"

"What do you think?"

"I think it's possible."

"What's the missing girl's name?"

"Nancy Showalter. That doesn't help. We'd have LENN, or any combination of those letters. But we don't know yet—" She stopped, struck by something. She glanced toward the pile of reports, but before she could pursue the errant thought Cochrane said, "His ego is a potential weakness. He's trying to say something without giving himself away, and thinks he's clever enough to do it. Have you talked to the local authorities about going public with the initials? Someone might recognize what he's up to."

"Detective Braden wants to release it. So far the police chief and the sheriff are against it. They're afraid of a citywide panic."

"If you find another body, you'll have the panic anyway."

"I know."

There was a brief silence. In it she felt the concern for her, and the passionate concern for the case she was working on, that defined Buddy Cochrane for her as a man and an FBI agent. "Take care of yourself," he said softly. "He's a monster. Don't get in his way."

"Not if I can help it."

After another beat he said, "We've been holding back on sending in a full-scale FBI task force. If he does strike again, we'll have to come out there in force."

"That won't make Braden happy."

"Is that important?"

"It might be," she said quietly.

RICHIE COULD NOT take his eyes off the television screen.

He paid little attention to the sound. Aside from moaning and crying out, the men and women depicted in the videos had little to say to each other, and what they did say sounded artificial even to Richie's ear. But the images were as graphic as a kick in the stomach.

He felt himself getting hot and excited. His heart pounded, his ears burned, and sometimes he felt dizzy. He couldn't bring himself to look at his father reclining nearby in the La-Z-Boy armchair, drinking beer and chuckling.

Some of the scenes were disturbing in ways other than sexual. The people involved—men and women, and sometimes, to Richie's surprise, women together—did not seem to like each other much in spite of their frenzied coupling. In the last video the naked woman had screamed and tried to get away, but the man, who had burst into her room at night, apparently surprising her, just laughed while he threw her down on the bed.

Richie had heard of such movies, of course—he could hardly miss seeing the Adults Only section at the local video store—but he had never actually *seen* one. He felt shame and embarrassment along with the excitement, but he couldn't stop looking.

The man on the screen slapped the woman, hard, and she suddenly stopped screaming. Her wide eyes stared up at the naked, hairy-chested man. Then she reached for him . . .

Richie heard his father's chuckle.

He felt himself getting hot again. He squirmed in his chair. His heart thumped so heavily he thought it was about to stop.

Ralph Beringer took another swig of beer and laughed aloud. "Time to grow up, Richie. Time to grow up."

KAREN SAT BOLT upright in bed. She felt clammy with perspiration. She peeled off the sweaty T-shirt she had worn for sleeping and padded into the bathroom. Toweling off, she tried to recall what had awakened her. Not a sound, not a nightmare this time, but—

She moved quickly back into her room. Her briefcase was still open, file folders stacked against it. She snatched one of the folders and thumbed rapidly through the reports it contained.

She stopped at one, staring.

That was what had prodded her awake: a name.

She could be all wrong, especially if the missing coed, Nancy Showalter, turned up as another victim.

It was 2:21 A.M. Buddy Cochrane had had a long day and night, probably hadn't got home before midnight; 5:21 A.M. there now.

She hesitated, sighed, then punched in a number. After four rings Cochrane's recorded voice said, "No one is available to answer your call just now. If you will leave your name and number, and the purpose of your call—"

He interrupted himself, cutting off the recorded message. "Cochrane."

"This is Special Agent Younger," she said quickly. "I'm sorry to do this to you, sir, but—"

"Don't apologize. It must be important."

"I think it might be," she said.

She explained how she wanted the parameters of the San Carlos name search to be extended through military and other records. She also added one new name to be run against all available lists.

"Care to tell me why?" Cochrane asked when she had finished.

When she explained, he was silent for a long moment. Then he said, "I'll get on it now."

The fact that it was still dark on a Sunday morning didn't matter.

Thirty-Two

SUNDAY WAS THE worst day for Glenda Lindstrom. With each passing hour her fear increased. Why hadn't they heard from Ralph? Where was Richie now?

In church that morning she found herself unable to pray. She went through the motions of the service numbly, sitting or standing or kneeling, aware of Elli beside her mimicking each move, of Dave silent and withdrawn.

Despair was the unforgivable sin—she couldn't give in to it. At the same time she felt hypocritical on her knees, staring up at the altar, her purse on the bench seat beside her holding not a prayer book but a small automatic pistol.

Finally some words came. She prayed for forgiveness for what she might do. The words seemed hollow.

She would not let Ralph destroy her family. Would Christ condemn a mother who fought for her children, her husband, herself—against a monster?

At the end of the service, emerging into the bright sunshine of an unusually warm autumn day, she fought off a black cloud of despair.

"Are you okay?" Dave asked, worried.

"Let's go home," she said.

"SURPRISE," RALPH BERINGER said.

Richie stared at his father, then past him in astonishment at the woman behind him, smiling broadly.

"Hi, Richie," Iris Whatley said.

It was early Sunday evening. Beringer had gone out an hour earlier, telling Richie to stay inside and warning him not to go near the phone. He had promised something unexpected when he came back. Richie had even speculated that Beringer might be going to see his parents. The temptation to pick up the phone and call home was overwhelming, but he was nervous about his parents' reaction. He knew he shouldn't have gone off without telling them what he was up to. He wished . . .

He was no longer sure what he wished.

The day had gone badly. During breakfast at a mall coffee shop Beringer had been surly and uncommunicative, responding to Richie's questions and comments curtly if at all, finally asking if Richie thought he could maybe keep his mouth shut for five minutes, just to see what it was like. When tears brimmed in Richie's eyes, all he could read in his father's stare was contempt. "You act like a goddam girl," Beringer said.

Things had been no better through the afternoon. Richie had been grateful for the pro football game that sporadically kept his father's attention. Even so, there had been periods when Beringer prowled the apartment like a lion in a cage at the zoo.

Finally he had gone out. Iris was his surprise—for Richie, a delightful one. Maybe his father would be in a better mood now, Richie hoped. Maybe they could have a good time together.

The waitress was very animated, talking in a voice that was higher pitched than Richie remembered, and giggling a lot, as if she were excited to be with them. They went out to Denny's to eat, Iris talking all through the meal while Richie stared admiringly at her, the waitress saying what a treat it was to be taken out to dinner, usually she was the one doing the serving and all. She joked about having to remind herself not to jump up and grab the coffeepot. Beringer said little. After a while Richie realized that Iris was more nervous than he was—that was why she talked and laughed so much. Her nervousness showed in little sidelong glances at Ralph Beringer. She also touched him often, putting her hand on his arm, or letting her fingertips brush his shoulder. Beringer didn't seem to notice.

It was dark when they returned to the apartment. Beringer had been silent in the car, but as soon as they were inside, the front door locked behind them, he told Richie, "Why don't you go on into the bedroom, kid."

"Uh . . . it's early, uh, Dad. I mean—"

"Do what you're told."

"HE'S A GOOD kid, I think you upset him," Iris said when they were alone. Her lips pouted in mock rebuke. "We could have waited a little bit," she added coquettishly.

"You think I give a shit what you think?" Ralph Beringer said.

He was in an ugly mood. He had been that way since the debacle Friday night with Nancy, his mood not improved by the circumstance that, for the next forty-eight hours, he had been stuck with the kid. It was one thing to tighten the screws on Glenda and her professor; it was another thing entirely to spend two days with a ten-year-old who didn't know when to shut up and who, if you said boo to him, acted like a girl.

The experience with Nancy—so keenly anticipated—had gone badly. First the whimpering in his car like a little girl, the same way Richie acted—that was all she was, really, a little girl in this big, overblown, beautiful woman's body. Then the sudden collapse that left Beringer frustrated, screaming with rage.

Once he had her in the car he had driven swiftly into the hills, knowing exactly where he was going. The girl blubbered and talked to herself, as if she were praying. Beringer realized she was talking to her parents. It was pathetic.

The regional park had been dark and deserted at that hour. Braking angrily in the empty parking area beneath the arms of a huge oak tree, Beringer had said, "Did you tell mommy and daddy how you were acting with your lover boy?"

Nancy went silent, her mouth open, eyes huge behind long wet lashes.

"You know what I'm talking about. Did you tell them about

dressing like a whore, making sure everyone could see those big tits?"

"I . . . I don't know what you mean."

It was over in an instant.

When Beringer hit her she went slack, mushy, as if this big lovely girl was nothing more than an envelope of skin, an inflated doll he had accidentally punctured.

Enraged by the lack of resistance, he didn't stop until his arms felt leaden, too heavy to lift. He went through his ritual, all of it, but there was none of the familiar, red-minded joy. He was left empty and disgusted, his rage unvented, still churning like a sickness in his belly.

It was like beating off alone in the dark all those years ago, while in the next room *she* howled and shrieked to climax with one of her transient friends . . .

"I'm out of here," Iris said, staring at him as if she had never seen him before.

"You're not going anywhere."

"Who says? You?" Her bark of laughter was derisive.

Beringer regarded her quietly, unmoved. He was between her and the door. "Go on in there. The kid's waiting."

Iris stared at him in disbelief. "You've gotta be kidding!"

"He likes you, you like him. It'll be good for him."

"Does he know about this?" She was incredulous.

"Don't worry, he'll get the idea quick enough if you show him. He's my son."

"You're sick!"

She tried to walk past him. Beringer grabbed her arm in the famous Beringer Pincer's Bite. Her bicep was surprisingly hard. His brain recorded the fact with a flicker of surprise but without alarm.

"You're goin' in there, one way or another. Why not the easy way?"

"Go fuck yourself!" Iris shouted, twisting free.

He hit her once, with an open palm rather than his fist, but not holding back. The blow rocked her on her heels, her eyes momentarily glassy. It also sent her a very clear message, which was what he intended.

His smile was cold, chilling her. "It's not like it's your first time. Just do it. Leave the door open," he added. "I'll be listening, so don't try to fake it."

TWENTY MINUTES LATER Iris stormed out of the bedroom, flinging the door behind her so hard it bounced off the wall. "I hope you're satisfied, you sick bastard!"

Behind her, shattered and in tears, the humiliated boy would not meet Beringer's eyes.

"Hey, how'd it go?" he questioned Richie.

"What do you care?" Richie rushed past him into the bathroom, slamming the door.

Beringer turned angrily on Iris. "What went on in there? I told you—"

"He couldn't handle it. For God's sake, what kind of a father are you? He's not ready! And neither am I—not for that kind of shit!" Iris shoved past him, heading into the living room. "You're no father, you're sick—and I'm out of here!"

Moving smoothly and without unnecessary haste, he caught her before she reached the small entryway. His fingers on her shoulders were like metal clamps. "You'll go when I say so."

"What the hell do you mean?" She was furious, almost as humiliated as the boy. She felt used and dirty. Iris had a healthy sexual appetite and few inhibitions, but this man had succeeded in turning joyful pleasure into something shameful and demeaning.

"Hey, calm down," Beringer said, easing his grip while his tone became more reasonable. "I brought you here, I'm taking you back, and that's it."

He was smiling now, but there was something in his eyes that frightened Iris and silenced her. They were like two small, deep, dark wells, with something swimming around down there that she suddenly did not wish to see more clearly. For the first time she felt something other than anger and disgust: a tickle at the back of her neck that caused hairs to rise.

"Don't move," he ordered her.

Richie was emerging from the bathroom. When he saw Beringer he tried to bolt past him. Beringer grabbed the boy, spun him around and held him easily while he struggled. "Get back in there, you little wimp. You're not going anywhere."

"I hate you!"

"Yeah, well, you're no prize yourself. You're staying here—I'm taking Iris back."

"I won't be here!"

Beringer smiled. Then he cuffed Richie across the mouth, splitting his lip and knocking him backward into the bathroom. Richie slipped on the tile floor and banged his hip against the counter of the sink. Tears sprang into his eyes. And in that instant, as his father's face swam before his eyes, blurred by the blow, he seemed to float outside of himself. He seemed to be up near the ceiling, staring down at a muscular man in a khaki uniform with stripes on his sleeve—at a soldier and a child. Richie watched in wide-eyed terror as the man's arm rose and fell, lashing again and again, each blow cutting across the child's screams like a scratch in a recording.

The bathroom door had a keyed lock. Beringer slammed the door shut. Richie heard the key turn and withdraw.

Then Beringer's voice, clear and harsh: "You touch that door, bitch, and I'll break your arm!"

After that there was only silence.

Thirty-Three

THE PHONE RANG as Karen Younger was coming through the door to her motel room. Expecting to hear Buddy Cochrane's voice—or someone on the line from Quantico—she ran to scoop it up.

"Younger?" Braden's voice, no preamble.

"I'm here. What's up?"

"We have another body. I'll pick you up. Ten minutes."

"I'll be out front."

In the car Braden said, "I tried to call you earlier."

"I was out for a walk. This weather is so unbelievable for October, it's hard to stay indoors," she explained, instantly guilty. "Is it the same pattern?"

"It's him, all right. Same slaughterhouse mentality with his fists. Same cutting. It's the girl who was reported missing Friday night."

"Nancy," Karen said, putting the letters together: L-E-N-N. Various combinations of the letters shed no new light. She frowned, thinking that her hunch had been wrong.

"This time there are some differences. For one, he wrapped her in a yellow fireman's coat that's been used recently. You can still smell the smoke and ashes." Braden did not look at her, concentrating on his driving as he cut in and out of traffic, his expression stony. "Second thing, Doc says this time he raped and cut her after she was dead. Definitely postmortem."

After a moment Karen said, "Those Nomex jackets should take prints." Her foot instinctively braced against the floorboards as Braden tapped the brake, found an opening and shot through an intersection.

"Prints are all over the coat, and I've a pretty good idea whose they are."

"David Lindstrom's," she guessed. "He's making a public announcement that he did it?"

His glance flicked toward her, searching for sarcasm. "Lindstrom reported the coat stolen from his car on campus last week."

"Then he's in the clear."

"Or he's thumbing his nose at us. That could be a slick way to deflect attention from himself—report losing something potentially incriminating ahead of time because you know you're going to use it."

"You don't give up easy, do you, Detective?"

"I don't like the coat any more than you do. It sucks. But I also don't like the way Lindstrom keeps popping up in each of these cases. I don't like coincidences at all, and I especially don't like three coincidences with three bodies."

"Have you wondered why the killer would steal Lindstrom's coat and then use it like this . . . if it wasn't Lindstrom himself?"

"I can't think of a reason that makes sense."

He ran a red light, siren whooping, and a driver in a Camaro approaching the intersection from the right was too busy talking on his car phone to hear the warning. At the last second the Camaro braked, fishtailing out of control. Braden swerved sharply left, gunned the Chevrolet's big engine and shot past the startled civilian. "Asshole," Braden muttered. "What's he think a siren is, the all-clear signal?"

"Unless someone had a grudge against Lindstrom," Karen persisted.

Braden shot her a startled glance.

"I came across a report in the file late last night about the Lindstroms' domestic problems."

"Yeah. His kid's missing. The parents were in the station Saturday morning. Seems the wife's ex-husband is making trouble. He called and told 'em the kid was with him—claimed he came on his own. Trouble is, that's not a crime. He's the boy's father."

He did not say that he could see no connection between a custody quarrel, however bitter, and the serial killer they were after, but Karen knew what he was thinking. She had asked herself the same question.

Speeding along a dark canyon beyond the city's edge, Braden swung sharply onto a two-lane road that climbed through blackened hills and ruined trees, legacy of the recent fire. Suddenly the terrain opened into a long narrow valley with green meadows, old shade oaks and, along a small creek, weeping willows trailing fingers in the water. Karen had a glimpse of picnic tables and barbecue pits.

"The regional park," Braden said as the Chevrolet rocked to a stop. Its headlights slashed across an expanse of asphalt toward the familiar sight of police cars, an ambulance and the medical examiner's van. This time, however, there were many other unofficial cars parked every which way as if there had been a massive pileup. Karen saw the call letters of one local TV station on the side of a van.

Pulling Karen along in his wake, Braden brushed past reporters who hurried toward them. "Coincidence number four," he muttered as soon as they were clear of the newspeople. "Keep them back!" he barked at a uniform.

"What do you mean?"

"This was the staging area for the firefighters a couple weeks ago. Which means Lindstrom was here."

A cluster of police and sheriff's deputies were grouped around the entrance to a concrete block public toilet facility. The sign over the entrance where they stood said MEN. Approaching the open doorway, Karen felt her stomach lurch. She fished a nasal spray from her purse and used it quickly. Law enforcement officials commonly exposed to the sight and stench of violent death resorted to various means of stemming nausea; the spray was hers. It didn't always work.

Nancy Showalter had been propped against a stained tile wall inside the restroom. She was a big girl, Karen saw, no more than eighteen or nineteen. The yellow slicker had been wrapped loosely around her shoulders, falling open at the front. She was naked under the coat.

As Karen stared down at her, the confluence of urinal smells and the sickly sweet odor of death caused her already queasy stomach to knot. She forced herself to take the time to examine closely what had been done to the girl—the battered features, the signature cuts, the indications of sexual assault. Then she pushed her way outside, where she stood leaning against the concrete block wall of the building, sucking in great gulps of cool night air. She shivered with nausea and shook with silent rage.

When Braden joined her outside, she asked, "How long has she been here?"

"Doc figures the best part of two days. That means the perp grabbed her at the powwow on campus Friday night and drove straight here. For whatever reason, the scene went bad on him. Doc's guess is he hit her too hard the first time and her heart stopped. Or she was scared to death."

Karen shuddered.

"Yeah," Braden said quietly. "As you can see, he was really pissed off."

Karen tried to erase the graphic images, lifting her face toward the purple night sky, taking deep breaths. When she trusted her voice she said, "He's unraveling, Braden. He's not sane anymore. God knows what he'll do next."

On the way to the beach Beringer drove past the Bright Spot without slowing. He saw Iris react, her hand reaching out in the direction of the diner as if in protest. "Let me out—stop this car!"

"Don't be in such a hurry."

Ignoring the fact that the Buick was speeding at fifty miles per hour along the coastal road, Iris grabbed at the door handle. Beringer backhanded her across the face, mashing her lips against her teeth. The car rocked back and forth as, steering with one hand, he grabbed Iris's nest of blond hair with the other and slammed her head against the seat's headrest.

Iris twisted her head and bit the heel of his palm.

Beringer roared. He released her, dug into his pocket jacket for the leather sleeve of steel balls. As he jerked it out, the end of the sleeve caught. The stitching, which had loosened without his noticing, opened up. Steel balls rolled onto the car seat, the floor, into Iris's lap. She grabbed one of the balls and threw it into his face.

His brain a haze of red, Beringer grabbed her hair and smashed her head forward against the dashboard—padded, dammit—jerked it back against the headrest, forward, back, over and over, the blood on the dash lost in the red mist of the night, not stopping until he felt her go limp. He pushed her head down and forward between her legs. She slumped sideways against the passenger door.

Beringer drove on to the beach, cursing and banging the steering wheel with the palm of his hand, ignoring the sting from his bite, the smear of blood on the wheel. Because of the unseasonally warm weather the beach had drawn huge crowds during the day, many of whom still lingered or, heading home, helped to create gridlock on the highway. The choicest parking lots within walking distance of the San Carlos Pier were still too full for comfort, and Beringer had to drive for more than a mile along the beachfront before he found a deserted lot. He pulled in, drove to the far end of the strip and parked.

He stared back along the parking area and the wide expanse of beach. Darkness pooled between widely spaced lights along the paved strip, and the beach itself was illuminated only by the pale light of a quarter moon. Some strollers far down the strand passed through the slant of a car's headlights. Closer, a jogger padded along the edge of the surf, keeping to the wet, packed sand, but he was moving in the opposite direction. A restroom near where Beringer had parked, which resembled a military bunker, appeared to be deserted. Beringer watched it for several minutes without seeing any sign of activity.

The cloudless sky created a nightscape not as black as Beringer would have liked, but the beach area he had chosen was dark enough for his purposes. The restroom reminded him of the final resting place he had found for the last coed, Nancy. Good enough for her, good enough for Iris.

The waitress had not stirred or made a sound in some time.

With a start of alarm, Beringer checked her pulse. It was strong and steady. Good! This, the prelude to the final act in the drama he had orchestrated, deserved his best efforts. After his disappointing adventure with Nancy, a living, vital Iris, awakening to terror, was essential.

Climbing out of the Buick, he tuned his senses to the night, watching and listening. Subdued brush of cars along the highway, but between those pulses, stillness all around.

He walked around the car, opened the front passenger door and caught Iris when she tumbled sideways toward him. He heard a soft moan. Lifting her clear of the door, he rested her dead weight across the front fender and hood.

As he turned to elbow the door shut with his free arm, Iris twisted out of his loose, one-handed grip, pushed off the vehicle and spun away.

Caught by surprise, Beringer reacted a split second too late. He grabbed for any piece of her—hair, arm, skirt—but she slipped free. Then she raced along the parking strip, quickly gaining speed.

Beringer pounded after her, cursing her cunning, his stupidity, the lingering beachgoers, the traffic, the clear night sky. Fucking bitch—she had tricked him!

He had underestimated Iris in more ways than one. He had brushed off her athleticism, a joking reference to working out. What kind of shape could she be in, waiting on tables? He had underestimated her courage and determination, or he would have taped her hands and feet before leaving the apartment garage. In his blinding rage he had not even considered that she might be clever enough to feign unconsciousness from the battering he had given her.

His breathing became labored, but Iris continued to run freely, not slowing. He had hardly gained on her at all. When he put on a burst of speed, designed to close the gap between them in a rush before she realized what was happening, Iris suddenly veered off the parking lot onto the soft sand, which was still warm from the day's heat.

Her toe stubbed on something buried in the sand. She stumbled. Beringer dove after her. His fingers closed on her trailing foot.

For a moment, exulting, he thought he had her. Then she kicked off her sandal, leaving it in his hand. As she leaped away she shed the other sandal and ran barefoot across the beach.

Stumbling after her, Beringer realized he couldn't take the time to remove his thick-soled Nikes. While he struggled, the soft sand dragging at his shoes, she seemed to fly across the sand, widening her lead.

Iris shouted, "Help! Help me, please!"

"Fat chance," Beringer raged aloud.

But even as he spoke he saw the cluster of people farther down the beach stop, alerted by the outcry. Several heads turned.

"Help!" Iris screamed.

Beringer pulled up. A stitch caught at his side. He bent over, wheezing, hands on his knees. He could never reach her in time. Some of the people on the strand had already started forward to meet the running woman.

A sudden realization of his own danger chilled Beringer's rage, shocking him to his senses. He turned at once and trotted back in the direction of the Buick, veering onto the asphalt parking strip for easier footing. As he broke into a run he calculated distances, the reaction times of strangers confronting a hysterical woman, the uncertainties that would initially beset Iris's rescuers.

The Buick loomed out of the darkness. No way anyone could intercept him before he reached the highway, or follow him afterward. What were the risks, then? Iris could describe but not identify him—he had never given her his real name. But she knew Richie's first name, she could identify the Buick—and she knew where the apartment was.

He hadn't lost the game, Beringer thought as he reached the Buick, jabbed the key into the ignition and spun the car around. The timetable had moved up, that was all.

Damn the bitch! But he had to forget about her. Use the boy now, as he had planned, but do it tonight. It would be some time before Iris was able to tell a coherent story to the police. Plenty of time for Beringer to clear out of the apartment, take the boy with him in the Taurus. Iris had seen him only in the Buick.

Time for the last act. He hadn't needed I for Iris, anyway. Lennie would still get the message.

He wouldn't have to look far for an E.

AT THE CRIME scene in the park Tim Braden berated himself for the latest death. He had not done enough to warn the young women of San Carlos and the college, he fumed. The reluctance of his superiors and the FBI to cause widespread panic or to give away too much information about the killings had silenced him. Not any longer, he said.

"The media vultures want something. I'm gonna give them the story."

"Wait a minute, Braden, the sheriff and your chief—"

"That girl might be alive if I'd scared her badly enough."

Karen's protest dried up. She knew he was right. She also understood that there was only so long the full story of the killer and his bizarre trademarks could be contained. In fact, she was surprised that no one from the San Carlos PD or the sheriff's department had leaked the story before now. In New York or Philly, she thought, it would have made page-one headlines a week or more ago.

Braden walked toward the press corps, barricaded behind crime scene tape. Lights and cameras swung toward him. Reporters began to shout, their words trampling over each other.

Braden held up both hands, flat palms gesturing for silence. "Okay, okay, listen up! You'll get your story." He paused, waiting for the hubub to die down, ignoring shouted questions until some of the reporters, realizing Braden was not going to talk until he could be heard, took charge. Gradually a silence fell.

"I'm only going to say this once, so listen carefully," he said. "No questions, no nothing. I'm just going to tell this once and then I'm going back to doing my job while you do yours." He blew out a long breath. "We have a serial killer here in San Carlos, and he's left his mark on each of his victims . . ."

When he had finished Karen watched him fight free of the reporters and, at a deputy's signal, march over to his car to take a radio call. Five minutes later, ignoring the pandemonium he had ignited, Braden grabbed Karen Younger's arm and hustled her toward his car. "This is the way it's gonna be from now on," he growled. "A goddam circus."

"Maybe not," Karen said, although she no longer felt as confident about her earlier intuition.

Braden looked at her sharply.

"Let's get out of here," she said.

Thirty-Four

PERIODICALLY RICHIE LINDSTROM turned off the vent fan in the bathroom to listen. But from the moment the silence in the apartment first told him he was alone, he had been working on the lock of the bathroom door.

He was sweating. The small, enclosed room was warm. The fan hardly seemed to stir the air.

It had taken a long time for his heart to stop hammering wildly. He kept thinking about Iris in the bedroom, taking off her blouse with nothing underneath it, stroking his cheek and murmuring, "Don't be scared, honey . . . it's all right." As he remembered the hot gush of sensation his cheeks burned with shame, guilt, humiliation. "It's okay, honey," Iris had said, but he recalled her stiff, angry gestures when she pulled her blouse closed over her breasts and smoothed her skirt over her thighs with the palms of her hands.

"I'm sorry," Richie had whispered, not sure what he had done wrong.

"Oh, you poor kid." Iris had pulled him to her, hugged him fiercely for a long moment, before she leaped up and threw the door wide, shouting at Beringer, "You sick bastard!"

Richie pawed through the drawers of the bathroom counter, searching for something else to try on the door lock. He was mechanically inclined, always asking how things worked, and he had seen actors on television or in movies a thousand times using a credit card or similar piece of plastic to work open a simple door lock. So far he had tried strips of stiff cardboard, a thin comb, a piece of plastic he had cut from the front of a package containing a pair of toothbrushes. Nothing had worked. The sweat ran down from his forehead into his eyes. He wondered how long his father had been gone and when he would return—and in spite of the warmth and the sweat, he shivered.

Nothing had gone the way he had expected. Discovering his missing father had been exciting at first, but events had chilled his enthusiasm. At various times Richie had seen hostility, contempt, cold appraisal in Ralph Beringer's eyes—never warmth or affection. Sometimes Beringer had simply looked at him as if he were a bug on a slide. In such moments Richie had experienced a visceral fear; he quivered inside, stomach churning, without knowing exactly why.

In a side drawer of the cabinet he came across a package of stiff, narrow, gritty sticks. Emery boards, he recalled. His mother used them. Taking one of the strips, he slid it between the door and the jamb, pushing against the latch of the lock.

He felt it give.

His heart began to race. He pushed carefully at the latch but the emery board slipped off it. He started over. The sweat poured down his face. His vision swam, and he had trouble breathing, as if the enclosed bathroom were running out of oxygen.

Click!

Richie froze in place. For a moment he dared not move. Then, still holding the plastic strip in place, he slowly reached for the doorknob and turned it cautiously to the left.

The door sprang free.

Richie rushed out into the cool of the apartment. He remembered where the phone was in the living room—Beringer had used it to call Pizza Hut. Richie ran to the phone and picked it up in a shaking hand. For an instant his mind went blank, he couldn't remember his own telephone number. He told himself to calm down, he *knew* the number! Then it popped into his head.

As Richie jabbed at the buttons, the door into the apartment opened. Caught with the phone in his hand, Richie stared at Ralph Beringer.

"What the hell do you think you're doing?" Beringer said.

The angry voice seemed to come from the distant past, harsh and frightful. Trembling, Richie dropped the phone and backed away.

In the car Richie sat as far away from his father as he could. He sensed the fury consuming the man, and behind it a darkness as cold and empty as a black hole in space.

Beringer had gone through the apartment like a tornado ripping through a mobile home park. Ignoring Richie, cursing savagely to himself, he had thrown clothes, shoes and shaving gear into a single large duffel bag, which already held most of his clothes and personal effects, as if he had always been prepared to leave quickly. He had dragged Richie with him down a back stairway to the garage, where they got into the gray Taurus.

Now, sneaking furtive glances at Beringer, Richie noticed details magnified by his fear. A deep scratch on his father's cheek. The smooth leather gloves on his hands that Richie had seen him wear once before—and also glimpsed under the folds of a towel on the floor of the shower stall, as if they had just been cleaned. The bulge at his waist under his jacket. Richie had had a glimpse of it when Beringer got into the car and the jacket pulled up. It was a gun.

Suddenly the Taurus swung off the road into a gas station. Beringer pulled past the pumps over to the side of the station, where there were two telephone booths. He turned in the seat to glare at Richie without pity or concern. "Beat it," he said.

"What? I don't—"

"You wanted to make a phone call, right? So go ahead—give Mommy a call. You got twenty cents?"

"Uh . . . yes . . ."

Richie could hardly believe this was happening. His hands shook with excitement as he fumbled in his side pocket for his change, "Will I . . . I mean, are you gonna . . . ?"

"Be around?" Beringer laughed, a sound no more pleasant than a saw ripping through a knot. "Hey, count on it. We'll be seeing each other soon. That's a promise."

"Uh . . . is Iris . . . did she say anything?"

"Forget Iris. She's just another cunt, that's all. Didn't you even learn that much?"

D AVE, WHO HAD picked up the phone, said, "Stay where you are, Richie. You hear me? Stay right there—I'll be there in ten minutes."

Glenda was on her feet. "Thank God—I'll come with you. We can—"

"No," Dave said sharply. "If Beringer is the kind of man you think he is, this could be some kind of trick to get at you. You stay here with Elli." He spoke again into the phone. "Are you alone, Richie? Can you talk?" He listened for a moment. "Good. Just stay put. I'm on my way—wait a minute, your mom wants to talk to you."

He handed Glenda the phone. The joy and relief in his face caused her heart to twist.

"Richie? This is Mom. Are you okay?"

Richie began to cry, unable to speak. Through choking sobs he mumbled something about a woman, and a word that sounded like the name of a flower—iris.

Dave was already on his way out the door.

D RIVING BACK TOWARD San Carlos from the regional park, Karen Younger felt Braden's contained anger pervading the car like a radiant force. She thought of the burdensome television image he carried on his back, the image of a cop who was a loose cannon, and realized how out of character the picture really was.

"It's not Lindstrom," she said after a moment.

"What did you mean back there?"

"I know you liked Lindstrom as the killer, but—"

"Yeah, I did, but it's all too damned pat. Wrapping this last girl in Lindstrom's coat, that's too much." He paused. "Besides . . . that call I got back there, couple minutes ago? The Navajo Tribal Police over in Arizona heard from Jim Roget. He says Lindstrom was with him that Friday night from midnight till maybe six in the morning."

Karen felt something click into place in her brain.

Braden said, "Someone is jerking my chain."

"The real killer."

"Yeah." He was silent a moment. The planes of his face were sharp-edged in the intermittent flicker of streetlights. "My problem still is, Lindstrom is connected somehow, and he's all I've got."

"I've thought the same thing. And there's a wild card there we haven't been looking at."

"I've been hoping you'd get around to telling me."

She had wondered how he would react to her holding something back. Not that she had deliberately kept anything from him; she simply hadn't been sure enough. She still had doubts; Nancy Showalter's name didn't fit the pattern she had perceived.

"All along I've had misgivings about this killer," she said. "In some ways he acts exactly like a hundred other serial killers—the seemingly random choice of victims, the acting out of sexual fantasies, the escalating violence—but in other ways he's very different. He's like two different people."

"I don't buy that," Braden objected.

"Neither do I, not this time. It's one man, but it's like he has two agendas. Or to put it another way, he has one agenda, and the killings are only incidental to it. Which, if anything, is even more horrifying."

"You're saying we've been concentrating too much on the killings themselves, not what's behind them."

"Yes. And he's spelling out this real agenda in the names of his victims." Karen paused. "Did you happen to note David Lindstrom's wife's name?"

"Well, uh, it's . . ."

"Glenda."

It took a moment for Braden to react. "You were looking at the LEN cuttings." He scowled. "Nancy doesn't fit there."

"I know, and I can't explain that. But I think Glenda's the connection, not David Lindstrom. The wild card is her ex-husband, Ralph Beringer, the one who has their son. Last night, when I reread the file on the Lindstroms and her name jumped at me—that was before Nancy became a definite part of the picture—I finally asked myself, where's this ex of hers been—and where did he come from? So I called Quantico and asked for some expanded lists of military records, including deserters and soldiers who went AWOL, pushing the time frame all the way back to Lisl Moeller's murder, and I added Beringer's name to those we're screening against the lists."

"And?" She heard the thread of excitement in his voice.

"I've been waiting all day to hear." Braden's Chevrolet had both a police radio and a car phone, she reminded herself. "Can you patch me through to Quantico on that phone? Maybe through the dispatcher?"

"I think so. But it's Sunday night. Even Quantico must be shut down Sunday night."

"I have Buddy Cochrane's home number."

When the call went through it was picked up on the first ring. Karen pictured the oak-paneled library she had seen on her only visit to Cochrane's home, a room lined with walls of books and memorabilia—one whole wall filled with framed photographs that offered a biography of one man's lifetime career with the FBI— Cochrane with Hoover, Webster and other directors, Cochrane shaking hands with Jack Kennedy, Cochrane with Nixon, Reagan, other presidents and senators.

"Yes?"

"Director? This is Agent Younger. Have your people been able to run those lists I requested?"

"You have another victim?"

"Yes . . . the girl who disappeared Friday night."

"That's three consecutive Friday nights. That's a clear pattern—"

"I don't think the nights are important," Karen said. "He's not going to wait another week. I need those lists as soon as I can get them."

"I'll see what we have. Stay on the line."

Karen and Braden rode in a tense silence, Braden slowing along Washington Boulevard as he neared the center of town and traffic thickened. "I was going to drop you at your motel, but I think Captain Hummel's gonna have something to say to us when he sees the special news bulletins on TV."

Before she could answer, Buddy Cochrane was back. "Those lists you asked for came in earlier this evening. The faxes went out about an hour ago. You have your portable fax with you?"

"No," she admitted, chagrined. "It's in my room." And the phone had been ringing with Braden's call when she returned to her room. In her haste she had not checked the fax machine.

"I can have them sent again." There was no rebuke in Cochrane's measured tone.

"That shouldn't be necessary, sir." She looked at Braden as she rang off. "How fast can you get me there?"

BRADEN USED THE siren and his turret lights. In less than five minutes they saw the sign for the Red Roof Inn ahead. Braden careened into the circular drive in front of the motel as his car radio squawked.

"Ten-four, this is Braden. Whatcha got?"

"A radio car picked up a woman some people brought in from the beach. They flagged the patrol car. Woman claims assault and attempted murder. Officer reports someone worked her over pretty good, smashed her face in."

"Where is she now?" Braden cut in.

"Officer reports taking the woman to Little Company of Mary. They're baby-sitting her."

"I'm on my way," Braden said tersely. He stared at Karen. "My gut tells me it's him. You coming, or do you want to follow up on your thing?"

"That's a long shot," she said dubiously. Would their serial killer have attacked someone on Sunday at the beach?

"You said this guy's unraveling. If it was him at the beach, and this is one who got away, his luck's running out. The son of a bitch isn't invincible anymore."

Karen nodded. "I'll be here checking those faxes from Quantico. Let me know what you find."

Braden's tires squealed as he shot back onto the street, red and blue lights a miniature carnival against the darkness. For a moment Karen stared after him. Then she rushed inside.

Thirty-Five

GLENDA LINDSTROM HALF listened to the sound of the television set in the den. Unable to remain still, she paced between the kitchen—where she wondered if Richie had eaten dinner—and the living room, knowing that it was too soon to expect to see the headlights of Dave's Nissan returning.

Richie was safe, that was all that mattered. He was coming home—he *wanted* to come home.

What had Ralph done to reduce the boy to hysterical tears? She dreaded the answer to the question. Glenda understood well Ralph's desire to torment her by keeping Richie with him, but she also knew how short-lived that pleasure would be—and how any change in Ralph's mood might cause him to turn on Richie . . .

"*. . . interrupt this program . . .*"

. . . and take out his anger on the all too human and vulnerable reminder of his reason for coming to San Carlos.

"*Detective Timothy Braden—still known to many of our viewers as the Corkscrew Cop—revealed that the serial killer who has stalked and terrorized San Carlos for the past three weeks has left a grisly signature on each of his victims, carving their first initials on their abdomen.*"

Glenda stopped pacing the living room, riveted by the television newsman's voice from the nearby den.

"*The latest victim, Nancy Showalter, joins two other San Carlos College students who have been murdered on successive Friday nights. Like the first two victims, Edith Foster and Natalie Rothleder, Nancy Showalter was described by friends this evening as a beautiful, warm-*

hearted and generous young woman without an enemy in the world. True to the stalker's pattern, her initial N was cut into her flesh by her brutal assailant . . ."

Glenda stood rigid. A quiver ran through her body.

N-E-N, she thought.

"Police believe that the killer is spelling out a hidden message concerning the motive behind his horrific crimes. This reporter has learned that the Federal Bureau of Investigation is entering the case with an expanded task force . . ."

"Not N-E-N," Glenda whispered aloud. "E-N-N."

She swayed, her legs turning to jelly. She had to put a hand out blindly, grabbing the arm of a wing-backed chair to keep from falling.

She was suddenly clammy, cold, as if she had come down with the flu or a fever.

She stumbled along the short hallway to the door of the den and stared across the room at the television set. But the cheerful duo of TV anchors had already moved on to other news. Researchers in Pennsylvania had discovered a fat gene previously unknown. Soon, they speculated, it would be possible to gorge on chocolates and remain thin. The false cameraderie of the doll faces on the screen seemed grotesque, like the orchestra playing as the *Titanic* sank into the icy waters of the North Atlantic.

It was a coincidence, Glenda told herself. It had to be. What she was thinking was unthinkable.

She knew instantly that there was no mistake. The full horror of what she comprehended enveloped her like a cloud of noxious gas. She couldn't breathe. Her heart pounded.

Unable to stand, she sank into a chair facing the TV set, but she no longer heard the words above the roaring in her head. What had she started all those years ago? All she had wanted was to be free, a chance to be herself. Instead she had thrown open one of the gates of hell.

In a dark corner of her mind she had always known that Ralph would keep his promise—that it would never be over for her. But never in her most anguished moments had she dreamed that innocent women would die because of her.

Edith. Natalie. Nancy. E-N-N.

For Lennie. Ralph, who had never liked the name Glenda—it sounded snooty, he said—was spelling out the nickname he had given her. He was the only one who had ever called her Lennie.

Spelling the name in bodies.

Her pain was unbearable, but it could not silence the shrill dartings of her mind. And one of those thoughts brought Richie's babblings back. In their brief time over the phone the boy's words hadn't seemed to make coherent sense. Something about a woman and a flower. But he hadn't meant a flower—he was telling her a name. *Iris!*

Glenda moaned aloud. Something had happened to Iris.

E-N-N-I. Only two letters missing. Could there be another victim, her ravaged body yet undiscovered, whose name began with L? Or was that letter reserved for Glenda herself? That left only the last—

Oh my God! Elli!

She screamed her daughter's name. "Elli!"

The reply came almost immediately, oddly plaintive. "Mommy?"

Glenda bolted to her feet. "Elli? Where are you? I'm coming!"

Glenda's fear momentarily paralyzed her. Where had the cry come from? Not upstairs—closer. The kitchen?

"Mommy?"

The child's cry came from the kitchen—a small, frightened voice. Glenda knew what she would find even before she got there. It was as if she had always known.

She rushed into the kitchen. Her whole world seemed to stop, like a moment in a movie when the soundtrack goes silent and the actors freeze in place. Glenda Lindstrom, housewife, mother, her anguished cry locked in her throat, standing rigid in the doorway. Pretty fair-haired child, image of her mother, her blue eyes brimming with tears, gazing up apprehensively at the man who holds her by the hand. Ralph Beringer, tanned, athletic, at ease, his eyes obscured behind the tinted lenses of his glasses, smiling as Glenda bursts into the room.

"Well, well—Lennie," he said. "Isn't this a surprise?"

* * *

BRADEN FLASHED HIS shield and had himself buzzed through the locking door to the emergency room's treatment area at Little Company of Mary Hospital in San Carlos. Iris Whatley was sitting on a table by herself behind a drawn curtain. When Braden's eyes met hers, there was an instant flash of recognition.

"I know you," he said. "The Bright Spot."

"Everybody's favorite punching bag," Iris said with a lopsided smile.

Braden identified himself, studying her closely. Her face was badly bruised, one cheek and the area around her left eye swollen. Her full lower lip had been cut. It was puffy but no longer bleeding. She was holding some kind of pack against the side of her head. She was wearing a pretty flowered print blouse and matching skirt, as if dressed for a special occasion. No pantyhose or stockings. Braden wondered what had happened to her shoes.

"You've been in the diner a few times. Coffee straight, am I right? Cinnamon roll?"

"That's right. You want to tell me what happened, Iris?"

Her face went blank for a moment. "You're a homicide detective?"

Braden nodded. "If the man who attacked you is the one we think he is, you're very lucky to be sitting here."

"Oh jeez, you don't mean . . . he's not the one who's been . . ." The words trailed off. The blood drained from her face. "It was on TV tonight—I saw it out there in the emergency room while I was waiting—after they brought me in here."

"I'm hoping you'll be able to help us find him. Tell me what happened. Start at the beginning. How did you meet this man?"

"Same way I meet any guy," Iris said with a trace of weariness. "Same way I met you, Detective . . . at the diner."

She described her first meeting with the man she knew as Ted, though she now doubted that was his real name. A boy had been with him the last time he came in—Saturday, that was—a cute kid named Richie. She was pretty sure that was the boy's real name because the man had used it several times. He was Richie's father. The boy was the real reason she had agreed to a date with the stranger, Iris said—because he had brought his son to the diner to meet her. Who would expect a problem after that?

Braden tried to keep the excitement out of his voice. "You had a date with him tonight?"

"We went out to dinner, the three of us." When she came to the scene in the apartment after dinner, Iris could not meet Braden's eyes. "He forced me—forced the kid. Threatened me if I didn't do what he said. I should've stopped right there, but . . . he's scary."

"Don't start blaming yourself," Braden said.

"It didn't go down the way he wanted, so Ted was really pissed off. He locked Richie in the bathroom, which should've told me something if I needed anything more, and we went down to his car. We weren't talking then. He was so mad he was grinding his teeth, but I was just as mad. I thought he was going to dump me at the diner, but when we got there he just kept driving. I knew I was in trouble then—that I was with a real crazy. I tried to open the door and jump out while we were moving—I didn't care what happened. That's when he grabbed me by the hair and started playing hit-the-nail on the dashboard with my head as the hammer . . ."

When Iris had finished describing her escape along the beach with her attacker in pursuit, Braden wondered if she really understood how close she had come to dying.

"You should be proud of yourself," he told her.

"After what happened with the kid? I guess not."

"You had no choice." He was not sure if he completely believed that, but it seemed important for Iris to believe it. "You were dealing with a psychopath—a man who likes to hurt people."

Iris stared at him. One hand went to her swollen cheek, fingers trailing along her jaw.

"Where is this apartment? The one where he locked the boy in the bathroom?"

"I can't give you the number but I could take you there. It's on San Anselmo, right near the mall. Vista something."

"You're in no shape to be going anywhere. Describe it."

Iris remembered the building, what side of the street it was on, approximately how far it was from the mall—the second block north, she insisted. More importantly, she also remembered the apartment number: 110.

An emergency room doctor pulled the curtain aside and stopped, scowling at Braden. "Are you a relative?" he asked.

"I'm a homicide detective," Braden said, fishing out his shield. "Asking her some questions."

"This woman has a concussion," the doctor said. "She also needs stitches for that cut on her scalp. I'm going to have to ask you to leave."

Braden gave him a cool, level stare. Then he turned to Iris. "I'll talk to you again later. Remember what I said—you did fine."

"Hey, come by for a cup of coffee, okay?"

KAREN YOUNGER STARED at the name: Ralph Beringer.

It was on not one but four computer-generated lists. The United States Air Force was looking for him because he had gone AWOL four years ago while stationed in Germany. Air Force Intelligence was investigating him for suspected black-market dealings and illegal surplus weapons sales. Interpol wanted him for questioning on a drug distribution charge. Ralph Beringer was bad news.

The fourth and most crucial match was to military personnel stationed at Wiesbaden, Germany, eight years ago.

Ralph Beringer had come home, and now three young women in San Carlos were dead.

She tried to reach Detective Braden without success. He was away from his car, the radio dispatcher told her. She left a message for him. She found David Lindstrom's home telephone number in the case file. She let the phone ring, stopping her count at ten.

They were a family unit, she thought. They had a five-year-old daughter. Where were they at ten in the evening? Out looking for their son Richie?

Feeling uneasy and very much alone, Karen went out to her rented Ford Contour.

The streets of San Carlos were quiet. Sunday night, she thought. Families should be home tonight, watching television, gearing up for the week ahead. A school day tomorrow, young children should be in bed sleeping. Where were the Lindstroms?

She regretted not being able to reach Braden. She remembered telling him that she wanted him there when she came face-to-face with the monster. *"You're pretty damned sure of yourself. What do you need us ordinary cops for?"* he had demanded. She remembered her answer clearly. *"Because I'm going to catch the son of a bitch, Detective. And when I do, I don't want to be alone."*

Paranoia, she thought. There was a reasonable explanation for the Lindstroms not answering their phone. If the killer—Ralph Beringer—had actually assaulted a woman at the beach tonight, the last place he would go would be the Lindstroms' house.

She didn't want Beringer to be there. She didn't want to confront him alone. Driving through the night, she felt the presence of the incarcerated killers she had interviewed as part of VICAP's Criminal Personality Research Project. She remembered their smiles, and their eyes looking at her. They had scared her out of the field, and they had all been confined.

No, she corrected herself. They had unnerved her, but the one who had exposed a weakness, altering her psyche forever, was the man who had brutalized Lisl Moeller under a Rhine River bridge eight years ago.

She knew, with an irrational but unalterable conviction, that she was racing through the night to meet him at last.

No backup. And no turning back.

Thirty-Six

WHEN BRADEN REPORTED in on his car radio from the hospital parking lot, the dispatcher told him, "We've been trying to reach you, Detective. That FBI Special Agent, Younger? She's been real anxious."

"Where is she? Lemme talk to her."

"She left you a message—said she had a match." *We've got him!* Braden thought reflexively. "Said to tell you she would be at the Lindstrom place."

Braden's elation instantly cooled. "Get me David Lindstrom—I don't have the number but it's on record and it's listed."

"Ten-four."

Braden started the Chevrolet and made his way toward the exit while he waited for the call to go through. The killer's run was about over, he thought. They had a victim and an eyewitness to battery; that would hold Beringer long enough for the rest of the evidence to fall into place.

"There's no answer, Detective."

Braden swore. For a moment he hesitated at the exit from the parking lot. Which way? Go for the boy at the apartment—or trust Younger's instincts about the killer?

She had been right about him. Her instincts were good.

He swore again, made a sharp turn in front of traffic and hit the button for the siren. *Don't do anything stupid, Younger,* he muttered aloud. *Just don't do anything stupid.*

＊　　＊　　＊

"HE'S THERE!" RICHIE cried.

They were a block from the house. Dave Lindstrom swerved instinctively at his son's shout but he didn't want to brake—not now, not this close to home. "What do you mean?"

"His car—that's his car! The gray Taurus—"

"Beringer? I thought you said he drove a Buick."

"No—he's got two cars." They drove past the Taurus by the side of the road. Richie stared ahead as their house loomed out of the darkness, familiar and welcoming—and suddenly different, as if an ominous shadow had fallen across it. He whispered, "He's here."

Dave Lindstrom heard the fear in his son's voice.

Bands of tension tightened around his chest. He careened into the driveway and jerked to a stop halfway onto the front lawn. He spilled out of the car, shouted at Richie, "Stay back! Go to the Johnsons—call the police!"

Dave ran up the steps to the porch. For an instant Richie hesitated. He looked across the street at the Johnsons' house. Then, as his father burst through the front door, Richie heard a scream.

He bolted up the steps into the house.

GLENDA'S PURSE WAS on one of the kitchen chairs beside the oak dining table, where she often dropped it when she came into the house from shopping. She backed away from Beringer toward the table. He watched her, smiling—but with eyes empty of feeling, the dead eyes she remembered from her nightmares.

"You killed those women," she whispered.

"Hey, you got my message? Good for you. I was afraid you'd never tumble. You look great, by the way, Lennie, you never let yourself go."

"All those innocent young women . . ."

"Innocent? Don't make me laugh—"

Glenda's fingers brushed across the top of her purse. She saw a flicker of concern cross Ralph's face. She was surprised that, after eight years, she could still read him so clearly. As he could read her.

He wouldn't give her another chance. It was now or never.

She seized the purse. Her hand dug inside, found the hard shape of the gun. Dragging it clear, keys and tissue and lipstick spilling out as her hand came free, she remembered the safety.

Ralph threw Elli across the room. She hit the wall with a small, splintered cry and sank toward the floor. With a scream of rage, Glenda fumbled for the safety—where was it? Why hadn't she spent more time practicing? *There!*

She raised the compact AMT .380. Ralph's hand closed over hers, forcing it down. Her trigger finger squeezed—

Nothing!

She had forgotten to chamber a bullet with the slide action. She had been afraid to do it ahead of time, heeding a mother's deep-seated anxiety about loaded weapons around children. She jerked her hand free, wrenched at the stiff-acting slide, felt it clash into place.

Ralph laughed. He caught her wrist again and twisted savagely. The gun spilled to the floor. He kicked it away. In despair she watched it skitter across the tile floor.

They both heard the front door crash inward. Dave shouted. Ralph pushed Glenda aside. The swing of his right arm toward his hip exposed a gun in a leather clip holster at his waist. He seemed to coil like a spring as he turned, dropping into a crouch. Dave blundered through the dining room, banging a hip against a chair, before he filled the kitchen doorway.

Dave's face had a wildness Glenda had never seen in it before—or expected to see. The expression shifted almost imperceptibly—panic laced with relief—when he saw Glenda braced against the counter where Beringer had shoved her. He took in the scene at a glance—Elli across the room on the floor, Glenda crying out a warning, and, facing him, the broad-shouldered, muscular figure of the man who had terrorized his family.

With an animal snarl Dave hurled himself at Beringer.

*   *   *

HE MOVED SMOOTHLY, economically, easily evading Lindstrom's
rush. He pivoted as he stepped aside and drove his right fist flush
against Lindstrom's jaw. The blow straightened Lindstrom up. A
second punch, a left hook that started around Beringer's waist,
knocked the professor off his feet. He spilled backward across the
kitchen table. The table skidded sideways, a chair crashed to the
floor. On his back, Lindstrom looked dazed.

Smiling happily, enveloped in the familiar red haze, Beringer
flexed his fists. He was wearing his trademark black goatskin gloves,
his only regret that he didn't have his personal value pack, the
leather pouch of steel balls. Watching Lindstrom struggle to his
feet, Beringer told himself that he didn't need the extra weight in
his fists, not this time. Nor did he need his gun. He didn't want
this to end too quickly. He had waited too long to enjoy it. . . .

OUTSIDE, KAREN YOUNGER saw Lindstrom's Nissan Sentra parked
halfway onto the lawn in front of the two-story house. The driver's
door hung open. Her bowels froze with dread. The front door to
the house was open. It gaped like a wound.

Her hands were locked onto the steering wheel. She tore them
free. Stumbled out of the car and sucked in air. Fear caught at her
throat. She wanted to run. Instead, on quivering legs, she drove
herself toward the porch. Once she was moving, her fear acknowledged, training took over. One hand released the flap of her hip
holster. She seized the grips of the Smith & Wesson .38 revolver
she had never fired away from a shooting range.

She held it before her in both hands as she went up the steps.
She moved sideways when she reached the door. Jumped as something crashed inside the house. The empty hallway beckoned, the
dark tunnel of her sweat-drenched dreams.

A craven thing in the recesses of her mind screamed, *"Don't
do this!"*

Karen ignored it, stepped through the doorway. The coward skittered away like a mouse in the dark, and she felt herself go cold and hard and determined.

RICHIE SAW DAVE Lindstrom bounce off the wall and, like a broken doll, slide loose-limbed to the floor. Blood smeared his face, and his nose was mashed like rotten fruit. In a corner of the room Elli sprawled where Beringer had thrown her, one thin arm upraised as if to ward off what she was seeing.

Near his sister's feet, Richie saw the gun on the floor.

Richie's mother flew at Beringer, clawing as his eyes. She shrieked in a voice Richie had never heard before. Beringer laughed. Able to fend off Glenda's blows effortlessly, he seemed content at first merely to avoid being scratched or stabbed in the eye. Then one of her small fists struck through his guard and a fingernail raked his cheek. It trailed a thin red line.

For an instant Beringer's laughter cut off as if a plug had been pulled. Then it began again, but with a difference. Richie was reminded of the laughter on some television shows, a sound just slightly off kilter that his dad called canned laughter.

Almost casually, Beringer hit Glenda across the side of her face. The blow rocked her back on her heels. Her eyes lost their brightness. Her feet did a rubbery little dance on the tile floor.

"No!" Richie yelled.

He scooped up the small automatic pistol from the floor near Elli's feet.

Dave had dragged himself to his feet again, using one of the kitchen chairs as a crutch until he was standing. Beringer saw him out of the corner of his eye. The canned laughter stopped. He looked as if he couldn't believe what he saw. Dave wasn't supposed to keep getting up again and again. Glenda wasn't supposed to fight back. The family was not supposed to hold together like this . . .

Beringer glanced at Richie, saw the gun. "Give it to me, son."

"No!"

"Don't play games with me."

"I . . . I won't let you hurt them anymore."

"Okay, okay, it's over. Now gimme the gun."

"Promise me—you've got to stop!"

Beringer frowned. He watched Dave Lindstrom while he fended off Glenda and talked to Richie. He was in control. He wasn't having any trouble with them, it was as easy as he had always known it would be, but the son of a bitch kept getting up off the floor and Beringer was losing patience.

"Okay, I promise. Now gimme the goddamned gun."

"Richie!" his mother cried. "Don't believe him—you know you can't believe him!"

Even without his mother's plea, Richie knew he couldn't let his father have the gun. He knew exactly what would happen if he did, as clearly as if Beringer had spelled it out for him. He felt tears like scalding water on his cheeks. Beringer glared at him with an expression of disgust, but Richie could not stop the flow of tears. He couldn't stop the tears or the way his hand shook holding the gun.

Dave Lindstrom chose that moment to hurl himself at his rival. Richie's mother screamed. The cry echoed down a corridor of years. At the far end a door in Richie's memory burst wide open, a barrier that had been sealed against unbearable pain and fear.

At that moment someone behind Richie yelled, "FBI— freeze!"

Incredulous, Beringer spun toward the unexpected voice. In the same smooth motion his hand drew his own weapon, a Walter PPK 9mm double action, already cocked and loaded.

"Don't—"

Richie felt the gun buck in his hand. There was a roaring in his ears, chaos all around him. He saw Ralph Beringer stagger, an expression of blank surprise replacing the baleful rage in his face. He stumbled backward, falling against the kitchen table. Redness pooled on his shirtfront.

Richie dropped the gun. He clapped both hands to his ears, as if he might block off the sound of his own screams.

Thirty-Seven

SPECIAL AGENT KAREN Younger stayed on a week in San Carlos while the unwieldy machinery of the criminal justice system dealt with the ramifications of an agent shooting resulting in death. On Wednesday of that week she visited Tim Braden's small unit near the beach.

They lingered on the balcony after dinner—take-out burritos from a small local Mexican restaurant washed down with a bottle of Carta Blanca.

After a while she murmured, "Have you talked to Dr. Nakashimi?"

"Yes. It wasn't your bullet that killed Beringer. Not that you FBI Special Agents can't shoot straight . . ."

"The boy never has to know."

"No." Braden paused. "How's Richie doing?"

"They have him with a child trauma specialist at UCLA. I guess it'll be a long time before they know how he's going to come out of this. Having a family like that, though . . . I think he has a good chance."

"How do you think the parents will do?"

"I think they'll do just fine. That woman . . . she's strong, Braden. Real strong."

They settled into companionable silence. The air turned cooler as a bank of fog crept inland. The weather pattern was changing, Braden had said. Summer was over. Temperatures would be dropping all the way down into the fifties. There was even a chance of rain.

Karen said, "You're good, Detective—did I tell you that? A good cop, I mean."

"Glad you clarified that."

"You should be one of those fast-track guys—a sergeant by now, even a loo."

"I was derailed. Maybe you heard the story."

"Even so. You should've been able to ride over that incident." She considered what she was saying. "I've seen something of politics in big-city police departments. I've seen it in the FBI."

"No kidding!" Braden sounded aghast. "In the Bureau?"

She ignored his sarcasm. "I can see why you'd make your superiors nervous. You're good, so they'd want to use you to make themselves look good, but you'd be a threat to them also. They wouldn't want to help you onto that fast track."

"I can see the advantages of having a resident shrink to explain these things to me."

"I'm not exactly a resident."

"You could consider it," Braden said lightly.

This time she was silent for a long time. "I want you to know, Detective, it's not a suggestion I'd reject out of hand. But I'm not ready. I discovered something about myself these past few weeks . . . that I can do what I do. Even if I'm scared."

"I could've told you that." He hitched his aluminum and plastic–webbed chair closer to hers, put his hand over hers. She didn't withdraw it. Her skin felt hot to the touch. "Maybe you should stay the night, sort of a mini–trial run, you might say."

"Well . . ."

As if in response to the suggestion, there was movement from inside the apartment. Karen heard nails clicking across the hardwood floor. A large dog joined them on the deck, a female golden retriever. She had long, silken, golden hair, a broad skull, a very cold nose that she pressed against the side of Karen's hand, asking for a caress. She also had thick scar tissue on the back of her head and she dragged her left rear leg slightly when she walked.

Karen stroked the dog's head. "You're pretty good at keeping secrets, Braden. Until tonight I never knew you even had a dog. All this time you never mentioned her."

"I put her in the kennel when this business started. I knew I wouldn't be around here much, and it wasn't fair to Duchess." He paused. "She worries when she's left alone too long."

Something in Braden's voice caught her attention.

He smiled. Duchess reacted immediately, coming over to him and trying to push her head in his lap. She settled for resting it on his knee while he fondled her ears.

"I got her from the vet. She's spent a lot of time there. I think she thinks of it as a second home. They all make a fuss over her."

"She was injured? In an accident?"

"She's a rescued dog," he said after a moment. "She was abused—beaten with a length of chain, among other things. That's why she has that scar tissue here on her neck and back."

Karen shivered. "She seems so friendly, so happy . . ."

"It took her a while to trust again, but she has so much in her it wanted to come out."

They fell silent again. Traffic rumbled by along the beach road. A seagull drifted overhead, circled and landed on the railing at the far end of the balcony. Braden said, "You finish that burrito?"

"Every last crumb."

"Not good for 'em anyway."

The seagull walked along the railing for a moment before giving up and flying away. It flew into the thick cloud bank across the road and was swallowed up, like a figure in a vintage movie set in London.

"I could get used to this," Karen murmured.

"The offer still goes. And you could find work here."

"I already have a job . . . and I'm not finished."

"There are still monsters out there."

"Yes . . ."

She was amazed how comfortable it was, sitting there with him on his tiny balcony, watching the slow march of the huge gray cloud bank, feeling the air change.

"One less, now," Braden said.